Imperial Scandal

Also by Teresa Grant

Vienna Waltz

Imperial Scandal

TERESA GRANT

KENSINGTON BOOKS
www.kensingtonbooks.com

KENSINGTON BOOKS are published by

Kensington Publishing Corp.
119 West 40th Street
New York, NY 10018

All Kensington titles, imprints, and distributed lines are available at special quantity discounts for bulk purchases for sales promotion, premiums, fund-raising, educational, or institutional use.

Special book excerpts or customized printings can also be created to fit specific needs. For details, write or phone the office of the Kensington Special Sales Manager: Kensington Publishing Corp., 119 West 40th Street, New York, NY 10018. Attn. Special Sales Department. Phone: 1-800-221-2647.

ISBN-13: 978-0-7582-5424-5
ISBN-10: 0-7582-5424-5

First Kensington Trade Paperback Printing: April 2012
10 9 8 7 6 5 4 3 2 1

Printed in the United States of America

For Jennifer, with thanks

...war and lechery confound all!

—Shakespeare, *Troilus and Cressida*, Act II, scene iii

ACKNOWLEDGMENTS

As always, any errors of research or plotting are entirely my responsibility, but I am grateful to a number of people for assistance, support, and inspiration in the writing of this book.

My editor, Audrey LaFehr, and my agent, Nancy Yost, offered invaluable support, advice, insight, and friendship and helped make this book what it is. I could not have done it without them. Thanks as well to Natanya Wheeler of Nancy Yost Literary Agency and Martin Biro of Kensington Books for answering questions, sending out ARCs and coverflats, and generally helping make a writer's life easier. To Paula Reedy for shepherding the book through copyedits and galleys with an eagle eye for detail. To Barbara Wild for the careful copyediting. To Kristine Mills-Noble and Judy York for another sumptuous cover that evokes the hectic glamour of pre-Waterloo Brussels and once again really looks like Suzanne. To Alexandra Nicolajsen for the superlative social media support. And to everyone at Kensington Books and the Nancy Yost Literary Agency for their support throughout the publication process.

Thank you to Gregory Paris and jim saliba for creating and updating my Web site. To Raphael Coffey for the best author event photos a writer could have. To Bernard Cornwell for answering my query about his research on the Duchess of Richmond's ball for his magnificent novel *Waterloo*. To Robert Sicular for a fabulous custom album of Brussels pictures that was the next best thing to actually going there myself. To Jayne Davis for the grammar advice. To Patrick Wilken for recordings of Korngold's "Pierrot's Lied," which to my mind achingly evokes Harry's feelings about Cordelia.

To Jami Alden, Bella Andre, Catherine Coulter, Barbara Freethy, Carol Grace, Anne Mallory, Monica McCarty, Penelope Williamson, and Veronica Wolff for writer lunches and e-mail brainstorming, and always being there to share the fun and headaches of a writer's life. And to Monica for introducing me to Scrivener, which made the writing of this book inestimably easier. To Veronica for wonderful writing dates during which much of *Imperial Scandal* was written and revised (and during which many words of encouragement were exchanged). To Penny for always being there to talk through book issues and for being the most supportive friend imaginable. And to Kate Perry for suggesting (during a writing date with Veronica) that a brothel would be a good location for an action scene.

To Lauren Willig, wonderful friend and equally wonderful fellow writer of Napoleonic spies, who understands plot and research issues I can't explain to anyone else. To Kalen Hughes for answering questions on the intricacies of early nineteenth-century clothing, and to Candice Hern for the wonderful fashion plates on her Web site, which inspired the gowns worn by Suzanne, Cordelia, and the other female characters. To the History Hoydens for insights, fun, and being a font of information on period detail. To Tasha Alexander, Deborah Crombie, Catherine Duthie, C. S. Harris, and Deanna Raybourn for their support and the inspiration I find in their own writing.

DRAMATIS PERSONAE
*indicates real historical figures

Allied and Prussian Commanders

*Arthur Wellesley, Duke of Wellington, commander of the British and Dutch-Belgian Allied army
*Marshal Blücher, commander of the Prussian army
*William, Prince of Orange, commander of the I corps of the Allied army
*Henry Paget, Earl of Uxbridge, cavalry commander
*General Peregrine Maitland

French Commanders

*Napoleon Bonaparte, Emperor of France
*Marshal Ney, commander of the left wing of the French army
*Marshal Grouchy, commander of the right wing of the French army
*General d'Erlon, commander of the I corps of the French army
*General Flahaut, aide-de-camp to Napoleon
*General de la Bédoyère, aide-de-camp to Napoleon

The Rannoch Family

Malcolm Rannoch, British attaché
Suzanne Rannoch, his wife
Colin Rannoch, their son
Addison, Malcolm's valet
Blanca, Suzanne's maid and companion
Valentin, their footman

Brigitte, their housemaid
Aline Blackwell, Malcolm's cousin
Dr. Geoffrey Blackwell, her husband
Edgar Rannoch, light dragoons, Malcolm's brother

The Davenport Family

Lady Cordelia Davenport
Colonel Harry Davenport, intelligence officer and aide-de-camp to
Wellington; Cordelia's husband
Livia Davenport, their daughter
*Lady Caroline Lamb, Cordelia's childhood friend

The Ashton Family

Lady Julia Ashton, Cordelia's sister
Captain John Ashton, British Life Guards, her husband
Robbie Ashton, their son

The Chase Family

Major George Chase, aide-de-camp to Lord Uxbridge
Annabel Chase, his wife
Captain Anthony Chase, 95th rifles, George's brother
Jane Chase, his wife
Violet Chase, George and Anthony's sister
Watkins, George's batman

Allied Staff Officers and Family

*Lord Fitzroy Somerset, military secretary to Wellington
*Emily Harriet Somerset, his wife

*Sir Alexander Gordon, aide-de-camp to Wellington
*Colonel Canning, aide-de-camp to Wellington
*Baron Jean de Constant Rebecque, chief of staff to the Prince of Orange
*Sir William De Lancey, quartermaster general to the Allied army

The Richmond Family

*Duke of Richmond, commander of the reserves in Brussels
*Charlotte, Duchess of Richmond, his wife
*Lord March, their son, aide-de-camp to the Prince of Orange
*Lady Sarah Lennox, their daughter
*Lady Georgiana Lennox, their daughter
*Lord George Lennox, their son, aide-de-camp to Wellington
*Lieutenant Lord William Lennox, their son

Others

Raoul O'Roarke, guerrillero leader from the Peninsular War
Lord Carfax, head of British intelligence
David Mallinson, Viscount Worsley, his son
Simon Tanner, David's lover
*Sir Colquhoun Grant, head of British military intelligence
*Sir Charles Stuart, British ambassador to the Hague
*Baron Müffling, Blücher's liaison officer with Wellington's Headquarters
Jean La Fleur, French soldier and British agent
*Mr. Creevey, British expatriate
*The Misses Ord, his stepdaughters
*Lady Charlotte Greville, British expatriate
Comte de Vedrin, Belgian aristocrat
Captain Dumont, Dutch-Belgian army
Henri, Vicomte de Rivaux, lieutenant in the Dutch-Belgian army
*Comtesse de Ribaucourt, Belgian aristocrat

Rachel Garnier, prostitute at Le Paon d'Or
Colonel Mortimer, 95th rifles
Pierre, son of one of the women at Le Paon d'Or
Madame Longé, dressmaker
Lucille, her assistant
Captain William Flemming
Major Hamish MacDermid
Philippe Valery, French agent

&ep; 1 &ep;

Outside Brussels, Belgium
Wednesday, 14 June 1815, 1:00 am

Malcolm Rannoch swung down from his horse in the moonlit courtyard. His kid-soled dress shoes made a soft thud on the flagstones. He patted his horse's sweat-dampened neck. It had been a hard half-hour ride from Brussels. A mere half hour. Odd to think that little more than thirty minutes ago he had been holding his wife in his arms, waltzing in the British ambassador's candlelit ballroom. Odder still to think that he had been waltzing at all, rather than hiding out in the library behind the fortifications of a book or newspaper. The past six months had changed him a great deal. Or perhaps the change was owed to his wife.

He slid his hand beneath the Bath superfine of his evening coat and drew out his pistol. The man he was meeting was a friend. In theory. But with the Allied army headquartered round Brussels, and the French army under the recently restored Napoleon Bonaparte in Paris, only a few days' march away, one never knew.

He drew his mare, Perdita, into the shadows of the gatehouse and gave one last pat to her forehead. She nuzzled his hand in response. No need to worry she wouldn't stay where bidden.

The moonlight threw a blue-black sheen on the flagstones and showed the outline of the old iron gate. He turned the handle and eased the gate open. The loamy scent of earth damp and the fragrance of roses and violets greeted him. He paused for a moment to get his bearings, to pick out the dark lines that delineated hedges and benches and statuary. The solid dark blur to his right was the château itself. He could see the lacy filigree of a balcony railing against the lighter stone of the walls.

He stepped forward along the pale line of a gravel path and gave a low sound close enough to the call of a thrush to fool all but the most adept ornithologist. No answering call greeted him. Well, though there wasn't enough light to see his pocket watch, he was probably a bit early. Wellington had been most insistent when he gave him the message, and he'd ridden hard.

He leaned against the trunk of what he thought was a lime tree, secure in the shadows. A gust of wind rippled through the trees. An owl hooted. A real owl? No way to be certain.

Ten minutes had passed if he counted correctly. He reached beneath his coat and unhooked the watch his wife had given him their second Christmas together. As he snapped it open, his thumb slid over the quote from *Romeo & Juliet* inscribed on the inside cover. He peered at the dial, his eyes now more accustomed to the moonlight. Nearly one-fifteen. La Fleur was almost a quarter hour late. Anyone could be delayed, especially these days. But in the two months he had been giving intelligence to the British, La Fleur had been almost painfully punctual.

A faint creak sounded from the shadows, followed by three thrush calls in quick succession. Malcolm stepped away from the tree.

"Sorry. Had to reconnoiter." Jean La Fleur, for the past two months one of their best sources of intelligence within the French army, stepped into the garden. He moved without haste, his pale hair gleaming in the moonlight. A few feet off, he stopped and scanned Malcolm in the shadows, taking in the evening coat and white net pantaloons and silver-buckled shoes.

"Dancing?" La Fleur's voice had the ironic lift of a soldier addressing a civilian.

"All in a day's work. Where else does one collect intelligence?"

"I could name you some possibilities. More interesting than a ballroom." La Fleur leaned his arm against a stone statue that looked to be some sort of Greek goddess and cast a glance at the house. "What is this place anyway? Something Wellington keeps for assignations?"

"The property of one of our Belgian allies. Conveniently empty and conveniently close to Brussels." Malcolm studied La Fleur in the shadows. The negligent line of his arm, the self-assured tilt of his shoulders. In all their months of dealings, of passing papers and money back and forth, Malcolm had never asked the Frenchman what drove him to betray his comrades. The thought left a faint tang of distaste in Malcolm's mouth. Which was absurd. What was intelligence if not betrayal, often of multiple people at once? "La Fleur? What's happened? Wellington said you indicated it was urgent."

La Fleur shook his head. "Sounds like a cliché, doesn't it, but for once I don't think I'm exaggerating. Listen, Rannoch—"

Malcolm grabbed La Fleur's arm and went still, senses keyed to every creak and vibration in the garden. Then he heard the sound again. A faint scrape and stir. Not an animal. Boot steps. In the garden of the supposedly empty château.

Malcolm leveled his pistol.

Suzanne Rannoch stirred the heavy perfumed air with her silk-painted fan. The youth and beauty of the Allied army swirled on the dance floor before her. Hussars, dragoons, Horse Guards, and Life Guards in brilliant crimson or blue and gold or silver lace, staff officers in dark blue coats, riflemen in dark green, Dutch-Belgians in green or blue, and a host of other uniforms. The soldiers circled the floor with girls in gauzy frocks of white and pink, primrose and forget-me-not, champagne and ivory. The candlelight glanced off gold and silver braid, gleaming medals and decorations, pearl necklaces, diamond eardrops, silver thread embroidered on sleeves and hems.

It might have been any ball in any elegant house. Save for the profusion of military brilliance and the dearth of sober dark civilian coats. This waltz had been a favorite at the Congress of Vienna, where Suzanne and her husband had spent the fall and winter. But even in Vienna military uniforms had not so predominated. The threat of war had hung over the Congress, but as a consequence of council chamber quarrels, a constant ripple beneath the surface of balls and masquerades and champagne-filled salons. Then Napoleon Bonaparte had escaped his exile on the island of Elba and returned to power in France and everything had changed.

The British, the Dutch-Belgians, and the Prussians were spread out along the border between Belgium (now part of the Netherlands) and France, the British and their Dutch-Belgian allies to the west of the old Roman road from Bavay to Maastricht, the Prussians to the east. Eventually, when their Austrian allies were ready, they would move into France. But if Napoleon, as seemed likely, crossed the border first they would close in and trap him. At least that was the plan. It was a long border and there were any number of ways the master strategist Napoleon Bonaparte could move. Together, the Allies and the Prussians outnumbered the French. But if he could separate them, Napoleon would have the advantage.

Suzanne's fingers tightened round her fan. Whatever the outcome of the confrontation between the Allies and Napoleon, it was sure to shake her to the core and test the limits of everything she was. And it could not leave her unchanged. Or her marriage.

"Standing about?" Sir Charles Stuart, Britain's ambassador to the Hague and the evening's host, put a glass of champagne into her hand. "We can't have that. Where's your husband got to?"

Suzanne took a sip of champagne and gave Stuart her most dazzling smile. "Surely you don't believe my husband and I spend the evening in each other's pockets, sir? Have I learned nothing in two and a half years as a diplomatic wife?"

"Off on an errand, is he?" Stuart gave her a lazy grin. "Wonder who sent him."

"It wasn't you?"

"In the middle of my own ball? No, ten to one he's been seconded by the military."

Malcolm had met her gaze across the ballroom an hour since, raised his champagne glass to her, and then slipped between two stands of candles and melted away through one of the French windows. Even she didn't know where he had gone. Malcolm had come to trust her a great deal in the two and a half years since they had entered into their oddly begun marriage of convenience, but there were some secrets a good intelligence agent didn't share, even with a spouse. She understood that better than anyone.

Stuart put a familiar arm round her and squeezed her shoulders, left fashionably bare by the ruffled neck of her gown of pomegranate gauze over a slip of pale pink satin. "You're a damned fine hostess, Suzanne. Couldn't have pulled the party off without you."

"Nonsense. You were an excellent host long before I met you."

"Lisbon was different from Brussels." Stuart kissed her cheek, managing at once to be flirtatious and brotherly. "He'll be safely back before dawn, never fear. We're weeks away from fighting."

"Weeks?" Even were Napoleon really still in Paris, he was only a short march from Brussels.

"Well, days at any rate."

"Mrs. Rannoch." A tall man in an austere black evening coat, his fine-boned face distinguished by a distinctive hook nose and piercing blue eyes, materialized out of the crowd. "You look lovelier every time I see you."

Suzanne held out her hand to the commander of the Allied army. "Is that the secret of your success, Your Grace? Always knowing precisely the right thing to say?"

Arthur Wellesley, Duke of Wellington, gave one of his brusque laughs. "Hardly. My brother's the diplomat in the family. Like your husband. Where's he disappeared to?"

"I fear I haven't the least idea," Suzanne said. "Though I thought perhaps Your Grace might."

Wellington gave her a shrewd look. "Possibly, my dear. Possibly. Don't let it get about that I said so, but diplomats can often prove remarkably useful."

Despite the heat in the candle-warmed room, a chill coursed through her. She knew Wellington was fond of Malcolm. And she also knew the duke wouldn't hesitate to sacrifice her husband or anyone else if he thought it necessary to achieve victory.

Malcolm tightened his grip on La Fleur's arm and kept stone-still until he could make out the shadowy form standing just inside the gate. Then he hurled himself across the garden in three strides, kicking up a hail of gravel, and knocked the man to the ground. They crashed through a hedge. Branches broke. Something prickly jabbed Malcolm in the eye. He gripped his fallen adversary by the shoulders. *"Qui êtes-vous?"*

"Easy, Rannoch. Don't take my head off." The other man's voice was hoarse but acerbic. "Your French is impeccable, but I know damn well it's you."

Those incisive, mocking tones were unmistakable. Malcolm sat back on his heels. "Davenport. What the devil are you doing here?"

"Warning you." Harry Davenport pushed himself up to a sitting position and stared at La Fleur, who had crossed the garden to them. "You must be La Fleur. Hanging back from a fight that isn't yours?"

"Never know what the hell Rannoch's up to. Seemed better to stay back. Who the devil are you?"

"Lieutenant-Colonel Harry Davenport," Malcolm said. "Aide-de-camp to the Duke of Wellington. Currently seconded to Colonel Grant."

Colquhoun Grant was the head of British military intelligence, keeping watch for movement of French troops near the border.

"Grant sent me." Davenport pulled himself free of the hedge and reached for his hat. "He intercepted a dispatch that implies the French may have broken one of our codes. Which means you could be compromised, La Fleur. We need to extract you tonight and get you back to Brussels."

"See here," La Fleur said, "selling you information's one thing. If you think I'm going to turn my back on everything—"

"You should have thought of that before you started selling out your fellows," Davenport said.

La Fleur whirled on him, hand raised. "Damn you—"

Malcolm grabbed La Fleur's arm. "Who knows where—"

Shots rang out. Malcolm flung himself down and heard Davenport and La Fleur slam into the gravel beside him.

Davenport lifted his head. "What the devil—"

Another shot whistled overhead from the direction of the garden wall. Malcolm rolled onto his back and fired off an answering shot.

"Compromised, you say?" La Fleur aimed a shot at the wall. "What the hell have you got me into?"

"Risks of the trade." Davenport fired as well, as a fresh hail answered from the wall. Whoever they were, they had the devil's own skill at reloading.

Malcolm jammed fresh powder into his pistol. A cry sounded from above, and he caught a glimpse of stirring blue fabric and pale hair. A light glowed behind one of the windows of the château. What the devil—

La Fleur flung himself over Malcolm just as a fresh volley rang out. Malcolm felt the impact of the bullet that struck La Fleur, an instant before the other man collapsed on top of him.

❧ 2 ❧

"Suzanne." Georgiana Lennox, the petite, elfin-faced third daughter of the Duke and Duchess of Richmond, fell upon Suzanne, dragging Malcolm's cousin Aline Blackwell by the hand. "What have you learned? What was the duke saying?"

"Everything to be charming and reassuring, nothing of substance." Suzanne met the gaze of the chief footman and nodded to him to open more champagne.

Georgiana groaned. "No matter now much ice water Wellington has in his veins he can't be completely sanguine."

"I am quite sure that he isn't." Suzanne glanced at the dance floor. A quadrille had just begun. The nearest set was made up of two young lieutenants partnering a blond girl in white and a brunette in pink. The soldiers were laughing as though they hadn't a care in the world.

Suzanne took Georgiana and Aline by the arm and steered them to an ivory damask bench against the wall.

"Have you thought of leaving?" Georgiana asked as she sank down on the bench, her eyes wide and candid. "Going to Antwerp or even back to England?"

England. An alien land Suzanne had only visited once and to which she only belonged by marriage. She touched the younger girl's arm. "It's not as though there's a great deal waiting for me there."

"It's Malcolm's family's home." Georgiana cast a glance at Aline. "They'd look after you."

"Yes, the Rannochs and the Dacre-Hammonds could be counted on for that." Aline settled the peach muslin folds of her skirt. "At least some of us. But no sense pretending it's easy living among the English ton, Georgy. Goodness knows I've never felt I properly belonged, and I was born one of their number."

"Are you thinking of leaving, Georgy?" Suzanne asked.

Georgiana shook her head. "My parents wouldn't dream of it, with Father in command of the reserve forces and my brothers in the army. But the Mertons and Grandisons have left. Does Dr. Blackwell want you to go home, Allie?"

Aline snorted. "Geoff knows better than to tell me what to do." Her cool, dark gaze turned serious as it settled on the young soldiers in the quadrille. "I didn't marry a military doctor to sit across the Channel wondering what would become of him."

"But you're going to have a baby. And Suzanne already has one."

Aline touched her stomach, nearly flat beneath her embroidered muslin gown, as though she still couldn't quite make sense of the fact that she was pregnant.

Suzanne saw her son's bright-eyed face when she'd kissed him good night before they left for the party. "Colin was born in the midst of a war, and Malcolm and I dragged him across the Peninsula. Perhaps it was selfish of us to have kept him with us, but he seemed to thrive on it. I often think that's why he sleeps so well through the night. He's used to being jolted over rough roads in an ill-sprung carriage with musket fire in the distance."

Aline's gaze moved from the young lieutenants in the quadrille to a group of riflemen talking on the edge of the dance floor. "The French aren't monsters if it comes to that. Even if we're taken prisoner, there's another seven months before my baby's born. And more of a chance Geoff will be here to deliver it."

Georgiana shuddered. "How can you joke about it?"

"Difficult to do much else," Aline said, her smile sharp with irony.

"I'm sorry." Georgiana pushed a light brown ringlet behind her ear with an impatient tug. "I'm all right most of the time. And then I look at my brothers and Lord Hay and our other friends—"

Suzanne squeezed Georgiana's shoulders. "We're all frightened, Georgy. We just have different ways of showing it."

Georgiana smiled. "Where's Malcolm? He's always so wonderfully sensible."

"Hiding out in the library I suspect," Suzanne said, shutting her mind to images of the danger her husband might be in. "I got one waltz out of him and count myself fortunate."

"I saw you dancing. I'd give a great deal to have a gentleman look at me the way Malcolm was looking at you. I wish—Good heavens!" Georgiana exclaimed. "I didn't realize she'd come to Brussels."

"Who?" Aline asked, looking round the ballroom.

"Cordelia Davenport. By the door with Caro Lamb. They're great friends. Not surprisingly, they share a penchant for scandal. But I wouldn't have thought Lady Cordelia would dare show her face here."

Suzanne turned her gaze to the door. Lady Caroline Lamb had entered the room, clad in one of her trademark clinging gauzes, her feathery curls clustering close to her delicate, pointed face. Beside her stood a woman Suzanne had never seen before. She was not particularly tall, but she held herself with a presence that somehow radiated across the room. She wore a gown of claret-colored silk, cut close to her body and veiled in black net drapery. Stark and dramatic among the pastels of the other ladies. Her bright gold hair was dressed in Grecian ringlets and threaded through with a diamond filet that caught the light from the branches of candles framing the door.

"Why are you surprised to see her here in particular?" Suzanne asked. Society in Brussels was popularly held to be looser than that in London.

"Because her husband's one of Wellington's officers," Georgiana said. "Harry Davenport. I don't think they've set eyes on each other for four years."

Davenport dragged La Fleur off Malcolm. Malcolm drew a ragged breath and fired off a shot from his reloaded pistol. He reached toward La Fleur and felt the spreading sticky warmth of blood. He yanked at his cravat, undid the twists of linen (there were advantages to favoring simple styles), and pressed the fabric to the wound in La Fleur's chest.

"Don't worry 'bout me." La Fleur's voice was a hoarse rasp. "Get the bastards."

"Got it covered." Davenport fired off a shot. A scream sounded from beyond the garden wall.

Another hail of fire came from the wall. Another scream sounded, this time from above, startlingly high-pitched.

Malcolm could feel blood seeping through the folds of linen. The sickly smell choked the air. Davenport jammed fresh powder into his pistol, but the garden had gone almost eerily still. Crashing sounded from the underbrush beyond the wall, not approaching but retreating.

"Made 'em run," La Fleur said in a faint voice. "Good for you."

Malcolm increased his pressure on the wounded man's chest. Blood welled between his fingers. "Don't waste your energy."

"Done for in any event," La Fleur muttered. "Listen, Rannoch." He switched to his native French. "The Silver Hawk."

"The what?"

"Be careful. Don't trust—"

La Fleur's head fell to the side. Even in the murky moonlight, Malcolm saw the life fade from the other man's eyes. He put his fingers to La Fleur's neck for confirmation. No blood pulsed beneath his touch.

"Poor blighter," Davenport murmured. "Though at least he's out of whatever the rest of us bastards are going to be up against in the next weeks."

"If he hadn't flung himself over me—" Malcolm stared down at the still features of the dead man in whose place he could so easily be lying. Suzanne's and Colin's faces swam before his eyes. Fear squeezed his chest. Sometimes he thought he hadn't known the true meaning of fear until he was a husband and father. "Why in God's name—"

"Don't waste time questioning it, Rannoch. Just be grateful that if La Fleur had to be an idiot he was the sacrificial sort. You're lucky."

"Damned lucky."

"Not that." Davenport picked up La Fleur's pistol and stowed it in his pocket. "You're lucky that you actually care whether you live or die."

Malcolm cast a sharp look at the other man, but Davenport was looking down at La Fleur. "What's the Silver Hawk?" Davenport asked. "It sounds like something out of a lending library novel."

"I don't know." Malcolm closed La Fleur's eyes, as he had closed the eyes of too many soldiers and civilians in recent years. He glanced up and saw the light still glowing behind one of the French windows on the first floor of the château, illuminating the balcony before it. A pale mass lay behind the wrought-metal fili-gree of the balcony railing, a mass that had not been there when he arrived. The stir of blue fabric and pale hair registered in his con-sciousness for the first time.

"What the devil—" Davenport had seen it as well.

Of one accord, the two men reloaded their pistols and got to their feet. They made their way up the shallow stone steps to the terrace. A glance at the balcony confirmed that it would be too dif-ficult to climb without rope. Malcolm's picklocks made quick work of one of the French windows off the terrace. They stepped into a room that held the faint, musty smell of lack of use. Shadowy blurs round them seemed to be furniture under Holland covers. Some sort of sitting room or salon.

They moved over the floorboards, Malcolm going first, Daven-port covering him. His eyes now adjusted to the dark, Malcolm found a door and turned the handle. A passage stretched before them, lit faintly by a shaft of moonlight coming through a single window at one end. Thank God for the lighter walls favored in Belgian houses. Much easier to see than if they had faced a mass of

English oak paneling. He could make out a staircase at the end of the passage farthest from the window.

He moved forward, testing the floorboards for squeaks, grateful now for his kid-soled evening shoes. Davenport was booted but was managing quite well behind him. Up the stairs, keeping close to the wall where the treads were solider. A window on the half landing let in a bit more light. At the stair head, a glow of candlelight came from a partially open door. Malcolm went still for the length of several heartbeats, senses keyed to any sound or movement. But nothing indicated the presence of any living creature but themselves.

Sliding his feet over the narrow strip of carpet, he picked his way down the passage to the open door. Davenport followed several paces behind. Malcolm flattened himself against the wall beside the door that was ajar. Through the narrow sliver he could make out the glow of a single candle. It stood on a small, round table against one wall, casting warm light on the flowered wallpaper. A dark mass on the opposite side of the room looked to be a four-poster bed. A breeze stirred the filmy curtains at the French window. The window was open.

Malcolm slipped into the room. Cool night air, dust, and a whiff of jasmine and iris. Not from nature, but expertly blended. Two and a half years of sharing a dressing table with his wife in cramped quarters had taught him to recognize the scent of good perfume.

He crossed the room and pushed open the unlatched French window. A tangle of robin's egg blue fabric and pale blond hair lay against the railing. Even as his mind screamed a hundred questions, Malcolm knelt beside the fallen woman. The smell of blood washed over him. She lay on her side, curled toward the railing. He pushed her hair, half fallen loose from its pins, back from her face, and felt the base of her throat. Sticky blood met his fingers. The bullet had gone through her carotid artery. He could feel no pulse.

"Good God." Davenport had dropped down beside him.

The woman's fashionably cropped ringlets fell over her face. Malcolm touched her shoulder and rolled her onto her back.

Her pale blue gown was a robe fastened with diamond clasps

over a slip of white satin. A ball gown. Her tangle of hair still obscured her face. Malcolm smoothed the disordered curls back from her forehead.

She was young, probably close to his wife's one-and-twenty. Delicate features, a retroussé nose, a faint wash of rouge on her creamy skin, pale blue eyes that stared up at him with the fixed glassiness of death. She looked familiar, but he couldn't place her. Though Brussels society was confined, one still met a score of people at each entertainment.

He felt Davenport's sudden stillness. Malcolm turned to look at the other man. Davenport was staring down at the dead woman as though a musket ball had pierced his memory.

"Do you know her?" Malcolm asked.

"You could say so." Davenport's voice was without expression. "It's my sister-in-law."

3

Suzanne studied Lady Cordelia Davenport. "Of course, her husband must be Harry Davenport." She had known Davenport since her days in the Peninsula when she first married Malcolm. A quick mind, a caustic wit, a general impatience with humanity. He'd never mentioned a wife that she could recall. "Colonel Davenport hasn't been home on leave in four years?"

"I remember now." Aline watched Lady Cordelia and Caroline Lamb as they advanced into the ballroom. "I was still in the schoolroom, but I heard the gossip in Mama's drawing room. There was another man involved, wasn't there? Not that that would be so shocking, particularly not to Mama's set, but I remember someone commenting that Lady Cordelia was 'positively flagrant' about it."

Georgiana nodded. "My sisters and I could talk of nothing else for weeks. It seems quite beastly of us now, but when one's a child one just feels the ghoulish fascination of the story."

Stuart, always quick to recognize pretty women, had crossed the room to greet Lady Caroline and Lady Cordelia. Suzanne watched him bow over the two ladies' hands. Her time on the Peninsula and in Vienna had given her an acquaintance with many of the soldiers and diplomats present tonight. She knew how to make herself at home in a Spanish farmhouse or on a rocky patch of ground, and she could negotiate a diplomatic salon and make her way among Continental royalty. But London society still remained uncharted territory for her. Her brief visit to Britain with Malcolm a year ago had only left her with a sense that it was an alien land set with mines and governed by a code to which she would never discover the key.

She watched Lady Cordelia, who had advanced into the room and, without so much as waving her fan or lifting a white-gloved finger, acquired a crowd of gentlemen about her. Two were offering her glasses of champagne, and the others appeared to be clamoring for the next dance. "Colonel Davenport learned of his wife's love affair?" she asked.

"It sounded as though he was just about the last person in London to be let in on the secret," Aline said, as Lady Cordelia tossed off the second glass of champagne and moved onto the dance floor on the arm of a handsome young subaltern. "The story was that he caught them in bed together—"

"Allie!" Georgiana protested.

"Well, where else would a husband catch his wife and her lover?" Aline pushed back an ash-brown ringlet that had escaped its pins and fallen over her forehead. "That is, they may not have actually been in a bed, but he found them having criminal conversation, as the courts would say."

A few of Harry Davenport's more sarcastic quips echoed in Suzanne's memory. A man who seemingly didn't care for anyone. Which often meant the person in question had once cared very much indeed. "Was there a duel?" she asked.

Aline frowned. "I don't think so. But there was a rather ghastly scene at a musicale—or was it a Venetian breakfast?"

"A concert of ancient music of all things," Georgiana said. "I think the two men actually came to blows. What was the lover's name—Charlton? Chalmers?"

"Chase," Aline said. She might not have much interest in gossip, but like Malcolm she had a keen memory for detail.

"That's right, George Chase. One of the Derbyshire Chases."

"Major Chase?" Suzanne asked.

"Yes." Georgiana's eyes widened. "Oh, good God, he's—"

"In Brussels as well. And at the ball. Though I don't see him at present." Suzanne cast her gaze over the ballroom. "Perhaps Lady Cordelia came to Brussels to see him."

"I doubt it. Their affair ended years ago." Georgiana studied Cordelia Davenport, now waltzing expertly if too closely for propriety in the arms of the subaltern.

"Lady Cordelia hasn't lacked for lovers according to the stories one hears," Aline said. "Of course neither does my mother, but she's a duke's daughter and has somehow managed to avoid open scandal. It's not what one does, it's the finesse with which one does it, she often says. Though I have to say Mama's quite egalitarian about whom she receives. The last I saw Cordelia Davenport was at Mama's in the autumn." Aline glanced at Suzanne. "Before I went to Vienna to stay with you and Malcolm. Cordelia was with Lord Eglinton then."

Georgiana watched as Lady Cordelia left the dance floor with the subaltern only to be besieged by a new crowd of admirers. "I think the last time I saw her must have been at her sister's."

"Her sister?" Suzanne asked. She was aware not just of the throngs of admiring gentlemen but also of the sharp-eyed stares of a number of the ladies present. She felt a flash of kinship with Lady Cordelia. Suzanne knew all too well what it was to be an outsider. One way and another, she had been one all her life. In ways even her husband didn't know.

"Lady Julia Ashton," Georgiana said. "Julia Brooke that was."

"Captain Ashton's wife?" John Ashton was a captain in the Life Guards. Suzanne had met him and his wife a handful of times. She had a vague image of a fair-haired woman, with cameo features and pale blue eyes. Lady Julia lacked Lady Cordelia's presence, but one could see how they could be sisters.

"They were the incomparable Brooke sisters when I was in the schoolroom," Georgiana said. "I remember hanging over the stair rail to get a peek at their ball dresses. No fortune of their own—"

"Their father had gambled it away," Aline put in.

"But they had throngs of suitors."

"Some things don't change," Aline said, eyeing the crowd round Lady Cordelia.

"They couldn't have made more different matches," Georgiana said. "Julia and Captain Ashton are quite devoted."

"Perhaps *that's* why Lady Cordelia came to Brussels," Suzanne said. "To see her sister."

"Perhaps." Georgiana frowned. "The scandal can't but have made things awkward for Julia. The sisters used to be quite close, but obviously Lady Cordelia's position in society makes matters more difficult now. Though I must say Cordelia's always been very kind to me."

"I wonder if Julia knows her sister is in Brussels?" Aline said.

"So do I." Georgiana cast a glance round the ballroom. "Where is Julia Ashton? I don't think I've seen her since supper."

Malcolm stared down at the clouded blue eyes of the woman on the balcony, then turned his gaze to Davenport. "Your sister-in-law? Your brother's wife?"

"My wife's sister."

Malcolm had first met Davenport four years ago when the other man had been posted to the Peninsula after buying a commission and Malcolm had been an attaché at the British embassy in Lisbon. Malcolm had dined with Davenport on occasion, had played chess against him, had listened to the advice layered beneath Davenport's caustic comments, had relied on his wits on one or two missions. He had never heard the other man mention his wife. Malcolm had never asked. But he had heard of Davenport's marriage from his friend David Mallinson long before they met, and he had heard the inevitable rumors that followed Davenport to the Peninsula. "Of course. You married Cordelia Brooke."

"So I did. Though I forget it myself half the time."

"So her sister is—"

Davenport's gaze moved over the dead woman. His face was expressionless, but his cool eyes had gone dark. "Julia Ashton."

"Johnny Ashton's wife?" That was where he had seen the woman, at a reception a few days before, clinging to Ashton's arm. "I knew them both a bit as girls. Their family lived not far from my friends the Mallinsons in Derbyshire." Malcolm had a brief image of two fair-haired girls in white dresses. Cordelia had been wilder, as he recalled. Julia had been the decorous one. "I think your sister-in-law was at Stuart's ball this evening." He frowned, conjuring up an image of the salon and ballroom. Suzanne in his arms as they waltzed, the crowd on the dance floor, the other couples swirling. A crowd by the archway to the supper room. A fair-haired woman in a pale blue gown. "She was definitely there. But as to how the devil she got here—"

Davenport reached out and brushed the glossy ringlets back from Julia's still forehead. His face was set in its customary harsh lines, but he touched her as though he were running his fingers over something breakable. "The last time I saw her she was scarcely more than a girl. I remember her on the terrace at her father's Richmond villa, playing with a throng of King Charles puppies."

"But you knew she'd married Ashton." Malcolm made the words not quite a question.

"I do keep up with the news from home. Academic interest if nothing else."

Malcolm cast a sideways glance at Davenport. The Peninsula had been a good place to hide oneself. He'd done much the same, joining the diplomatic corps and turning his back on his fragmented family after his mother's death. "Ashton came over to Brussels with the Life Guards. You'd have been with Grant at the border."

"Of course." Davenport dropped his hand from his sister-in-law's face. "I forget Wellington's so desperate for troops we're sending over Hyde Park soldiers."

Malcolm turned his gaze back to the body and gently lifted Julia Ashton's head. His fingers met an exit wound at the back of her neck. "The bullet passed clean through," he said. "See if you can feel anything on the balcony beneath her."

Davenport's fingers closed round something. "Here," he said in an expressionless voice. "A musket ball."

"It went in at an upward angle," Malcolm said. "She was caught by the snipers firing at us, though in God's name why they were firing so high—"

"You've done this before," Davenport said.

"Unfortunately, one comes upon dead bodies on intelligence

missions. And I investigated a murder in Vienna." Malcolm shut his mind to the memories. The wound had barely begun to heal.

He glanced at the open French window and the glow of the candle flame within. "I didn't see the candle when I first arrived. Did you?" Davenport shook his head.

"So she must have got here while we were talking with La Fleur. She was in the bedchamber, she heard the shots. She must have run out onto the balcony. But as to *why* she was here—Would your sister-in-law have known Edouard de Vere? The château belongs to his family."

Davenport shook his head. "She might have been on intimate terms with Napoleon Bonaparte for all I know of her life in recent years."

Malcolm got to his feet and returned to the bedchamber. By the light of the single taper, he could see two more candles on the dressing table against the wall. He took a flint from his pocket and lit them.

A four-poster bed, the curtains looped back, a dressing table and wardrobe, the small, round table that held the candle, a wing-back chair near the French windows. A bundle of dark fabric was tossed over the chairback. Malcolm picked it up and shook it out. A lady's cloak of dark blue velvet lined in white satin. On the chair beneath it lay a reticule, pale blue silk stitched with a multitude of tiny crystal beads that sparkled in the candlelight, suspended from a steel filigree frame. The sort of frivolous, impractical little thing his own eminently practical wife loved.

He carried the reticule to the dressing table and undid the clasp. Davenport came to stand beside him as he spilled out the contents in the candlelight. A silver perfume flask, a rouge pot, a handkerchief with *J.A.* and a forget-me-not embroidered in one corner, a small silk purse that proved to contain Belgian currency, an ivory comb, a paper of pins. And at the bottom, a folded piece of hot-pressed notepaper. Malcolm unfolded it and held it beneath the candlelight.

Château de Vere. 1:30.
W.

The black ink had smeared, as though the writer had been in a hurry and had not taken time to dust it with sand. The handwriting was a swift, angular scrawl that tugged at Malcolm's memory.

"So she came here to meet someone." Davenport's voice held an edge of anger, barely leashed.

"Yes," Malcolm said. "The question is who?"

❧ 4 ❧

Suzanne left the dance floor, breathless from an energetic waltz with Lord Fitzroy Somerset. Fitzroy, Wellington's military secretary, was a kind man and a good dancer, but the swift tempo of the music and his agreeable conversation had not stilled the knot of unease growing ever tighter beneath her corset laces. Ridiculous. Malcolm had gone off on missions throughout their marriage. But somehow the specter of the looming confrontation with Napoleon's army lent heightened urgency to everything. Her husband had now been gone for over two and a half hours.

Fitzroy procured glasses of champagne from a passing footman. Instead of moving off, the footman turned to Suzanne. "Madame Rannoch?" he said in Belgian-accented French.

"Yes."

He pressed a paper into her hand, a single sheet torn from a notebook. She unfolded it to see her husband's quick scrawl.

The Garden.
M.

"Is everything all right?" Fitzroy asked.

"I need to find Malcolm." Suzanne took a quick sip of champagne and returned the glass to Fitzroy.

"So he's back?" Fitzroy said.

"You knew he'd gone?"

"I've learned to have an eye for such things. Trouble?"

"I'm not sure. Cover for me?"

"Of course."

Suzanne slipped through one of the French windows onto the terrace. A welcome breeze greeted her after the heat of the ballroom, bringing the scent of roses and jasmine. Torches flanked the steps down to the garden, casting a molten glow on the gray stone. The rest of the garden was washed by cool moonlight.

An expert thrush call alerted her to Malcolm's location, on the side of the terrace to the left. As she rounded the terrace, he detached himself from the dark blur of trees and came toward her. The tension coiled so tight within her eased at the sight of his familiar features, sharp and distinct even in the shadows.

"You were gone almost long enough for me to worry," she said, going forward to take his hands. His fingers closed hard and reassuringly solid round her own. Then she caught a proper look at him in the moonlight. His dark hair fell over his forehead in disarray. Smudges showed on his face and some trails of sticky red that could only be blood. His neckcloth was missing and more blood showed on his shirt collar. "Good God, darling—"

"I'm all right." His fingers tightened over her own. "The blood isn't mine. But things didn't go at all according to plan. We need your help."

"*We?*"

Another man stepped from the shadows, slightly taller than Malcolm. "Mrs. Rannoch. I'd say it's lovely to see you again, but under the circumstances perhaps we'd best dispense with the social niceties."

"Colonel Davenport." Suzanne put out her hand automatically. The moonlight accentuated the lean planes of Harry Davenport's face and the mocking line of his mouth. He, too, had smudges and blood on his face and linen.

"Can you get Stuart and Wellington into a room that opens off the garden?" Malcolm said. "We need to talk to them without going into the ballroom and making a scene."

"Of course." Suzanne cast another glance at Harry Davenport. The timing was dreadful, but he had to be warned. "Colonel Davenport, I don't know if you realize that your wife just arrived in Brussels. She's in the ballroom."

Davenport's eyes widened. For a moment, Suzanne caught a glimpse in their depths of something she could not have put a name to, save that it looked strong enough to break glass. "Thank you, Mrs. Rannoch. But after all these years that really can't be any concern of mine."

Stuart stared at Malcolm and Davenport across a side salon hung with cream silk. "Dead? Julia Ashton can't be dead. She's in the ballroom."

"She *was* in the ballroom," Malcolm said. "She must have left about the same time I did and ridden straight to the Château de Vere. We found her horse in the stables."

"What have you done with the body? Bodies." Wellington was scowling at a pastoral watercolor on the wall opposite.

"We brought them back to Brussels in a cart we found at the château," Davenport said. They had hitched Davenport's horse to the cart and tied Lady Julia's and La Fleur's mounts behind. "They're in the stable with two of your grooms sworn to secrecy. Though sometimes that only makes people more likely to talk."

"We searched the château thoroughly," Malcolm added. "The only signs of her presence we found were her cloak and reticule."

Stuart shook his head. "Why in God's name would she be—"

"Perhaps this will shed some light on it." Malcolm held out the note they had found in Lady Julia's reticule.

Stuart stared at it. "Oh, Christ. I should have guessed."

"A scandal's all we need just now." Wellington crossed the room and took the note from Stuart. His sharp-boned face, tanned from years in the saddle, drained of color. "God in heaven."

"I know it's surprising," Stuart said. "She and Ashton always seemed so devoted, but one never knows—"

"Not that," Wellington said, as though a love affair was of little moment. "Whom the damned note is from."

Malcolm frowned at the Allied commander. He had known Wellington through the difficult years of the Peninsular War and had rarely seen the general so rattled. Had Julia Ashton been having an affair with a member of Wellington's staff? It seemed odd even that would so concern the commander.

Davenport, who had fallen to staring into the fireplace, snapped his head up to look at the duke. "Who?"

Wellington lifted his gaze from the paper and cast a sharp look from Davenport to Malcolm to Stuart. Malcolm could see him weighing the risks of disclosure. At last he gave a harsh sigh. "Our esteemed ally. The commander of the I corps. His Royal Highness, Prince William of Orange."

Suzanne accepted a fresh glass of champagne from a passing footman and took an automatic sip. Malcolm was back, and though his mission had clearly proved dangerous, he was unhurt. She should be relieved. Instead she found it harder than ever to keep in place the smiling mask she had perfected as a diplomatic wife.

Whatever Malcolm and Colonel Davenport were discussing with Wellington and Stuart, it was clearly very serious. But they had been teetering on a knife's point of danger in Brussels for weeks. For that matter, she had lived with danger for most of her life. There were even stretches of time when her own survival had not been a matter of very great moment to her.

A waltz came to an end. Couples swept from the dance floor and others hurried to take their place for the *écossaise* that was forming. She took another quick sip of champagne. The coming confrontation with Napoleon Bonaparte's forces had scraped at her nerves for months. She knew all too well how high the stakes were, for the future of the Continent and for those she loved. And for her personally. But the tension roiling within her now wasn't fear, it was frustration. Malcolm was closeted in a salon sharing whatever had happened this evening with Wellington and Stuart, while she was relegated to the sidelines. She had got used to sharing her husband's adventures.

Whatever had happened tonight might mean that the confrontation between the Allies and the French was that much nearer. Her blood quickened at the implications. Yet here she was sipping champagne on the edge of the dance floor.

An iron grip closed round her arm. "What on earth is going on?" Georgiana Lennox demanded.

"What? Have we run out of champagne?" Suzanne tightened her hold on her own glass before it could topple over from the force of Georgiana's grip.

"Don't be provoking. Wellington and Stuart left the ballroom a quarter hour ago."

Suzanne straightened the crumpled folds of Georgiana's lace scarf. "I daresay Stuart wanted to give Wellington a glass of his good port."

"And just now I saw Stuart come back into the ballroom—"

"Well, then."

"—and leave again with the Prince of Orange. Have they had news? Is Bonaparte marching?"

"Georgy, darling." Suzanne slipped her arm round Georgiana's shoulders. "It's a truism of diplomatic life that balls are often the scene of negotiations. I think half the decisions at the Congress of Vienna were made in the midst of masquerade balls. I daresay Wellington needed to have a talk with the prince and thought it would be more easily accomplished here than at Headquarters."

"Do you really think so?"

"Yes, though if you ask me they really may be drinking port." Suzanne cast a glance round the ballroom searching for distraction. A splash of red and black caught her eye. Cordelia Davenport was leaning against one of the French windows in a pose of casual nonchalance, laughing up at a hussar and a dragoon who were both offering her glasses of champagne. For a moment Suzanne saw Harry Davenport's harsh face and intense eyes when she'd told him his wife was in Brussels.

"Was Colonel Davenport already a soldier when he married Lady Cordelia?" Suzanne asked. Harry Davenport had never seemed to her entirely suited to the life. She'd more than once caught a glint in his eyes that signaled frustration at orders.

"Oh no," Georgiana said. "He was fearfully bookish in those days. He was a classical scholar. I think he studied the Julio-Claudians."

Who would make poor Harry Davenport's own scandal look positively tame. "It doesn't sound as though he and Lady Cordelia were well suited," Suzanne said.

"A hopeless mismatch. I don't know what they found to talk about."

"So Harry Davenport bought himself a commission to escape his failed marriage?" Suzanne had had too many other matters to contend with in the past two and a half years to spare a great deal of thought for the enigmatic Colonel Davenport, but he had always puzzled her.

"He went to the Peninsula and ended up on Wellington's staff. My brother March knows him." Georgiana's brother Lord March had also been an aide-de-camp to Wellington until he'd been seconded to the Prince of Orange's staff. "March says he's brilliant, but one can never be sure what he'll say. I don't think he's been back to Britain since, not even when Wellington was in London last year before the Congress. A lot of people thought he'd sue for divorce, but I expect he didn't care for the scandal. I don't think they're even formally separated."

"Do they have any children?"

Georgiana's lips tightened. "A little girl. Born some months after Harry left England. She bears his name, and I don't think he's ever made any effort to repudiate her."

"But of course there's talk," Suzanne said, thinking of her own son.

"Of course."

"Lady Julia's death is tragic and the prince's involvement is a damnable inconvenience," Wellington said to Malcolm and Davenport when Stuart had left the room to fetch the Prince of Orange. "But when all's said and done it's La Fleur's death and why it happened that's the real concern. What convinced Grant the French had broken our code?"

"It seemed the logical assumption when we intercepted a dispatch of theirs that contained information they could only have obtained from our coded communications," Davenport replied.

Wellington frowned. "Damned shame. La Fleur was an invaluable asset. So the French followed and took him out?"

"It seems the obvious conclusion," Malcolm said.

Wellington shot him a swift look. "Why seems?"

"Just that in that case I wonder why they retreated without killing Davenport and me as well."

"Perhaps they ran out of ammunition. You say you hit one of them."

"So it seemed."

"If it wasn't the French—"

"Quite," Malcolm said.

Davenport was watching Malcolm closely. "Not that I have a great deal of faith in the understanding of French soldiers. Or British soldiers if it comes to that. But the whole thing was a bit rum. If—"

The door swung open on his words and His Royal Highness William, Prince of Orange, strode into the room, Stuart following in his wake.

Malcolm had known the Prince of Orange, more commonly referred to as Slender Billy, since boyhood. The prince had been only three when his family had fled to England to escape the French. Billy's parents were friends of Lord and Lady Carfax, the parents of Malcolm's friend David Mallinson. Malcolm had met the prince at Carfax Court. Four years Malcolm's junior, Billy had been brash and eager and had enthusiastically embraced Britain and the British. Later, he had served in the Peninsula as an aide-de-camp to Wellington, when Malcolm was an attaché at the British embassy. Billy had been betrothed briefly to the prince regent's daughter, Princess Charlotte, but Charlotte had broken off the engagement.

"What's the kickup?" the prince asked, his gaze sweeping the company. "Don't tell me Boney's on the march already."

"Not so far as we know." Wellington surveyed him. Theirs was a somewhat delicate relationship. The prince had once served on

Wellington's staff, but more recently Billy had been the commander of the Allied army until Wellington arrived from Vienna to take control. The prince had relinquished his command with every appearance of respect, if not out-and-out hero worship, but Wellington's relationship with his father, King Frederick, and the relationship in general between the British and their Dutch-Belgian allies was a more complicated thing.

Stuart leaned against the closed door panels, while Malcolm and Davenport watched from the sidelines.

Billy straightened his thin shoulders, reverting to the young aide-de-camp before his admired superior. "What is it, sir?"

"I didn't realize Your Royal Highness had an engagement that would take you away from the ball this evening."

Malcolm saw the color flare in Billy's cheeks—he'd never been good at lying. "An engage—I don't know what you're talking about."

Wellington reached inside his coat and held out the note Malcolm had found in Lady Julia's reticule.

The prince's face turned as white as his starched shirt points. "Oh, Lord. It isn't—"

"It's no concern of mine whom you choose to take to bed," Wellington said. "Though I must say, it isn't good for morale if it gets about that you're bedding the wife of one of my officers."

"I never meant—"

"For it to become public knowledge. So I should hope. Had you met Lady Julia at the Château de Vere before?"

The prince dug the polished toe of his shoe into the Brussels weave of the carpet. "Edouard de Vere is a friend of mine. I knew the château was empty. It seemed discreet—"

"And tonight?"

"I never left the ball. Julia sent me a note saying we'd best not meet after all."

"When did you receive it?"

"Just after I arrived here. One of the footmen gave it me."

"Do you still have it?"

Billy reached inside his shirt cuff. Malcolm flicked a glance at

Davenport and knew they were thinking the same thing. An intelligence agent would have burned it at once.

The prince held a scrap of paper out to Wellington, who regarded it with a closed face, then handed it to Malcolm and Davenport. A torn piece of notepaper to which a faint odor of jasmine clung. *H.R.H. the Prince of Orange* was written on one side in a flowing hand with loops and flourishes. Malcolm turned the paper over. On the other side, in the same hand, the words:

> *Not tonight. I'll explain later.*
> *J.*

"Interesting," Wellington said. "Because the thing is, Lady Julia did go to the rendezvous."

"Why the devil would she do that?"

"I don't know. But I'm afraid she had the misfortune to stumble into a French attack on an agent in our service." Wellington drew a breath. "I'm very sorry to tell you this, Your Royal Highness, but I'm afraid Lady Julia was killed this evening."

For a moment, Billy stared at the duke in blank incomprehension. Then the prince swayed on his feet. Malcolm pulled a chair forward and pushed Billy into it. Davenport crossed to a table with decanters, poured a glass of brandy, and put it in Billy's hand. The glass slipped from the prince's nerveless fingers, spattering cognac on his dancing shoes. Davenport caught the glass before it could fall to the floor and held it to Billy's lips.

The prince gulped down some brandy and coughed, his shoulders shaking. "But she can't be—"

"I'm afraid she most definitely is," Malcolm said. "Davenport and I saw her. A terrible tragedy."

Billy stared up at him with numb eyes. "If I'd gone to meet her—"

Malcolm gripped the prince's shoulder. "She told you not to. Something went terribly awry."

"Who else knew you and Lady Julia planned to meet at the château this evening?" Wellington asked.

"No one." Billy gulped down some more brandy.

"You're sure? You didn't mention it to any of your friends over port—"

"What sort of an idiot do you take me for? I wouldn't put Julia's reputation at risk."

Davenport's head snapped up, but he bit back whatever he had been going to say.

"How long had the affair been going on?" the duke said, in the same measured voice.

The prince stared at the splashes of brandy on the toes of his shoes, as though wondering how they had got there. "A month. Since early May. It was at the opera. She was so lovely. I never thought—"

"One doesn't usually in such situations," Wellington said.

"It didn't seem—It's the way marriages are conducted in the English ton."

Davenport didn't so much as draw a breath, but Malcolm felt the tension radiating off him like waves of heat from a smoldering fire.

Wellington, whose wife was home in London and who was himself engaged in what was at the very least an agreeable flirtation in Brussels with the very-much-married Lady Frances Webster, regarded the prince with drawn brows. "Not all English husbands are complacent. I don't pay much heed to such things, but from what I've observed, John Ashton gave the impression of being very much in love with his wife."

Billy blinked. "Julia said they had an understanding. She—" He looked up at Malcolm with the confused gaze Malcolm remembered from boyhood. "Are you sure it was Julia? Perhaps you made a mistake—"

"It was quite definitely Julia," Davenport said.

"She's your wife's sister, isn't she?" Stuart said on a note of surprise. "I forgot—"

"That I'm married?" Davenport asked. "I do the same myself much of the time."

Wellington stared at the prince for a long moment, flicked a glance at the brandy glass, looked pointedly at Davenport. Davenport refilled the glass and returned it to Billy.

"Drink that down," Wellington said, "and pull yourself together. You need to return to the ballroom as though nothing has happened."

"But I can't—"

"I assume you would not wish any scandal to attach to Lady Julia's memory. Nor would you wish for any ill feeling between yourself and her husband and his fellow officers. Difficult, I know, but I have no doubt Your Highness is equal to the task."

Billy's shoulders straightened perceptibly at this compliment from the mentor he admired. He swallowed the second brandy and got to his feet.

Wellington gave an approving nod and clapped the prince on the shoulder. "You'll do, lad. Stuart, you'd best go with him."

Stuart inclined his head and took Billy's arm. "Your Royal Highness."

Wellington watched the door close behind the two men. Then his gaze snapped to Malcolm and Davenport. "What you just heard stays within these walls."

"Sir—" Malcolm said.

"There's enough tension between the Dutch-Belgian forces and our lads as it is."

"Billy's popular among our officers," Malcolm pointed out. "One of their own."

"Even so. We don't need a damned scandal distracting everyone." Wellington crossed to a table that held a brace of candles and held Billy's note to Lady Julia·to one of the candle flames. "You never saw this," he said as the paper dissolved to black ash on the cherrywood tabletop. "Ideally Lady Julia was never at the château."

"And Julia's husband?" Davenport asked.

"He'll have to be told something." Wellington swept the crumbs of ash into his hand and tossed them into the cold grate. "But I don't think he'll want a scandal any more than we do."

Davenport had crossed to a pier table that held a single candle. He was holding Julia's note to the prince to the light. Not to burn it, to study. He stared at it with drawn brows.

"Best burn that as well," Wellington said.

"Not just yet I think." Davenport looked up from the paper. "It appears to be a forgery."

❧ 5 ❧

"What?" Wellington said. "You hadn't seen Lady Julia in four years. How the devil can you recognize her handwriting?"

"I can't. But I know a forgery when I see it." Davenport carried the note over to the duke. "See the breaks in the line? As though the writer wrote with painstaking care. Here he or she even traced back over. We don't do that when we write ourselves. We scrawl the words without thinking."

Malcolm studied the note, remembering Davenport giving him a similar lecture three years ago over an intercepted French dispatch. "He's right," Malcolm said. The breaks in the lines were obvious now Davenport had pointed them out. "Davenport usually is."

Wellington looked from Malcolm to Davenport, as though he'd just glimpsed an extra regiment of enemy troops lying in wait right before a battle. "That would mean—"

"That someone knew of the rendezvous and went to great lengths to ensure the prince wouldn't arrive for it," Malcolm said.

"And that Julia would be there alone," Davenport added.

The implications hung in the air like smoke after a cannon blast. "No one could have known the French would ambush you," Wellington said.

"Unless it wasn't the French shooting at us," Davenport said.

Wellington swung his gaze to the colonel. "You think someone who knew Malcolm was meeting La Fleur tonight lured Lady Julia to the château, shot at all of you, and killed La Fleur, just to get rid of Lady Julia?"

"I admit it's far-fetched. But it's not impossible. It's also possible that someone who knew nothing about Rannoch's meeting with La Fleur planned to confront Julia at the château and then hung back because of the gunfire."

"Was Johnny Ashton in the ballroom all evening?" Malcolm asked.

"I—" Wellington bit back the words. "I can't swear to it." His gaze was like ice. "But one way or another, Lady Julia's husband is the next person we need to talk to."

"Mrs. Rannoch?"

Suzanne turned to find herself looking into the bright eyes of Lady Caroline Lamb. Lord Byron's erstwhile mistress, the estranged wife of Malcolm's friend William Lamb, one of the most scandalous women in Britain. Suzanne smiled at her. She liked Lady Caroline despite—or perhaps because of—the stories of her outrageous behavior. Unlike many, Caro Lamb had never raised her brows at Malcolm Rannoch's foreign-born war bride.

"I don't believe you've met Lady Cordelia Davenport," Lady Caroline said, indicating the woman who stood beside her. "She's just this afternoon arrived in Brussels and is staying with me."

Suzanne exchanged greetings with Harry Davenport's wife. Close up, Lady Cordelia was not as tall as she had appeared when she entered the ballroom. Her presence lent her the illusion of height. The smile that had dazzled the ballroom was warm and direct, but Suzanne saw lines of strain behind Lady Cordelia's artfully applied eye blacking, and her face was pale beneath her wash of rouge.

"Caro says you're one of the most sensible women in Brussels, Mrs. Rannoch," Cordelia said. She had a low-pitched, musical voice. "And one of the best dressed. The second of which is quite obvious."

"She's half-French," Lady Caroline said. "She was born with an advantage."

"And that you've had all sorts of adventures in Spain with your intrepid husband."

Suzanne smiled. "No more than anyone else caught up in the midst of a war."

"And I daresay most of the arrangements for tonight's entertainment were yours," Lady Caroline said. "Stuart is fortunate to have you. Mrs. Rannoch, we need your help. You have a wonderful knack for knowing what is going on and to all intents and purposes you're the evening's hostess. Have you seen Julia—Lady Julia Ashton, that is?"

"She's my sister, you see," Cordelia Davenport said. "She doesn't know I've arrived in Brussels, and I've been looking everywhere for her."

Perfectly natural for Lady Cordelia to be looking for her sister, yet there was a tension in her voice that implied something more urgent than a sibling reunion. Suzanne cast a glance round the ballroom and then thought back through the evening. "I think the last time I saw Lady Julia was at supper. But there's such a press of people I don't think I've seen half the guests in the course of the evening."

"Of course," said Lady Cordelia. "I'm sure we'll find her eventually." But the tension seemed to tighten between her perfectly groomed brows.

The Honorable John Ashton, third son of the Earl of Langdon, had been in Malcolm's year at Harrow, though he'd bought a commission when he left rather than going on to Oxford as Malcolm had done. Malcolm remembered Ashton as an agreeable fellow, good at sports, a bruising rider, popular but not arrogant with those less well favored. Malcolm had helped him with Latin translations once or twice and Ashton had seemed genuinely grateful.

Ashton came into the salon to which Wellington had summoned him with a quick step, the light of the chase in his eyes. For him, like the Prince of Orange, secret councils implied Bonaparte was finally on the move. "Sir—" he said, then came up short at the sight of Malcolm. "Good God, Rannoch, what happened to you?" His gaze slid to Davenport and froze in confusion.

"Colonel Davenport," Wellington supplied. "One of my aides-de-camp, seconded to Colonel Grant."

"Pleased to meet you, we're relying on you lot." Ashton extended his hand, then frowned. "You're—"

"Cordelia's husband." Davenport shook Ashton's proffered hand. "I'm afraid we aren't meeting under the best of circumstances."

"Sit down, Ashton." Wellington put a hand on the captain's shoulder and pressed him into the same chair the Prince of Orange had earlier occupied. "Did you know your wife had left the ball?"

"Julia? Don't be absurd, she's been on the dance floor all evening. I just saw her at supper—" Ashton broke off, as though realizing how long ago that had been.

"Rannoch and Davenport had a meeting with a French contact at the Château de Vere tonight," Wellington said in brisk tones. "They were ambushed, and their contact was killed in the exchange. Unbeknownst to them, your wife was inside the château. She came out on the balcony and was struck by a musket ball. I'm very sorry to say that she is dead."

Brisk as a bucketful of cold water, a soldier's way of breaking bad news and probably the best choice in these circumstances.

Ashton stared up at his superior, a man who has had a knife plunged in his guts but is in too much shock to yet feel the pain. "But she couldn't—There has to be some mistake," he said, echoing the Prince of Orange.

"I'm afraid not." This time it was Davenport who addressed the question. "It was undoubtedly Julia. I knew her well at one time."

Ashton turned his gaze to the brother-in-law he had just met. "But if she was called away, why wouldn't she have told me?" He caught himself up short as he said this last, the obvious, painful explanation showing clearly in his heretofore-unshadowed blue-gray eyes. "No," he said. "Julia wouldn't—I won't let you slander her."

"No one," Wellington said, "would dream of slandering your unfortunate wife. But I think you may have to accept, Ashton, that we often know less than we think we do about those closest to us."

Davenport dropped a hand on Ashton's shoulder. For a moment, behind the colonel's controlled gaze, Malcolm glimpsed wounds that had lain festering for years.

Wellington was regarding Ashton, weighing his options. Tell Ashton the truth and risk a confrontation between the young captain and the Prince of Orange. Withhold the truth from Ashton and risk the outraged husband stumbling upon it himself to infinitely worse effect.

Perhaps Ashton's solid, confused gaze convinced him. This was a man bred up to put his country first.

"Ashton." Wellington seemed to measure his words even as he spoke. "We have reason to believe your wife had an assignation with the Prince of Orange at the château this evening."

"With the—"Ashton surged out of his chair. "That's a damned lie."

"I'm afraid the prince has admitted it."

"Then he's—" Ashton broke off, unable to come up with a logical reason why a man would falsely claim to be having an affair with another man's wife.

"The prince says your wife sent him a note canceling the rendezvous. Ashton, can you tell us if this is your wife's hand?"

Davenport held out Julia Ashton's supposed note. Ashton frowned at it. "It's like her hand." He traced the letters, as though seeking an echo of his wife's presence. Then he frowned. "But there's something a bit odd. The lines don't flow properly."

Davenport nodded. "It was forged."

Ashton shook his head. "First you tell me my wife had a rendezvous with the Prince of Orange, then you say someone forged a note so the prince wouldn't go to the rendezvous—In God's name why?"

"It's difficult to make sense of it," Malcolm said. "Do you know of anyone who might have wanted to meet with your wife secretly at the château?"

"Of course not. I didn't even know she'd—I still can't believe—"

Ashton pressed his hands over his face, his fingers shaking. Then he dropped his hands and looked from Malcolm to Davenport to Wellington, his gaze hardening. "Are you accusing me of setting this up? So I could confront her about her...her indiscretion? Of which I knew nothing—"

"No one's accusing you of anything, Ashton." Wellington rested a hand on the captain's shoulder. "You've suffered a great shock and a terrible loss. Unfortunately, this comes at a time when we can none of us dwell on personal matters. I think I need hardly tell you how disastrous any tension between our troops and the Dutch-Belgians would be just now."

Ashton's mouth drew into a tight line. "You're telling me not to plant the Prince of Orange a facer," he said in a tone that indicated he wouldn't soil his hands with the other man. "Or call him out."

"Among other things. Believe me, I can understand the temptation, but it could do incalculable harm. As well as casting scandal upon your wife's memory. Which, despite everything, I don't believe you would wish to do."

"No," Ashton said. The single word held a raw grief, just beginning to break through the shock. "But I want to understand—"

"So do we all," Wellington told him. "Your wife wasn't the only one to lose her life tonight. We lost one of our most valued agents. We need to discover precisely what happened to both of them."

"How—"

Wellington jerked his head at Malcolm. "Rannoch investigated a murder in Vienna."

"Murder?" Ashton said. "No one's suggesting Julia was—"

"No, of course not. But Rannoch's good at unraveling puzzles and putting the pieces back together. Malcolm?"

Malcolm had already seen where the conversation was leading. In truth, he wouldn't have been best pleased to have the matter put in someone else's hands. "I'll do my best, sir."

"You'll tell me what you discover?" Ashton said. "At least whatever relates to Julia?"

Malcolm looked into Ashton's pleading eyes and found himself saying, "Yes, of course," though he knew even as he framed the words that it might be a difficult promise to keep.

"Do you want someone to see you home?" Wellington asked. "I can understand you're not—"

"No, I'll manage. I just—Oh, Lord." Ashton grimaced. "Cordelia. She's here. In the ballroom. Just arrived in Brussels. She's been looking for Julia. We'll have to tell her—"

"I'll do it," Davenport said.

Ashton looked at him for a moment, blinking through his own distress. "Are you sure—?"

"No." Davenport gave a twisted half smile. "But when it comes to Cordelia I don't think it's possible for me to make matters any worse."

ଶ 6 ଶ

"Cordelia. What in God's name are you doing here?"

Cordelia Davenport turned from her conversation with Caro and Suzanne Rannoch to see a tall, broad-shouldered man with close-cropped golden-brown hair and an all-too-familiar smile striding along the edge of the dance floor.

"Major Chase." Cordelia extended her hand. "Why shouldn't I come to Brussels? All the world seems to have flocked here. I'm not usually so behind the fashion."

George brushed his lips over her hand, a bit stiffly. He met her gaze as he straightened up. "For God's sake, Cordy, it's dangerous."

"I doubt Wellington would care to hear you say so. You know Lady Caroline, of course," Cordelia said, grateful for the mask of social convention. "Have you met Mrs. Rannoch? Her husband is on Stuart's staff."

George nodded at the other two ladies with one of his quick, disarming smiles. "Forgive my informality. Cord—Lady Cordelia and I have known each other since we were children. I'm in the habit of worrying about her."

"A fatal mistake, Major Chase," Caro said. "Cordelia could look after herself at the age of six, and nothing puts her in such a temper as being fussed over."

George grinned. "With Cordy I've always been slow to learn my lessons." The look he turned to Cordelia was a mix of ruefulness and regret. It reminded her of the way he'd used to turn his head to meet her gaze one last time before he stepped into the carriage to return to Eton or Oxford, knowing it would be many months before they met again. Against all instincts to the contrary, her throat went tight.

George turned to Suzanne Rannoch. "I knew your husband a bit as a boy when he used to visit the Mallinsons at Carfax Court in Derbyshire. Always thought he'd do something remarkable."

"He was frighteningly clever," Cordelia said, recalling the tall, gangly boy with intent eyes and a quick wit. "And inclined to spend all his time in the library."

Suzanne Rannoch smiled. "Some things don't change."

"I hear Wellington claims Rannoch's the civilian he could least do without," George said.

"My husband would say one can't believe everything one hears in Brussels these days."

"You seem very sanguine, Mrs. Rannoch."

"As a diplomat's wife, one of my first duties is to calm the panic."

"And yet"—George cast a glance at the couples circling the floor—"I fear life in Brussels is not the picnic it appears."

Cordelia unfurled her fan, willing her fingers to hold steady against the ebony sticks. "Have you sent your own wife back to England?"

She heard George suck in his breath. He looked directly into her eyes, his own shadowed with...guilt? Apology? "No, Annabel's somewhere in the ballroom as it happens. I'm stationed at Ninove, on Uxbridge's staff, but we've taken a house in Brussels. We talked about Annabel taking the children back to England, but we—She felt it would be harder to be separated at such a time."

"How sweet." Cordelia took a sip of champagne and then cursed herself. She was being spiteful and neither George nor Annabel deserved that.

"It's different for Annabel," George said quickly. "She's a soldier's wife—"

"So am I if it comes to that. I don't suppose it occurred to you that I came to Brussels to see Harry?"

The look on George's face might have been comical had she been able to muster up anything remotely approaching laughter. "I'm sorry, Cordy," he said. "I should have realized—"

"Oh, don't look so apologetic, George. Harry isn't even in Brussels as it happens. I came here to see Julia, only I can't seem to find her anywhere in the ballroom or salons. Have you seen her?"

George frowned. "Not since supper, I think. But she's bound to turn up before long. Julia's not the sort to fade into the woodwork. She'll be glad to see you."

"I hope so," Cordelia said, for once speaking the unvarnished truth.

George touched her arm. "Don't be silly, Cordy. Whatever else, Julia will always be your sister. Ladies."

George inclined his head to Caro and Suzanne Rannoch and walked off along the edge of the dance floor.

Cordelia felt Caro's concerned gaze on her and Suzanne Rannoch's appraising one. How much of the story had Mrs. Rannoch heard? Not that it mattered. She was damned in any case. "George and I've known each other since we were both in the nursery," she said.

"Old friends know one in a way no one else quite does," Suzanne Rannoch said. Cordelia could see her trying to piece together the past, yet there was a surprising lack of judgment in her gaze. Not what Cordelia was accustomed to from respectable happily married women.

"Damnable, isn't it?" Cordelia said, throwing out the curse like a challenge. George was talking with two cavalry officers, head bent at a serious angle. A bit of a change. The old George would have been dancing with a pretty girl.

"Quite damnable." With two words Suzanne Rannoch picked up the challenge and rendered it irrelevant.

Caro touched Cordelia's arm. "Cordy—"

"It's quite all right, Caro. If I couldn't confront my past I'd never be able to go out in society."

"Lady Cordelia?"

Cordelia turned to tell the footman she didn't need any more champagne and saw that he was holding out a square of paper. "A gentleman asked me to give you this."

Cordelia took the paper.

I'm sure you find this as awkward as I do, but I have important news to impart. I beg you will grant me a few moments of your time. I fear I'm not fit for the ballroom.

H.

She knew the precise, slanted handwriting at once. Speaking of confronting one's past. She folded the paper between fingers that had gone nerveless. "Where is he?"

"In one of the salons."

Cordelia turned to Caro and Mrs. Rannoch. "Pray excuse me. It seems I need speak with my husband."

Caro made a quick move toward her. "Dearest—Do you want me to go with you?"

Cordelia drew together defenses carefully built over the past four years. "No, I shall be quite all right. I knew I might encounter Harry in Brussels after all. And I've just dealt with George. How bad can this be?"

The footman guided her along the edge of the ballroom and then held open a white-painted door. Cordelia stepped beneath the gilt pediment, feeling like Anne Boleyn on her way to her execution.

Oh, that was absurd. She wasn't a fanciful girl anymore.

It was a small room hung with cream silk and lit by a candelabrum and a couple of additional tapers. She caught a whiff of brandy in the air, overlaying the wood polish and lemon oil.

Harry stood on the far side of the room. Though his face was in shadow, she'd have known the mocking angle of his shoulders anywhere. For a moment she was a girl of twenty, her eye caught by the broody-looking young man with disordered brown hair and intense blue eyes, hovering on the edge of the Devonshire House dance floor. A quadrille that had been all the rage that season had been playing, and she'd wanted to avoid dancing with Toby

Somerton. How different would their lives have been, hers and Harry's, if she hadn't crossed the room to speak with him that night?

"Thank you for coming." He stepped forward as she pushed the door to. The light from the candelabrum fell across him, and she saw that his face had hardened into sharper planes and angles and that lines she didn't remember bracketed his mouth. He wore riding dress, not his uniform. His coat and breeches were splashed with mud and—Good God, was that blood?

"Harry—" She crossed to his side in three quick steps, her hand extended. "Are you hurt—"

"No." His voice forestalled her before she could touch him. "The blood isn't mine. It belonged to a poor French bastard who was selling us information and got caught. At least that's what seems to have happened."

She let her hand fall to her side and clasped her gloved fingers together. "That's why you're back in Brussels."

"Yes, in a roundabout way. I'm sorry, I don't suppose you expected to see me."

"I knew it was a possibility. But then we're foolish to think we can avoid each other forever. At some point you'll come back to England."

"I suppose anything's possible."

"Perhaps it's easier to see each other first here rather than in London with the ton staring at us like fish in a bowl. Was that why you asked to see me?"

"No." He ran a hand over his hair, an uncharacteristic gesture. "Cordelia—Perhaps you should sit down." He reached out a hand as though to take her arm, then let it fall to his side and instead pulled a shield-back chair forward.

There was something in his eyes that was suspiciously like pity. She jerked away from it and from the proffered chair. "For God's sake, Harry, don't be silly. I'm not some missish girl. Whatever it is you have to tell me say it straight out."

Harry swallowed. She saw that beneath the grime and blood and the layer of tan from years in the field his skin had gone pale. "I went to a château just outside Brussels this evening to warn

Malcolm Rannoch and this agent of ours that our communications had been rumbled. We were caught in a French ambush. It was only afterwards that we realized someone else had been in the château and had died in the cross fire. A woman." His gaze fastened on her face with a gentleness she had never thought to see again when he looked at her. "It was Julia. I'm sorry, Cordy."

For a moment the room swam before her eyes, a dark void she could not look into. A roaring filled her ears and a silent scream echoed in her head.

Strong fingers closed on her arms. She clung to him, her fingers digging into the cloth of his coat. The smell of blood and stale sweat washed over her, and beneath it a whiff of spice, a scent she had not smelled in so long it was half forgot.

His quick intake of breath stirred her hair. Then he steered her to the side and pressed her into the chair. A moment later he put a glass into her hand and guided it to her lips. She choked down a sip of brandy.

"You're sure it was Julia?" Her sister's laughing voice echoed in her ears.

"I'm sure." He knelt beside her, his hand hovering near the glass in her hand.

"You haven't seen her in four years—"

"Cordy, I'm sure. I don't forget so easily."

She darted a quick look at him but saw none of the usual mockery in his expression, only a sympathy that cut her to the quick. "I'd been trying to find her ever since I got to the ball. If I'd arrived sooner—"

His hand closed over her own. No doubt to keep the glass from falling from her fingers. "Guilt will get you nowhere."

"She left the ball and went—What in God's name was she doing there?"

"I don't know," he said. But she saw the flicker in his eyes, a shutter drawn closed over whatever he knew.

"You mean you won't tell me."

"Yes, I thought there hadn't been enough tragedy tonight, I'd throw in some lies to top it off." Harry sat back on his heels. "Whatever Julia was doing at the château, it had nothing to do with Rannoch's meeting with La Fleur, which was what took me there—"

"That doesn't mean you don't have more information." She jerked her hand away from his and took a quick swallow of brandy. It stung her throat. All her senses came flooding back. "She was there for a rendezvous, wasn't she?"

"Cordelia—"

"Oh, for God's sake, why else would a woman slip off in the midst of a ball and go to a lonely château? After all, I'm an expert in such matters. Don't tell me you were avoiding the nasty truth to spare my sensibilities, that would be too rich." She looked down into his face, closed now as a book in an unknown tongue. "It's because of whom the rendezvous was with, isn't it? Someone you think it's too sensitive for me to know about."

His gaze remained steady, but she could tell from the quick flash in his eyes that she'd guessed correctly. She could still read Harry well, for all she'd never properly understood him.

"Damn you." She pushed herself to her feet, scraping the chair against the floorboards. "My sister's dead and you're covering it up like a good little soldier."

He got to his feet as well. "It would seem that way to you, I suppose. Though I doubt any of my commanding officers would agree that I've ever been anything remotely approaching a good little soldier."

He had retreated behind that caustic mask that had always driven her to distraction. One could never air anything with Harry in a proper fight. "*Seem?* Don't play your word games with me, Harry. We're talking about my baby sister. Or are you just as glad to have one less Brooke in the world?"

"I was smiling all the way back to Brussels. For God's sake, Cordelia." He didn't raise his voice, but the words stopped her like a slap to the face. "Julia was—" Memories cracked open the reserve in his eyes. "Julia welcomed me to the family. She was always kind to me."

"A great deal kinder than I was." The anger drained out of her, leaving a sick feeling in the pit of her stomach. "A pity for you it wasn't me who died."

Something jerked in his eyes that might have been anger. "Hardly. That would have entailed entirely too many complications."

She shot a sharp look at him.

"I've never wished you harm, Cordy." He swallowed. Harry had always been frighteningly honest. "At least not—"

"After the first few weeks?" she asked, the ashes of memory bitter on her tongue.

His mouth twisted. "It's odd how angry one can be over commonplace trivialities."

Cordelia swallowed the last of her brandy and clunked the glass down on the nearest table. "None of this changes the facts. My sister's dead, and you're under orders to cover it up for fear of embarrassing the army."

"Quite. With Boney about to march, avoiding embarrassment is obviously Wellington's top priority."

"So he's taking no interest in the matter at all?"

Harry leaned his hand on a chairback. "Wellington's asked Malcolm Rannoch to look into it. From what I've seen of Rannoch, he won't rest until he uncovers the truth."

"And when he does uncover it?" She closed her fingers on her elbows, nails digging into the silk of her gloves. "Just who will be told this elusive truth?"

He met her gaze without flinching. "I'll tell you what I can."

"What you *can.*"

"You know I can't promise you more, Cordelia."

"I suppose if nothing else we've learned not to make false promises to each other." She glanced into the empty depths of her brandy glass. "Does Johnny know?"

"Wellington told him himself."

"And Johnny's agreed to hold his tongue. Duty first, stiff upper lip, 'lov'd I not honor more,' and all that. Does he know Julia had a lover?"

Harry's gaze darkened. "He does now."

"Poor Johnny. So perhaps love isn't entering into it so very much."

"No, I'd say Ashton's grief for Julia's loss overwhelmed all else.

He reacted much better than I did in similar circumstances," Harry added, as though he were speaking of someone quite disconnected to him.

"Well, if I'd died, you'd have had more incentive to be noble."

His gaze moved over her face, sharp and probing. "Did you know, Cordy?"

"Know what?"

"That Julia had a lover."

"We don't confide in each other as much as we used to. I'm a bit too scandalous for Julia to be seen too much with me, though I have to say Johnny's always been very kind—Oh God." She closed her arms across her chest as nausea welled up in her throat. "Where is she?" she asked, when she could force out the words.

He hesitated, though he did not pretend to misunderstand her. "We brought her back to Lisbon in a cart. It's in Stuart's stable at present."

"I want to see her."

He gave a curt nod. "I'll take you."

She'd been prepared for argument, but then whatever else he'd been as a husband, Harry had never been overprotective. He moved to a French window that led to the terrace and held it open for her. She swept past him.

A breeze rippled across the garden, fresh with the incongruous scent of roses and lilies. Wrong somehow that the world could still smell so fragrant in the face of such horror.

Harry didn't attempt to take her arm, but he led her across the garden, walking close but not so close that his arm brushed against her own or her skirts fell over his boots. He stopped before a gate in the back wall. "Cordelia—" he said, his hand on the latch.

"I've seen a dead body before," she told him. "I was with my father when he died."

"But you haven't seen someone who died by violent means. It's—"

"Quite horrific, I daresay, and there's no way to prepare one for it." She pulled the folds of her net scarf tighter about her. "So we'd better just get on with it."

He nodded and held open the gate. She stepped through, met

by the smell of manure and leather and saddle soap. A lantern at one end of the mews drew her eye to the dark outlines of what must be the cart. She hesitated, sickeningly grateful when Harry stepped up beside her, close enough that she could feel the warmth of his body. "La Fleur, the French agent, is in the cart as well," he told her. "It's all right," he called to the groom who stood beside the cart. "This is the lady's sister."

The lantern cast a discordantly warm glow on the rough wood slats of the cart. Cordelia took a determined step forward. She caught a whiff of blood. The lobster patties and champagne from supper rose up in her throat.

Within the cart lay two dark bundles. Two bodies, wrapped in coarse brown blankets. Harry moved to her side and pulled down a corner of one of the blankets with fingers that were surprisingly gentle.

Her sister's eyes stared up at her. Or rather what had been her eyes, for it was all too clear that the life had fled. The brilliant blue that scores of ardent young gentlemen had likened to cornflowers or sapphires had frozen and faded to a watery gray. Her side curls were shorter than when Cordelia had last seen her in London. Her mouth, carefully painted with lip rouge, was parted slightly, not in pain but perhaps in surprise. Beneath the lip rouge, it had a bluish cast. Her skin, always so smooth and glowing, had a waxen quality, like a creature at Madame Tussaud's.

For the first time, Cordelia understood properly that Julia was gone. A cry stuck in her throat, too raw to be given voice.

Blood congealed round a gaping wound at the base of Julia's throat. The bullet must have struck an artery.

"It would have been very quick," Harry said at Cordelia's shoulder. "She wouldn't have felt anything."

She nodded. Her fingers dug into the side of the cart. She was afraid if she let go she'd collapse on the cobblestones. She drew a breath and brushed her free hand against Julia's cheek. She tried to lean over, but the cart was too deep. She put a foot on one of the spokes of the wheel and pulled herself up. Without speaking, Harry gripped her waist and steadied her as she bent over Julia's body.

The smell of blood washed over her again, but this time she did not recoil. She bent down and touched her lips to her sister's brow. Cold, no blood flowing beneath the skin. The final confirmation of what a part of her mind still refused to accept.

When she straightened up, Harry lifted her down and kept his hands on her waist to steady her. She looked up into his face. The lamplight lent his skin unexpected warmth. "Thank you."

His eyes glinted with something she could not name. "I did little enough."

"No. It was a great deal." She stepped out of his hold. Harry had got her through the past quarter hour, and she would be forever grateful for that. One more debt to add to the balance of what she owed him.

But for what lay ahead he would not be an ally and might quite possibly be her enemy. Because she was going to learn what had happened to Julia and see her avenged.

The consequences to the Allied army be damned.

ᑋ 7 ᑋ

"I'm sorry, my dear." Stuart materialized out of the crowd at Suzanne's side. "Unexpected complications. Any damage here?"

"A few people commented on you and Wellington having disappeared, and then Georgy Lennox noticed that you had fetched the Prince of Orange. No sooner had I calmed her down than Mr. Creevey noticed it as well. Rumors started that Bonaparte was on the march. For a moment I thought we were on the verge of a full-scale panic, but then I said that you'd mentioned you had some particularly fine new port you wanted to share with Wellington and the prince. That seemed to quiet things down."

"Clever girl." Stuart squeezed her arm. "I knew you could be relied upon. Sounds as though I should circulate though. If you hear any comments on Slender Billy having gone home, you might mention that he drank one too many glasses of that port. Malcolm should be back with you in a bit. He's having a chat with one of the footmen."

"Sir—"

Stuart turned back to look at her.

"Is Malcolm injured?" Suzanne asked.

"Didn't he assure you he wasn't?"

"Of course. But he would, wouldn't he?"

Stuart grinned. "Just so. Take my word for it, Suzanne, on this occasion you'll have him home in one piece. Though it looks to be a long night for all of us."

Harry Davenport walked Cordelia back to the house. It seemed the least he could do, though he could not imagine she took any comfort in his presence. He didn't try to take her arm or otherwise touch her. Nor did he speak, for which he sensed she was grateful. She walked with deliberate steps, her head held high. Cordelia had always had courage, he'd give her that.

He held open the gate to the garden. They proceeded down the gravel paths and up the terrace steps to the French window that opened onto the salon in which they had spoken a quarter hour since. He wondered if it felt as much an eternity to her as it did to him.

He held the French window open for her, then pulled it to behind them and nodded at the door to the ballroom. "I'd best not go in. There's no way to explain the state I'm in. I can arrange for a carriage—"

"Thank you." Cordelia's voice was level though it trembled a bit. "I need to find Caro."

"Caro?"

"Caroline Lamb. I'm staying with her."

Of course. Caro Lamb was a childhood friend of Cordelia's. Harry had never been quite sure what to say to the quixotic Lady Caroline, though he'd got on well with her husband, William. Which perhaps was not a good omen, given what had become of William and Caro's marriage.

Cordelia put up a hand to her cheek. "Is there—Do I have blood on my face?"

He took a step closer so he could see her better in the candlelight. "No. Just a smudge on your jaw. To the left." He started to wipe it away for her, as he would once have done unthinkingly, but his own hands were so filthy he'd do more damage. And despite the way she had clung to him in shock, he couldn't imagine she'd want him touching her.

Cordelia opened the steel clasp on the reticule that hung from her wrist and took out a silver-backed mirror. He studied her as she wiped the smudge from her jaw, pushed loose strands of hair back into their pins, rubbed at the blacking that had smeared below her eyes. To his shame, he could still trace the bones of her face from memory. But her skin was stretched more tautly over those bones, and there were fine lines he didn't remember about her eyes and at the corners of her mouth. The eyes themselves still held the wounds of this night's revelations. And perhaps other scars as well.

He had thought a ridiculous number of times—in a camp bed, hidden in prickly bracken, wading through icy streams, bored at a regimental ball—of what he'd say to her if he saw her again. How she'd look, how he'd respond, what he would and wouldn't admit. Julia's death rendered that all completely trivial.

Cordelia returned the mirror to her reticule and snapped the clasp shut. "More or less in order. At least able to go back on-stage."

He shifted his position, resting his bad arm on a chairback.

"You *are* hurt," Cordelia said, her gaze going to his arm.

"No. Not tonight." He'd been unaware he was favoring it. "Bad break at Salamanca. Didn't set properly." And was a constant, gnawing pain. Like other things. "Bit of a nuisance."

Cordelia watched him with a frowning gaze he couldn't interpret. He'd got used to reading people. He forgot she'd always been a cipher. He started to reach out a hand to her, then let it fall. "I don't know how much longer I'll be in Brussels. If you need—"

"Thank you. I'll be fine."

He gave a twisted smile. "I'll do my best to stay out of your way."

"That's not what I meant. But I'm rather good at looking after myself."

Her life was elsewhere, she might as well have said. Which was true. As was his. And yet—He might never see her again. A battle loomed in the not-so-distant future, and like any battle it could well prove to be his last.

Perhaps that was what drove him to speak, when every instinct of rationality called for silence. "Cordy."

She was already reaching for the door handle. She turned over her shoulder to look at him.

A few brief lines in one or two letters. Unthinking words from an acquaintance who didn't know the true state of his marriage. How many times had he told himself it didn't matter? Which it didn't. Shouldn't. "How is ... the child?"

Her fingers tightened round the door handle. "Surely you know her name, Harry."

"How's Livia?" The name felt odd on his lips. Had he ever voiced it before? Most people were careful not to speak to him of her.

"She's fine. She's at Caro's with her nurse."

Harry stared at his wife. "I always underestimate the risks you'll run. You've brought her to Brussels?"

"Where else would she be? I'm her mother."

He took two steps toward her and seized her wrist. "This isn't a game, Cordelia, whatever the holidaymakers thronging to Brussels may think. It was dangerous enough two months ago, but now we could be at war at any moment. If you choose to play dice with your own safety that's your affair, but to drag the child into it—"

She jerked away from his grip. "What right—"

"A father's. At least in name."

She smoothed the links of her diamond bracelet, twisted by his grip. "You've never set eyes on her or written to her. You've scarcely even asked after her. How dare you—"

"How dare I what?"

"Presume I don't have her interests at heart." She snapped a link back into place. "Presume to know me at all."

A harsh laugh broke from his lips. "You're right. That was always my error." He stared for a moment into the eyes that had caught him across a ballroom all those years ago. "Can you honestly tell me you *wanted* me to ask after her? To try to see her? To be anything approaching a father? To come anywhere near either of you?"

"I—" She swallowed. "I didn't ask you to leave."

"It would have been a bit crowded if I'd remained."

The tension drained from her shoulders. She closed her eyes for a moment. "You did more for Livia than anyone could have expected," she said, in a tone that reminded him of a rifleman after an exchange of fire. "But that doesn't—"

"Give me the right to interfere?"

"Harry—" She put out her hand, then snatched it back. "I warned you I'd make you a damnable wife. You didn't believe me."

"No." For a moment it was five years ago and he was stripped as raw as he'd been when he met her. "Even through my haze of infatuation I believed you. It was just that having you on any terms seemed infinitely preferable to not having you at all."

Harry went into the adjoining salon, where he knew Malcolm Rannoch had been interrogating the footmen. He found Rannoch alone, frowning at the notebook in his hand.

"Any luck?" Harry asked.

"The note was left on a footman's tray among the champagne glasses. Just about any of the guests could have put it there."

"So someone wanted to confront Julia at the château alone. Someone who knew about her rendezvous with the prince."

"So it would seem." Rannoch looked up at him. "Did you talk to your—To Lady Cordelia?"

Harry nodded. "And took her to see her sister's body. She insisted on it."

Rannoch didn't express the surprise or horror he expected. "Many people shy away from looking at the dead, but it makes it easier to accept the loss, I think. In the long run. Did Lady Cordelia know about her sister's affair?"

"She claimed not to."

"But—?"

Harry dropped into a chair. "She knows more than she's admitting. I've never been very good at reading Cordelia, but I could tell that much."

Stuart poked his head round the door. "I've got evening clothes laid out for you in a room upstairs."

"Thank you." Harry glanced down at his stained coat. "But

there's no need for me to go into the ballroom. I expect I'll be leaving Brussels by dawn—"

"Not according to Wellington. He says he's keeping you here to work with Rannoch. Expect I've breached protocol by telling you myself, but sometimes can't see the sense in waiting for official channels. Third bedchamber by the top of the stairs, Malcolm. You know the way. Have to get back to the party or there'll be more rumors of God knows what."

"I'm sorry," Malcolm said when Stuart had ducked out. "You were eager to return to Grant."

"Couldn't wait to be back sleeping on the hard ground, but I'll make do with a featherbed and proper sheets if duty calls." One could not very well voice one's qualms about being in the city with one's estranged wife. Not to mention the child one had never met.

Rannoch moved to a side door. "If it's any comfort, I'll welcome your assistance. Particularly as you know the individuals involved."

"Not being blind or dumb, you've no doubt realized my wife and I are not precisely on convivial terms."

"But you know her."

Harry didn't even attempt to contain the bitterness of his laugh. "I think I know Cordelia less now than the day I married her."

Rannoch regarded him for a moment with a gaze that, Harry feared, saw far more than he would have wished. "There are different types of knowing. If it's any comfort, I've been married two and a half years and I still feel I'm coming to know my wife. But last autumn I learned the risks that can come from keeping secrets."

Harry had little faith in the long-term success of any marriage, but he'd always been struck by the easy rapport between Malcolm and Suzanne Rannoch. He thought back to his brief glimpse of Suzanne Rannoch when she had met them in the garden upon their arrival at Stuart's house. Even in the moonlight, her exquisite features had been plain to see, the pointed chin and winged brows and generous mouth, but what had been most striking was the quick, direct exchange between her and Rannoch. Almost as though they were comrades in arms rather than spouses or lovers.

Even in his most deluded romantic moments, it had never occurred to Harry to think of his wife as a comrade.

"You're a fortunate man, Rannoch," he said. "You have a wife you can talk to. Talking never worked very well for Cordelia and me. But then we were about as spectacularly ill-suited as one could imagine." He hesitated, then added, "I don't believe she'll let the question of Julia's death go."

Rannoch regarded him for a moment. "Neither will we."

"No." Harry knew Rannoch's reputation as a fair man who went his own way. But Rannoch was also bound to report to Wellington and Stuart and accede to their instructions. As was Harry himself. But in Rannoch's case, duty wasn't complicated by the fact that Julia was his sister-in-law. Harry wasn't at all sure where he'd come down when they knew the truth behind Julia's death. This wouldn't be the first time he'd bent the rules when it came to orders.

Rannoch was watching him with shrewd eyes. "But you're worried about what Lady Cordelia will do with the answers?"

"Cordelia's never been one to shy away from scandal. Nor from the truth."

"I've no desire to tarnish your sister-in-law's memory, Davenport. Nor have I any stomach for being part of a cover-up."

Harry inclined his head and moved to the door. He still didn't know Rannoch well enough to say more.

$\approx$ 8 $\approx$

Cordelia Davenport knocked at a shiny blue-painted door in Rue Royale. From her sister's letters, she knew that this house with the neat brass knocker was where Julia and Johnny had been staying in Brussels.

If she had arrived in Brussels two hours sooner, if she hadn't stopped on the journey from Ostend so Livia could have milk and cakes in the coffee room of Les Trois Reines, if instead of dressing for the ball and talking to Caro she'd gone straight to Julia's the moment she arrived in Brussels—If somehow she'd managed to speak with her sister before the ball.

Cordelia drew a breath that shuddered against her corset laces. The questions would be with her until the day she died.

A footman whose crumpled neckcloth and unfocused gaze suggested he had been dozing in the hall pulled open the door.

"I'm here to see Captain Ashton," Cordelia said.

The footman blinked at her with sleep-flushed eyes. "Madame, it's—"

"I'm his sister-in-law." Cordelia pushed past him into the entrance hall. Marble tiled with pale blue walls and crisp white moldings. Small but exquisitely proportioned. Cards of invitation spilled from a silver filigree box on a pier table. A trace of familiar jasmine and iris scent lingered in the air. Trust Julia to find an elegant abode. She always—She *had* always—Damnation.

"Where's Captain Ashton?" Cordelia demanded before tears could betray her.

"The study. But, madame—"

It was a good guess that the double doors beneath the ornate doorcase to the left led to a library. She pulled open the dark paneled door beyond them. Candlelight and the smell of brandy greeted her. Johnny sat slumped in a leather wingback chair, a glass in his hand, a single taper burning on the table beside him. He looked up at the opening of the door, but it seemed a moment or two before he made sense of her presence.

"Cordelia." Her name was almost a question.

Cordelia pushed the door to and advanced into the room. "Harry told me."

A spasm crossed his face. "Should have told you myself. But I couldn't face—"

"You needed to get out of there before you collapsed. It's just as well. I needed to hear what Harry had discovered. And he took me to see Julia."

"You *saw* her?" Johnny stared at her for a moment, then shuddered. "Dear God, I should have—I didn't even—" A flame of desperate hope lit his eyes. "Was it her? Are you sure?"

Cordelia sank down on a footstool beside her brother-in-law's chair. "I'm afraid there's no doubt, Johnny." She laid her hand over his own.

"No. Of course not." He took a quick swallow of brandy, then stared into the glass as though he were looking into the gates of hell. "Did you know?"

"That Julia was dead? Of course not, how—"

"That she was the Prince of Orange's mistress." Johnny's lips twisted with uncharacteristic bitterness as he framed the words. And with a sort of disbelief, as though even now a part of his brain refused to make sense of it.

"The Prince of Orange?" Cordelia drew a sharp breath. So that was what Harry hadn't wanted to tell her. Dear God, what had her sister been up to? "Johnny, I haven't seen Julia since you left England."

"She writes—wrote—to you every week. More sometimes. She always confided in you. Especially—"

"You think one adulteress confides in another?"

Johnny flinched.

"I'm sorry," Cordelia said. "That was uncalled for. You were never quick to judge me."

His fingers tightened round the glass. "Were there…others?"

For an incongruous moment she saw Harry, not tonight, but four years ago, before his face had acquired the bitter lines it now bore and his eyes had grown bleak and closed. His gaze had been uncharacteristically open that night and so vulnerable, and when she answered his questions she'd seen her words smash home in his eyes.

"Johnny, Julia was—"

"I thought she loved me. I thought we were happy."

Cordelia pressed her fingers over the black net and claret satin of her gown. The fabric gleamed bloodred between the white of her gloves. "Johnny, just because a woman strays it doesn't necessarily mean she doesn't love her husband. Or even that she isn't happy."

"But—"

"After all, that's what gentlemen always say about their *chère-amies*, isn't it?"

He opened his mouth to protest, then frowned. "So there *were* others?"

She sorted through a weight of suspicions and half-truths balanced against the fragility in her brother-in-law's eyes. "I'm not sure. I do know she was very happy when she married you."

"I thought she was. But I thought I was sure of a lot of things about her." Johnny took another swallow of brandy. "God. Do you think Robbie—"

Cordelia drew a sharp breath at the thought of her nephew. "He looks just like you, Johnny."

"I can never see it properly."

"One can't often with one's own children." She saw Livia for a moment when she had gone in to kiss her good night before the ball, curled up peacefully in her bed at Caro's. And then she saw Robbie with his bright eyes and quick smile. An eager little boy who would now grow up without a mother. "How is he?"

"What—" Johnny ran a hand over his hair. "He's fine. Asleep. I looked in on him when I got home. Needed to be sure he was all right somehow. But I didn't—Dear Christ, how do you tell a two-year-old his mother's dead?"

Cordelia touched his hand again. "I can come back in the morning if you like. But he needs to hear it from you."

Johnny gave a quick nod, his gaze fixed on his brandy glass. "If I hadn't brought them here. If I'd made them go back to England—"

"I've been thinking the same thoughts myself." She crossed her arms, pressing her fingers against her rib cage. "They get one nowhere."

He hunched his shoulders as though fighting off a wave of—Pain? Guilt? "I can't even remember the last moment I saw her. Across the supper room, I think." The bitterness in his voice had given way to the ache of loss. "Wellington and Rannoch said someone arranged for her to arrive alone at the château tonight. Who—"

"Johnny, this is important." Cordelia took the brandy glass from his hand and set it on the table beside the taper. "Had Julia done or said anything out of the ordinary in recent days?"

He cast a glance at the glass, then frowned at her. "No. I told you, I had no idea—"

"Not about her affair with the Prince of Orange. Did she seem distressed?"

"She didn't—" Johnny frowned in a seemingly genuine effort of memory. "We've been flitting from one event to another. And with me being called to my regiment so much, there were whole days when we saw each other only in the carriage on the way to some damn dinner or ball. Oh God, do you think—"

"It takes more than that to make someone stray." Although God knows boredom could play far more of a role in infidelity than she'd like to admit.

"She seemed—More restless perhaps. Her eyes had that glitter they get sometimes, and I don't think she was sleeping well. She'd started taking laudanum drops. And when I suggested two days ago that in view of the situation she might take Robbie back to England, she nearly bit my head off. It was the worst row we've had since—"

"Since you found out about her gambling debts?"

Johnny turned his head away. "That was years ago. When we were first married and foolish. I—"

"You had every right to be angry. Johnny, was Julia gambling again?"

"Of course not." He swung his gaze back to her. "What makes you ask that?"

"Perhaps our father's example. Once a gamester, always a gamester."

"No. Not Julia. She promised me—" He gave a harsh laugh. "That's rich, isn't it? But I'd swear she hasn't played more than silver loo since all that nonsense." He picked up the brandy glass and turned it in his hand, as though searching for answers in the cut glass.

Cordelia studied him. She'd known Johnny since they were all in the nursery, playing in Hyde Park under the supervision of their nursery maids, riding their first ponies, sharing iced cakes and cambric tea at birthday parties. Johnny had always been kind and dependable, quick to smooth over a fight, to rescue a doll tossed into the duck pond, to play patiently with the younger children. He was one of the most open people she'd ever encountered. Looking into his ravaged gaze now, she knew without a doubt that his grief was genuine.

But she had a niggling certainty, sharp as a knife stab, that there was something he wasn't telling her.

Malcolm made his way across the ballroom, stopping to speak to Fitzroy Somerset (who ran a shrewd gaze over his not-quite-perfectly fitting coat) and to several others who didn't seem to have the least idea he'd been missing from the party. He found his wife at last by the French windows, talking to a tall, thin man with a shock of dark hair, a fine-boned face, and intense gray eyes.

"O'Roarke." Malcolm held out his hand. "I was wondering where you'd got to."

"I was wondering the same, Rannoch." Raoul O'Roarke shook Malcolm's hand.

"You know my habit of disappearing into the library at entertainments. My wife often bemoans it. I spent a bit longer with David Hume than I intended."

"Indeed." O'Roarke's gaze told Malcolm he saw a good deal more. Raoul O'Roarke was no stranger to intrigue. Half-Spanish, half-Irish, he was a friend of Malcolm's parents and had been involved in the United Irish Uprising in 1798. In more recent years he had worked with the *guerrilleros* who had allied with the British in driving the French out of Spain during the war in the Peninsula. "Rumors were circulating through the ballroom like wildfire for a bit," O'Roarke added, "but they seem to have died down. Your wife has formidable diplomatic skills."

"Vienna taught me a whole different set of skills from the Peninsula," Suzanne said, curling her hand round Malcolm's arm.

"Quite so." O'Roarke smiled. "I must be off. I still have to pay my respects to the Duchess of Richmond."

Malcolm squeezed Suzanne's hand as O'Roarke strolled across the ballroom. "Sorry for deserting you for a bit."

Suzanne's gaze moved over his borrowed clothes. "That coat doesn't fit quite as well as the one you arrived in."

"I know, I think Fitzroy noticed and probably O'Roarke did as well. But hopefully most people will just think they missed the bad tailoring the first look round. It's not as though I'm known for my sartorial splendor."

"Tell that to Addison."

Malcolm grinned. His valet, Addison, was a good agent in his own right but also meticulous about the fit of coats and the proper amount of starch in a cravat and champagne in boot polish. "Thank God Addison isn't here. I'd never live this down."

Suzanne tilted her head back to look up at him. "How bad is it?"

He let his gaze roam over the ballroom. Wellington was standing beside his latest flirt, Lady Frances Webster, surrounded by a knot of people, laughing and apparently entertaining them with an anecdote. Stuart was circling the room, champagne glass in hand, the picture of a relaxed host. "Not good. And I'm going to need your help."

She smiled with something like relief. "I'm glad I at least don't have to argue with you about that."

"After Vienna? I wouldn't dream of it."

He could see the questions chasing themselves behind his wife's alert gaze, but she knew better than to voice them in public. In the event, it was another hour before he was able to answer her questions. They had to wait until the guests began to drift from the ball. Social life in Brussels had been frenetic all spring. Guests seemed to linger longer and longer at social engagements, as though determined to extract every last moment of pleasure as the prospect of war loomed ever nearer.

Harry Davenport strolled up beside Malcolm and Suzanne as the earliest guests were leaving. "Considering I wasn't properly invited, it seems only tactful to make myself scarce. I'll see you at Headquarters in the morning."

"You have somewhere to stay?" Malcolm asked him.

"Wouldn't be much of an agent if I couldn't scrounge up lodgings at a moment's notice." Davenport inclined his head to Suzanne. "Mrs. Rannoch."

Wellington stayed until almost the last of the guests had left, talking, laughing, dancing one or two waltzes, giving no appearance of a man about to face the most important military engagement of his career. He stopped on his way out and touched Malcolm on the arm.

"Come round to Headquarters in the morning, Rannoch."

"Of course, sir."

Wellington nodded and smiled at Suzanne. "My thanks for your efforts this evening, my dear."

"Purely routine, Your Grace."

"As are all of ours, my dear girl. That doesn't make them less necessary."

Stuart came up to them ten minutes later. "That's all but the stragglers. You two should be off. Wellington will want you before noon, Malcolm."

And given the talking he and Suzanne still had to do, Malcolm doubted he'd get much sleep. Not that he felt remotely tired.

At last he and Suzanne were free to return to the house they had taken in the Rue Ducale. For the first time in their married life, they had a whole house to themselves. They could even, he supposed, have taken separate bedchambers, as was the accepted practice with most couples in their set. He'd wondered, fleetingly, if Suzanne would prefer that when they'd first seen the house. But she'd pointed out the bedchamber she thought could be theirs with just the faintest of questions in her voice and eyes. And he'd nodded matter-of-factly, answering her unvoiced question without addressing it, aware of an unlooked-for rush of relief.

The truth was, it would be damnably odd not to have the warmth of her curled beside him, not to smell her scent and face powder when he stepped into the room, not to see lacy bits of her clothing strewn about. But of course he couldn't say so. There were still certain boundaries they didn't cross in their marriage.

They looked in on their son, sleeping peacefully in the glow of the tin-shaded night-light in his room next door to their own. Difficult to believe Colin would turn two tomorrow—or rather today—Malcolm thought, twitching his son's blanket straight. It seemed only yesterday he had been kneeling by Suzanne's bedside, holding a basin of hot water and holding on to his self-command for all he was worth. Nothing in his life had equaled the wonder of the moment when Geoffrey Blackwell placed the squirming baby in his arms.

When they stepped into the quiet of their bedchamber Suzanne gave a sigh of relief, as though relinquishing her armor for the first time that evening. She dropped her gauzy shawl and ribboned reticule on the dressing table, unfastened her garnet necklace, and began to peel off her gloves. Malcolm went to a side table that held the whisky he'd brought from Scotland and poured them each a glass.

Suzanne took the glass he gave her, perched on the dressing

table bench, and waited for him to speak. Malcolm shrugged out of his coat and draped it over the damask armchair, then dropped down on the chair arm. He tossed back a smoky draught of whisky and stared into the glass for a moment. "I lost a man tonight. A French soldier who was a contact."

Concern flashed in Suzanne's eyes. "That's whom you went to meet?"

"Wellington got a message from him at the ball. His name was La Fleur." It was the first time he had mentioned La Fleur specifically to his wife. Even with her, his ingrained instinct to hold his contacts close to his chest held true.

"I'm sorry." Suzanne got up and moved to perch beside him. She slid her arm round him and leaned her head against his chest. "But you must know it wasn't your fault."

"Did I say I thought it was?"

"No, but I can tell what you're thinking. What you think when you lose anyone you feel remotely responsible for."

He slid his fingers along the nape of her neck and into her hair. "He flung himself over me. Damned fool. If he hadn't—"

She sat back, catching his hand in her own. "I'll be forever grateful to him."

He recognized the look in her eyes. He'd felt the same on more than one hair-raising occasion when she'd nearly been shot, knifed, drowned fording a river. Circumstances that, more often than not, she'd been in because she happened to be his wife.

"So will I," he said. For a moment the prospect of Suzanne left alone in a foreign country, their son growing up without a father, hung starkly before him. It was an ever-present risk in this life they lived. "But that doesn't lessen—"

"Guilt is singularly wasteful, Malcolm. I've heard you say so yourself on more than one occasion."

"And you expect me to actually take my own advice?" He took another sip of whisky, but the pungent bite couldn't wash away the bitter taste of the night's events. Suzanne's fingers tightened round his own.

"That wasn't the whole of what happened tonight," he said, and went on to tell his wife about Harry Davenport arriving with the warning that the code had been broken, the ambush, finding Julia Ashton's body.

"Cordelia Davenport's sister?" Suzanne said.

He nodded. "And Harry Davenport's sister-in-law."

Suzanne's winged brows drew together. "You know Cordelia Davenport arrived in Brussels tonight? That she was at the ball?"

Malcolm nodded. "You spoke with her?"

"She was trying to find her sister. Did she—"

"Davenport told her. And showed her Lady Julia's body."

Distress flickered through Suzanne's gaze. "That can't have been easy. According to Aline and Georgy Lennox, Cordelia and Harry Davenport haven't seen each other in four years."

"That's more or less the story I got from Davenport."

Suzanne's frown deepened.

"What?" Malcolm asked.

"It's just that Cordelia Davenport seemed more anxious to find her sister than one would expect if it was just a sisterly reunion. Almost as if—"

"She knew Julia was in some sort of trouble?"

"Precisely." Suzanne fingered the tasseled gold cord that confined her gown at the waist. "When a woman slips away from a ball to visit an empty château, there's an obvious explanation that springs to mind."

"And apparently in this case the obvious explanation is the correct one." Malcolm told her about Julia Ashton's affair with the Prince of Orange.

Suzanne's sea-green eyes widened. "Oh, dear God. You know I've always been fond of Billy, but he does have the most astonishing knack for blundering in just where he can cause problems."

"With a vengeance."

Malcolm told her about the note the prince had received canceling the rendezvous and Davenport's discovery that the note had been forged.

Suzanne stared into her whisky glass. "Someone went to a great deal of trouble to get Julia Ashton to the château alone." She looked up at him. "Do you think she was the real target of the ambush?"

"That the shooters' goal was to kill Julia Ashton and they were just shooting at Davenport and La Fleur and me for cover? I did wonder. Though it's the devil of a complicated way to try to commit murder. Assuming someone wanted Julia Ashton dead."

"Did her husband know about the affair?"

"He does now. Unless he's a very good actor, I'd swear he didn't know before." Malcolm grimaced at the memory of John Ashton's bewildered expression, like a man who had received a blow to the back from which he'd never recover. "Poor bastard. I think he was genuinely in love with her."

Suzanne looked at him for a moment. "It does happen between husbands and wives."

He curled his fingers behind her neck and tilted her face up to his. "So I've heard tell."

She pressed a light kiss against his lips, lingering for a moment. Her mouth tasted of champagne and marzipan. The bones of her face felt fragile beneath his fingers. "I need to not go on missions so I can make sure you eat at entertainments," he said, studying the hollows beneath her cheeks, deeper than they'd been in Vienna.

He caught a flash of something in her eyes, then she gave one of her brilliant smiles. "And to think you're the one who complains about being fussed over. One would think by now you'd have learned how sturdy I am. Could Captain Ashton have sent the note because he was planning to meet his wife at the château alone and confront her about the affair?"

Malcolm ran his fingers through his wife's carefully arranged side curls. "Again only if he has the abilities of an actor. Or an agent."

"Which he isn't?" Suzanne said, a faint question in her tone.

He tucked a walnut-brown curl behind her ear. "Have you ever heard me mention that he is?"

"No, but you don't tell me everything. You're much too good an agent yourself."

"I try. But unless someone hasn't let me in on the secret—which is entirely possible—Johnny Ashton isn't an agent. Besides, if he'd wanted to confront Julia, one would think he'd have tried to catch her with her lover, not on her own."

Suzanne turned her whisky glass in her hand, watching the crystal catch the candlelight. "Someone else who disapproved of the affair then? Who wanted to warn her off? But even if whoever sent the forged note planned to confront Julia Ashton, they didn't arrive at the château."

"Unless they arrived in the midst of the ambush and turned away when they heard the gunfire. Or got there after we left." Malcolm went to the side table and splashed more whisky into his glass and Suzanne's. "Relations are tense enough between the British troops and our Dutch-Belgian allies. Wellington's concerned about the havoc the news of the affair could wreak on morale. Particularly if Ashton made an issue out of it, which I don't think he will. One could imagine a Dutch-Belgian or British commander trying to warn Julia Ashton off if he knew. In many ways it's the likeliest scenario."

Suzanne scanned his face. "But you don't believe it?"

Malcolm returned the decanter to the table, clunking it down a little harder than necessary. The crystal rattled. "Perhaps I'm so used to looking for plots within plots that my vision's become warped. But it feels too easy. As though there's a piece we're not seeing." He returned to the chair and slid his arm round his wife's shoulders. "Can you get Cordelia Davenport to confide in you about her sister?"

Suzanne smiled. "I can try."

"Good," he said, and lowered his mouth to hers.

❧ 9 ❧

"Cordelia."

Caro's voice stopped Cordelia as she climbed the stairs of the house in the Rue de Belle Vue, candle in her hand. Caro stood on the first-floor landing, the light from the open door behind her outlining her disordered ringlets and the white gauze of her gown.

"You didn't need to wait up," Cordelia said.

"Stuff." Caro took her arm. "You can lock up, Georges," she called to the footman in the hall below, and then dragged Cordelia through the open door of the salon where she had been waiting. She flung her arms round Cordelia and hugged her hard. "Dearest. I'm so sorry."

Cordelia clung to her friend for a moment. "Don't, Caro, or I'll quite fall to pieces."

Caro pushed her into an armchair, put a glass of brandy in her hand, and perched on the sofa beside her. "I looked in on Livia, and she's sleeping like an angel, so you needn't worry."

It was a reversal of their usual roles. Normally it was Cordelia who held Caro's hand, smoothed her hair, convinced her to eat or sleep through the ups and downs of her marriage and in particular the volatile days of her affair with Lord Byron.

Cordelia stared at the glass in her hand, seeing Johnny hunched over his brandy in his study. Nausea choked her. She set the glass on the table beside her, aware that her fingers were shaking.

"How was Johnny?" Caro asked.

"Devastated. Angry. And—"

"What?"

Cordelia snatched up the glass and tossed down a sip. "I think there's something he isn't telling me."

Caro picked up her own glass. "You haven't talked about the other part of the evening."

"Harry."

Cordelia tossed down another swallow of brandy. "I knew I'd probably see him in Brussels."

"But not—"

"Over my sister's body."

Caro's eyes darkened. Before she'd left the ball to call on Johnny, Cordelia had told her friend about Julia's death and that Harry had taken her to see Julia's body. Remembering now her clipped words, she thought Caro must have thought her mad.

Cordelia turned her glass in her hand. "Poor Harry. Marrying into our family seems to have led him from one coil to another. We had a beastly quarrel about Livia. He accused me of being unfeeling in bringing her to Brussels. I accused him of not caring about her at all. Not that there's any reason he should be expected to."

Caro tucked her feet up under her on the sofa and leaned toward Cordelia. "Cordy, you have every right to be—"

"I don't have a right to be anything." Cordelia clunked her glass on the table, so hard, drops of brandy splashed onto the polished mahogany. "When it comes to Harry I long ago forfeited the right to anything."

Caro's eyes darkened in her thin face. Marriage was a difficult subject with her. "Harry wasn't—"

"Harry was a fool. But he didn't deserve what he got when he married me." Fragments of memory chased through her mind. The candle doused in their alien bedchamber, awkward touches. Uncomfortable silences across engraved silver and gilt-edged wedding china. Bending over a book in the library, her hair brushing his own, a sudden moment of understanding. His gaze following her across the ballroom. Coming home alone from an entertainment and glancing into the library to see him hunched over his books.

She grabbed the brandy glass and tossed down a swallow that burned her throat. "I knew I'd made a mess of my life. I thought Julia had done better."

"But you knew—"

"That her marriage wasn't as perfect as it appeared on the surface? Whose is?"

Caro grimaced and hugged her arms across her chest.

Cordelia's fingers tightened round the glass. "Perhaps the fools are the ones who actually expect fidelity."

"Cordy, that's dreadful. You sound like William. My husband was always much more of a cynic than I am."

Cordelia smiled at her friend, against the memory of scandals and tantrums and hysterical outbursts. "You're an incurable romantic, Caro. I often think life would be much easier for you if you weren't."

"Just because Harry wasn't—"

"Oh, for God's sake. Blame my affairs on boredom or lust or the need to provoke. But they aren't motivated by a search for my one true love." Except for the beginning, and she wasn't going to let her mind dwell on her youthful folly now.

Caro wrapped her arms round her knees. "I was in love with William when I married him."

"I know." Cordelia reached over and touched her friend's hand. She had a vivid memory of Caro's bright face on her wedding day. She'd been trembling when she hugged Cordelia before she climbed in the carriage outside Melbourne House for the wedding journey, but the gaze she had turned on William Lamb had burned with adoration. "You married for much more honest reasons than I did."

"And Julia?" Caro asked.

Cordelia frowned into her glass. "I told Johnny tonight that I was sure Julia loved him when she married him. But I think that was because I had some mad urge to offer comfort. The truth is I've felt I knew Julia less and less in recent years. At first I thought it was the scandal, that she was uncomfortable round me."

"And so of course you pulled back and spent less time with her to make it less awkward for her."

"I suppose so. Yes." Cordelia pushed her fingers into her hair, knocking several hairpins to the floor. "And then suddenly I realized the little sister who used to confide in me was almost a stranger. But it began long before. I remember on their wedding day telling her she was fortunate to have made such a happy match. And she laughed and said we all had to make compromises."

Caro's eyes widened. "You think she thought she was *compromising* in marrying Johnny?"

"I don't know." Cordelia saw her sister on her wedding day, fragile and exquisite in figured gauze over white satin, eyes bright, delicate lips curved with...happiness? Satisfaction? Triumph? "She was certainly determined to secure him. Poor Violet. Julia practically snatched Johnny right out of her arms."

Caro wrinkled her nose. "Violet's in Brussels, you know. I saw her chatting quite civilly with Julia at a military review."

"Julia wrote me that she'd seen Violet. I assume Violet's seen Johnny in Brussels as well. What was between them was a long time ago."

Caro gave Cordelia a hard look. "First loves don't die easily."

"No." Memories shot along Cordelia's nerve endings. "But they can become irrelevant."

For a moment Caro looked as though she was about to press the matter, but instead she asked, "Do you think Julia left the ball to meet a man?"

"Apparently she was having an affair with the Prince of Orange."

"Good heavens. That does explain the secrecy."

Cordelia studied her friend. "You don't seem particularly shocked."

"Don't forget I grew up among the Devonshire House Set. It

takes a lot to shock me. Do you think Julia fancied herself in love with the prince?"

Cordelia tried to imagine her elegant sister beside the awkward, impulsive prince. "Impossible to say. But I doubt she'd decided Slender Billy was the love of her life. You saw her these past weeks in Brussels, Caro. Did you notice anything between her and the prince?"

"No. I don't even remember them dancing together particularly. But then lovers often go to great lengths not to give public clues to their relationship. That is—" Caro flushed. Her affair with Lord Byron had been played out very much on the public stage. In fact, Cordelia had always suspected there was more to it in public than in private.

"We have different reasons for entering into love affairs," Cordelia said. "Julia was never the sort to want to make a scandal."

"Everyone called her the perfect wife. Said how devoted she and Captain Ashton were. Which only goes to show—" Caro sat bolt upright. "Oh God, Cordy, I'm a wretch. I'm supposed to be comforting you, not—"

"No, I need to understand." Cordelia pushed her fingers into her hair again, dislodging more pins. "I need to understand Julia if I'm to learn who did this to her."

"But—" Caro stared at her. "You said she was killed because she was caught in an ambush. That Harry and Malcolm Rannoch were meeting with a French contact."

"That's what Harry told me."

"You think Harry was lying?"

Cordelia got to her feet, stalked across the room, and splashed more cognac into her glass. "I think Harry would like to tidy this whole nasty business away with no uncomfortable scandals or questions about the Prince of Orange sleeping with a British officer's wife."

"Cordy—" Caro scanned her face. "Do you really want—Is there any purpose to be served by dragging Julia's name through the mud? We both know what it's like—There's Julia's little boy to think of."

"I am thinking of Robbie. He deserves to know what happened to his mother. I don't think we've begun to learn the whole of it."

Harry Davenport was already in the outer office at Headquarters when Malcolm arrived at five minutes to twelve the next morning. Davenport was shaved and neatly attired in his staff officer's dark blue coat, white pantaloons, and black stock.

"Do you ever sleep, Davenport?" Malcolm inquired, closing the door.

"About as much as you do, I expect. And I didn't have a family to command any of my attention this morning."

The words were spoken in neutral tones, as though Davenport were making a statement about the weather or the condition of the roads.

"It's my son's birthday as it happens," Malcolm said. "Once he'd opened his presents, he was insistent on time spent tossing his new ball. Or rather rolling, but I like to think he has the arm of a cricketer."

Fitzroy Somerset, the only other occupant of the room, looked up from the stack of papers on the desk before him. "Young Colin has a capital arm. He's going to be splendid on the playing fields of Harrow."

"Assuming we don't decide to educate him at home. It's odd how being a parent makes one loath to put one's child through what one went through oneself."

"Not odd at all." Fitzroy's serious face relaxed into a grin. He was a new father of a baby daughter. "It's ridiculous how cautious it makes one. Though I suppose if I was really cautious I'd have sent Harriet and the baby back to England."

"I doubt Harriet would have gone," Malcolm said, "any more than Suzanne would."

"Very true. And I could scarcely argue with her own uncle saying it's perfectly safe." Fitzroy's young wife was Wellington's niece. Fitzroy jerked his head at the door to Wellington's office. "He's expecting you. But have a care. Last night strained him more than he'll admit, and he's not happy with the news from the Prussians."

Malcolm exchanged a look with Davenport, and they moved to the door with one accord. Malcolm, more at home at Headquarters than Davenport in recent weeks, rapped on the door panels. A few moments later a curt voice bade them come in.

Wellington was seated behind his desk, frowning at the papers before him, but he looked up at their entrance. "Learned anything new?"

"Not since last night, sir," Malcolm said.

"No, I suppose not." Wellington waved them to two straight-backed chairs that stood in front of the desk. "Davenport, you spoke with your—with Lady Cordelia last night?"

Davenport nodded, face guarded. "As I said."

"And?"

"My wife is a number of things, but she cared about her sister. She was upset, as you can imagine. And she insisted I show her her sister's body."

Wellington raised his brows. "Intrepid woman. Could she shed any light on her sister's actions last night?"

"Cordelia only arrived in Brussels last night herself. She said she hadn't seen Julia before arriving at the ball."

"*Said?*" Wellington repeated.

Malcolm shot Davenport a sharp glance.

"I have no reason to think Cordelia was lying about that."

"But—" Wellington said.

Davenport shifted his position against the hard slats of his chair. "I think Cordelia may know more about Julia than she admitted to me last night. I'm not the likeliest person for her to confide in."

Wellington's gaze slid to Malcolm. "Could Suzanne—"

"I've already asked her to speak to Lady Cordelia." Malcolm glanced at Davenport. "My wife has assisted me in the past."

"I've heard stories of her exploits. Your marriage is remarkable, Rannoch," Davenport said, in a tone that indicated he still hadn't made up his mind whether that was a negative or a positive.

"Right." Wellington tapped his fingers on the ink blotter. "Let's get back to La Fleur and his warning. Tell me again precisely what he said?"

Malcolm exchanged a glance with Davenport. "'Don't trust the Silver Hawk.'"

Wellington frowned. "It sounds like a code name."

"So it does. But not one I've ever heard of. Davenport?"

Davenport shook his head.

"I have contacts in Brussels we can approach," Malcolm said. "Unless—" He glanced at Davenport.

"You've been in Brussels more than I have in recent weeks," Davenport said.

Wellington gave a curt nod. "Go carefully."

"I always do, sir," Malcolm said.

"Hrmph," said the commander of the Allied army.

"I swear it's as though mysterious deaths follow the two of you about." Blanca Mendoza, Suzanne's confidante, maid, and friend, added a yellow block to the gatehouse she, Suzanne, and Colin were building on the salon carpet in the Rue Ducale house out of the blocks that had been among Colin's birthday presents.

"I'd say that's a function of our work." Suzanne cupped her hand round Colin's own and carefully helped him put a red block atop the yellow one, completing the tower over the archway.

Blanca shot a sharp look at her. "You can't go on like this forever."

"Who said anything about forever?" Suzanne watched her son pick up one of his new wooden horses and gallop it through the archway. The weight of the future pressed against her, as it had more and more of late. An iron band round her temples drawn ever tighter. "I'm just trying to get through one day at a time."

"That's what worries me," Blanca said.

"No sense fussing. We've come this far. Careful, darling." Suzanne stopped Colin before he could plow the horse into the blocks. "I don't think the gatehouse could stand up to Mercury's hooves."

"You always say that," Blanca said, "but this time—"

A rap sounded on the door. "Forgive me, madame." Valentin, the footman they'd engaged when they came to Brussels (how odd to have a footman), stepped into the room. "You have a caller. A Lady Cordelia Davenport."

⁓ 10 ⁓

Suzanne had been mulling over ways to approach Lady Cordelia. She had not expected it to be this easy. Years in the intelligence world had taught her to be wary of anything that was too easy. She got to her feet and shook out the crumpled cambric folds of her skirt. "Please show her in, Valentin. And perhaps you could ask Brigitte to send in some coffee?"

Colin stared up at Suzanne as Valentin withdrew. He was already adept at reading situations. "Yes, I know, darling," she said, scooping him up in her arms, "but I need to talk to Lady Cordelia. You can meet her, and then Blanca's going to take you out in the garden for a bit."

Colin regarded her with a steady gaze. An early childhood that had taken him from the war-torn Peninsula to the frenetic pace of the Congress of Vienna had made him blessedly adaptable. "Play later?"

"Promise." Suzanne kissed his forehead.

From the doorway, Valentin gave a discreet cough. "Lady Cordelia Davenport."

Cordelia Davenport paused on the threshold, taking in the scene before her. Beneath the pleated violet silk of her bonnet, her face was shadowed with strain and exhaustion, but she gave a sudden smile as her gaze settled on Colin.

"Lady Cordelia, will you allow me to present my son, Colin?" Suzanne set Colin on his feet. "This is Lady Cordelia, Colin."

"Master Rannoch." Cordelia advanced toward him and held out her hand. "It's an honor."

Colin shook her lilac-kid-gloved hand with great concentration. "Lady Cordelia," he said carefully, only slurring the last syllables slightly. He studied her for a moment, then added, "It's my birthday."

"Happy birthday. I'm sorry I didn't know so I could bring you a present. Very remiss of me."

Colin grinned. "That's all right, Mummy and Daddy gave me lots."

"Very satisfactory of them."

"And Blanca Mendoza, my companion," Suzanne said.

Lady Cordelia again shook hands, showing no surprise at being introduced to someone's maid.

"Thank you," Suzanne said when Blanca had taken Colin off to the garden. "I like to give him practice."

"Very sensible. It makes it so much easier to take children places. My daughter turned three in January," Cordelia added. "She was an intrepid traveler on our journey to Brussels."

"Was she very stubborn about doing things on her own at two?" Suzanne gestured for Cordelia to be seated on one of the two striped satin sofas ranged before the fireplace and sat opposite her.

"Incorrigibly," Cordelia said with another smile. "She insisted on walking herself, though it took twice as long as being carried or pushed in her carriage."

Valentin returned with a coffee service and biscuits. Suzanne poured out the coffee and handed Lady Cordelia a cup. Cordelia took a quick swallow, as though she wished it were something stronger.

"Lady Cordelia." Suzanne leaned forward. "I'm so very sorry about your sister."

"Thank you." Cordelia returned the silver-rimmed cup to its saucer with great care. "I've just written to my mother and stepfather. Mama will take it hard, she was so proud of Julia. But my stepfather's a sensible man, thank God. Far steadier than any of us." She took another sip of coffee. "I expect you wonder why the devil I called on you."

"I imagine it's something to do with last night's events."

"I was hoping to find Mr. Rannoch here." Cordelia gave a brittle laugh. "Not the best word choice. When I call asking for husbands, wives usually fly into an alarm."

Suzanne settled back on the sofa with her own cup of coffee. "Given the life my husband leads, if I took alarm at every unexpected person who called asking for him, I should live in a constant state of anxiety."

Cordelia shot her a quick look. "Is he—"

"He's gone to Headquarters."

"Of course."

"But I expect him back shortly. Won't you wait?"

Lady Cordelia hesitated, her posture taut, as though she feared every wasted moment. Suzanne recognized the desperate need to be doing something, anything, in the wake of grief and loss.

"It shouldn't be long," Suzanne said. "And I imagine you'll feel better when you've seen him."

Cordelia drew a sharp breath, then collapsed back on the sofa. In the light from the windows, the shadows beneath her eyes were more pronounced. Suzanne wished she had stirred some sugar into the coffee she'd given her guest. Cordelia Davenport appeared to be existing on sheer nerves.

"I only met your sister a handful of times," Suzanne said, "but she was so charming. She was very kind to Colin. We met her walking out a few times with her own little boy."

"It's going to be beastly for Robbie. Not that it's not beastly for the rest of us, but he's only a little boy. He shouldn't—Oh damn." Cordelia put her hand to her face as tears sprang unbidden to her eyes.

Suzanne got up without hesitation, moved to sit on the sofa beside the other woman, and pressed a handkerchief into Cordelia's hand. "I can't imagine what you must be going through."

Which was true. She'd had her own losses, but grief was different for everyone.

"Julia would despise me," Cordelia said into the handkerchief. "She had no use for watering pots."

"That depends upon the circumstances. There are times when crying is by far the most sensible thing one can do."

Cordelia blew her nose. "How much did your husband tell you of what happened last night?"

Suzanne hesitated. But if she was to get Lady Cordelia to confide in her, they needed to be able to talk freely. "Very nearly the whole. At least according to what I know of it."

"A husband who trusts his wife. How novel."

Suzanne swallowed. She knew full well that Malcolm trusted her. Far more than he should. "Malcolm and I have learned to rely on each other."

Lady Cordelia shot her a look over the rim of her coffee cup. "It seems almost unimaginable."

"What?"

Cordelia tossed down a swallow of coffee. "Relying upon one's spouse."

Malcolm led Harry Davenport through the door of Le Lion Vert. They stepped into the smell of Belgian ale and Turkish tobacco and a medley of voices speaking French, Dutch, English, German. The common room was dark, with heavy oak beams and thick glass in the windows, but the oil lamps showed the red coats of British soldiers, the green jackets of riflemen, the blue of Horse Guards, one or two staff officers in dark blue, and the blue or green of Dutch-Belgian uniforms, as well as a number of dark-coated civilians. The turning of newspaper pages and the whiffle of cards stirred the air. And underneath it all, speculation about the military situation, as palpable as the tobacco smoke and the sour smell of the ale the potboys carried from table to table.

Malcolm and Harry lingered for a time watching a chess game in progress between a white-haired man and a young Dutch-Belgian lieutenant. When the door opened to admit a trio of British hussars, Malcolm wandered to the back of the common room, stopping to exchange greetings with Alexander Gordon, who was lounging with a glass of red wine in one hand as though he hadn't a care in the world and was a civilian rather than one of Wellington's aides-de-camp.

Davenport moved behind Malcolm, but not too closely. Malcolm heard him call a greeting to one or two acquaintances. Malcolm strolled up the age-darkened oak stairs at the back of the common room and heard Davenport's soft, sure treads on the steps behind him. At the head, Malcolm led the way down the passage and pushed open a door.

Davenport followed him inside and glanced round the neat, whitewashed private parlor. "Is your contact invisible or late?"

"She'll be here." Malcolm picked up the decanter of red wine that stood on the round table in the center of the room and poured a glass.

Davenport dropped into a chair. "She?"

"Rachel Garnier." Malcolm handed the glass to Davenport. "My best source in Brussels. She has access to a wealth of information."

"A shopkeeper?"

"A bird of paradise." Malcolm poured a second glass of wine and took a sip of the quite acceptable Côte de Rhone. "She's employed at a house frequented by Belgians with French sympathies. Several of her regular clients are French agents. In fact, there's a small spy ring that uses the brothel for meetings."

"But you haven't taken them in because that would put a stop to one of your best sources of information."

"Quite."

Davenport took a sip of wine and studied Malcolm over the rim of the glass. "Your marriage appears to be more complicated than one would think at first glance. Or perhaps more commonplace."

"Suzanne's met Rachel."

"Intriguing. Do—"

Davenport's words were cut short by the opening of the door. A slender young woman in a spring green gown stood on the threshold, a plumed hat set at a rakish angle on her auburn curls. She smiled at Malcolm. "I must say, I was quite pleased to get your message—" She went still as she caught sight of Davenport.

"It's all right," Malcolm said. "He's a friend."

Rachel regarded Davenport, her dark brows tightly drawn. "Who says friends are to be trusted?"

"A good point," Malcolm conceded. "But this friend is also a colleague without whom I might very well not have survived last night's adventures. Mademoiselle Garnier, may I present Colonel Davenport?"

Rachel regarded Davenport with a frank gaze. "You'll forgive my suspicions? One learns to watch one's back these days."

"The best way to avoid taking a knife between the shoulder blades." Davenport got to his feet and gave a half bow.

Rachel smiled and dipped in a precise curtsy. She was a lace-maker's daughter, or so she had told Malcolm, but she had acquired the manners of a duchess. "You're the man who was in the ambush with Monsieur Rannoch last night."

"You heard about the ambush?" Malcolm looked up from pulling out a chair for Rachel.

"Haven't you learned how quickly news travels in Brussels?" Rachel slid into the chair. "It was the talk of the house into the early hours of the morning."

Malcolm poured a third glass of wine and handed it to her. "Have you heard of the Silver Hawk?"

Rachel took a sip of wine. "Is it a code? It sounds like something out of a novel."

"We were told to beware of it."

"By La Fleur?" Rachel set down her wineglass and leaned forward, fixing Malcolm with a direct stare from her blue eyes.

Malcolm dropped into the chair across from her. "What do you know about La Fleur?"

Rachel began to strip off her gloves. She had the instincts of an actress and enjoyed playing the drama of the moment. "That he was killed last night and both of you were caught in the attack as well." She looked between Malcolm and Davenport. "La Fleur had been rumbled."

Malcolm flicked a glance at Davenport. "We knew. Davenport came to warn La Fleur and me. But it was too late. The French had sent someone to ambush us."

"It's not quite so simple." Rachel laid her lemon-colored gloves atop the table. "One of my regulars came to see me last night. Or rather early this morning." She glanced at Malcolm. "Étienne Bouret."

"A soldier?" Davenport moved to a chair at the table. It was no secret there were a number of Bonapartist sympathizers in the Dutch-Belgian army.

"Not this one." Rachel reached for her glass again and took a sip of wine. "Étienne runs a café. He's a primary source for passing along information. When he came to me last night he'd just got wind that La Fleur had been killed. He was shocked."

"Shocked?" Malcolm said.

"Apparently just before he came to see me he'd learned of La Fleur's death from a source who's the sweetheart of one of Sir Charles Stuart's stable boys."

Davenport frowned. "But—"

Rachel took another sip of wine, savoring the moment. "According to Étienne, they'd just learned La Fleur was selling secrets to the British, but they hadn't known he was meeting you last night. If Étienne's to be believed, it wasn't the French who shot at you."

"Clever woman," Davenport said as he and Malcolm left the tavern. "You're to be congratulated."

"Yes, I'm fortunate in my agents." Malcolm kept his gaze fixed straight ahead.

Davenport shot a look at him.

"But as it happens I'm not sleeping with her."

"You can't seriously expect me to believe you're blind to her charms."

"I didn't say that."

"So?" Davenport sounded like a man investigating an obscure theorem.

"I could say I take vows seriously, but I'd sound like a pretentious prig. I could say I love my wife, but I've never been one to talk about my emotions."

Davenport regarded him a moment longer with that incisive gaze. "You're the last man I took for a romantic, Rannoch."

"Somehow I don't think that's a compliment."

Davenport turned his gaze to a young Dutch-Belgian lieutenant and a girl in a Flemish lappet cap holding hands beneath the lacy ironwork of an overhanging balcony. "Illusions are a dangerous thing."

"Speaking as someone who once had them?"

"If I did, it's so long ago I don't speak the language anymore. I suppose you want to look in at home."

"You think I'm tied to my wife's apron strings?"

"No, I think you want to consult with her. An excellent idea. Mrs. Rannoch's a clever woman. I'll look into some things myself and call on you later in the afternoon."

Malcolm returned to the Rue Ducale to be informed by Valentin that Madame Rannoch was in the garden with a guest. He made his way to the back salon. Through the French windows that opened onto the garden he saw his son kneeling on the flagstones, pushing a trowel into an empty patch of earth beside a bed of primroses with great concentration. Suzanne sat at the wrought-metal table beneath the lilac tree with Blanca and a lady with fair curls escaping a violet bonnet. The fair-haired woman turned her head, and Malcolm realized he was looking at Harry Davenport's wife.

He opened the French window and stepped into the garden, silently applauding his wife's celerity in taking Lady Cordelia into her confidence.

"Darling." Suzanne sprang to her feet. "I'm so glad. Lady Cordelia called in the hope of being able to speak to you."

Malcolm bent to hug Colin, who tugged at his boot as he walked past, then moved to the table and bowed to Lady Cordelia. "Lady Cordelia. I'm sorry we meet again under these circumstances. My sympathies on the loss of your sister."

"Thank you." Cordelia Davenport got to her feet. She was shorter than Suzanne, but she carried herself with an air of command. Her voice was tranquil, but beneath the brim of her bonnet her face was pale and her eyes bleak. "I remember you were always kind as a boy."

"You flatter me. I fear I was remote. And damnably self-absorbed."

"As most of us are at that age." Cordelia smiled and Malcolm caught a flash of the mischievous girl in the white dress he'd met at Carfax Court all those years ago.

"I am at your disposal," he said. "Shall we go into the salon?"

Lady Cordelia cast a glance at Suzanne. "Would you—Mrs. Rannoch, might I prevail upon you to come with us?"

"Certainly, if you wish it."

Malcolm held open the French window, and the two ladies preceded him into the salon. Suzanne dropped down on one of the sofas, but Lady Cordelia remained standing, her hands clasped in front of her.

"Mr. Rannoch, I understand you've been charged with investigating my sister's death."

Malcolm stood opposite Cordelia Davenport where the light spilling through the French window gave him a good view of her face. "Wellington and Stuart have asked me to look into last night's tragic events."

"And you think my sister's death was an unfortunate sidelight to those events. That she was quite literally caught in the cross fire."

Malcolm hesitated. He wasn't yet ready to share what he had learned from Rachel. "We know too little at this point to be entirely sure what happened."

The light flashed in Cordelia's eyes as she lifted her chin. "But you think my sister was a foolish woman who was in the wrong place at the wrong time."

"I hope I've learned not to make such swift judgments about anyone."

Her gaze moved over his face, and he had the oddest sense he was being put through a test. "Yes, you look like someone who examines the evidence. But I can guess where the evidence thus far must have led you. A spoiled, pampered woman who was betraying her husband. Whose love affair would cause more problems if it became public."

Malcolm took a step forward. "Are you suggesting I don't want to get to the truth of your sister's death, Lady Cordelia?"

"I'm suggesting that Wellington and Stuart might prefer that you not get to the truth of Julia's death."

"And yet you came to see me."

Lady Cordelia's gaze flickered to Suzanne and then back to Malcolm. "I decided it was worth a chance."

"What was?"

"That you'd believe me." Cordelia Davenport drew a breath and clasped her hands together. "Mr. Rannoch, I came to Brussels because Julia wrote me a letter a fortnight ago." Cordelia undid the clasp on her reticule and drew out a creased sheet of hot-pressed paper.

Malcolm took the paper and unfolded it. A faint hint of jasmine clung to the single sheet. An elegant loopy hand, similar to the writing on the note the Prince of Orange had received at the ball but without the painstaking care and retracing of the letters that Davenport had noted on the forgery.

> *Rue Royale*
> *22 May 1815*
> *Cordy darling,*
> *Why, oh why, aren't you in Brussels? You're always at the center of everything. It's an odd thing at my age to realize one needs one's elder sister, but I find myself wishing desperately that you were sitting on the chaise-longue, sipping champagne and offering me advice. Advice which I was often not sensible enough to take, yes, I confess it. And don't say you're the last person who should be offering advice. You've always been much better at sorting out other people's problems than managing your own.*
> *I'm in trouble. Quite ghastly trouble, the sort I never thought I'd encounter in my lovely perfect life. I'm not sure how I managed to do it. I've always been so good at*

organizing things, at least on the surface. Far better than you if truth be told. I've always known what I wanted from life. And I had it. The life I was supposed to have, the perfect polished life that was everything I'd aspired to. It was years before I realized it wasn't what I wanted at all. At least not the sum total of what I wanted. Even then I thought I had things under control, but it's all gone terribly wrong.

I can't say more, not in writing. But if you should hear that anything befalls me—I know it will sound nonsensical, but promise you won't be too quick to believe what you're told should you hear ill news of me. And that you'll look after Robbie. He'll always have Johnny, of course, but you have a knack for talking to children.

The thing is—Oh, poison, I must go, I have to dress for a military review, and I want to get this in the post.

The thing is, Cordy, outrageous as it sounds, I fear for my life.

Your distracted sister,
Julia

❧ 11 ❧

Malcolm read the last paragraph over three times, then looked up and met Cordelia's taut gaze. "May I show this to my wife?"

Surprise flickered through Cordelia's eyes, but she nodded. Malcolm held the letter out to Suzanne. She came to his side and drew a quick breath of surprise as she scanned Julia Ashton's words.

"My sister wasn't given to dramatics or hysterical fits," Cordelia said in a tight voice.

"Was she in the habit of confiding in you?" Suzanne asked.

"When we were girls. In recent years she's ceased to do so much at all."

Malcolm glanced at the closing paragraphs again. "Perhaps not, but she wanted you to come to Brussels."

"She doesn't ask me to."

"No, but she says she can't tell you more in writing. With the clear implication that she *could* talk to you in person."

A glint of appreciation lit Lady Cordelia's eyes. "I drew the same conclusions myself. And it certainly had that effect on me. If I had been able to talk to her—Oh, the devil." She pressed her hands to her face. "I know it's folly to refine upon the past, but I can't seem to stop doing it."

Suzanne went to Lady Cordelia and put her arm round her. "Won't you sit down? Then we can all talk about this properly."

Cordelia permitted Suzanne to pull her down on one of the sofas, though her spine remained taut. Malcolm sat in a chair opposite them.

"Do you have any idea what your sister meant?" he asked. "What she thought she hadn't managed properly and what had gone so horribly wrong?"

Lady Cordelia smoothed her hands over her lap, pressing the sheer lilac fabric of her gown smooth. "As I said, Julia hadn't been in the habit of confiding in me in recent years. We move in quite different circles these days."

And Julia was the one who had pulled away. Malcolm read that clearly in Lady Cordelia's eyes. Cordelia Davenport's scandal had created distance between the incomparable Brooke sisters.

Cordelia tugged at the ribbons on her bonnet and lifted it from her head. "Given what Johnny told me last night about her affair with the Prince of Orange, one might suspect the possible repercussions of the liaison were what concerned Julia. But while a love affair can do incalculable damage, one wouldn't think it would make Julia fear for her life."

"Could she have feared the consequences if her husband learned of the affair?" Malcolm asked.

"Of course she'd have been worried, Johnny would have been devastated. Is devastated. He adores Julia. But that doesn't—" Cordelia's gaze froze on Malcolm's own. "You think Julia feared for her life because of *Johnny?*"

"Husbands have been known to lose control. Like most Shakespeare plays, *Othello* is grounded in reality."

"Yes, but—" Cordelia frowned for a moment as though trying to conjure the possibility in her mind, then shook her head. "No. Not Johnny. I've known him since we were children. He's not violent."

"He's a soldier."

"On those grounds, most of the men in Brussels right now would be capable of murder."

"But wouldn't have the motive." Malcolm leaned forward,

holding her gaze with his own. "I was in the Peninsula during the war. I saw men who seemed the soul of honor—men who fought on all sides—commit the most unspeakable acts. One can never be sure what a person might be capable of under the right circumstances."

Cordelia's hands locked on her elbows. "Perhaps. Perhaps Johnny would be capable of snapping in a moment of rage. But for Julia to foresee it, weeks before she was killed—"

She broke off as the French window opened with an almost soundless click, and Harry Davenport strolled into the salon. "Forgive me for coming in unannounced," he said as he pushed the window to. "I've got used to avoiding front doors, and I thought it might be prudent for us not to be seen too much in conversation. I—" His gaze fell on his wife. Something flashed in his eyes, too quick for Malcolm to put a name to it. "Cordelia. My skills must be failing. I didn't predict this."

Lady Cordelia lifted her chin. "I needed to speak to Mr. Rannoch."

Davenport rested his shoulders against the window, his face tilted back into the shadows. "Perhaps it's as well. You may be able to shed some light on what I've discovered. Rannoch?"

"By all means," Malcolm said. "Lady Cordelia's insights are proving invaluable."

"Pray be seated, Colonel Davenport," Suzanne said.

Cordelia was staring at her husband. "You've learned something about Julia? How?"

Davenport flung himself down in a chair beside Malcolm. "I should hope I've learned something. I'd be slipping if I went through someone's things without making some sort of discovery."

"You—" Cordelia stared across the sofa table at him. "Johnny let you into the house?"

"It seemed better not to bother Ashton." Davenport stretched out his legs and crossed his booted feet at the ankles. "I climbed in through her bedchamber window."

"What—"

"I am a spy after all. Didn't see a need to change tactics just because we're among friends."

Malcolm leaned back in his chair. "You make me look positively orthodox, Davenport."

"Never that, Rannoch." Davenport let his shoulders sink into the green satin chairback. "I thought we should go through Julia's things as quickly as possible, and I wasn't sure you'd agree to my methods."

Cordelia was studying her estranged husband as though he were a stranger wearing a familiar mask. Davenport cast a glance at her. "I've acquired some new skills since last you saw me, Cordelia. Though I fear my Latin's got a bit rusty."

"Out with it, Davenport," Malcolm said. "I know the look of an agent back from a successful mission."

Davenport grinned. This, Malcolm suspected, was the closest the other man came to enjoying himself. "Nothing hidden in Julia's dressing table beyond the usual powders and paints and jewels. Her writing desk was more informative. A number of cards of invitation. Bills from her dressmaker and milliner. Calling cards—her own and those of others, though no one particularly surprising." He reached inside his coat and drew out a folded paper. "A half-finished letter to her sister."

Lady Cordelia snatched the paper from his fingers. She started to unfold it, then looked up at her husband. "Did you—"

The mockery left Davenport's gaze. "I had to read it, Cordy. It's my job. It seems to follow upon another letter. The reason, I assume, that you came to Brussels?"

The paper crackled between Cordelia's fingers as she unfolded it. She glanced through the contents, drew a sharp breath, then held it out to Suzanne. "We can't afford secrets."

Malcolm rose and went to read over his wife's shoulder.

> *Rue Royale*
> *7 June 1815*
> *Dearest Cordy,*
> *What must you think of me after that last letter? I don't know what possessed me to write it, save that I haven't been sleeping well. Blame the letter's outrageous contents*

*on laudanum drops and one too many glasses of
champagne the night before. I've fallen prey to fancies. Not
like me, I know, but then I think everyone in Brussels is on
edge with war drawing ever nearer. Johnny will actually
be going into battle. I can't quite comprehend it. I knew I'd
married a soldier, of course, but I think I thought he'd
always be stationed in London, looking dashing in his
uniform and defending St. James's Palace from invaders.*

    *In any case, please forgive my sad lapse into lending
library novel language. I trust you're too sensible to have
worried, and that you've treated that letter as the fiction it
was. Hopefully entertaining fiction, though I fear I'm no
novelist.*

    *I am quite well and perfectly safe. That is, as well and
safe as anyone in Brussels just now, with Bonaparte only
a few days' march away and my husband in uniform. But
do not fear. The duke is calmness itself, and should it
prove necessary, he assures me there will be plenty of time
to disembark for home. Not that he even admits the
possibility of defeat, of course. Johnny's been inclined to
fuss, but Robbie and I shall be quite all right, as I've told
him more than once.*

    *One way and another I hope to see you soon, though I
confess to quite longing to see Paris. If—when—our forces
achieve victory—*

The writing broke off. A streak of black ink across the bottom of
the paper suggested Lady Julia had flung down the pen.

Cordelia picked up the earlier letter her sister had sent her and
held it out to her husband without speaking.

Davenport met her gaze for a moment with raised brows, then
glanced through the much-creased paper. "Julia should have
known you'd be halfway across the Channel long before she could
post the second letter."

"The first letter wasn't a fancy," Cordelia said.

Davenport folded the letter. "You seem very sure."

"I knew my sister that well."

He handed the letter back to her. "For what it's worth I'm inclined to agree with you."

"She protests a bit too much about her husband in the second letter," Suzanne said.

Davenport turned his gaze to her. "Insightful as usual, Mrs. Rannoch."

Cordelia pushed herself to her feet as though too impatient to sit still. "She was frightened, she wanted me to come to Brussels. And then she changed her mind. Which either means she wasn't frightened anymore—"

"Which is rather belied by the fact that she did lose her life," Davenport said.

"—or she decided she was more afraid of the consequences of me coming to Brussels than of whatever caused her to write the letter in the first place." Cordelia paced to the fireplace. "Why?"

"Perhaps because you knew her so well," Suzanne said. "She knew she couldn't keep secrets from you."

"But I'd have helped her whatever was wrong." Cordelia spun round, her lilac gown vivid against the white marble of the mantel. "Julia should have known I'd never betray her."

Davenport tilted his head back to study his wife. "You know, Cordy, from you idealism is either deeply ironic or oddly touching."

Cordelia shot a look at him.

"A love affair wouldn't have shocked you," Davenport said. "At least, I don't think it would?"

Cordelia paced to the windows. "Don't be clever, Harry."

"That's one of the nicer things you've called me. So if adultery wouldn't have done it, what might Julia have done that would strain your sympathies to the breaking point?"

"She was my sister."

"What if she'd killed someone?"

Cordelia spun toward her husband, skirts snapping about her. "What else did you find in Julia's room?"

"Nothing to suggest she even contemplated murder. I'm just trying to gauge your moral limits. As relates to Julia, of course."

"Whatever it was, she wanted Lady Cordelia to come to Brussels and then she changed her mind," Malcolm said, stepping into the cross fire between the Davenports. "So either the situation changed, or her analysis of it did."

Davenport reached inside his coat and drew out a cream-colored square of paper. "What sort of terms was Julia on with Violet Chase?"

Cordelia took a quick step toward him. "You said none of the calling cards was surprising."

"I said none of the calling cards was *from* anyone surprising. I don't see anything particularly surprising in Julia receiving a card from Violet Chase. I know perfectly well how close your family has always been to the Chases. What's surprising is what's written on the back." Davenport turned the card over between his fingers. " 'The Allée Verte. 10:00 tomorrow.' "

Lady Cordelia squeezed her eyes shut. "You might have mentioned this from the first."

"I wanted to see your reaction to Julia's letters without this to cloud the issue."

"Damn you, Harry—"

"From an investigative standpoint."

Cordelia swallowed. "Dear God. I knew Violet was in Brussels, but—"

"I remember the Chases," Malcolm said, thinking back to his boyhood visits to Carfax Court in Derbyshire. "They have the estate neighboring your family's, Lady Cordelia?"

Cordelia nodded. "We grew up with them. With them and the Ashtons. We were always in and out of each other's houses as children. Violet and Johnny were betrothed—well, betrothed in all but name—before Johnny married Julia."

Davenport's eyes narrowed. "Julia took Ashton from her?"

"I don't know that it was quite so simple. From childhood, everyone always assumed Johnny and Violet would marry. Then one night at Lady Cowper's Johnny asked Julia to dance. He must have danced with her a score of times in the past, starting with our first attempts in the schoolroom with me at the piano. But something was different that night. I saw it when he crossed the room to us and asked Julia for the next waltz. Johnny danced two waltzes with Julia, took her in to supper, and followed her with his gaze all evening. I don't think he had eyes for anyone else after that."

Davenport regarded his wife steadily. "Odd how that can happen."

Cordelia dropped down on the sofa beside Suzanne and rubbed her temples. "I think Violet knew before I did. Perhaps even before Johnny and Julia did. I remember her standing beside me that night, watching Julia circle the floor in Johnny's arms. The look in her eyes—It made me—"

She broke off.

"What?" Davenport asked.

Cordelia met his gaze without flinching. "It made me wonder if I'd ever done that to another woman."

"Ashton was the one who was already promised," Davenport said. "It was still his responsibility."

"Miss Chase has two brothers," Malcolm said, matching present knowledge with his memory of children's parties at Carfax Court. "I remember playing cricket with them and my friend David Mallinson. And they're both in the army now."

"Yes." Cordelia's gaze was fixed on the bowl of moss roses on the sofa table. "Anthony is a captain in the 95th. George is an aide-de-camp to Lord Uxbridge." She drew a breath. "And because you'll no doubt put two and two together before long, George was the subject of Harry's and my marriage going so spectacularly wrong."

Davenport tugged out his handkerchief and brushed at the film of dust on his boots. "I expect it would have happened in the end without good old George. But he certainly helped hurry things along."

"Were the Chase brothers angered when Captain Ashton turned his attentions away from their sister?" Suzanne asked.

Lady Cordelia rubbed her arms. "They were both out of England at the time."

Davenport shifted his position in the chair, easing his bad arm. "I saw George and Tony on a handful of occasions in the Peninsula. George and I've got over the urge to throttle each other. Odd how one realizes things that once seemed earthshaking are really quite trivial."

Lady Cordelia looked into her husband's eyes for a moment. "Tony came home on leave just before Johnny and Julia got married. There was an unpleasant incident."

"Chase challenged Ashton to a duel?" Malcolm asked.

"No. He planted him a facer in the card room at Boodle's. Supposedly the fight went out into the passage and down the stairs before some of their fellow officers broke it up."

Davenport gave a rough laugh. "God. Suspiciously like George and me. I always secretly feared my behavior was a cliché." He cast a glance at Malcolm.

Lady Cordelia looked between the two men. "You can't think Tony Chase would have killed Julia because of something that happened years ago. Johnny was the one he was angry at. I know you're searching for motives, but—"

"No, it doesn't seem likely," Malcolm said. "But we should talk to Chase."

"Tony got married when he was home on leave a couple of years ago," Lady Cordelia said. "To Jane Sanderson. She's Johnny's cousin as it happens."

"Good God." Davenport stared at his wife. "Don't you lot admit anyone else to your charmed circle?"

"Yes, I know," Lady Cordelia said. "It probably shows a fatal lack of imagination. Or some sort of dreadful incestuous impulses. In any case, Tony and Jane are in Brussels. Violet's with them."

"Do you know if your sister and brother-in-law had seen Miss Chase in Brussels?" Malcolm asked.

Cordelia nodded. "Caro said last night that she'd seen them talking at a military review. Julia wrote that she'd encountered Violet and Jane in the park in early May. She said it was a bit awkward, but they were quite civil."

"And yet Violet Chase wanted to see your sister. In private. To make accusations? To heal the breach?" Malcolm cast a glance at his wife. "Suzette?"

"You want me to talk to Miss Chase."

"I think she's more likely to confide in you."

"She doesn't know me."

"But you have a way of creating instant trust. Davenport and I will try to track down her brother."

Suzanne turned to Cordelia. "Lady Cordelia? By any chance would you be willing to go with me?"

Cordelia's eyes widened with surprise and, Malcolm thought, something like relief. "Certainly, if you wish it. Though I don't know that Violet is particularly happy with any of the Brookes."

Suzanne got to her feet and smoothed her skirt. "Sometimes being able to provoke someone is an advantage."

❧ 12 ❧

Cordelia Davenport glanced at Suzanne as they stood before the house that Anthony and Jane Chase had taken in the Rue du Musée. A light breeze stirred the ribbons on Lady Cordelia's bonnet and blew strands of hair across her face. "Thank you."

Suzanne held her skirts taut against the breeze. "I'm the one who should be thanking you for coming with me."

"If I hadn't I'd have gone mad for want of something to do." Cordelia pushed the hair back from her face with an impatient gesture. "You saw that."

"Perhaps. But I also genuinely wanted your help."

Cordelia's gaze flickered over Suzanne's face. "You've lost someone yourself, haven't you?"

Blood on cobblestones. Screams. Light fading from young eyes. Suzanne swallowed, forcing down a host of memories she couldn't afford to dwell on. "Which of us who was in the Peninsula during the war didn't?"

"Someone very close to you."

Suzanne started to draw her expertly built defenses round her like the folds of her gauze scarf. But when she met Lady Cordelia's bruised gaze, she said simply, "Yes."

Cordelia gave a quick nod.

"Do you think Violet Chase will agree to see us?"

"I'm not sure. Violet's not—She's not what one would expect of the girl who stood on the sidelines at a ball while another woman bewitched her fiancé. It will be interesting to see how she responds."

"If she agrees to see us."

Lady Cordelia lifted the polished brass knocker. "There's only one way to find out."

A liveried footman took their cards and said he would inquire if Madame and Mademoiselle Chase were at home. Suzanne and Lady Cordelia were left alone in an elegant entry hall with café-au-lait-colored walls, white moldings, and graceful mahogany furniture. A single, unexpected splash of color caught Suzanne's eye beside one of the tapered legs of the ivory damask bench. A bright red top. "Do the Chases have children?" she asked Lady Cordelia.

"One, I think. No, perhaps two now."

After only a brief interval the footman returned to say Madame and Mademoiselle Chase would be pleased to receive them. Suzanne heard Lady Cordelia release her breath. The footman escorted them up a slender staircase to a sunny salon hung with pale blue silk.

Two ladies got to their feet as the door opened. The shorter of the two, a startlingly pretty young woman with glossy chestnut ringlets and a heart-shaped face, came forward in a stir of airy jaconet edged with flounces of beaded French work.

"Cordelia, dearest." She took Cordelia's hands in both her own. "I'm so very sorry about Julia. I could scarcely believe it when we heard the news."

"Thank you." Cordelia returned the pressure of the other woman's hands, a note of surprise in her voice.

Violet Chase drew back and scanned Cordelia's face. Her almond-shaped eyes were wide and dark beneath perfectly plucked brows. "Oh, dear. You think I'm a shocking hypocrite. But truly, Cordy, that was all over and done with years ago. And in any case, can you imagine I'd have wished such a fate on anyone?"

"I'm sorry, Violet." Cordelia gave her a quick hug. "I'm not thinking clearly."

"I can't see how you possibly could be." Violet Chase returned Cordelia's embrace, then drew back and looked at her for a moment.

Cordelia returned Violet's gaze, then turned to Suzanne. "May I present Mrs. Rannoch. Mrs. and Miss Chase. Two of my oldest friends."

Jane Chase came forward, shook Suzanne's hand, and pressed Cordelia's. "I'm so sorry, Cordy." Her tone was more restrained than Violet's and yet somehow held a sterling note her sister-in-law's had lacked. She looked to be in her midtwenties like Cordelia and Violet, a slender woman possessed of a direct gaze, a generous mouth, and dark hair dressed in somewhat disordered curls. Pretty, but lacking Violet Chase's exquisite polish.

Suzanne understood Cordelia's saying Violet was not what one would expect of a lady whose suitor had left her for another woman. Whatever had drawn John Ashton to Julia Brooke, it wasn't simply the allure of a beautiful woman. He had already been betrothed—in all but name—to a beautiful woman. Suzanne suspected it had been an unusual experience for Violet to find herself ignored.

Violet turned her gaze to Suzanne while Jane Chase greeted Cordelia. Suzanne caught the other woman's quick appraisal of her cambric high dress and Angoulême spencer, the pearl earrings showing beneath her peach blossom satin hat, the rosettes on the kid slippers peeping out beneath her skirts. "You're Malcolm Rannoch's wife."

"I understand you knew my husband when you were children."

"He used to visit Carfax Court, which isn't far from our home in Derbyshire." Violet's gaze continued to linger on Suzanne. Suzanne knew that look. In British society she was the Continental adventuress who had snagged one of the beau monde's most eligible bachelors. "I suppose he's looking into Julia's death."

"Violet." Jane Chase stretched out a hand to her husband's sister. "There's no need—"

"Everyone knows Mr. Rannoch investigated a murder in Vienna. It's only natural Wellington would turn to him."

Cordelia smiled at her childhood friend. "Actually, Mrs. Rannoch and I have something in common. Wellington's turned the matter over to both our husbands."

Violet stared at her. "To—Harry?"

"He's still the only husband I've had."

"Do sit down," Jane Chase said. "I've sent for tea."

The footman returned with a tea tray. The smell of pungent China tea and fresh-cut lemons filled the air.

Suzanne more than half-expected Violet to press the matter of the investigation into Julia's death, but instead Miss Chase arranged her skirts with care and smiled at Cordelia as her sister-in-law poured out the tea.

"How's your little girl? Lydia's her name, isn't it?"

"Livia. After Caesar Augustus's wife."

"You were always better than me at lessons, but I never took you for a classicist."

Cordelia gave a smile with the sweetness of lemon ice as she tugged at the ribbons on her bonnet. "My husband is."

"Of course." Violet smoothed her French work ruff, discomfited by the mention of Cordelia's estranged husband. Or perhaps, Suzanne thought, deliberately drawing attention to the discomfort. "How's Livia?"

"Thriving." Cordelia lifted her bonnet from her head and began to strip off her gloves. "Chattering away. Delving into whatever books she can get her hands on."

Violet squeezed a wedge of lemon into her tea. "I met Julia in the park walking with her son. Did she tell you?"

Cordelia tugged the second lilac glove from her fingertips. "She mentioned it in one of her letters."

"Such a sweet boy. Julia's hair and eyes, but he looks so like his father." Violet carefully spooned two lemon seeds out of her tea. "How's Johnny?" She tossed the spoon down. "Oh, what a ridiculous way to put it. I can't imagine what this must be like for him."

"He's devastated." Cordelia laid the gloves atop her reticule. Suzanne could see her watching Violet closely.

"I sent a note round to him this morning," Jane Chase said. "It seemed too soon to call."

"Of course he'd be devastated." Violet pulled out a handkerchief and mopped up the tea she'd spattered when she tossed the spoon down. "He adored Julia. I still remember the way he followed her round the room with his eyes that night at Lady Cowper's. I think I knew the moment I saw him bow over her hand."

"Violet—" Mrs. Chase touched her sister-in-law's hand.

"It's all right, Jane." Violet gave her a tight smile. "It's not as though we don't all know the history." She glanced at Suzanne, as though she had forgot she was there. "Forgive me, Mrs. Rannoch. Events like these have a way of making conventions fly out the window."

Suzanne stirred milk into her tea. "Entirely understandable, Miss Chase."

"I was hurt, of course," Violet said, gaze on her tea. "But I don't think I was jealous precisely. It was so very clear they belonged together."

Cordelia clunked her teacup back into its saucer. "Nonsense."

"I beg your pardon?"

"You have more self-respect than that, Vi. You wanted to scratch Julia's eyes out and rightly so. Julia was lovely, but she wasn't an enchantress."

"She—" Violet shook her head. "What does it matter? It was years ago."

"The past has a way of echoing into the present." Cordelia unclasped her reticule and drew out Violet's calling card. "We found this among Julia's things."

Violet froze, her cup halfway to her lips. "I called on Julia after I met her in the park. What's so surprising in that?"

"The note on the back makes it sound as though you wanted to meet her away from her house."

Violet returned the cup to its saucer, sloshing tea onto the forget-me-not-splashed porcelain. "I knew it. Is this why you brought Mrs. Rannoch here? To ask questions about Julia?"

"I brought Mrs. Rannoch because she's been kind to me, and I find it difficult to be alone just now."

Violet twitched her skirt smooth. "I wanted to talk to Julia."

"Why?"

"I don't see what this has to do with—"

Cordelia returned her cup to the table with a clatter of china and leaned forward, arms on her knees. "Violet, Julia was afraid of something before she was killed. Anything that happened to her in the last weeks may be relevant."

Violet drew back in her chair, spine very straight. "I heard she was killed in a French ambush."

"It may be more complicated."

"And you think—" Violet stared at Cordelia. "You think I'm still upset over what happened three years ago?"

"You wouldn't be human if you weren't, darling."

"I have a dozen men clamoring for each dance at every ball we attend."

"You haven't married any of them."

Violet glanced away and drummed her nails on the lacquered arm of the sofa. "I was engaged once. Twice, but the second one wasn't announced."

"It can take a long time to get over someone. I wouldn't—"

Violet swung her gaze to Cordelia. "You think I arranged to meet Julia to—what? Ring a peal over her? It's not her fault that Johnny loved her more than me."

"Vi—"

"Good God, Cordy, do you think I had something to do with her death?"

"Of course not, but—"

"Oh, for heaven's sake." Mrs. Chase clunked down her teacup. "Violet, why didn't you tell me?"

Violet cast an impatient glance at her sister-in-law. "Jane, it's nothing to do with—"

"You knew, didn't you?"

"Knew what?" Violet asked in seemingly genuine confusion.

"Oh, dear God, you did." Jane Chase's mouth twisted in a bitter smile. "Is that what all this was about?"

"Of course not." Violet tightened her grip on her teacup. "That is, I don't know what you're talking about."

"It was sweet of you to try to sort things out, love, but there was no need for you to interfere." Jane Chase squeezed Violet's hand, then turned a calm hazel gaze on Suzanne and Cordelia. "Mrs. Rannoch, forgive me, but you seem to be in the midst of this, and if your husband's looking into Julia's death he'll learn soon enough. Violet didn't arrange to meet Julia Ashton because of what happened three years ago. I believe she arranged to meet her because of something much more current. Julia was involved in a liaison with my husband."

Inquiries at Headquarters, where, in addition to Fitzroy Somerset, Malcolm and Davenport found Colonel Canning and Alexander Gordon, two more of Wellington's aides-de-camp, elicited the information that the officers of the 95th were in the habit of drinking at La Rose Blanche off the Grand Place. Three lieutenants and a captain, tossing dice in the back room of La Rose Blanche, said they hadn't seen Anthony Chase since Stuart's ball the night before, but one of the lieutenants volunteered that Chase's closest friend in the regiment was Colonel Mortimer. When asked for Mortimer's whereabouts, the lieutenant said he was probably visiting his mistress, whose house was—where the devil was it again?—somewhere off the park.

Further inquiries led them at last to a neat little blue-painted house with drawn curtains. Malcolm rang the bell three times and then rapped at the door with no response. Davenport snatched up a handful of gravel and threw it at the French window off the first-floor balcony. At last Colonel Mortimer poked his tousled head out the window and demanded to know what the devil they wanted.

"Assuming he isn't sharing the bed with you and your mistress, where's the likeliest place for Anthony Chase to be?" Davenport shouted up to him.

"Chase?" Mortimer blinked. "Why the devil—"

"Orders."

"But—"

"*Chéri*—" a sleepy voice called from inside the house.

"It's nothing, Adèle," Mortimer said, turning toward the house. He looked back down at Davenport and Malcolm. "Why on earth—Oh, devil take it."

Mortimer vanished back into the house. A few moments later

he stuck his head out the front door. "Why the hell do you need to find Chase so urgently?"

"We just need to talk to him," Malcolm said. "Wherever he is, it won't get him in trouble."

Mortimer's gaze shot from Malcolm to Davenport. "Why should Tony be in trouble?"

"He isn't." Davenport grabbed the side of the door before Mortimer could pull it closed.

"Oh." Mortimer tugged at the neck of his dressing gown. "Well, after his morning ride, he often has a glass of beer by the bridge in the Allée Verte. See here, Rannoch, what the devil—"

"Thanks," Malcolm called over his shoulder, running after Davenport, who was already halfway down the street.

The Allée Verte was the most fashionable promenade in Brussels. Leafy lime and elm trees lined the broad carriage road, with pedestrian walkways on either side. On one side of the road, the blue waters of the canal that led toward Antwerp shimmered peacefully in the afternoon sun. On the other, placid green meadows rolled into the distance. It was late for morning rides and early for afternoon promenades, but Malcolm and Davenport passed a handful of officers out for a stroll or a ride, ladies with sunshades walking or tooling phaetons, nursemaids pushing baby carriages or accompanied by children rolling hoops.

As they neared the end of the mile-long promenade, the wail of an organ and the thud of a tabor cut the air. At the end of the allée, near a bridge that crossed the canal, a German-style beer garden had been set up. Like the allée itself it was not as crowded as it would be later in the day, but soldiers in a variety of uniforms and a few Bruxellois and British expatriates in civilian coats lounged on benches and wooden chairs, sipping wine and beer in the bright sun.

Malcolm and Davenport strolled through the crowd to the far end of the beer garden. Two young Dutch-Belgian officers were sitting to one side, a chessboard between them. A fifty-something Prussian major was turning the pages of a newspaper. And by the edge of the canal, flaxen hair catching the sunlight, was a young officer in the green jacket of the 95th, a glass of lager cradled in his hands.

Davenport strolled up to the bench. "Good afternoon, Chase."

"Davenport?" Chase blinked up at him against the sunlight. "What—"

Davenport dropped down on the bench beside him. "Sorry to interrupt your tête-à-tête with a glass of beer, but I'm afraid we're in need of information. I believe you know Malcolm Rannoch."

"Chase," Malcolm said, pulling up a chair. "Cricket on the lawn at Carfax Court seems a long time ago now."

Tony Chase stared at him. His jacket was unbuttoned, his black leather stock loosened, his gaze unfocused. A day's growth of stubble showed on his face. "Never thought you'd turn into a man of action, Rannoch."

"Hardly that." Malcolm dropped into the chair. "I'm a diplomat."

"And an agent." Tony took a gulp of beer. "What do you want with me?"

"Wellington's asked us to look into Julia Ashton's death," Malcolm said.

"*Julia.*" Tony slumped back against his chair. "Why—"

"You and your brother and sister grew up with Julia and Cordelia Brooke," Malcolm said. "And with John Ashton."

Tony ran his hand over his disordered hair, which looked as though it was customarily expertly tousled. "Our families have neighboring estates in Derbyshire. We saw a lot of each other as children. You know that. But it was years ago. Ashton's in a different regiment—"

"You drew Ashton's cork at Boodle's three years ago," Davenport said.

Tony swung his gaze to Davenport. "How do you know—"

"My wife told me. It sounds sadly like my unfortunate confrontation with your brother."

"What the devil—"

"Cordelia also told me that John Ashton was almost your brother-in-law. The fact that he didn't become your brother-in-law led to the assault."

Tony tugged at his loosened stock. "I don't see what ancient history between Ashton and my sister has to do with Julia's death."

"Perhaps it doesn't." Davenport was turned sideways on the bench, arms folded across his chest, regarding Tony with a steady gaze. "But the fact that you were her lover does."

Malcolm shot a look at Davenport. He'd been thinking the same himself, but he wouldn't have put it into words. Not yet.

Beer sloshed over the rim of Tony's glass. "Wh—what makes you think that?"

"You're drunk. And it's not yet three o'clock."

"Christ, Davenport, if you claimed every man who was drunk before three o'clock had been the lover of—"

"Blue shadows under your eyes. You haven't slept. Red-rimmed eyes, you've been crying. You haven't shaved or combed your hair, and I suspect your valet would be shocked at the state of your linen. Then there's the mingled guilt and grief in your voice when you say her name. Shall I go on?"

Tony drew a breath. Then he slumped forward and took a long drink of beer. "Oh God, what's the use?" He put the glass down on the bench with shaking fingers. "I was in love with her. What man wouldn't have been?"

"A surprising number actually," Davenport said. "Or this investigation would be quite impossible."

Tony stared at him. "How can you talk so coolly about it? Julia's your—"

"Wife's sister. And rather kinder to me than Cordelia was. Just because I choose not to indulge my grief in front of you doesn't mean I'm not feeling it."

"You cold-hearted bastard."

"But don't worry, I've long since given up any delusions about defending the honor of the Brooke sisters," Davenport said. "How long had the affair been going on?"

"I don't see what—"

"The events that led to Lady Julia's death were more complicated than they at first appeared," Malcolm said.

"Are you saying someone deliberately killed her?"

"Possibly."

Tony gripped the edge of the bench. "But who on earth—"

"So we need to know everything possible about her life these past few weeks." Malcolm put a hand on the glass of beer before Tony's grip on the bench could send it tumbling to the ground. "Who she saw, what she did—"

"But—" Tony's horrified gaze fastened on Malcolm's face. "Good God, Rannoch, you can't think I killed her."

"We need—"

"Don't be stupid, Chase." Davenport grabbed Tony's arm, loosening his grip on the bench. "Lovers are always suspects. Like husbands and wives. Tell us why you went from pummeling John Ashton to seducing his wife."

"I didn't—It wasn't like that—" Tony glanced to the side, his gaze clouded with memories. Malcolm felt his throat go tight, his own loss of a few months before fresh in his mind. "Oh, the devil, I don't suppose there's any chance you'd understand."

"Try us," Malcolm said in a soft voice.

Tony stared at the placid waters of the canal. "That business three years ago—it was stupid. But Johnny was as good as promised to Violet. When I got home on leave I could tell how distressed she was. Vi doesn't show her feelings easily. But she cared about Ashton. Or her pride was hurt. Or maybe both. Dash it, a fellow doesn't like to see his sister—"

Malcolm and Davenport sat back and let Tony's voice trail off. Tony snatched his glass from Malcolm and took a sip. "I scarcely even considered Julia in the midst of it all. She was barely out of the schoolroom when I went out to the Peninsula. I still remembered her arranging tea parties with Violet for their dolls."

Davenport leaned back on the bench. "Doing it much too brown, Chase. You aren't blind."

"Of course I knew Julia was lovely, but she was practically my sister. Violet's very pretty, too. I couldn't understand Ashton—" He lifted his glass with both hands and took a long swallow. "It was awkward after the fight. My wife is Johnny's cousin. You probably know that. Johnny and Julia were at our wedding. But I was in the Peninsula, and Johnny was a Hyde Park soldier. We didn't see much of each other. Then in Brussels there they were. I don't know how it is, but Julia—"

"Didn't seem like your sister anymore?" Davenport asked.

"She took my breath away."

"Odd how that happens."

Tony stared at the tea garden across the canal. The house at the center of the garden was surrounded by a moat, a relic of an older age, but Tony seemed to be looking into his own past. "I went into the card room at Lady Charlotte Greville's. Julia was playing piquet with Freemantle and Sarah Lennox and some Belgian fellow. Vedrin his name is. I was drinking port with Kincaid, but the game caught my eye. Well, Julia caught my eye. Her eyes were bright and her color high, but it was obvious she was distressed. She—" He cast a sideways glance at Malcolm. "Did—"

"Rannoch knows Julia had a weakness for cards," Davenport said. "So did her father. How badly was she losing?"

"Badly." Tony stared down at the water lapping against the canal wall. "She flung down her cards and ran from the room. I followed." He looked up at Malcolm and Davenport. "We've been friends from childhood, even if I hadn't seen her so much of late. I wanted to see if I could be of service."

"Naturally you were concerned," Malcolm said, in a tone calculated to elicit confidences.

Tony dug his fingers into his hair. "I found her in tears in an antechamber. I gave her my handkerchief, poured her a glass of brandy." He curved his fingers round his own glass of beer. "I think she was desperate for someone to talk to. She told me the whole. She'd been playing deep since they'd come to Brussels. The Comte de Vedrin had her vowels."

"How much?" Davenport asked.

Tony's gaze slid to the side.

"It's a bit late to be protecting Julia's memory."

"A bit over five thousand pounds. Apparently she'd got badly in debt just after her marriage. Ashton had settled things for her, but he wasn't happy about it. She was terrified of telling him again." Tony turned the glass between his hands. "She was in an impossible situation. So I did the only thing I could. I settled the debt for her."

"All of it?" Malcolm asked.

Tony nodded. "She protested of course. But I said we could consider it a loan, and she could pay me back whenever it suited her, but that there was no hurry now. Or ever."

Davenport regarded Tony as though he had transformed into a particularly repellant type of reptile. "You paid Julia's gambling debts."

"Yes, I just told you—"

"And then she became your mistress."

"Yes. No. That is, one didn't lead to the other." Tony met Davenport's hard stare. "Good God, you can't think—"

"You rescued Julia from an impossible situation," Davenport said, his tone like a succession of level, precise pistol shots. "She was indebted to you financially, and you were possessed of information that could have ruined her marriage. You can't seriously expect me to believe that none of that came into play when she went to your bed."

"Damn you—" Tony half-rose, then dropped back onto the bench with a thud. "What's the use? I doubt you even know the meaning of love."

Davenport kept his gaze steady on Tony's face. "One can understand a thing without experiencing it oneself."

"Nothing happened the day I told her I'd paid off the debts. I didn't even kiss her hand."

"You said she took your breath away," Davenport said. "Do you expect us to believe you didn't want to—"

"Of course I wanted to." Tony drew a breath. "But I didn't. There are rules about that sort of thing."

"Rules often more honored in the breach than the observance," Malcolm said.

"I'm not proud of everything I've done, but I still consider myself a gentleman. Later we found ourselves standing next to each other in line at the buffet at the ball at the Hôtel de Ville. We started talking just to fill the silence—about the waltz that was playing, the crowd, the quality of the champagne. It wasn't what we said, it was the way her eyes lit up—" He shook his head. "I've been in love before of course. This was different." He gave a lop-sided grin that women probably found endearing. At least they would if he weren't three sheets to the wind, with greasy hair and bloodshot eyes. "God, I'd say that in any case, wouldn't I? But it was. Not just the thrill of the chase, the lure of the moment, but—"

"I'd say it takes about a decade to test whether or not that's true," Davenport said.

Tony fixed him with a hard gaze. His red-rimmed eyes were suddenly focused. "I was going to marry her."

❧ 13 ❧

Suzanne studied Jane Chase across the gleaming tea service. A typical British officer's wife in her flounced muslin and strand of pearls. Young, fresh, quite pretty, if not an obvious diamond of the first water like Violet Chase or Julia Ashton. But Jane's bright eyes were tinged with a hint of worldly wisdom, and her full-lipped mouth curved with irony. She held her chin high and her gaze steady as the other three women took in the bombshell she had exploded over the tea table.

It was Violet Chase who broke the stunned silence. She gripped her sister-in-law's arm. "Don't be ridiculous, Jane. Tony adores you—"

"Oh, for heaven's sake, Violet." Jane Chase detached her sister-in-law's hand from her arm. "Do you really think this is the first time it's happened?"

Violet's carefully plucked brows drew together.

"Dearest." Jane squeezed Violet's hand. "Your faith in your brother is touching."

"But he—"

"He's a man." Jane turned her gaze to Suzanne and Cordelia. "My apologies for the domestic drama. My husband is expert at persuading women he's in love with them. And at persuading himself he loves them, to be fair. I imagined you knew that, Cordelia."

"Tony was always tumbling in and out of love."

Jane Chase smoothed her finger over a crease in her skirt. "I think he actually believed he loved me. He was remarkably ardent and oddly sincere." She reached for her tea and took a careful sip.

"But—" Violet plucked at the Valenciennes lace on her sleeve. "You seemed so—"

"Happy?" Jane gave a dry smile. "The first liaison hurt, of course, because I'd fancied myself quite desperately in love with Tony. I had mad thoughts of leaving him or doing other quite unspeakable things. The second was easier to bear. With each one I grew a bit more numb. Now—" She shrugged. "We've learned to rub along, as most couples do. I suppose you could say we're happy, after a fashion. At least I don't expect we're any more miserable than the average couple you'd have found at the ball last night."

Violet stared at her sister-in-law as though she'd transformed into a creature from another world. "You can't expect me to believe—"

Jane twitched her skirt smooth, gaze fastened on a scalloped flounce. "I knew the first time I saw him pointedly ignore Julia at Catalani's concert. There's only one reason he'd ignore such a beautiful woman."

Violet shook her head, her chestnut ringlets whipping about her face. "This doesn't make any sense, Jane. You can't be so sanguine—"

"Life isn't a fairy tale, Vi."

Cordelia was watching Jane Chase, eyes dark with unexpected concern. "My apologies, Jane."

"There's no need for you to—"

"On my sister's account."

Jane reached for the teapot and refilled the cups. "Johnny may blame Julia. I don't. If it wasn't Julia someone else would have caught Tony's eye."

Violet's lips tightened. "Julia had no right—"

Cordelia turned her gaze to her childhood friend. "She took Johnny from you and then she took your brother from his wife. You had every reason to be angry at her."

Violet grabbed her teacup and took a swallow as though she wished it were something stronger. "Spare me the false sympathy, Cordy."

"Violet." Cordelia leaned forward. "I always felt badly about Julia taking Johnny from you. I never understood what was in my sister's mind, but that wasn't her finest moment."

Violet turned her head to the side and gave what sounded suspiciously like a snort.

"And I'm dreadfully sorry for what Jane's had to go through."

"Why?" Violet spun her gaze to Cordelia. "Why should you be remotely sorry for any of it? After what you did with George—"

"I see." Cordelia straightened up. Her color was high, but her gaze remained steady.

Violet clunked her cup down in its saucer. "You think you're excused everything because you and George were madly in love and somehow destined for each other."

"Violet," Jane said.

"Don't you?" Violet's gaze was trained on Cordelia.

Cordelia's fingers curled inward, nails pressing into her palms. "If George and I were destined for each other, something has obviously gone sadly wrong."

Violet was still staring at Cordelia. "You think you and George should be forgiven anything—"

"Thought, perhaps." Cordelia uncurled her fingers with deliberation and reached for her teacup.

"And after all that, you didn't even stay loyal to him. Any more than Julia stayed loyal to Johnny."

"Violet—" Cordelia drew a sharp breath. "For what it's worth, I don't always like myself very much."

"And then after George there were God knows how many others," Violet said, gaze still fixed on Cordelia.

"For heaven's sake, Violet," Jane said.

"It's no more than the truth, Jane." Cordelia took a sip of tea. "But that's between me and Harry." She returned the cup to its saucer. "Why did you arrange to meet Julia, Violet?"

"I don't see—"

"Vi, please. I just want to learn what happened to my sister."

"Violet." Jane touched her sister-in-law's arm. "I think the truth can only help now. If Mr. Rannoch and Colonel Davenport are looking into Julia's death there are bound to be questions. Better to answer them now." Better, her gaze implied, to speak before Suzanne rather than her husband.

Violet sprang to her feet and paced to the window. She stood for a moment looking out at the leafy oak tree in the garden behind the house. "I came into the drawing room one day last week. Tony was writing—which was odd in and of itself, Tony has never been much of a writer. He pushed whatever he was writing between the pages of a book when I came into the room."

"Naturally you were curious," Cordelia said.

"Don't be spiteful, Cordy."

"I'm not. I'd have been curious myself."

Violet curled her fingers round the window frame. "Tony received a summons from his commanding officer and had to leave the house at once, so of course he couldn't retrieve the paper. As soon as he was gone, I looked at it." She cast a defiant glance over her shoulder. Neither Cordelia nor Jane rose to the challenge.

"It was a love letter to Julia." Violet paced to the fireplace, gripping her elbows. "Julia, of all people. She'd done enough damage to our family. Tony should have known—It was a dreadful insult to Jane."

"And an insult to you," Jane said in a quiet voice.

Violet fingered a card of invitation to the Duchess of Richmond's ball, tucked into the gilt frame of the mirror that hung over the mantel. "I was going to confront Tony. I had all sorts of terribly satisfying things worked out to say to him. But the more I thought about it, the more I was convinced Julia had done something to make him stray—"

Jane gave a dry laugh.

"—and men can be so foolishly stubborn. So it was no good talking to Tony, I needed to talk to Julia. I sent her a note. That note, the one Cordy found." She made a gesture toward the square of paper on the sofa table.

"What were you going to say to her?" Suzanne asked.

Violet spun round, eyes wide with justified outrage. "What damage she was doing. That it had to stop."

"And you thought she'd stop just like that?" Jane asked.

"I thought she'd listen to reason. Not that Julia was ever that reasonable. But we used to be friends. I thought—" Violet shrugged, fluttering the knots of seafoam ribbon on her bodice. "I just needed to talk to her."

"Did she meet you?" Suzanne asked.

"Two days ago. She was on time, I'll give her that." Violet rubbed her arms. "She didn't seem to have the least suspicion what it was about. She thought I wanted to talk about Johnny. Which I did, in a roundabout way. I said that having taken him she might at least have had the decency to appreciate him. Even then she didn't seem to know what I was talking about until I told her I'd found Tony's letter to her. Then she said—" Violet's gaze slid to the side.

"It's all right, Vi," Jane said. Her eyes held concern for her sister-in-law, but beneath it Suzanne thought she detected a lingering trace of bitterness. "I think I'm quite past Julia's ability to hurt me."

"She said when I was married myself I'd understand these things." Violet's mouth twisted. "As though she was a font of wisdom, and I was—I told her I didn't need to be married to understand perfectly well that she was betraying her husband and interfering in my brother's marriage. Julia said—" Violet bit her lip and fixed her gaze on the moss roses in the hearth rug. "She said Jane wouldn't be hurt by what she didn't know about, and if I were sensible I'd keep quiet about the whole thing. The affair would end as these things always do, and Jane would be none the wiser."

"Tony's charms appear to have worked less well than usual," Jane murmured.

"I rather lost my temper then. She was so hideously self-assured, and she didn't have the decency to be properly in love with Tony, any more than she had been with Johnny. That was the only possible excuse for what she'd done with Johnny. I'd even half-convinced myself I couldn't stand in the way of their grand passion, and I'd done something noble by stepping aside. But if she was going to toss him aside like last season's gowns—I called her all sorts of names. Julia didn't even—"

"Have the decency to lose her temper back?" Cordelia said.

"No."

Cordelia nodded. "She was like that from childhood. One of the nursery maids would come in to find me yelling, and Julia looking at me with those wide blue eyes, and I'd inevitably be punished for losing my temper with my sweet little sister." Cordelia bit her lip, perhaps at the memory that her sweet little sister was gone.

"I galloped off in a temper," Violet said. "It wasn't until I got home and I'd flung my riding hat and gloves across the room that I realized somehow I'd ended up feeling I was the one in the wrong." She cast a glance at her sister-in-law. "I'm sorry, Jane. I'm sorry Tony put you through this. I thought he was more decent than George. Even after I knew about Julia, I thought it was just the one lapse."

Jane got to her feet and went to Violet's side. "Tony isn't your responsibility, Vi." She squeezed Violet's shoulders.

"Did you see Lady Julia at the ball last night, Miss Chase?" Suzanne asked.

Violet dashed a hand across her eyes. "Across the room briefly early in the evening. We didn't speak. I didn't speak to her again after that morning in the Allée Verte." She took a step toward Cordelia. "I'm sorry she's dead, Cordy. Truly. However angry I was, I'd never have wished that on her."

Cordelia met Violet's gaze. For a moment, Suzanne would have sworn that what passed between these two women who were both masters of artifice was bone-deep and genuine. "Thank you, Vi."

The organ and the tabor sounded unnaturally loud in the sudden stillness. A splash cut the air. Across the canal, two young boys who had escaped their mothers in the tea garden were tossing pebbles into the water.

Davenport shifted his injured arm and ran his gaze over the man who had just claimed it was his intention to marry the very-married Julia Ashton. "Forgive me for dwelling on petty details, but I was under the impression that you and Julia were both already married."

Tony flushed. "Of course. We knew it wouldn't be easy—"

"You were taking a leaf from Lord Uxbridge and Lady Charlotte Wellesley's book?"

Lord Uxbridge's elopement with Wellington's sister-in-law and their subsequent divorces from both their spouses had been the scandal of the beau monde seven years ago. The events had been talked of again recently when Uxbridge was appointed to command the cavalry under Wellington. Wellington had merely said he'd take good care Uxbridge didn't run off with him. He didn't care about anyone else.

"We—" Tony swallowed. "Julia and I were going to go away together. Naturally there would have been unpleasantness—"

"Two divorces."

"—but eventually we would have married."

Davenport folded his arms across his chest, cradling the elbow of his bad arm. "Were you planning to run off and consider the world well lost for love before or after war breaks out?"

A muscle tensed in Tony's jaw. "I'm not a coward."

"And?"

"Of course we wouldn't have left before Bonaparte attacked. After the battle we were going to go to Italy."

"Comforting that you're confident of such a quick victory."

Malcolm leaned forward. "Lady Julia had agreed to go away with you?"

"Of course. I told you, we were in love. There was no other alternative really, given how we felt about each other. Difficult, as I said, a lot of loose ends—"

"Children," Davenport said.

Tony took a sip of beer, though he seemed to find it bitter. "That was the hardest for Julia, her son. But in the end she decided it wasn't fair for him to grow up with a mother who was miserable."

"So she was going to leave him with his father?" Malcolm asked.

"Ashton adores the boy. Of course Julia hoped she'd be able to see him eventually."

"And your own children?" Davenport was observing Tony with the expression Geoffrey Blackwell wore when he looked at something particularly disagreeable under the microscope. "You have two, I believe. Were you planning to exercise a father's rights and keep them with you? Take them to your exile in Italy and let Julia be their stepmother?"

"I—" Tony ran a hand over his hair. "I hadn't thought that far."

Davenport continued to lean back in his chair, but from the look in his eyes and the tension in his arms, he wanted nothing more than to plant Tony a facer. Malcolm, thinking of his own son, was of much the same mind, but such an action would be sadly unproductive in the investigation.

"Did Lady Julia ever seem to you to be afraid?" Malcolm asked.

"When I first met her she was terrified of Vedrin and the hold he had on her with her gambling debts."

"And more recently?"

Tony appeared to give the question genuine consideration. "She felt guilty. About Ashton, about her son. But afraid—No. What makes you think she was afraid?"

"She wrote to her sister that she was."

"Cordelia?" Tony's gaze flickered to Davenport. "Your wife."

"She goes by that name."

"But that doesn't make any sense." Tony frowned into his beer glass. "I know Julia was in the habit of corresponding with Cordelia, but she told me she found it harder and harder to write to her of late. Since our affair began. Because of course she couldn't write to her about that so she had to fill the letters with trivialities."

"Why?" Davenport said.

"She had to have something to put in the letters."

"Why couldn't she tell Cordelia about the affair?"

"Tell her sister she was involved with another man and about to leave her husband and child—"

"You think Cordelia would be scandalized? You've known my wife since she was a child."

"That doesn't—"

"And your brother was her lover."

Tony's gaze slid to the side. "For God's sake, Davenport—"

Davenport raised his brows. "Considering you've admitted to betraying your own wife, having an affair with a married woman, and planning to run off with her, I don't see what you're caviling at saying. Unless you're embarrassed by referring to the fact that I was cuckolded. Believe me, I got over it years ago."

Tony's gaze locked with Davenport's own. "I think Julia was afraid Cordelia would advise her to act differently based on her own example."

Davenport stretched his legs out toward the edge of the canal. "That doesn't sound like Cordelia."

"Julia said her sister had changed in the last few years."

"That doesn't sound like Cordelia, either."

Tony's gaze settled on Davenport's face. It looked a little less unfocused than it had previously. "But then it's been some years since you've seen your wife, hasn't it?"

"Fair enough. And of course in the end your brother and my wife didn't run off together and seek release from their respective marriages. Did you ask your brother why he didn't marry Cordelia?"

Tony's gaze widened. "I thought—"

"That I stood in the way of a divorce? My dear Tony, why would I seek to keep a woman who so obviously didn't want me?"

"You didn't—"

"Cordelia never asked me for a divorce as it happens. I saw no need to put us both through it. But we've rather drifted from the point. Julia did write the letter to Cordelia saying she was afraid. That she feared for her life."

"*Feared for her life?*"

"Are you sure Vedrin had stopped bothering Julia?" Malcolm asked.

"He had no reason to continue. I'd paid off the debts."

"You'd paid off the debts she told you about. You don't know that she told you about all of them."

Tony tugged at his stained shirt collar. "She didn't actually. I got Vedrin to tell me the full amount. And then I paid it all."

"You don't know that she hadn't acquired more debts since," Davenport said.

"She stopped gambling."

"You've spent every moment with her since the affair began?"

"She promised me. She swore to it."

"And lovers never lie."

"Julia wouldn't have." Tony's eyes were wide and blue and earnest. "Not to me."

"For a man capable of leaving his wife and children, you have a touching romanticism."

Malcolm shifted his chair to avoid the glare of the sun off the pavement. "Where were you last night, Tony?"

"Where you were. At Stuart's ball."

"I slipped out as it happens. I was at the Château de Vere when Julia was killed."

"You—"

"And I managed to get back to the ball without anyone except my wife realizing I'd gone. Amazing how easy it is to do that at a large entertainment."

Tony stared at him. "You're suggesting I could have—You think I rode to the château and killed Julia? Good God—"

"Can you tell us who you spoke with between midnight and two?" Davenport asked.

Tony ran a hand over his hair. "I took Sarah Lennox in to supper. I danced with her afterwards. I danced with my sister and with Catherine Somerset and then with—My wife. Then I realized I hadn't seen Julia since supper. I went looking for her. Wandered through the ballroom and salons. Exchanged greetings, but I wasn't noting whom I spoke to."

"When did you learn she'd been killed?" Davenport asked.

"This morning. At breakfast. Freemantle called round and told my wife and Violet and me."

"For God's sake, Chase," Davenport said, "this will go a lot faster if you avoid lying. You obviously haven't slept. You learned last night."

Tony swallowed. "All right, I saw Ashton leave the ball alone." He glanced to the side, then met Davenport's gaze. "I followed him home. I knew something was wrong. I was afraid Ashton had discovered the truth, and he and Julia had quarreled. I never guessed—After I saw him go into the house alone I bribed the footman for information."

"Do you think Ashton did know about the affair?" Malcolm asked.

"No. That is—" Tony stared from Malcolm to Davenport. "You don't think Ashton—"

"We don't have enough information yet to think anything," Malcolm said. "But lovers and husbands are obvious suspects."

Tony looked from Malcolm to Davenport. The sun fell hard and clear over his face. "I didn't kill her. I know you don't believe me, but I hope to God instead of wasting time on me, you'll discover who was behind her death. And then I'll finish the bastard myself."

❧ 14 ❧

Suzanne cast a sideways glance at Cordelia Davenport as they left the Chase house. Lady Cordelia had tugged on her gloves, adjusted her bonnet, and taken her leave of Violet and Jane Chase with every appearance of composure. More composure than either of the Chase ladies had shown. But now her face was set in firm lines beneath the brim of her bonnet. As though she were hanging on to her self-command by her fingernails.

As the footman pushed the front door to behind them, Lady Cordelia's foot slipped on the sand-scoured steps. Suzanne caught the other woman's arm in a firm grip. Beneath the light muslin of her gown, Cordelia was shaking and, despite the sticky heat, her skin was ice-cold.

"I'm sorry," Cordelia said. "I—"

"Entirely understandable. We both need fortification." Suzanne retained her grip on Cordelia's arm as they descended the remainder of the steps, and then steered the way down the street and round the corner. A blue and gold sign, slightly faded but still bright in the sunlight, proclaimed Les Trois Roses café. It had become a favorite haunt of Suzanne's during her weeks in Brussels for the excellence of the coffee, the quality of the wine, and the discretion of the staff. She said nothing until she and Cordelia were seated at a table in a secluded window alcove and supplied with glasses of Bordeaux.

Lady Cordelia curled both hands round the glass. It shook in her fingers. She took a quick sip, then set the glass down with great care. She stared into the deep red of the wine, eyes dark with the ghosts of memories. "Of all the names I've justifiably been called, I never thought of myself as missish. What a poor creature you must think me."

"On the contrary." Suzanne draped her scarf over the chairback and stripped off her gloves. "I'm amazed you maintained your composure so well. It's never easy to confront the past." She took a sip of wine. It tasted more bitter than she remembered.

Cordelia laced her fingers together round the stem of her own wineglass. "We all grew up together. The Chases didn't have a feather to fly with and neither did Julia and I, but none of us understood about mortgaged estates and the lack of proper dowries yet. We lived in a sort of charmed, golden world. Picking strawberries, sneaking bottles of champagne from our parents' wine cellars, playing with the Mallinsons at Carfax Court and the Devonshire House children at Chatsworth."

"Where you met Lady Caroline Lamb."

Cordelia's mouth twisted. "Next to Caro I used to be considered the stable one. We got up to all sorts of mischief." She took another sip of wine. "The two Devonshire girls—Little G and Harryo—always looked a bit askance at us. They approved of Julia, who was always much better behaved than I was. As was Violet, though Vi had more of an adventurous streak." Her mouth curved as happier memories seemed to drift through her mind. "Johnny was ridiculously honorable even as a boy. But he tagged along after us to make sure we didn't get in too much trouble. He was following Violet round in those days. And he and Tony Chase were friends. Hard to believe—" Her fingers tightened round the stem of her glass.

"People grow up."

"And change." Cordelia's mouth twisted. "George Chase and I—We were the oldest in our respective families, the most daring, the ones who organized the amateur theatricals and the secret moonlight picnics by the lake. I decided I was going to marry him when I was twelve, though it was more like realizing something I'd always known than making a conscious decision. When I was sixteen, I looked at him over the Christmas punch bowl and realized that marriage entailed a great deal more than I'd previously considered."

"But that didn't change your mind about whom you wanted to marry?"

"On the contrary. I was more convinced I wanted George than ever. And George wanted me. I knew that when he kissed me under the mistletoe and then later in the birch coppice when we were delivering Boxing Day gifts. It all seemed so easy and so perfect. We were desperately in love. The way one only is the first time."

"So I remember," Suzanne said, though her own first love had been a good deal more complicated.

Cordelia pushed her glass away across the table. "George proposed at my come-out ball when I was eighteen and he was just down from Oxford. In my parents' conservatory. Such a cliché, but that night all I could think was how perfect my life would be. Odd now to remember I was ever such a romantic."

"Your parents forbade the match?"

"How did you guess?"

"Something stopped you from marrying him."

Cordelia rubbed a hand over her eyes. "George went to my father the next day. I thought it was purely a formality. I could scarcely believe it when I saw George stalking out of the house. Then Papa summoned me to his study. He said he couldn't condemn me to a life of poverty. When I protested that I loved George, and we'd be happy as long as we were together, my father said that I'd learn soon enough that love didn't outlast privation. It's odd, Papa never seemed very interested in either Julia or me, but in that moment he was almost tender."

The light ironic tone could not quite disguise the pain beneath. "I don't imagine you took it easily," Suzanne said.

"I cried. I railed. I slipped out of the house and tracked George down in a gambling hell. I wanted to go straight to Gretna Green. George persuaded me to wait. With time, surely our parents would come round." Cordelia hunched her shoulders and pulled her wineglass back toward her. Her gloves pulled taut over her knuckles. "That Christmas, George went to a house party in Hampshire and became betrothed to Annabel Lovell. An heiress with a fortune of sixty thousand pounds."

Suzanne saw the knife-cut heartbreak of an eighteen-year-old girl in the cynical gaze of the woman before her. "It must have been unbearable."

"It probably saved us both from the rude awakening my father warned me of. I don't think either George or I was suited to love in a cottage. Though it would have been easier on Harry and on Annabel Lovell if George and I had inflicted ourselves on each other instead of on them. I wouldn't believe the betrothal was real until I heard it from George himself. When I saw him in London after the holidays, he told me there'd been no alternative. We couldn't have been happy with nothing to live on, and he had to see to his brother and sister. I called him a coward and worse. We didn't part well." She rubbed her arms. "George married Annabel Lovell at St. George's Hanover Square, then bought a commission. He went off to the Peninsula shortly after his honeymoon. For about six months I was certain I would die."

"And then?"

Cordelia snatched up her glass and took a sip of wine. "I realized I was going to survive, like it or not. I flung myself into the Season. I'd always liked pretty things. It occurred to me life had other sources of pleasure to offer besides love. Which I was still certain I'd never feel again." She frowned. "Not that I have precisely come to think of it."

"A first love is different from the ones that come after."

"Assuming any do come after." Cordelia brushed a speck of lint from the tablecloth. "The next spring at a ball at Devonshire House I met Harry. He was clever, different from the usual boys just down from Oxford who flirted with me and tried to look down my bodice and trod on my toes. And he had a handsome fortune." She lifted her gaze and met Suzanne's own, her eyes defiant.

"Naturally having given up on love, you'd be prudent."

"Or cynical. Harry and I were wildly unsuited. He liked to stay home with his books, I liked to go out every night. I couldn't bear to be still, because I didn't much like the thoughts I had when I was. All the same, we managed to rub along. Until George came home from the Peninsula on leave."

Suzanne recalled the force of the tension between the Davenports in her salon that afternoon. Such tension only came in the wake of emotions that had once run very strong indeed. "That must have been unspeakably difficult."

Cordelia's gaze moved to a pastoral print on the wall, then to the window. "I was arrogant enough to believe I was indifferent to him. Love was a conceit, so how could I fall victim to it? I'd gone from being a romantic fool of eighteen to an arrogant fool of twenty who thought I was beyond love."

"And when you saw him—?"

"It all came back. I held out for a bit. Told myself it was just the tug of memories, that I was tougher than that, that I knew it was a sure path to ruin." Her hands locked together on the tabletop. "Not because I valued my virtue or because I had any particular loyalty to my husband. I've never been a very good person, you see. But I was determined never again to make myself so vulnerable. A determination that barely lasted the length of a brief meeting in the country and a reception at Melbourne House. Caro was with me when George walked into the room. She told me to have a care. Whatever people have said about her and Lord Byron, I was just as much of a fool. If I made less of a scandal, it's only because my lover wasn't a poet who was the talk of the ton."

Suzanne read the self-disgust in the twist of Lady Cordelia's mouth and the hollowness of her gaze. "My husband and I were in Vienna before we came to Brussels. Intrigue of all sorts was the order of the day, romantic as well as diplomatic. It wasn't so much what people did that caused the scandal. It wasn't even the liaisons that were public knowledge. It was the liaisons that became such public knowledge no one could even pretend to look the other way."

"It's the same in England, though the gossip sets in a bit more quickly." Cordelia tugged at a loose thread in her puffed sleeve. "Harry seemed to be the last to know. The more flagrantly George and I behaved, the more he buried himself in his books. I almost—"

"Wanted him to notice?"

Cordelia gave a harsh laugh. "That would be delightfully simple, wouldn't it? The straying wife who really just wanted the attention of the husband she loved deeply. If that isn't a play, it should be. But the truth is I scarcely had a thought for Harry. I scarcely had a thought for anything but George and our grand passion."

The last was delivered with all the cynicism of the former romantic. A cynicism Suzanne had never been enough of a romantic herself to feel.

Lady Cordelia tossed down another swallow of wine. "But apparently Harry really didn't know. Because when he decided to surprise me at Lady Bessborough's concert of ancient music and found me in George's arms in an antechamber—" Her fingers tightened round the glass. For a moment Suzanne thought it would shatter. "I'll never forget the look in his eyes."

"Angry or hurt?"

"Hurt first. As though he'd been punched in the stomach and stabbed in the back at the same time. Then angry. Like a husband who actually cared for his wife. Far more than the wife realized. Or perhaps his pride was simply hurt. I've never claimed to understand Harry very well. He was quite cerebral in those days, but he planted George a facer. George struck back and they went crashing into an ormolu table. Sally Jersey walked into the room thirty seconds later with Corisande Ossulton. The story was all over the house within minutes and all over London by morning."

"Leaving you no chance to sort things out."

"I doubt we could have done so in any case. I went home and told Harry he could divorce me. Harry asked if I intended to marry George. I couldn't even think that far. Though I was sure I could never bear to be parted from George again. Which I said. Harry simply stared at me with a look like a frozen moor and said that in that case I'd better go to my lover."

"Giving you his permission in a way you'd never forget."

"I turned and walked from the house. I didn't even summon a carriage. I went to Caro at Melbourne House and sent George a note. We left for the country the next day. Harry bought himself a commission. He was gone within the week. I didn't speak to him again until the ball last night."

"Appallingly bad circumstances."

"I knew I might see him in Brussels. I knew it would be ghastly. The odd thing is if anyone had told me Harry would be kind to me I'd have laughed in their face."

"You couldn't have foreseen—"

"That my sister would die. Even then, Harry surprised me." Cordelia jabbed a curl beneath the brim of her bonnet. "George and I stayed in the country for a fortnight. We were going to go off to America together. But then George got word that Annabel was pregnant. Reality set in once again."

Suzanne studied Lady Cordelia. She must have been pregnant herself at about the same time, but she made no reference to it. Had she learned she was expecting a child before or after George Chase left her? And did she know who the father was?

"It's ancient history," Cordelia said, reaching for her wineglass. "Or I thought it was. But if Julia and Tony acted out the same folly I did with his brother—" She shuddered. "Julia always seemed immune to such madness. She didn't even let herself love Johnny. I always thought the reason she was determined not to give way to love was my sad example."

"Was there anything between her and Anthony Chase when they were younger?"

Cordelia shook her head. "I think Julia thought Tony was too young and callow. How she could have thrown her life away—"

"Cordelia." Suzanne reached across the table and laid her hand over Cordelia's own. "You could have been here in Brussels the whole time, offering her sisterly advice every night, and it would have made no difference."

Cordelia gave a wintry smile. "You can't know that."

"I know how people behave when they're in love. Or in lust. Or whatever one chooses to call it."

"Julia couldn't have been all that lost in love. Or even lust. She was bedding the Prince of Orange as well."

"At least now we can see why she said her life had got complicated and was out of her control."

"But none of this explains why she was afraid."

"How would Tony Chase have reacted if he'd known his mistress had another lover?"

Cordelia's eyes widened. "Tony never seemed the knight in shining armor Johnny did. But I can't imagine—"

"You said it yourself to Violet Chase. Someone was behind your sister's death."

"You're right." Cordelia grimaced. "I don't suppose I make a very good investigator."

"I'd say you're managing amazingly well. It's more difficult when it's people one knows."

"Have you been in this situation with people you know?"

"I've never faced the fact that someone I grew up with might have killed my sister. But yes, I've had to investigate people I was close to."

"With your husband."

Suzanne took a sip of wine. "When I married Malcolm I married his work. It was that or sit home waiting like Penelope."

"You don't seem to mind."

"On the contrary. It was part of the attraction."

"You fell in love with an adventurous man."

"I married an adventurous man."

Cordelia raised her brows.

Suzanne stared into the bloodred depths of her glass. Her wedding day, a stuffy room in the British embassy in Lisbon. Malcolm repeating his vows with a sincerity that bit her in the throat. Wonder. Fear. Guilt. "You're the one who said you didn't believe in love." She twisted the stem of the glass between her fingers. "Did you expect an argument from me?"

"You're an intriguing woman, Mrs. Rannoch."

"After today, don't you think you'd better call me Suzanne?"

Cordelia smiled. "If—"

The door of the café opened with a squeak, letting in a warm breeze. Cordelia broke off. Suzanne glanced over her shoulder and found herself looking at the petite, dark-haired person of Blanca Mendoza.

She refrained from rising from her chair, but her fingers closed on the edge of the table. "Colin?" she asked in as conversational a tone as she could manage.

"He's fine." Blanca stopped in front of the table and dropped a curtsy to Cordelia.

"Sit down, Blanca. You can talk in front of Lady Cordelia."

Blanca drew up a chair from a neighboring table and reached into the straw basket that dangled over her arm. "This message came for Mr. Rannoch. It's in code, but I recognized the seal. I wasn't sure where to find him. I asked the Chases' footman, and when he said you'd left I thought you might be here."

Suzanne glanced at the single sheet of paper. The pale blue rose-shaped seal and the slanted handwriting belonged to Rachel Garnier. There were only a few words and Suzanne knew the key to the code. She pulled a pencil from her reticule and quickly sketched out the plaintext.

Urgent. Come at Once.

❧ 15 ❧

"I never cared for Anthony Chase much," Harry Davenport muttered as he and Malcolm walked back along the Allée Verte in the glare of the afternoon sun. "I didn't know why until now."

"His grief seemed genuine."

"Seemed." Davenport scowled at a lime tree.

"How good an actor do you think Tony Chase is?"

"If he's that good an actor, I wouldn't be able to tell."

"False modesty doesn't become you, Davenport."

Davenport gave a sideways grin. "I never saw Tony as brilliant, but he has an uncanny ability to make women believe he's in love with them. To make himself believe it. Any man who can do that—"

A party of officers cantered past on the carriage road, letting up a cloud of dust. "His eyes," Malcolm said.

Davenport shot a look at him, his own eyes a white gleam in the shadows of the overhanging trees. "You noticed it, too."

"They weren't as unfocused later in the interview as they at first appeared. And at one point I'd swear he deliberately made his fingers shake."

"Vienna didn't blunt your abilities, Rannoch."

"If you noticed it as well, why didn't you say so from the first?"

"Because I wanted to see if you noticed it."

"Glad I passed the test."

"You're a good sort, Rannoch."

From Davenport, Malcolm suspected that was a high compliment. "If Chase had learned about Lady Julia's affair with the Prince of Orange—"

"You think he lured to her to the château to confront her? It's possible. He falls out of love easily himself, but I doubt he takes kindly to the same behavior in his mistresses. But then who was doing the shooting?"

They hadn't had a chance to discuss the logistics of the shooting since Rachel's revelation that the French hadn't been behind the ambush, but the implications were obvious and troubling. "For the ambush to have been an attempt to get rid of Lady Julia, someone would have had to know we'd be there," Malcolm said, "as well as knowing about her rendezvous with the Prince of Orange."

"Quite. Who knew you were meeting with La Fleur?"

"Only La Fleur and Wellington and me as far as I know. And you. Whom did you tell?"

"Only Colonel Grant. Or rather he told me."

Malcolm glanced at a man in a hussar's uniform who had stopped to speak with a lady in a green and gold barouche. "Do you think Lady Julia would have really run off with Chase?"

Davenport kicked aside a loose pebble. "I've scarcely proved myself the best judge of what a woman will do for love. Though her simultaneous affair with the prince suggests Julia wasn't as lost in love as Chase claims to have been." Davenport stared ahead, eyes narrowed against the sunlight slanting through the trees to glare off the paving. "Cordelia could give a better analysis."

"You'll talk to her?"

"I think your wife should. Cordelia appears to trust her. That's hardly the case when it comes to me."

The barouche clattered down the allée, the hussar and the lady now putting their heads together beneath the shelter of her lace parasol. "Your sister-in-law's life was undeniably complicated," Malcolm said. "But we still haven't discovered any real danger."

"You said it yourself. One can never be sure who will turn violent. It never occurred to me I'd find myself planting Anthony Chase's brother a facer."

Malcolm cast a glance at Davenport. Beneath the dappling shadows of the trees, his face was set in lines of determined control, his mouth twisted with self-derision. "You had considerable provocation."

"It seemed so at the time. If I'd managed to get over my feelings for Cordelia sooner, we'd have all been spared an uncomfortable scene. But the fact remains I found myself behaving with a lack of control of which I'd have thought myself incapable."

"You didn't—"

"Kill my wife? No, oddly enough that didn't even occur to me. There's no accounting for responses."

Malcolm stopped walking and touched the other man's arm. "Davenport—"

Davenport swung round to look him full in the face. "I'm hardly the most disinterested party when it comes to the Chase family or to my wife and her family. On the other hand, I'm known to be a cold-blooded bastard. I should be able to muddle through without entirely losing my perspective. Though it's probably just as well I have you to keep an eye on me."

"Thank you."

"Don't let it get about."

"Monsieur Rannoch." A towheaded boy darted down the path toward them. "I've been looking all over for you."

"What is it, Pierre?" Malcolm asked, looking down at the boy's freckled face and serious blue eyes. "You have a message?"

Pierre was the son of one of the women at Le Paon d'Or, Rachel's brothel. He ran errands for the brothel, and Rachel had more than once employed him to send messages. At the age of eight, he was more reliable than many men of five-and-thirty.

Pierre cast a sideways glance at Davenport and shifted his weight from one foot to the other.

"It's all right," Malcolm said. "This is Colonel Davenport. You can talk in front of him."

Pierre drew a breath. "Mam'selle Rachel didn't give me a written message. She just said you were to come at once."

Malcolm dug his purse from his pocket. "Thank you." He pressed a coin into Pierre's hand. "You'd best take a roundabout way back to Le Paon d'Or."

"I know the drill." Pierre pocketed the coin with a grin, then bowed his head formally and ran back down the path.

"From Mademoiselle Garnier?" Davenport asked.

"Do you want to come with me?"

"Delighted you asked. That will save me following you."

"Le Paon d'Or. Off the Place Royale."

Davenport regarded Malcolm as a yellow-wheeled cabriolet tooled by a young buck with high shirt points rolled past. "You're going to walk right into a brothel? Not exactly the discretion I'd expect of one of Britain's finest agents."

"Usually I meet Rachel away from Le Paon d'Or, but sometimes it's easier for me to go there than for her to leave. There's a side entrance that some of the more discreet customers use. We won't attract as much attention there. If we are seen going in, people will just assume we're there for obvious reasons."

"Won't it look suspicious for the last faithful husband in the beau monde to be seen going into a brothel?"

"I said I wasn't unfaithful to my wife, not that others believed it. In Vienna everyone assumed I had a mistress."

Davenport cast a sideways glance at him. "You have unexpected depths, Rannoch. Is your mistress-in-name-only still in Vienna?"

For a moment Malcolm's throat felt as raw as if he'd swallowed acid. "She's dead."

"I'm sorry."

Malcolm fixed his gaze on the shifting shadows cast by the overhanging branches, though Tatiana's image was still etched sharp in his memory. "She wasn't actually my mistress."

"But her death meant something to you. Unless my powers of observation are quite failing me."

Malcolm jerked his head toward the end of the Allée Verte. Davenport was almost as sharp-eyed an observer as Suzanne.

Which could be damnably inconvenient.

*   *   *

There were disadvantages to being the wife of a man connected to the most powerful families in the British ton, Suzanne thought as she stood in the shadows cast by a walnut tree across the street from Le Paon d'Or. For instance, it made it much more difficult to enter a brothel undetected than she would have found it a few years ago. Not that she cared so very much for her reputation, but gossip would be tiresome for Malcolm. Though he didn't listen to it himself, a scandalous wife could be a detriment to a diplomat's career.

A diplomatic wife was supposed to practice discretion. She owed Malcolm that much. Besides, becoming a social pariah would make it difficult to investigate. Women like Violet and Jane Chase wouldn't be so quick to confide in her.

She tugged at the brim of her gypsy hat so it enveloped her face and pulled the folds of her plain blue kerseymere shawl more closely about her shoulders. Blanca had brought the hat and shawl in the basket that now dangled over Suzanne's arm and had taken away Suzanne's hat, spencer, and gauze scarf. At the bottom of the basket were bottles and flasks, which let off a fragrant scent. Suzanne could pass for a shopgirl making a delivery from a parfumerie.

She waited until three British officers had descended the steps of Le Paon d'Or, exchanging tense nods with two Dutch-Belgians who were going in. Then she darted across the street just before a fiacre clattered by in a cloud of dust. Two young ensigns jumped down from the fiacre. Even with her limited peripheral vision thanks to the deep brim of the hat, she'd swear one was Teddy Fairbanks, whom she'd danced with last night at Stuart's ball. His gaze swept past her as though she were part of the area railings.

As Teddy and his friend climbed the steps to the front door, Suzanne descended the area steps and rang a bell. A maidservant in a crisp green print dress and a starched apron opened the door.

"I'm here to see Mam'selle Garnier," Suzanne said, softening her voice into the accents of Belgian French. "She ordered some new perfumes from Lamier's. I'm new there, I wasn't sure which door to go to."

"You can go through the kitchen." The girl stepped aside to allow Suzanne into the room. Copper pans hung on the wall and enamel tins lined the shelves. The air smelled of salt and lemon peel and wine from the decanter and glasses that stood on a tray on the long deal table. It might be the kitchen in any town house in Brussels.

The maid led the way across the kitchen, through a door, and up a narrow pine staircase. A flirtatious laugh came from above, followed by the sound of a door slamming. Memories shot through Suzanne, sharp as a palm connecting with her cheek. Her hand closed on the railing, sending a sliver through her glove, but the maidservant was walking ahead and there was no one else to see.

The maid left her to wait in a small sitting room with lamps shaded in pink silk and graceful gilded furniture. Suzanne gave her a card that was from Lamier's parfumerie but had a code scribbled on the back. A few moments later Rachel Garnier appeared in the doorway, a gauzy pink shawl thrown over her sprigged muslin dress. She closed the door and stared with raised brows. "What on earth—"

Suzanne tugged at the ribbons on the gypsy hat and pulled it from her head. "Your note sounded urgent. It seemed faster to come here than to try to track down my husband."

Rachel's gaze swept over Suzanne. "So you came to a brothel."

"It seemed the simplest solution."

"I knew you were a surprising woman the moment I met you, Madame Rannoch. Well, the very fact that your husband introduced you to me confirmed it. But apparently I didn't realize the half of it. If Monsieur Rannoch finds out—"

"He'll only want to know why you summoned him so urgently."

"Do you know, I think you may be right?" Rachel tilted her head to one side, considering. "Monsieur Rannoch is a man of surprises himself." She took a quick step forward. "Madame Rannoch—"

A crash and a cry from the passage drowned out her words. Of one accord the two women ran to the door. As they stepped into the passage, a girl raced by, gold ringlets tumbling down her back, clad only in a large flowered silk shawl and stockings worked with pink clocks.

A Dutch-Belgian lieutenant and a British major had apparently tipped over a demilune table and sent a vase crashing to the floor. They were now pummeling each other on the carpet. The lieutenant, who was on top for the moment, drew back his fist to punch the major in the jaw. The major brought up his knee and hit the lieutenant in the groin. The lieutenant rolled off with a cry and landed on the shards of broken vase.

A door was flung open. A bare-chested man with his breeches unbuttoned ran out and hurled himself into the mêlée on the floor. A redheaded girl in a chemise followed and flung a pitcher of water over the men. None of the men responded.

A girl with nut-brown hair poked her head out a door down the passage. "Brawl," she shouted at Rachel. "Best take cover."

Instead Rachel and Suzanne ran down the passage.

Malcolm and Davenport slipped through the side entrance to Le Paon d'Or. They were in a narrow, dimly lit passage, but the smell of perfume and the strains of a waltz played on a pianoforte drifted from ahead.

And then a raised voice. "Bloody frogs. Can't keep your hands off our women."

"If you can't satisfy your women yourselves—" That voice was Belgian accented.

"Here now," said a third voice with a Scots burr. "Plenty of girls to go round. Give us a kiss, Marie."

A flirtatious giggle. Then a curse. "It's not the girls here. Their damned prince took the wife of one of our officers to his bed."

"That's a filthy—"

"Can't the blighter get his own women without poaching—"

"How dare you insult His Royal Highness—" Another Belgian voice.

"If he's a rutting bastard—"

The sound of a fist connecting with flesh. A girl screamed. Something heavy crashed to the floor. Malcolm and Davenport took a step back. Two men hurtled round the corner, pummeling each other, and careered into Malcolm and Davenport. One of them drew back a fist and hit Malcolm in the eye rather than his opponent.

Malcolm ducked. The man grabbed him by the shoulders. "Can't get away so easily, you frog coward—"

"As it happens, he's not—"

Davenport's words were cut off as the other man landed him a blow to the jaw. In the room beyond, glass shattered.

Malcolm jerked away from his opponent, pulling out of his coat, which was cut more for comfort than fashion. He whirled round and caught the man's arm as he drew it back to land another blow. "Look." He spun his opponent round, holding the man's arm twisted behind him. "I'm not Belgian. And I'm not interested in fighting."

Three more shadowy forms hurtled into the darkened passage. One aimed a blow at Malcolm's opponent, knocking him from Malcolm's grip. The other struck Malcolm. Pain slashed through Malcolm's ribs. He dropped to the ground and rolled across the floor. He sprang to his feet in the room beyond, wincing at the pain in his ribs, just as a bottle went sailing across the room and smashed into the gilt-framed mirror over the mantel.

The smell of good Burgundy filled the air. Two girls clad in clinging white dresses, one fair-haired, the other a brunette, stood on oval-back chairs, screaming. Another girl, chestnut hair fallen from its pins, flung a bucket of ice over the dragoon and the man in civilian clothes who were pummeling each other on the floor.

"Slimy bastards. That mirror belonged to Madame Grès's grandmother."

With a roar of rage, a Belgian lieutenant knocked a man in a powdered wig and footman's livery into a shelf of books against the wall. Leather-bound volumes and sheets of newspaper went flying. Malcolm pushed himself to his feet. The man who had thrown the bottle grabbed another bottle from the drinks table and brought it down on the head of a Belgian sergeant who was staggering to his feet. The Belgian sergeant slumped back to the floor and would have collided with Malcolm if Malcolm hadn't dodged out of the way.

A scream sounded from the hall beyond. Not a cry of rage, but an actual scream of pain and terror. Malcolm ran across the salon, dodging the two men battling on the floor, broken glass crunching beneath his boots.

A man in his shirtsleeves with a dragoon's sabre thrust through his belt had a flaxen-haired boy pinned up against the wall at the base of the stairs. The boy's face was drained of color, his eyes wide and desperate. The dragoon's hand was round his throat.

Malcolm launched himself at the dragoon's back. The dragoon whirled round and struck Malcolm across the face. The flaxen-haired boy slid to the floor.

"How dare you interfere," the dragoon said.

"I wasn't aware strangling children had become part of military duties."

"Impertinent puppy." The dragoon whipped his sword from its scabbard and brought it down on Malcolm's arm. Malcolm staggered back.

"Fight like a man, you frog coward." The dragoon lunged after him.

"Rannoch." Davenport's voice came from the archway to the salon, rising over the thuds and cries and crash of broken glass. Malcolm risked a quick glance over his shoulder. Davenport held a cavalry sabre, which he sent spinning through the air. Malcolm caught the sword and brought it up to meet the dragoon's relentless attack.

The blades slid against each other, disengaged, met again. Malcolm turned, holding the blade of his sword taut against the dragoon's, and backed up the stairs. The dragoon followed, pressing his attack. His cuts were swift and reckless. Malcolm could have dodged beneath his guard, but he had no desire to wound the other man.

Malcolm's boot slipped on the polished mahogany. He caught himself on one hand. Pain shot through his arm. The dragoon's blade slid along his cheekbone. Malcolm pushed himself to his feet and engaged the other man's blade, forcing it down.

He jumped backward up the last two steps, parrying for all his life was worth.

A pistol shot cut the air. The dragoon dropped his sword and whirled round, clutching his shoulder. "What the devil—"

Suzanne lowered her smoking pistol. "Sorry. But I rather take exception to someone trying to kill my husband."

16

Suzanne regarded her husband's erstwhile opponent. High cheekbones, sandy hair, a face flushed with drink. Blue eyes fixed on her as though she were one of Titania's minions, tumbled out of the midsummer night.

"You impertinent doxy—"

"Careful," Malcolm said, lowering his sword. "I may have to challenge you to fight all over again."

"He's lying," Suzanne said, over the sound of a crash from below. "My husband wouldn't really get into a fight to defend my honor. He knows I can take care of myself."

The dragoon took his hand away from his arm and stared at the smears of crimson on his fingers. "I'm bleeding."

"I only meant to wing you." Suzanne stepped closer and peered at his shoulder. Red was seeping through the fine linen of his shirt, but not enough for her to have hit anything serious. She tugged a handkerchief from her cuff. "Yes, I thought so. I very seldom miss."

"You damned—"

"Hold still." She bound the handkerchief round his shoulder. "There. Go downstairs and put some brandy on it and then swallow some yourself."

The dragoon stared down at her, anger given way to utter bewilderment. "Who—"

"I'm a mother. It's excellent training for patching people up. Well, living through a war helped as well."

Another shot rang out from below, followed by two more in quick succession.

"Madame Grès," Rachel said, as the tumult below went abruptly still. "That should get things under control."

"Let's see how bad the damage is, darling," Suzanne said. "Mademoiselle Garnier, could you fetch me that bottle of cognac? I hate to waste it, but it's the closest alcohol to hand."

It was a quarter hour since Madame Grès's pistol shots had restored order to her establishment. Those of the brawlers who had not been summarily tossed out by Le Paon d'Or's footmen were being served coffee in the salon and presented with a bill for the damage. Suzanne, Malcolm, Davenport, and Rachel were back in the sitting room with the pink-silk lamp shades.

"My compliments, Rannoch," Davenport said. He was slumped in an armchair, a towel full of ice pressed to his face. He had a split lip and a bruise beneath his eye and he was holding his bad arm close to his side, but he showed no sign of wounds.

"Where did you get the sword you tossed me?" Malcolm asked, wincing as he struggled with the buttons on his waistcoat.

"Off another dragoon who was trying to bring it down on my head. Seemed a good idea to get it away from him. I dealt him a right hook and snatched up the sword."

"My thanks." Malcolm dropped his hand from the waistcoat, the buttons half-undone, breathing hard.

Suzanne leaned over him to undo the last of the buttons. "Good God, darling." Blood had welled through his shirtsleeve, but more bright red stained his side, where it had been covered by the waistcoat. "If I'd known how much damage the dragoon had done, I wouldn't have just winged him."

Malcolm glanced down. "It wasn't all him. Someone knifed me earlier."

"Who?" Davenport pulled the ice away from his face.

"I couldn't tell." Malcolm glanced at Suzanne and tugged at the folds of his cravat. "It was when we were in the passage. There must have been five or six men, and I couldn't see anyone's face."

Rachel crossed to Suzanne, carrying a decanter of cognac. "We get brawls every now and then. More lately with so many soldiers in Brussels. Two start fighting over a girl or a wager or God knows what, and it seems to spread. But this is the worst I can ever remember. Do you know what started it?"

Malcolm flicked a glance at Davenport. "The British and the Dutch-Belgians. Apparently Julia Ashton's liaison with the Prince of Orange is no longer secret."

Suzanne took the ends of the cravat from her husband's fingers and unwound the folds of linen. "You heard the soldiers quarreling about it?"

Malcolm nodded. "Wellington isn't going to be happy."

"Take your shirt off, darling. I don't think we'll offend Mademoiselle Garnier's sensibilities."

He glanced up at her, an ironic glint in his eyes. "You're going soft, sweetheart. This is nothing compared to Spain."

She helped undo his shirt cuffs and pull the torn shirt over his head. The blood was already clotting in the scratch on his shoulder, but the wound on his side was still bleeding. Her throat tightened. It was true she'd seen her husband more badly injured, but each time was a reminder of the reality they lived with every day but tried to cheerfully ignore. That she could lose him at any moment.

She unstopped the decanter and poured cognac onto a cloth. "Besides the two of you, who knew about Julia Ashton's affair with the Prince of Orange?"

"Wellington. Stuart." Malcolm winced as she pressed the brandy-soaked cloth against the wound in his side. "The prince himself. John Ashton."

"My wife." Davenport dropped the dripping towel into the ice bucket beside his chair. "But though Cordelia's capable of a lot of things, I doubt she'd have let anything slip. She tends to keep her word. At least about some things."

Suzanne recalled Lady Cordelia's haunted gaze across the café table less than two hours before. "No, I wouldn't think she'd have talked," she said, dabbing at the scratch on Malcolm's shoulder. "But—"

"Lady Julia or the prince could have let something slip to someone else," Malcolm said, the muscles in his arm tensing beneath her touch.

"The timing's suspicious though." Davenport pushed himself to his feet and strode across the room. "The news apparently got out right on the heels of Julia's death."

"Wellington and Stuart wouldn't have talked," Malcolm said as Suzanne wound linen round his ribs. "And I don't think Ashton would have based on what we saw last night. But Slender Billy's never been the best at keeping secrets. I imagine when he left the ball he sought refuge in a bottle. Which would have made him all the more likely to talk."

"Damage is done." Davenport frowned at the Corinthian pilasters that flanked the mantel as though they held answers to unasked questions. "Though I doubt this will be the last brawl it's an excuse for."

Malcolm turned to Rachel. "Why did you send for us in the first place?"

"I'll show you when your wife's finished bandaging you."

When Suzanne had the bandage in place and had helped Malcolm back into his bloodstained shirt, with waistcoat and cravat covering the stains, Rachel picked up the cognac decanter and glanced into the passage. She nodded that the way was clear, then led them down the passage, still littered with shards of the broken vase, and opened one of the white and gold doors. The door gave onto a bedchamber with a large four-poster bed draped with gauzy white hangings. The peach satin coverlet was rumpled, and beneath the smells of tuberose perfume and lavender a faint musky odor hung in the air. Rachel walked to the wall behind the bed and pressed one of the flowers in the peach damask wall hangings. A panel slid open.

"Concealed room. For people who like to watch," she said matter-of-factly. "It's all right, Henri. You can come out now."

A young man ducked through the secret door. He was tall and

lanky, with curly dark hair that fell over his thin, sharp-boned face. His coat was unbuttoned, but it bore the insignia of a lieutenant in the Dutch-Belgian army.

"Lieutenant Monsieur le Vicomte de Rivaux," Rachel said. "Monsieur and Madame Rannoch and Colonel Davenport, Henri."

Despite the disorder of his attire, Rivaux put his feet together and bowed with the formality of the ballroom.

Rachel gestured toward the chaise-longue and chairs by the fireplace. "Perhaps we'd best sit down. We can count on privacy here."

They disposed themselves about the fireplace, Suzanne and Malcolm on the chaise-longue, Davenport and Rivaux on the chairs. Rachel poured the cognac into five glasses set out on a side table and handed them round like a hostess in her salon.

"Henri is one of my best sources," she said. She glanced at Malcolm as she handed him a glass of cognac. "Our best sources."

Rivaux took a sip of cognac. "I have heard a great deal about you, Monsieur Rannoch."

"Brussels is a small town," Malcolm said.

"Not in the ballroom. In intelligence circles. You are much talked of. Even before you came to Brussels."

Malcolm settled back on the chaise-longue, wincing as he jostled his wound. "All sorts of speculation have run rampant in recent months. I didn't realize it had descended as low as the exploits of attachés."

"False modesty doesn't become you, Rannoch." Davenport tossed down a swallow of cognac.

"I've heard about Madame Rannoch as well." Rivaux inclined his head to Suzanne. "It is an honor to meet you both."

"You're very kind, Monsieur le Vicomte," Suzanne said.

Rivaux looked from her to Malcolm. "You investigated a murder in Vienna."

"We didn't solve it," Malcolm said, cradling his glass in his hand.

"Not officially. Rumor says otherwise." Rivaux leaned forward. "I believe you to be a man of honor. That's partly why I—But I'm getting ahead of myself."

"Henri came to me today with information I thought you should hear in person," Rachel said, dropping into a chair. "It was safer to summon you here than to take Henri to meet you. I'm sorry—"

"You couldn't have known," Malcolm said.

"Some weeks ago, shortly after the emp—Bonaparte escaped from Elba, I was approached by some of my fellow officers," Rivaux said in a quick, intent voice. "Men still loyal to Bonaparte. Who wanted Belgium to return to the Empire." He looked Malcolm directly in the eye. "It's no secret that I read Paine and Voltaire and have Republican sympathies."

"So do I." Malcolm took a sip of cognac. "So these fellow officers thought your Republican sympathies meant you would join them in plotting for Napoleon Bonaparte's victory?"

Rivaux nodded. "I was horrified. Whatever I think of the current government, I'm a soldier. We have made a commitment to our allies. I don't believe in going back on commitments."

"A somewhat novel position in international politics these days," Davenport murmured.

"I told Rachel—Mademoiselle Garnier. We were already—er—acquainted at that time." His gaze lingered on Rachel's face for a moment, with something that went far beyond the relationship between a client and a prostitute. His eyes held all the wonder of young love. Suzanne's fingers tightened round her glass. It was definitely not a way she and Malcolm had ever looked at each other. "I was going to report the men who had approached me to my commanding officer," Rivaux continued. "But Mademoiselle Garnier persuaded me I could be of more use by joining them and passing information on to her. I knew she was working with you. I believed you could be trusted. So you see, you benefited from your reputation preceding you."

"Not the first time I've had cause to be grateful for entertaining fiction," Malcolm said.

Rivaux's gaze flickered over Malcolm's face. "Mademoiselle Garnier says you've known about the spy ring for some time."

Malcolm nodded. "We've found it useful to keep track of it. You've been an important part of that."

Rivaux's shoulders straightened. "I don't need to be coddled."

"No, but I don't imagine you enjoy betraying your comrades. I thought it might help to know the value of your efforts."

Rivaux stared at Malcolm for a moment, eyes wide. "How did you know? That is, that I don't—"

"You seem entirely too decent for the espionage game."

Rivaux flushed. "Thank you. I think."

"Believe me it was a compliment."

Davenport stretched out his legs. "Some of us have been in the espionage game long enough to envy you your decency."

Rivaux turned to look at Davenport. "I heard about the ambush at the Château de Vere. I saw some of my associates last night, and they could talk of little else. I also heard about the death of the French officer La Fleur. According to our French sources, La Fleur was a traitor, but they had only just discovered it and weren't behind the ambush."

Malcolm nodded. "That fits with what Mademoiselle Garnier told me earlier today."

Rivaux leaned forward. "I came to Mademoiselle Garnier today to tell her what I'd heard. She said you already knew the French weren't behind the ambush last night. She also said you were looking for information about the Silver Hawk."

Malcolm didn't move a muscle, but Suzanne felt the shock of attention that ran through him. "You've heard of the Silver Hawk?"

"Last night. I wasn't supposed to. I'm not in the inner circle. I'm excluded from many of the most important discussions."

"Fortunately, I have other sources for those," Rachel said.

Rivaux cast a quick glance at her, his brows drawn.

"It's my job, Henri." Rachel touched his hand. "Not pretty, perhaps, but then it doesn't involve as many betrayals as espionage. Unless one happens to be combining the two."

Rivaux flushed. "No one could question your sacrifices—"

Rachel squeezed his fingers. "I'm good at my job. Both of them."

Rivaux's fingers twined round her own when she tried to draw her hand back. He looked at her for a moment, then turned back to the others. "Last night, one of the senior men and I were waiting for a contact who was late. We shared a flask of brandy. He let something slip. Eager to show off how much inside information he had, I think. The Silver Hawk is a code name."

Malcolm exchanged a look with Davenport. "We thought as much. For whom?"

Rivaux drew in a breath. "A British officer who's an agent for the French."

Davenport whistled. "Well, that's an interesting twist."

"Who?" Malcolm asked.

"I don't know his name. The Silver Hawk works on his own, and his identity is a highly guarded secret."

"One can see why," Davenport murmured.

"There's more, Monsieur Rannoch." Rivaux leaned forward. "That's why I had to see Mademoiselle Garnier today, and why she sent for you. Apparently the Silver Hawk had been ordered to assassinate someone."

Malcolm looked at Suzanne. Echoes of their adventures in Vienna. "Who?"

Rivaux swallowed. "You, Monsieur Rannoch."

❧ 17 ❧

Suzanne's hand moved involuntarily to her husband's arm. "Did your source say why the Silver Hawk wanted to kill Malcolm?"

"No," Rivaux said.

"But he used Malcolm's name?" Her fingers tightened on Malcolm's arm, feeling the solid warmth of his flesh beneath the linen.

"Most definitely."

Malcolm shook his head. "That doesn't make any sense."

"Rivaux said it." Davenport shifted in his chair, cradling his bad arm. "Your reputation preceded you to Brussels."

"It's preposterous." Malcolm glanced down at Suzanne's fingers on his arm, then met her gaze, an ironic glint in his eyes. "We're on the brink of war. Brussels is full of generals and kings and princes. I'm surprised anyone even knows who I am. Even granted the most highly romanticized stories about my supposed exploits, it would make no sense to kill me."

"It would put a crimp in British intelligence," Davenport said.

"A mild crimp."

"You must represent some sort of threat." Suzanne willed her heartbeat to be still. "Because of something you know?"

"Something that would identify this Silver Hawk person?" Rachel suggested.

"That would certainly give him a motive for killing me." Malcolm squeezed Suzanne's fingers and detached them from his arm. "Save that I hadn't even heard of him until just now."

"Unless it's something you know but don't realize you know," Suzanne said. "Even you can't put the pieces together when the picture's too murky, darling."

"However clever this Silver Hawk is, he hasn't actually managed to make an attempt on my life," Malcolm said.

"I'm not so sure about that." Davenport swirled the cognac in his glass, frowning into the golden-brown liquid. "Energetic as the brawl was, there weren't a lot of knives drawn. And yet if that cut to your ribs had been a few inches over, your lovely wife might be a widow. And we still don't know who attacked you."

Rachel clunked her glass down on a side table, spattering drops of cognac on the polished rosewood. "You think the brawl was an attempt to kill Monsieur Rannoch?"

"Not a very tidy assassination attempt." Malcolm took a swallow of cognac.

"But easy to cover up," Davenport pointed out. "If we were followed to Le Paon d'Or—"

"You think someone managed to follow us without either of us tumbling to it?"

"Lamentable, but supposedly this Silver Hawk is good at what he does." Davenport stretched his legs out and crossed his feet at the ankles. "If he saw us go in the side door, there'd have been time for him to go round through the front before the fight broke out."

"Barely."

"A house full of soldiers chafing at inactivity in the face of coming battle. All it would take is a few well-chosen words."

"Chancy," Malcolm said.

"Most attempts at murder are chancy," Davenport countered. "So which British officers might you know enough about to identify them as French agents?"

"My source didn't say the Silver Hawk had decided to kill Monsieur Rannoch," Rivaux interjected. "He said the Silver Hawk had been *ordered* to kill him."

"Even odder," Malcolm said. "I can't imagine why French intelligence would waste time on me."

Suzanne took a sip of cognac, forcing down a welling of panic and fury. "Something you know. But about what?"

Davenport tipped his glass back, draining the last of the cognac. "Perhaps whoever was behind the ambush last night wasn't after La Fleur or Julia. Perhaps you were the target."

Suzanne's fingers curled into her palm.

"The French said it wasn't their attack," Rachel pointed out, getting up and reaching for the decanter to refill the glasses.

"But as Rivaux said, the Silver Hawk works on his own. Perhaps someone very high up is running the Silver Hawk."

"I think so." Rivaux leaned forward. "Few people know about the Silver Hawk and even fewer know his identity. But last night my source was boasting. Implying he's in contact with the Silver Hawk. I tried to get him to reveal the Silver Hawk's identity, but there was only so much I could do without betraying myself."

"Sensible." Malcolm cast an approving glance at Rivaux. "I can't tell you how many promising double agents we've lost to clumsy, overzealous questioning. Who is this man?"

Rivaux hesitated a moment, then shook his head. "Foolish to cavil at betraying him now. It's Dumont. A captain in my regiment."

"You can't confront him," Rachel said. "You'd—"

"Blow our knowledge of the spy ring." Davenport met Malcolm's gaze and grimaced. "Devil of a fix."

"Dumont receives messages at the opera," Rivaux said. "I've seen it. One of the footmen brings them round with the champagne glasses and slips them into his hand."

"Messages from whom?" Malcolm asked.

"I don't know. The one night I was with him when he got one, he made a great effort to prevent my seeing it. But now we know he's working with the Silver Hawk—"

"Is it always the same footman?" Suzanne asked.

"The two times I saw him receive a note. The footmen are all tall and all wear powdered wigs, but this man has fading pox scars on his cheeks."

"So we get a look at one of these notes, and with any luck it will lead us to the Silver Hawk." Davenport took a sip from his refilled glass. "Of course intelligence missions are rarely so simple, but we can but hope."

"Dumont should be at the opera tonight," Rivaux said. "If he gets a note perhaps I can retrieve it before he sees it—"

"No," Malcolm said. "He'd be bound to suspect you. We need someone unassuming, someone above suspicion. Someone with a devastating skill at sleight of hand."

"Thank you, darling," Suzanne said. "I thought you'd never ask." She looked from Malcolm to Davenport. "I may need your help creating a distraction."

"We're at your service, Mrs. Rannoch," Davenport said.

"And if luck is extraordinarily with us, as Davenport says, this may lead us to the Silver Hawk," Malcolm said.

Suzanne gripped his arm again. "Darling—"

"I'll be on guard. And I'll have Davenport for backup."

"And me."

"And you." Malcolm lifted her hand to his lips and lightly kissed her fingers. "What could I possibly have to fear?"

"La Fleur warned you about the Silver Hawk," Davenport said. They had returned to the house in the Rue Ducale, where they could talk in private, and were again ensconced in the salon off the garden. "No doubt because he knew the Silver Hawk was trying to kill you. And we know the French had intercepted our communications with La Fleur. If the Silver Hawk knew you were meeting La Fleur at the château and knew La Fleur was warning you—"

"We've still got the fact that someone made sure Julia Ashton would be at the château alone." Malcolm took a sip of the coffee Suzanne had ordered. It was just past four o'clock, and they still had a long evening's work ahead of them. "If the Silver Hawk was behind the attack at the château, who sent the note to the Prince of Orange so he wouldn't show up for his rendezvous with Lady Julia? And why?"

"It's a damnable coincidence someone luring Julia there at the same time as the ambush." Davenport scowled into his cup. "I hate coincidences."

"What if—" Suzanne froze in the midst of pouring warm milk into her coffee, the jug tilted over her cup. "What if it wasn't a coincidence? What if the Silver Hawk wanted to get rid of Lady Julia as well?"

"My God." Davenport stared at her across the sofa table. "You are good."

Suzanne set down the jug before her cup could overflow. Droplets of milk spattered on the blue and white porcelain of the tray. "Lady Julia told her sister she'd tumbled into something that was beyond her control. Nothing we've learned about her so far explains why she feared for her life. But if she'd realized a man she was close to was a French agent—"

"It's a good theory," Malcolm said. "But there's no proof."

"Actually there is of a sort." Davenport leaned forward. "Whoever started the fight at Le Paon d'Or knew about Julia's affair with the Prince of Orange. As far as we know the only people privy to that information were Wellington, Stuart, you, me, Mrs. Rannoch, Cordelia, and the prince himself. And whoever sent that note to the prince canceling the rendezvous, the same person who may have been behind Julia's death. Far tidier if the person who sent the note to the prince also started today's brawl."

Malcolm took a sip of coffee. "It's only surmise that the Silver Hawk was behind the brawl."

"If he wasn't, we have another damned coincidence on our hands," Davenport muttered.

"And all we know about the Silver Hawk is that he's supposedly a British officer. There are hundreds of British officers in Brussels—"

"And Julia Ashton was married to one," Suzanne said, looking at her husband. "And mistress to another."

Davenport twisted his cup between his hands, as though answers were hidden in the transferware pattern. "Ashton would make the perfect spy. The upright Englishman who seems to actually believe all the scept'red-isle nonsense and looks as if he couldn't even conceive of the word 'betrayal.'"

"It would make him one hell of an actor," Malcolm said.

"Which the Silver Hawk is to hear young Rivaux tell it." Davenport took a sip of coffee and looked as though he was debating its degree of bitterness. "Of course Anthony Chase is a much more obvious choice. He plainly has no morals when it comes to his women, so why should he when it comes to his country?"

"If every officer who betrayed his wife betrayed his country, God help the British army," Malcolm said.

"Captain Ashton and Captain Chase are the most obvious possibilities, but there are others." Suzanne took a careful sip from her cup, which was full to the brim. The hot liquid scalded her tongue. "Society in Brussels is confined, and Julia Ashton was at the heart of it. In theory she could have stumbled upon information linking any British officer with the Silver Hawk."

Malcolm set his cup down with a quiet click of porcelain. "It's a tidy theory, Suzette. But you know as well as I do that you still need facts however clever the thesis."

"Then we'll have to find the facts." Davenport folded his hands behind his head. "And yes," he added, forestalling a protest from Malcolm, "without ignoring the possibility that the facts may lead us to some other theory. Though I somehow doubt that Mrs. Rannoch's theories often prove incorrect."

"Thank you, Colonel Davenport." Suzanne smiled at him across the coffee things. "I knew you were a man of sense."

"Assassinate Rannoch?" The Duke of Wellington's eyes widened in rare surprise. "Why the devil would anyone care about getting rid of Rannoch?"

"Precisely my reaction," Malcolm said.

"Nevertheless." Davenport met Wellington's gaze without flinching. "We have no reason to doubt Rivaux's story. And there's already been one attempt on Rannoch's life, possibly two."

"One of which could have been a tavern brawl, the other of which could have been an attempt to kill La Fleur or Julia Ashton," Malcolm said.

Wellington's gaze snapped to Malcolm. "False modesty isn't helpful, Rannoch."

"I thought you were on my side."

"I said I couldn't understand the French wasting their time trying to get rid of you. But this wouldn't be the first time French motives have baffled me." The duke picked up a sheaf of papers from his desktop and snapped them down hard on the polished wood, aligning the edges. He wore evening dress, the Order of the Garter pinned to his dark coat, but he was still in his office at Headquarters. He drew a harsh breath, gaze on the papers in his hands. "You'd never heard of this Silver Hawk before?"

"Not until La Fleur's warning," Malcolm said.

Wellington set the papers down on the desk, tightly controlled precision in each movement of his hands. "And he's a British officer?"

"According to Rivaux's source," Davenport said. "We can't confirm it, but Rivaux's intelligence has been trustworthy so far."

Wellington scowled at the papers. "Damnation." He slammed his hand down on the desk. "As if we don't have enough to contend with, with the French congregating round Mauberge."

"*What?*" Malcolm and Davenport said almost in one breath.

"Bonaparte was bound to move sooner or later." Wellington continued to frown at the papers. "No sense in doing anything until we have intelligence about where the main attack will come from. A wrong move could leave us dangerously exposed. But the last thing we need is further distraction among the troops. We couldn't even control the news about the prince's affair with Julia Ashton for twenty-four hours. Now we've got soldiers brawling, rumors flying—" His mouth tightened. "If it gets out that a British officer may be a French agent—" He realigned the edges of the papers he'd disarranged when he slammed his hand on the desk. "Learn what you can at the opera tonight. With Bonaparte on the move, time is of the essence." He glanced up at Malcolm. "You think you can intercept the communication for this Dumont?"

"I don't know." Malcolm cast a glance at Davenport. "But I'm quite sure Suzanne can."

Wellington's thin mouth curved in a smile. "Yes, I imagine she can. Keep me informed—"

A rap at the door interrupted his words. "Yes?" Wellington said with a frown.

"It's Uxbridge."

Wellington stared at the door for a moment from beneath drawn brows. "Come in," he said at last.

The Earl of Uxbridge, commander of the cavalry and the man who had eloped with Wellington's brother's wife seven years ago, strolled into the room. He wore hussar dress, brightly polished orders pinned to his frogged coat, his fur-trimmed pelisse hanging over one shoulder with a casual elegance no other officer could quite equal.

"Uxbridge." Wellington inclined his head. "No more news from Mauberge. I don't know that we'll hear more before morning."

"Nor do I. As it happens it's Rannoch and Davenport I've come to talk to. I heard they were here with you."

Wellington's brows lifted. "Unless this is an extreme coincidence, I take it this has to do with the events of last night?"

Uxbridge returned Wellington's gaze coolly. "It does."

"Were you planning to speak with them in private or am I to be in on this discussion?" Wellington inquired.

Uxbridge moved to a chair but did not sit. "If I'd wished to speak to them alone, I hope I'd have had enough wit to seek them out other than at Headquarters."

Wellington gave a reluctant smile and inclined his head for Uxbridge to be seated. The two men regarded each other for a moment. They were always perfectly civil, but there was a faint tug of distance between them. Malcolm was never sure if it was the legacy of Uxbridge's elopement with Charlotte Wellesley or simply the strong and differing personalities of the two men.

Uxbridge sank into the chair and crossed his legs. "The story that Julia Ashton was the Prince of Orange's mistress is running through town like wildfire. Is it true?"

Wellington gave a brief nod. "I'm afraid so."

Uxbridge's mouth tightened. "Was the prince there last night when she died? You can lie to me of course, but I think it will be easier if we tell each other the truth."

"God help me if I have to lie to my cavalry commander."

"Oh, I'm sure you're capable of it if required," Uxbridge said. "But in this case—"

Wellington nodded at Malcolm.

"The prince had an assignation with Lady Julia at the Château de Vere," Malcolm said. "But he received a note canceling the rendezvous. A note supposedly from Lady Julia, but in fact forged. Lady Julia went to the rendezvous. She was caught in the fire when we were ambushed."

"Good God." Uxbridge smoothed a crease from his sleeve. "John Ashton is one of my abler officers. I believe he adores his wife. And of course the prince is my fellow commander. A sad business."

Wellington leaned back in his chair. "If all you had to contribute was the observation that it's a sad business you'd be on your way to the opera now."

"True." Uxbridge adjusted the folds of his black cravat. Malcolm had never before seen the self-confident, sartorially splendid earl make such a nervous gesture. "In the general run of things, I'd think it the gentlemanly thing to keep it to myself. But under the circumstances—" He twitched one of the orders pinned to his tightly fitting coat. "It was just after I came to Brussels. At your concert ball, Wellington. I came upon Lady Julia crying in an antechamber."

"Had she been playing cards?" Davenport asked. His voice was level, but Malcolm could feel his quickening attention.

"What? I'm not sure." Uxbridge drew a breath. "I've known the Brooke sisters since they were children. Their late father was ahead of me at Oxford. I poured her a glass of wine, asked her what was the matter." He gave a wry smile. "Told her that when she was my age ten to one she'd realize whatever it was wasn't of such very great importance. The next thing I knew she was crying on my shoulder. Rather made a mess of my coat, but one makes allowances for pretty women." He shifted in his chair. "Then she lifted her lips to mine and pulled my head down to her own."

❧ 18 ❧

Davenport stared at the cavalry commander. "Are you saying Julia tried to kiss you?"

"I'm saying she did kiss me." Uxbridge met Davenport's gaze. "I sprang to my feet. I'm afraid I managed to spill the wine all over the floorboards."

"Interesting reaction," Wellington said.

"Julia was young enough to be my daughter."

"Many men don't find that a deterrent."

Uxbridge answered the challenge in Wellington's gaze. "I ran off with Charlotte. That doesn't mean I run off with everyone I get the chance to. Contrary to rumors."

"What did Lady Julia do?" Malcolm asked.

"Said she was sorry but that she'd wanted to do that ever since she was a girl. That I was her first love and perhaps her only love." Uxbridge's brows drew together.

"And what did you do?" Davenport asked.

"Told her I had a wife I loved in England. Reminded her she had a husband who was one of my officers. She got an odd look on her face, but she asked me to forgive her foolishness. Which I was only too ready to do. Until this."

"Dear God," Wellington said.

"This would have been before her affair with the Prince of Orange began," Malcolm said.

"Julia was always such a well-mannered little thing," Uxbridge said. "If it had been her sister, I'd have understood it better."

"People can surprise you," Davenport said.

"Oh, devil take it. I keep forgetting she's your wife. No offense meant, Davenport."

Davenport's gaze was steady and stripped of feeling. "None taken, sir."

Uxbridge's eyes narrowed. "Given my history, I don't suppose you think very well of me."

"On the contrary," Davenport said. "I take no responsibility for anyone else's marriage. I didn't even take much responsibility for my own."

Uxbridge's full-lipped mouth curved in a wry smile. "I've always been fond of Cordelia. But I'd never claim she was sensible. Particularly when it comes to men. I don't expect you've had an easy time of it. Which I'm sure sounds ironic coming from me."

"A great deal of truth can hide in irony, sir."

Uxbridge's smile deepened. "Quite."

"What happened next?" Wellington demanded, a note of impatience in his voice. "With Lady Julia?"

"Nothing." Uxbridge leaned back, elbows resting comfortably on the chair arms. "We've only met since in company. Naturally I had no desire to find myself alone with her, and she seemed to steer well clear of me. I thought it no more than an unfortunate incident, thankfully forgot. Until I heard rumors of Julia's affair with the Prince of Orange."

"The woman seems to have had an interest in men in positions of power," Wellington said. "Damned awkward."

"It's odd," Uxbridge said, "I never had the sense Julia took any particular interest in me in the past, even in a schoolgirl's infatuation sort of way."

Wellington looked at Uxbridge from beneath lowered brows. "You didn't say anything to Ashton?"

"What kind of fool do you take me for?"

"One might take the view that Ashton deserves to know of his wife's indiscretions."

"I wouldn't have done that to Julia. Besides, the last thing I need is one of my officers distracted."

"Which is precisely the situation we now have. And the rest of the army along with him." Wellington picked up a pen from his desktop and frowned at the nib. "Does this tell you anything?" He looked from Malcolm to Davenport. "Aside from the fact that there may be other men Lady Julia was involved with."

"Nothing beyond that." Malcolm didn't so much as glance at Davenport. By tacit agreement they said nothing of Lady Julia's affair with Anthony Chase.

Wellington tossed the pen down with decision. "Then your investigation continues. And I suggest you consider that Lady Julia may have been involved with other men. Which means there may have been others with reason to want her dead."

"Is it true?" Anthony Chase ran up to Malcolm and Davenport as they stepped into the outer office. He was neatly shaved, his dress uniform immaculate, his hair combed smooth, but his gaze was more wild-eyed than it had been in the beer garden that afternoon.

"Captain Chase." Malcolm put a hand on Tony's shoulder. "Perhaps we could talk in private."

Fitzroy Somerset, working his way through a pile of correspondence, glanced up briefly, then returned to his work with typical tact.

Tony held his tongue as they moved into an adjoining sitting room, still filled with a jumble of papers left by the officers who'd been working there that afternoon. But the moment the door was closed he said again in a hoarse voice, "Is it true?"

"Is what true?" Malcolm asked, voice carefully neutral.

"You know damned well." Tony's gaze shot from Malcolm to Davenport. "The talk was all over every tavern and café and brothel in Brussels by this afternoon. Julia and His Royal bloody Highness the Prince of Orange."

Davenport leaned against the wall, arms folded, legs crossed at the ankles. "You didn't know?"

"So it's true?" Tony's voice fairly shook with desperation.

"What do you think?" Davenport asked.

"Damn you—" Tony hurled himself at Davenport. Malcolm caught him by the shoulders.

"We were in love," Tony said, breathing hard. "She wouldn't have—"

"Then there's no need to ask us, is there?" Davenport smoothed his sleeve where Tony had gripped it.

"Lady Julia gave you no hint?" Malcolm asked.

"Of course not." Tony jerked out of Malcolm's grip and whirled to face him. The smell of cognac hung on his breath. "I told you—"

"Betrayal's not so amusing when the shoe's on the other foot, is it?" Davenport remarked.

"You don't understand." Tony pushed his fingers into his hair. "What we had wasn't like an ordinary affair. God knows I've had plenty of those. We had something in an entirely different key, something extraordinary—"

"Extraordinariness doesn't necessarily rule out betrayal," Davenport remarked.

Tony spun toward him. "What the hell do you know about love?"

"Nothing at all," Davenport conceded. "But it's often easier to judge from the outside."

"Just because you couldn't hold on to your own wife—"

"That assumes I wanted to keep her." Davenport crossed the room and stood regarding a print of a country farmhouse that hung on the wall. "But it's an erroneous comparison." He glanced over his shoulder at Tony. "We aren't talking about your wife, we're talking about John Ashton's."

Tony spun away, his hands balled into fists, then turned back to them. "It's true, isn't it?"

"We don't know what's true," Malcolm said. The news was out, the damage was done. There was nothing to be gained from denying it, and they needed to get whatever information Tony possessed. "But the Prince of Orange does claim to have had a rendezvous with Lady Julia at the Château de Vere the night she was killed."

Tony stared at him for a long moment, face drained of color. "So the prince was there? He was with her when she was killed?"

"No. He received a letter canceling the rendezvous. Supposedly from Lady Julia, but in fact a forgery."

Tony dropped into a ladder-back chair. "She said—She said she'd never really understood what love meant until—Why would she—"

"People have any number of reasons for entering into love affairs," Malcolm said. "You really didn't suspect?"

"Of course not. I can't believe she was pretending the whole time—"

Tony looked like such a woebegone schoolboy that for a moment Malcolm felt a tug of sympathy. "Love and fidelity don't necessarily go hand in hand."

"Spoken by a man who's never had cause to doubt his wife," Davenport murmured.

Tony stared up at Malcolm, eyes glazed with confusion. "You said someone sent a forged letter to the prince. So this person wanted Julia to be at the château alone? Why?"

"Possibly to confront her or to convince her to break off her affair with the prince." Malcolm studied Tony. The light from a brace of candles on the desk fell full on his face. The confusion in those wide blue eyes appeared as genuine as if it bore a sterling hallmark. "Or—"

"To kill her?" Anger shot through Tony's posture. "Is that what all this was about? Someone lured Julia to her death?"

"You have reason to think someone might have wished to do so?" Davenport moved toward Tony's chair.

"What? No. Julia didn't have an enemy in the world."

"She had a husband and two lovers." Davenport leaned against the desk. "Unless you're all remarkably compliant, that could create all sorts of enemies."

"You think Ashton killed her? Because he learned about us? By God—"

"Do you think your wife knew?" Malcolm asked.

Tony sprang to his feet, knocking his chair over. "How dare you insult Jane."

"I rather think it's you who did that," Davenport observed. "Rannoch just asked if your wife could have known you were betraying her."

"I know her. She's my wife. I'd have realized—"

"I know my wife," Malcolm said. "At least I think I do, as well as one can know anyone. I've trusted her with my life on more than one occasion. But I'd never claim to be privy to her every thought."

Tony spun away and stared at the papers that littered the desk. "Don't you think I haven't been tormented by the thought of what Jane will think when she finds out? She trusts me. She always has. And I know bloody well that I don't deserve it. I'd have noticed if there'd been any change in her. She's too honest for deception."

"She's better at it than you think," Davenport said. "She told Mrs. Rannoch and Cordelia she'd known about you and Julia almost from the first."

"She—" Tony whirled on Malcolm. "How dare you question my wife?"

"It's an investigation, Chase," Malcolm said. "Into why the woman you claim to have loved lost her life. Your sister knew as well."

"Violet—" Tony's face drained of color. "Oh God, that damned letter."

"Apparently."

"What are you suggesting?" Tony demanded. "That Jane sent that note to the Prince of Orange so she could confront Julia at the château? That she had something to do with her death—I could call you out for such a suggestion."

"Don't," Davenport said. "I doubt he'd agree to meet you, and Wellington will have our hides if you do anything to get yourself cashiered from the army. He's short of soldiers as it is."

Tony straightened his shoulders. "Are you so sure you can trust the prince?"

"We aren't sure we can trust anyone," Malcolm said.

"Well then. You claim I'd have been jealous if I'd known Julia had another lover. What if Slender Billy knew? I doubt he'd take kindly to it, either. Suppose he forged that note from Julia to give himself an alibi."

Davenport stared straight ahead as he and Malcolm left Headquarters, his gaze narrowed against the glare of the setting sun against the cobblestones. "It's all right," he said, without looking round. "I'm not going to waste time defending the honor of the sister of the woman to whom I happen to be married. But you have to admit it's odd."

"It keeps getting odder and odder." Malcolm kept pace beside Davenport, his own gaze fixed ahead. Two young officers strolled down the street ahead of them, arm in arm with Brussels girls wearing white lace mantillas. "Lady Julia made overtures to Lord Uxbridge. Not long after that she began a liaison with the Prince of Orange. While at the same time conducting an affair with Anthony Chase, who claims they were desperately in love and she was going to run off with him."

"A love affair that seems less and less probable. At least on Julia's side."

The officers and the girls in the mantillas stepped into a café down the street. Malcolm glanced at Davenport, then returned his gaze to the street ahead. "My mother flitted from one lover to another. She wasn't a very happy woman." Arabella Rannoch's restless blue eyes and discontented mouth flickered in his memory, as sharp and vivid as the Brussels street before him. "Though she'd have claimed she took them all lightly, I think she kept hoping the right man would make sense of her life."

Davenport turned to look at him for a moment. "That can't have been easy for you."

The events of the past autumn and the new things he had learned about his mother bit Malcolm in the throat. "No. Nor for my brother and sister."

"Your brother's a light dragoon, isn't he?"

"Yes. He's stationed near Ninove, so I haven't seen much of him in Brussels." Though in truth that was only half the story. Malcolm and Edgar weren't the friends they once had been, for reasons Malcolm didn't entirely understand, though the estrangement was rooted in their mother's death. "One's relationships with one's parents are always complicated."

"Mine did me the favor of dying when I was eight. Carriage accident. I'd just gone up to Eton."

It was Malcolm's turn to look sideways at Davenport. "That must have been—"

"Simpler perhaps, all things considered. The uncle I spent holidays with mostly left me to my own devices." Davenport kept his gaze fixed ahead. "If you knew about your mother's affairs even as a boy, she can't have been overly discreet."

"No. Nor was my father. They had an understanding of sorts. If you can say that of two people who cordially disliked each other. I think my mother enjoyed defying convention."

"Which one could say of Cordelia," Davenport said without a trace of emotion. "But not Julia. She indulged in reckless behavior, but she was still careful of her reputation."

"But she was troubled and her moods shifted, judging by her letters to her sister," Malcolm said. "My mother would swing between frenetic excitement and bouts of depression. According to Geoffrey Blackwell, she may have had an illness of the brain."

Davenport didn't dismiss the idea, as Malcolm more than half-expected, but instead considered it for several paces. "If that was true of Julia, it's something that came on suddenly. Or—No, I suppose I can't claim to have ever known her well enough to be sure. But whatever was going on with her, Wellington's right. We have to consider the possibility that there were other men. Do you think Uxbridge was telling the truth?"

"He had no reason to come to us with the story."

"Unless he decided it was better to come to us with his version of the truth before we discovered it in other ways."

"You think he was Lady Julia's lover?"

"I think it's a possibility we can't ignore. As we have to consider Tony Chase's suggestion about the Prince of Orange."

Malcolm nodded. "Any man involved with Julia might have been angered if he'd learned he wasn't her only lover. Or might have decided she was a liability. Or both."

"And it looks as though we may well be at war before we discover the answer. Damnable timing. I find I'm distinctly averse to the thought of dying without learning the truth."

❧ 19 ❧

"To think I thought Julia Ashton a bit insipid." Suzanne fastened the second of her diamond earrings. She had dismissed Blanca once her hair was dressed so she and Malcolm could talk while they got ready for the opera. "She seems more and more interesting with each revelation. And sadder."

Malcolm grimaced as he did up the buttons on his cream silk waistcoat. "The perfect wife who was actually a mass of discontent."

Suzanne turned round on the dressing table bench to look at her husband. The ghosts in his gray eyes were all too familiar. "Darling, she's not—"

"My mother." He fastened the last button and tugged his waistcoat smooth. "No, she most definitely isn't. Mama liked to flaunt her indiscretions in society's face. Lady Julia managed to maintain her decorous veneer."

Suzanne drew on one of her long ivory gloves, smoothing the fingers with care. "I can understand her attraction to men in positions of power. And I can understand her thinking she'd found true love with Anthony Chase, though it speaks poorly to her judgment of men. But the two at the same time don't make sense."

"No." Malcolm shrugged into the black superfine evening coat Addison had left draped over a chairback.

Suzanne picked up the second glove. "Do you think Anthony Chase is lying about the affair?"

"There was something odd about him this afternoon when Davenport and I spoke with him. But we have Violet Chase's account of finding his letter to Lady Julia and of the interview in which she says Lady Julia admitted to the affair."

"And Jane Chase claims to have known about it, too." Suzanne pulled on her second glove. "So unless a number of people are lying for no apparent reason the affair happened. But perhaps it wasn't quite the breathless idyll Captain Chase described."

"At least on Lady Julia's side. Chase's anger when he confronted Davenport and me this evening seemed genuine enough."

"Genuine enough to kill over?"

Malcolm frowned at the buttons on his coat as he did them up. "Who can say what sends anyone over the edge? But Chase has a temper, and I think he's lying about something. Which would fit if he already knew Julia had another lover and he killed her because of it. Or if he's the Silver Hawk and realized Lady Julia had begun to suspect him. Of course one could say the fact that I can see through him argues against his being the Silver Hawk."

Suzanne got to her feet and picked up her silver net scarf. "You're rather exceptional at seeing through people, darling."

"Fair to middling. God knows I've been wrong in the past."

"As have we all." She managed to keep her voice tranquil, but the words stuck in her throat. She forced herself to turn to the mirror and focus on adjusting the pearl clasp on her belt. The champagne crêpe of her round robe hung loose on her body. She was going to have to get Blanca to take her gowns in or Malcolm would start asking more questions.

Malcolm twitched his shirt cuffs smooth beneath his coat. "Lady Julia was playing a damnably dangerous game."

"Danger can be addictive." She took a step toward him, her mind filled with past sins and future terrors. "As we both know."

Their gazes met and held for a moment. A smile curved Malcolm's mouth. "I keep telling myself that one day we'll have a nice settled life filled with ordinary trivialities."

She closed the distance between them and put her lips to his.

"Careful what you wish for, dearest. If we had a nice settled life, I'm afraid we'd both go mad."

He returned her kiss with surprising urgency, then drew back, his eyes gone serious. "Wellington had news of his own. It looks as though the French have finally crossed the frontier."

Fear coursed unbidden through her. "Not another false alarm?"

"I think not. Wellington seemed very sure of the intelligence. He's waiting to see where the attack will come from."

"How long?" she asked, keeping her voice level. After all, she had known for months that this day would come.

"A few days at most, I should think." His fingers tightened over her own. "Sweetheart, if you want to go to Antwerp—"

She jerked her hands from his clasp. "Don't you dare suggest I run away."

"I'm not. But your hands are like ice."

She hugged her arms over her chest. "War is about to break out. I'm worried about our friends. I'm worried about my husband."

"I'm not going to be anywhere near the fighting."

"Liar." Screams echoed in her ears. Blood glistened on the cobblestones before her eyes. "I've already gone through one war with you, don't forget."

His gaze moved over her face. "I can't, Suzette."

"Can't what?"

"Promise to stay here in Brussels with you."

She swallowed. She'd made her choices a long time ago. She would have to live with them. "I wouldn't ask that of you. Any more than you'd ask it of me."

"Well then." He touched her arm. "This is nothing we haven't been through before."

For a moment she was sitting beside a camp bed where her wounded husband lay a few months into their oddly begun marriage, holding Malcolm's hand and staring at his ashen face, wondering if she'd ever have the chance to speak to him again. But even then . . . "It was different," she said, her voice rough. "We weren't—We didn't—We mean more to each other now. We have more to lose."

He drew her to him. "We'll have to make sure we don't lose it then," he said into her hair.

She resisted for a moment, then drew a shuddering breath and let her head fall into the familiar hollow of his shoulder. Her fingers dug into the fabric of his coat as though she could hold on to him, hold on to what was between them. But the problem with his words, as with most comforting words, was that they were more easily spoken than put into practice.

"Suzanne." Georgiana Lennox darted through the crowd in the entry hall of the opera house and seized Suzanne's arm. Her elder sister, Lady Sarah, was not far behind her. "Are the rumors true?"

"Which rumors?" Suzanne looked between the Lennox sisters. Malcolm had stopped to speak with Baron Müffling as the crowd eddied and pressed about them. "If you're hearing Bonaparte is on the march again—"

"Not Bonaparte. We've heard he's on the march so many times it's difficult to take it seriously." Georgiana cast a glance round the entry hall, crowded with silks, satins, ostrich feathers, gleaming uniforms. Orange-sellers moved through the crowd with baskets over their arms. She lowered her voice, though Suzanne doubted anyone could hear over the buzz of conversation beneath the fretted ceiling. "Julia Ashton."

"Georgy—" Sarah Lennox said.

"What about Julia Ashton?" Suzanne asked.

"People are saying she was killed last night when she tried to stop a duel between her husband and the Prince of Orange."

Suzanne bit back both a laugh and a curse. "Georgy, you were at the ball last night. You noticed the minute the Prince of Orange left the ballroom with Wellington and Stuart. Could he possibly have been absent anything close to long enough to have fought a duel?"

"I told you it was all an outrageous hum, Georgy." Lady Sarah shook her head.

Georgiana was regarding Suzanne with sharp eyes. "You said the Prince of Orange didn't fight a duel with John Ashton. You didn't say Julia Ashton wasn't the prince's mistress."

There were times when lies served no purpose. "No," Suzanne said. "I didn't."

Lady Sarah grimaced. "Oh, dear. I'd never have thought it. She and Captain Ashton always seemed so devoted."

The smell of oranges wafted through the hall. Suzanne found herself staring fixedly at a gentleman peeling an orange for the white-gowned lady at his side. The lady was smiling as though she didn't have eyes for anyone else in the world. Her husband? Or her lover? "One never really knows what goes on inside a marriage."

Georgiana frowned. "But if Lady Julia wasn't away from the ball because of a duel or because she was meeting the prince—"

"No one knows precisely what happened." Suzanne heard a loud, excited voice behind her. Without looking round, she knew the Prince of Orange had run up to Malcolm.

Georgiana cast a quick glance behind her, then darted a keen gaze over Suzanne's face. "You and Malcolm are investigating, aren't you?"

It was a pity a duke's daughter couldn't have trained as a spy, Georgiana would have made a good one. "Georgy—"

"For heaven's sake, Suzanne, you're not the sort to have false modesty."

"No." Suzanne nodded at Alexander Gordon and Colonel Canning, who had just come through the doors from the street. "But I do know the importance of discretion."

"It doesn't matter, we know perfectly well what you're doing. And the point is you need information. Do tell her, Sarah."

Lady Sarah frowned, tugging on the blond lace on her bodice. "Georgy, we don't know—"

"That's just the point. *We* don't know what it means, but Suzanne might."

"It's—"

"It's not gossip, it's evidence. Or it might be. You can trust Suzanne to be discreet." Georgiana seized her sister's hand. "If we slip between those two Dutch-Belgian officers, we can stand in the alcove by the base of the stairs."

Lady Sarah continued to frown but permitted her sister to pull her to the side. Suzanne exchanged a glance with Malcolm, who was steering the Prince of Orange in the opposite direction, and then followed the Lennox sisters.

"Lady Sarah?" she said. "If there is anything you think is important—"

Sarah fingered the ivory sticks of her fan. "I daresay it means nothing. But when I heard about Julia, and I remembered that they knew each other—"

"Who?" Suzanne asked.

"It was at the ball last night. A bit before supper. I left the dance floor only to find I'd torn a flounce, so I went into the ladies' retiring room to pin it up. I found her there, trying to sponge her skirt."

"Lady Julia?"

"No." Sarah hesitated a moment. "Violet Chase."

Suzanne forced her mind not to jump to conclusions. "It was a warm evening. A number of people went out into the garden. If she got mud on her skirt—"

"It was more than that. She looked as though she'd been crying. Miss Chase and I have never been on particularly familiar terms, but I asked her what was the matter. She said it was nothing. When I insisted that she was obviously in distress and asked if I could help, she said she'd gone into the garden with a gentleman, and he'd gone beyond the line of what was pleasing. But—" Lady Sarah frowned. "I can't put my finger on it, but I'm quite sure she was lying."

Georgiana cast an anxious glance at Suzanne. "Does it—"

"It could mean anything," Suzanne said. "And very likely it means nothing as far as Julia Ashton is concerned." She looked at Sarah. "But thank you for telling me. Any information about last night is helpful."

Lady Sarah gave a quick nod. "Violet Chase isn't—We've never been great friends, as I said. But I can't imagine—"

"I can't imagine Julia Ashton being dead," Georgiana said. "But she is."

Lady Sarah shuddered and then smiled as she caught sight of General Maitland. Suzanne had noticed Sarah spending more and more time in Maitland's company of late. Sarah's mother, the Duchess of Richmond, seemed unaware of the development, which was probably just as well. Suzanne suspected the duchess had her eye on titled husbands for her daughters.

"Violet Chase was practically betrothed to John Ashton," Georgiana said, as her sister went off on General Maitland's arm. "She wouldn't have been human if she hadn't disliked Lady Julia excessively. You don't think—"

"It's too early to think anything at all," Suzanne said.

Despite the crowd, Malcolm could feel the gazes upon him and the Prince of Orange, but at least the alcove afforded a modicum of privacy.

"I didn't tell anyone," Billy said in a fierce whisper. "You do believe me, don't you?"

"I have the utmost faith in you, sir," Malcolm said in a measured voice.

"You think I'm lying. You think I told someone about Julia." Billy stared at Malcolm, as woebegone as a schoolboy accused of cheating at cricket.

"I didn't say that."

"I can see it in your face. For God's sake, Malcolm, do you think I would talk at the expense of a lady's reputation? Especially after Wellington told me not to?"

"You were naturally distressed last night. You didn't confide in anyone—a friend, your valet—"

"I'm not a boy anymore, Malcolm." Billy straightened his thin shoulders. "I'm a commander myself. I know how serious this is. Especially when we could be on the march at any moment." He cast a glance over Malcolm's face. "Do you think it's true? That Bonaparte's finally on the move?"

"Wellington believes so. But he's waiting for further intelligence."

For a moment, the reality of the coming battle shot through Billy's young gaze. "And now of all times—The story about Julia and me is all over Brussels. The things I've had said to me—All deserved of course." He swallowed. "Should I offer Ashton satisfaction?"

"No," Malcolm said, in the tone he'd used when the fourteen-year-old Billy had wanted to visit a gaming hell. "Sir, I know how Lady Julia's death distressed you—"

Billy ran a hand over his hair. "The devil of it is, if I'd actually gone to the rendezvous I was going to end it."

"What?" Malcolm stared at the prince. "Last night—"

"I was shocked by her death." Billy shifted his weight from one foot to another. "It seemed no time to disparage her memory."

"You'd learned something about her?" Malcolm watched the prince closely. Had Billy known about Julia's affair with Tony Chase?

Billy swallowed, looked away, then met Malcolm's gaze. "The night before Stuart's ball—Julia and I—We were together. We— Well, the point is, I woke up to find her going through the pockets of my coat."

❧ 20 ❧

"You've discovered something." Aline Blackwell looked from Malcolm to Suzanne as they entered their box. "I learned to read that look on both your faces in Vienna."

Suzanne didn't risk a glance at her husband. The taut grip of his hand on her elbow as they'd climbed the stairs had told her he'd discovered something. She suspected that, being Malcolm, he knew she'd discovered something as well.

"I know better than to argue with you, Allie," Malcolm said, pulling out Suzanne's chair for her.

"But I don't suppose there's the least chance you'll tell us any of it." Aline turned to look at her cousin, elbow on the back of her chair, chin in her hand. "I was rather helpful in Vienna as I recall."

"You were invaluable. We'll be sure to come to you with any unbreakable codes."

Aline gave a mock sigh, grinned at him, then turned to her husband. "You don't seem the least bit curious, Geoff."

Geoffrey Blackwell looked up from a perusal of the programme (unlike many of those in the theatre, he had a genuine passion for music). "My dear, by the time you've reached my age, you learn life is quite complicated enough without embroiling oneself in the complications of others."

But despite his words, Suzanne caught the appraising gaze Geoffrey ran over Malcolm and then her. It held more than curiosity. It held concern. Geoff knew better than most the strain they'd both been under in Vienna.

Suzanne sank into the chair beside Aline that Malcolm had pulled out for her, lifted her opera glasses, and scanned the house. It was no more than everyone else was doing. The Chases were in a box to the right. Violet, her shoulders swathed in a cloud of orange blossom tulle, her chestnut curls threaded with ivory roses, was laughing up at two riflemen, her cheeks flushed bright. Jane Chase, decorous in primrose-colored crêpe, was engaged in conversation with a third rifleman who apparently hadn't been able to get Violet's attention. Jane's gaze held a trace of ironic amusement, but her hands were locked tight on the beaded reticule in her lap.

As Suzanne watched, a man in the uniform of a captain in the 95th came through the curtains at the back of the box. The light from the candle sconces glinted off his smooth, pale gold hair, and the smile he flashed was quick and engaging, though his gaze held a hint of strain. Captain Anthony Chase.

Another man followed Captain Chase. Taller, with hair that was more brown than gold, familiar from last night at Stuart's ball. Major George Chase. The man for whom Cordelia Davenport had left her husband.

A woman slipped into the box beside Major Chase. Fair-haired, small-boned. The wife Major Chase had returned to despite his and Cordelia Davenport's grand passion.

A stir rippled through the theatre. Suzanne turned her opera glasses. Cordelia Davenport and Caroline Lamb had taken their seats at the railing of a box to the left. A crowd of gentlemen in uniform clustered behind them, including Lady Caroline's brother Frederick Ponsonby. Cordelia wore black gauze over white satin. Her rouge stood out against her pale skin. She scanned the theatre with a tense, anxious gaze. Lady Caroline looked at her in concern. The gentlemen behind them seemed quite forgot.

A louder murmur ran through the crowd as the Prince of Orange stepped into his box. The prince held his head high, though through her glasses Suzanne caught a telltale flush on his cheeks. Georgy and Sarah's brother Lord March, a handsome, serious-faced young man, sat on one side of him. On the other was Baron Jean de Constant Rebecque, who had been the prince's tutor at Oxford and was now his chief of staff. Malcolm, Suzanne knew, had a great deal of respect for Rebecque, whom he described as a kindly man with a keen understanding, an excellent stabilizing influence on Billy.

"Poor young devil," Geoffrey murmured. As a military doctor, he knew the prince from the Peninsula.

Aline shot a sharp look at her husband. "I thought you weren't paying attention to the rumors."

"Not being deaf, I could hardly avoid them completely. Billy never impressed me as having an overabundance of wit, but I didn't think he was quite such a fool. Though all the rumors are almost comforting."

"Comforting?" Aline asked.

"That we still have leisure for gossip. These rumors are likely to seem positively quaint when we face what lies ahead. Ah, at last. The musicians are finally tuning up."

Malcolm leaned against the wall beside the door of the grand salon, where the operagoers crowded during the interval. Several waiters circulated among the crowd with trays of champagne. He knew Suzanne had her eye out for the waiter with the fading pox scars on his face. He could best help by turning a blind eye and waiting for her to slip the paper into his hand.

"Malcolm."

Malcolm turned round to find Fitzroy Somerset standing beside him. A line showed between Fitzroy's brows, a rare sign of unease. In the Peninsula Malcolm had seen his friend look less alarmed on the eve of battle. Of course, they were more or less on the eve of battle now.

"How's Harriet?" Malcolm asked.

"Well." A smile briefly dispelled the frown. "She decided to stay at home tonight with the baby. In truth I came partly because I was hoping for a word with you."

Malcolm scanned his friend's face. "Something's happened since I saw you at Headquarters?"

"I wanted to tell you in private. And oddly this seems more private than Headquarters."

"Crowds often are. You're learning an intelligence agent's tricks."

Fitzroy turned slightly, his back to the crowd. "Speaking of intelligence agents, the duke's asked you to look into last night's events?"

"Is that a statement or a question?"

"I'm no spy, but I'm not blind. Or deaf."

"Quite the opposite. You know something about last night's events?" Something Fitzroy hadn't wanted to repeat at Headquarters, which was damned odd.

Fitzroy grimaced, cast a glance over his shoulder, looked back at Malcolm. "Was Julia Ashton's death an accident?"

Malcolm kept his gaze steady on his friend's face. "It's beginning to look as though it may have been more complicated."

"I was afraid of that." Fitzroy's fair brows drew together again. "I hate to tell tales—"

Malcolm touched his friend's arm. He considered Fitzroy a rare example of a British gentleman in that he took the gentleman's code with the utmost seriousness. "We're on the brink of war, and Lady Julia's death seems to be caught up in that. If you know anything that could possibly shed light on what happened—"

"Quite." Fitzroy's mouth tightened. "Look, Malcolm, do I have your word you won't repeat this unless you find it necessary in your investigation?"

"Do you really have to ask that?"

Fitzroy gave an unexpected grin. "Just trying to salve my conscience, I suppose." He shifted his weight from one foot to the other. "Last night, fairly early in the evening—it was before supper, at any rate—I walked out into the garden for some air. Well, truth be told, I was avoiding being buttonholed by Mr. Creevey with more anxious questions about Bonaparte. I wandered down one of the gravel walks. As I passed a hedge I . . . caught sight of a couple who'd taken refuge behind the hedge."

Malcolm's gaze skimmed over Fitzroy's face. "Lady Julia?"

"No. Her husband."

"Well. That is a surprise."

"Damn you, Malcolm, are you so cold-blooded about everything?"

"On the contrary. I'd have sworn Ashton was madly in love with his wife. Did you recognize the lady?"

"Yes." Fitzroy swallowed. "It was Violet Chase."

Malcolm drew in his breath. "Interesting. Were they embracing or just talking?"

"She was in his arms, but—Malcolm, I've known Violet since she was a child. She's a bit of a madcap, but I'd swear she wouldn't—"

"I have no desire to cast aspersions on Miss Chase's virtue. I understand she and Ashton were once practically betrothed."

"Yes. There was some—unpleasantness—when it ended. But I was sure Ashton—"

"Was devoted to his wife. But people said the same about Lady Julia's feelings for him, and you must have heard today's rumors about her and Slender Billy."

"I own I was shocked. But this doesn't mean—"

"That Ashton and Miss Chase were lovers?" Malcolm sifted the possibilities in his mind. "Not necessarily. But it does mean that Ashton didn't tell us the whole truth last night."

The trick to spotting an individual in a throng all dressed alike, Suzanne had learned, was to focus in on details. Look at faces rather than powdered wigs and blue brocade coats, and the pox-scarred face of the man Rivaux had described was quite unmistakable. He was carrying a tray of champagne glasses. A cloth was spread over the tray, and peeping out from beneath it Suzanne saw a corner of cream-colored paper.

She cast a glance at Davenport, who was standing beside her in the grand salon. He coughed loudly. "Can't we get some champagne over here?"

While the footman's head was turned, Suzanne took a glass of champagne, palmed the paper, and slid another in its place. The work of a few seconds.

She moved across the room to Malcolm, who was standing by the door in conversation with Fitzroy Somerset and Lord March.

"It doesn't make a lot of sense for Bonaparte to attack through the Sambre and Meuse valleys," Fitzroy was saying. "The French have already destroyed the roads through there. It's not so much that the reports we're getting may be false as that these French attacks could well be a feint."

"With the real attack coming from the west," March said. "To cut us off from the sea and our supply lines."

"Quite."

"So there *is* going to be an attack?" Suzanne asked. "Don't worry, I'm not the sort to panic." Or at least she had the panic well under control.

"It looks that way," Fitzroy said. "But it's looked that way before."

For a moment, the remembered smell of blood washed over her. She looked at Fitzroy and March, so elegant and insouciant in their white net pantaloons, fringed sashes, and beautifully cut coats. Champagne turned bitter in her mouth.

"What have you done with Slender Billy?" she asked, slipping her arm through Malcolm's and sliding the note into his palm.

"Rebecque persuaded him to have champagne in his box." March grimaced. "Devil of a night."

"The talk will die down," Fitzroy said in the tone Suzanne had heard him use during innumerable hair-raising crises in the Peninsula.

"Provided nothing worse surfaces," March said.

"Do you have reason to think it will?" Malcolm asked, voice deceptively conversational.

"Just general apprehension. And a knowledge of Billy."

"He can't say more if there isn't more to reveal," Fitzroy pointed out.

"Thanks, Fitzroy, that's very comforting." March dug his shoulder into the wall behind him. "You should have heard the dressing-down I got from Wellington. I think in his mind part of my duties is to keep Slender Billy out of unfortunate entanglements. Which I would have done, if I'd known."

"Were you with Billy much of the night last night?" Malcolm asked.

"Enough to know that he couldn't have slipped off and fought a duel whatever the gossips are saying." March took a sip of champagne. "The odd thing is, you know who I did see slipping through a side door?"

"Who?" Malcolm asked, in the same conversational tone.

"Alexander Gordon. I asked him where he'd been, and he just gave me some roundabout story about smoking a cigarillo in the garden, which could have been true save that the way Gordon told it, it was plainly a farrago of nonsense. I didn't realize Gordon had a—" March broke off, flushing.

"A mistress in Brussels," Suzanne finished for him. "Surely you know me well enough not to think I'd be shocked, Lord March? For Gordon's sake, I do hope she's amusing."

"Gossip is a fascinating thing." Raoul O'Roarke stopped beside them before the embarrassed March could answer. "The Prince of Orange's indiscretion and Lady Julia's death have quite eclipsed the latest rumors that the French are on the march. I just heard someone giving even odds on whether fighting would break out first between the Allies and the French or the British troops and the Dutch-Belgians."

"I don't suppose you have any advice from the days when you tried to hold together five different *guerrillero* factions in the Peninsula, do you, O'Roarke?" Fitzroy asked.

Raoul gave an ironic grin. "Mostly I'm grateful not to be in the thick of it anymore. But as I recall, distraction is a great key."

"Speaking of which, the Ashton scandal's going to hang over my mother's ball tomorrow night," March said. "Mother wondered if it would be in better taste to call it off, but Wellington had a word with her."

"Sensible," Raoul said. "Canceling at the last minute would fuel rumors and panic. Not to mention emboldening the Bonapartists in Brussels."

"And hopefully the dancing will distract our troops and the Dutch-Belgians from quarreling." Malcolm took a sip from Suzanne's champagne glass. "If you'll excuse me, I must speak to Stuart."

Malcolm slipped out of the salon. Suzanne asked how Fitzroy's wife was getting on with her new baby daughter. A murmur from the crowd caught their attention. Fitzroy let out a low whistle. "One can't but sympathize, but it would have been so much easier if she'd remained in London."

Cordelia Davenport and Caroline Lamb had come into the salon. Half the crowd appeared to be looking at them, the other half at Harry Davenport, flicking a bit of lint from his lapel, and at George Chase, who was standing with three of his fellow cavalry officers.

"Poor Davenport," Lord March muttered. "Sharp tongue, but not a bad fellow. He certainly didn't deserve this."

Suzanne nodded. She had noticed something else that turned her blood colder than her expertly iced champagne. A sandy-haired man she recognized as Captain Dumont had come into the room and was making his way toward the waiter with the pox scars. No sign of Malcolm. No way to exchange the dummy note for the original.

"Evening, Chase." Davenport took a step toward George Chase. His voice rang out, slightly slurred. "A bit awkward, but I suppose there's a certain drama in our meeting at the opera."

The crowd froze with equal parts awkwardness and interest. Dumont couldn't move without drawing attention to himself.

A host of emotions flickered through George Chase's eyes. Surprise. Embarrassment. Guilt. Quickly as they had appeared they vanished beneath an easy smile. "Davenport." He moved toward the other man, his hand extended. "It's good to see you in Brussels. It looks like we're in for a bit of a hard run. I'm glad we'll have you with us."

Davenport stared down at George Chase's hand as though it were some unknown substance he'd stumbled over in the street. "Doing it much too brown, Chase. I doubt my presence brings you any comfort. In fact, I rather think you wouldn't care to find me at your back."

"Ancient history, Davenport."

"Is it? We could fight that duel we never fought and rival the opera. Though I must say I think Orfeo's carrying on a bit much about his wife being dragged off to the underworld. He might be better off without her. Oh, look." He cast a glance to the side. "There's my wife."

Cordelia Davenport stepped forward with a shrug of her shoulders that made her jet-beaded shawl flash in the candlelight. "Don't be tiresome, Harry. You can't possibly take it seriously after all these years. No one's interested in yesterday's scandal. At least"—she cast a glance round the company—"I wouldn't think they were."

Her words broke the crowd's stillness, like the crack of ice. Nervous laughter ran through the room, a way of asserting that they were not so ill-bred as to have been observing the domestic drama that had been played out before them. Gowns rustled. Glasses clinked. Dumont took a step forward.

Davenport swung back his fist and hit George Chase in the jaw. Or tried to. His blow glanced off Chase's chin. Davenport lost his balance and tumbled to the carpet. In the process he bumped into the pox-scarred waiter. The waiter's tray went flying. The crowd jumped back as champagne spattered and crystal cracked. The cream-colored note card landed by a gilded chair leg. Suzanne could see Dumont looking at it.

Fitzroy drew in his breath. March bit back an exclamation. Raoul O'Roarke, an expert at breaking up fights, started forward, then checked himself at a look from Suzanne.

"For God's sake, Harry," Cordelia said.

"Sorry." Davenport rubbed his hand. "Wanted to do that for years."

Dumont moved again. The door from the anteroom opened, and Malcolm stepped through.

"Easy, Davenport." Malcolm bent over the fallen Davenport and pulled him to his feet. "Let's get you some coffee."

The fallen note card now lay at a slightly different angle. Hopefully not different enough for Dumont to notice. The pox-scarred waiter bent to retrieve the broken glasses and blot up the spilled champagne. Cordelia looked from her husband to George Chase, eyes dark with a guilt Suzanne recognized all too well.

Malcolm helped Davenport to the door to the corridor. Cordelia cast a quick glance at George, then turned to go after her husband and Malcolm. As Suzanne moved to follow them, she saw Dumont out of the corner of her eye, bending down by the fallen note card as though to pick up a dropped programme.

Suzanne stepped into the corridor in time to see Cordelia run to Davenport's side and grip his arm. "Harry."

Davenport was still leaning against Malcolm as though suffering from the effects of drink. "Sorry, Cordy. Seem to have had a bit of a relapse. Thought I was over such idiocy years ago."

Lady Cordelia's finely plucked brows drew together. "I never thought—"

"That I still had feelings? Messy things, feelings." He glanced down at his wife's fingers, curled round his arm.

Cordelia dropped her hand to her side. "If you feel like hitting someone, it would make far more sense for it to be me."

"Never knew you to be a martyr, old girl. Much better not to hit anyone, don't you think? Though if we're parceling out blame, I'd say George had plenty to do with our sorry little drama."

Cordelia frowned at him. Then her gaze flickered down the passage to Suzanne. "I'm sorry you had to witness this, Suzanne. And you, Mr. Rannoch."

"It's already calming down in the salon," Suzanne said, walking down the corridor toward them. "Goodness knows everyone has enough other things to gossip about."

"Like my sister." Cordelia stepped back. Her gaze flickered from Suzanne to Malcolm and then rested on Davenport for a moment. "Harry. Are you—"

"What?" Davenport inquired, voice carefully slurred.

Cordelia regarded him a moment longer. "You're very good at what you do, aren't you?"

"Not at the moment. Spies are supposed to be above feelings."

"My point precisely." Cordelia touched his arm again with light fingers, then stepped back and looked from him to Malcolm to Suzanne. "You must have things to discuss. I'll go back to the salon and give them more reason to gossip. I daresay you could do with the distraction."

Davenport's gaze lingered on his wife as she vanished down the corridor. Then he turned, still leaning against Malcolm in case any more footmen passed by, and the two men and Suzanne moved toward an antechamber.

"Good show," Malcolm said when they were in the small white and gold room.

"Who says it was a show?" Davenport rubbed his hand, posture straight, gaze alert and focused. "I've wanted to hit Chase for years."

"If it wasn't a show you'd have actually hit him," Malcolm said.

Davenport gave a reluctant grin. "Possibly."

"Your wife's a discerning woman," Malcolm said.

"Yes." Davenport flexed his fingers. "I'm afraid she saw all too much."

"She'll keep quiet," Suzanne said.

Davenport's mouth twisted. "You sound very sure, Mrs. Rannoch. You only met her last night."

"I've seen enough of her in the past twenty-four hours to be sure of that."

"Odd. I've known Cordelia for five years, and I'm not sure of anything when it comes to her. Did you get a look at the note, Rannoch?"

Malcolm nodded. " 'The north salon, eleven o'clock.' Dumont has a rendezvous tonight. If it proves to be of the amorous variety, I shall feel a colossal fool."

"Dangerous to hope it will be with the Silver Hawk," Davenport said.

"Stranger things have happened."

Suzanne leaned against a chairback. "The north salon has tall windows with velvet curtains. Good for concealment."

"If Dumont and his friend are halfway good at their job they'll have someone keeping an eye on the corridor before the meeting," Davenport said.

"Yes, I was thinking of that." Suzanne moved to the antechamber's one window and drew aside the gold damask curtains. She pushed up the sash window and glanced out at the façade of the building. "Nice decorative detailing with footholds. We can go out the window here. It overlooks a side street. We shouldn't be seen."

Davenport gave a rare smile that was free of irony. "You're a remarkable woman, Mrs. Rannoch."

"A devious mind has its uses, Colonel Davenport."

৵ 21 ৵

Brittle conversation filled the air again when Cordelia stepped back into the salon. Glasses clinked, fans stirred the candle-warmed air. The fallen champagne glasses had been tidied away. Only a faint damp mark on the red and gold carpet showed where the contretemps had occurred.

Cordelia felt several gazes darted in her direction. She ignored them with the ease of long practice. George was across the room in a corner, talking to three fellow officers. She moved toward him, aware of a sharp look from Caro.

George turned as though aware of her approach. He froze for a moment, then murmured something to his companions and came toward her. "Cordy." He reached out as though he would take her hands but stopped a few feet off. "I heard about Julia this morning. I'm so sorry."

She nodded. For a moment she didn't trust herself to speak. Julia's death was a constant, gnawing ache in her chest. And then sometimes the reality of it would slam into her all over again, leaving her scarcely able to breathe.

He stretched out a hand again, then let it fall to his side without touching her. "If there's anything I can do—"

"There is actually." She looked directly into his eyes. People were watching of course, but they'd gossip regardless. "I need to talk to you, George. Alone."

"I'm not—"

"There's a reason. Beyond foolishness."

"Cordy—"

"Wait ten minutes into the next act and meet me in the antechamber. Through that door."

"Cordy, I can't possibly—"

"You owe me this much."

He drew a breath. "Yes. Of course."

As they resumed their seats for the opera, Caro leaned toward Cordelia under cover of settling her lavender gauze skirts. "Are you crazy?"

"Probably," Cordelia said, fingers not quite steady as she lifted her opera glasses. "But I need to talk to him."

"You needing him has always been the problem."

"Not in that way." Cordelia squeezed her friend's hand. "I'll explain later, dearest."

Caro's snort and concerned gaze followed her as she slipped from the box.

She would have given only slightly more than even odds on George actually meeting her, but before she had paced the length of the antechamber the door opened with a quiet click. "I don't know that this is a good idea, Cordy."

She turned and looked at him. The candlelight fell across his face, shadowing bones and hollows she could trace from memory. He didn't move a muscle, but she could feel his gaze shifting over her face.

"Probably not," she agreed. "But when has that ever stopped us?"

A smile shot across his face, then faded abruptly. He pushed the door to with a firm click. "It's not a joke, Cordy. It never was. We were just too young and foolish to see it."

"And now we're wise?"

"Hardly." George leaned against the door, his gaze trained on her face. "At least speaking for myself. I have barely enough wit to recognize a mistake seconds before I make it."

"I think we've already made all the mistakes possible, don't you?"

"Oh, don't you believe it for a moment."

She took a step toward him, to prove that she could do so. "I'm sorry about Harry just now."

George grimaced. "It was no more than I deserved. Save that I deserved to have him actually plant me a facer."

Harry's bleak gaze flickered in her memory. She'd been shocked at how much the wounds of their sorry past still lingered for him. And then she'd realized that it had all been an act, part of whatever intrigue he and the Rannochs were involved in. And yet—"Harry should be on my conscience, not yours."

"Are you saying you don't feel guilty about Annabel?"

Annabel. Cordelia had caught a glimpse of her tonight across the theatre, her white-gloved fingers curled round George's arm. Blond, sweet, in love with George. A much better wife than Cordelia was herself. "I know I have a reputation for heartlessness," she said, "but I'm not quite that bad. Of course I feel guilty about Annabel."

"I hurt people." George's fingers tightened against the door panels. "I hurt you."

"I did plenty of that myself. It's over and done with."

"It will never be done with." George's gaze moved back to her face. She could feel its pressure against her skin. "Not completely. If we had any doubts about that, Harry put them to rest tonight."

"I'm sorry, George." She folded her arms, fingers digging into her elbows, as though she could anchor herself. "But we need to talk about this."

"Talk about what?"

She drew a breath. Her throat was raw. "You must have heard the rumors today. They're all over Brussels. That Julia was the Prince of Orange's mistress."

George's gaze slid away. "I couldn't believe—Julia, of all people."

"Oh, for God's sake, George." Cordelia moved toward him, heedless of the risks. "You knew her. Julia wouldn't let morality stand in the way of something she wanted."

"Cordy, she was—"

"My sister. So I knew her."

"You're saying that Julia—"

"Was having an affair with the Prince of Orange. But that isn't the part I wanted to talk to you about. Did you know?"

"About Julia and the Prince of Orange?" George ran a hand over his hair. "Of course not."

"About my sister and your brother."

George stared at her, fingers dug into his hair. He'd looked at her in much the same way when she'd announced at the age of twelve that being a mistress sounded much more interesting than being a wife. "Oh, dear God."

"You *did* know?"

"Cordy—"

She grabbed his shoulders. "Damn it, George, how could you?"

"How could *I*—"

"How could you have let them be so stupid? How could you stand by and watch them make the same mistakes we did?"

George caught her wrists and detached her grip on his shoulders with gentle fingers. "I'm not Tony's keeper. Nor Julia's if it comes to that."

His skin still smelled faintly of citrus and cloves. His breath was warm and held a hint of red wine. "So you did nothing?"

"What would you have had me do?" George retained his grip on her hands, holding them in front of him. "Order Tony to stop? I haven't had any control over him since he was out of leading strings. If then."

Traces of a shaving cut showed on his jaw. She wondered if Annabel daubed the cuts the way she once had done. "You could have warned him of what he was risking."

His mouth tightened. "You think I didn't? Not that it did any more good this time than—"

"With his prior indiscretions?"

"I never said—"

"Jane admitted it."

George blinked in confusion. "Jane—"

"She knew about Julia. She said it wasn't Tony's first liaison since their marriage."

George glanced to the side.

"You knew that."

He grimaced. "I think Tony genuinely loves Jane. Or did when they married. But fidelity doesn't come easily to him."

"We both have cause to know about that."

George's fingers tightened over her own. Beneath his gloves, she could feel the calluses on his fingers and a rough spot where a bone had broken and not mended properly. "Tony threw my own past in my face when I tried to have a brotherly talk with him. He said—" George bit back the words, a pulse beating fast in his jaw.

"What?" Cordelia demanded.

George drew a rough breath, looked away, looked back at her. "He asked if I was really happy with the choice I'd made four years ago."

Cordelia jerked her hands out of her former lover's clasp. "Well, that should have been easy to answer."

"Should have been."

She folded her arms across her chest, her fingers digging into the silk of her gloves. "You could have written to me."

"What the devil would you have done?"

"Talked some sense into Julia."

"Told her you'd be happier if you were still living with Davenport?"

His words slapped against her skin. "Damn it, George—"

"I'm sorry. That was unpardonable."

"Johnny isn't Harry." Cordelia tightened her grip on her arms. "Julia was happy with him."

"Sweetheart—" George bit the word back before it was fully formed. "Can you really know what they were? You haven't seen much of Julia in recent years."

"All the more reason for her to know the consequences of playing with fire. I don't think she'd have fared as well as I've done as a social exile."

"Which is exactly why I thought the less said about the affair the better." George moved away from the door with sudden force, paced halfway across the room, turned back to her. "I thought they'd get over it. God knows Tony has tired of all the others."

"George—"

"Damn it—" He drew a rough breath. "Cordy, you have every right to be angry at me," he said in a more temperate voice. "But not about this. Don't let's waste time—"

"I'm not angry. I need to understand. Julia was afraid, George. She didn't write to me about her affair with Tony, but she wrote to me about that."

"What the devil did Julia have to be afraid of?"

"I don't know. Yet." She rested her hands on a gilded chairback. "Violet knew."

"That Julia was afraid?"

"About Julia's affair with Tony. She found a letter Tony wrote to Julia. She didn't confront Tony, but she did confront Julia."

The fear of an elder brother filled George's eyes. "Oh God."

"Yes, I can't imagine it was a very comfortable conversation."

George ran a hand over his hair. "I know how prickly Vi can be. But she was genuinely brokenhearted when Ashton married Julia. I don't think she ever properly got over it."

"Nor do I."

His eyes widened. "You can't think Julia was afraid of Violet—"

"Violet can be rather terrifying in a temper."

"Not to you. Not to Julia. You're both made of sterner stuff."

"I'm trying very hard not to let my thoughts run away with me. But someone was behind Julia's death." Cordelia studied her former lover. She'd once thought she knew him better than anyone in the world, but now she understood how impossible it was to ever really know another person. "How would Tony have reacted if he'd learned Julia was the Prince of Orange's mistress as well as his own?"

"He'd have been jealous, Tony has never been good at sharing." George's gaze froze on her face. "Oh no, Cordy."

"Don't say you can't imagine him doing it, George. We both know all too well just what depths people are capable of sinking to."

"It's a far cry from—"

"Adultery to murder?"

"We're talking about my brother."

"And my sister."

"Cordy." He closed the distance between them and reached for her hands again. "I know this must be unbearable. I know how desperate you must be to make sense of it—"

She pulled her hands away. "Don't you dare try to humor me."

"Perish the thought." He frowned. "A few days ago, Tony asked me if I'd look after Jane if anything happened to him. I said of course and I assumed he'd do the same for Annabel if I didn't survive the coming battle. He shot me the oddest look, as though he'd meant something else entirely. It was only later that I wondered—"

Cordelia stared at her former lover, chilled to the bone. "You think Tony was planning to *run off* with Julia?"

"You can hardly deny it's possible."

Her sister's face hung before Cordelia's eyes. Pale blond hair swept smooth, mouth curved in a decorous smile, cheeks tinged with the faintest hint of rouge, eyes bright but carefully veiled. "I can't imagine—"

"What?" George scanned her face.

"Julia throwing everything over. Giving up her husband, her child, her position—"

"You were willing to do it once."

"I'm not Julia." She folded her arms across her chest. "And I didn't have a child then."

She saw the flinch in George's gaze at the mention of Livia. "You didn't think Julia would take a lover, either, did you? Let alone two."

Cordelia stared at him, seeing the unlined face and clear, unshadowed eyes of the man she'd been ready to throw everything over for four years ago. "You suspected this, and you let them—"

"For God's sake, Cordy, it wasn't a question of letting. I told you, I couldn't control either of them."

"You said you were hoping it would end quietly. But once you realized they were going to ruin their lives—"

"Perhaps—" He stared at her for a long moment. She could feel the tension coming off him like waves of heat. "Perhaps I wasn't entirely sure they were ruining their lives."

Cordelia took a step back. "George—"

He glanced away, a muscle tense in his jaw. "We've been living in a different world these past weeks, Cordy."

"Caro told me. The picnics, the balls, the military reviews with ladies carrying their parasols and pink champagne afterwards. A soap bubble world. That's going to pop any minute."

"That's just it. When you know you may well be dead before the leaves turn color, it's amazing how trivial some things seem. There's a wonderful clarity, the sort that comes when the dawn light hits the cobblestones."

"As one staggers home three sheets to the wind."

"Sobering up. Aware of what really matters and what one wants."

A thread snagged in Cordelia's gown as her fingers closed on the gauze. "George. When we found out Annabel was with child, and I told you that you should go back to her—"

"We were in an impossible situation. You made a sacrifice, but I should have—"

"I wasn't being noble, George."

He shook his head, his gaze soft with tenderness in that way that had always twisted her heart. "Oh, Cordy. I know how terrified you've always been of the least hint of sentimentality. But I've always understood—"

"No." She heard her voice bounce off the gilt and plaster walls of the room. "The truth is, George, when I sent you back to Annabel I could already see the end."

"You knew what we'd have to go through—"

"I knew what we felt for each other wouldn't last."

He looked like a child who's been told fairy tales are only make-believe. "You can't mean that. After everything—"

"It's precisely because of everything we've been through that I can mean it. Love's very amusing, but it doesn't last. Especially not in the face of privation."

His gaze moved over her face. "I hate that I made you into a cynic."

"You didn't make me into anything that I wasn't already. We did more than enough damage, but Annabel saved us from the worst. Falling out of love."

He stared at her for a long moment. "Speak for yourself, Cordy," he said at last, in a low, rough voice. Then he turned on his heel and left the room.

The sash windows to the north salon opened with relative ease under the force of Malcolm's picklocks. The creak made him profoundly grateful that they were twenty minutes ahead of schedule. It was only to be hoped that neither Dumont nor his contact was that early for their rendezvous.

Malcolm swung his foot over the sill, suppressing a twinge at the stab through his side. He paused for a moment, but he could hear nothing but the stir of wind from outside and the faint rattle of carriage wheels a street over. He pushed aside the heavy damask curtains. A single brace of candles lit the room, casting long shadows on watered cream silk wall hangings, but there was no sign of a human presence. He reached back and handed Suzanne through the window, and then Davenport.

Davenport rubbed his bad arm once he was on solid ground. Suzanne cast a glance at him, then ran a sharp gaze over Malcolm's side where a bandage was wound round his ribs beneath shirt and waistcoat and coat. Malcolm shook his head and reached for her hand. They slipped behind the curtains of one of the two windows, Davenport behind the other. Malcolm wrapped his arm round his wife so they'd take up less room in the cramped space. He felt her soft exhale of laughter against his throat. She reached up and pressed a kiss against his cheek, then went still in the circle of his arm.

He remembered a time, early in their marriage, when they'd stood in a similar position in the loft of a Spanish barn. For all that they were sharing a bed, there had been an intimacy in holding her against him, straw tickling their noses, that had seemed out of place in their oddly begun marriage. A great deal had changed since then. Danger had brought them together at the start. Danger had also broken down the barriers between them.

The door opened with a faint creak. Footsteps sounded, of the sort made by soft-soled evening shoes on a good carpet. A man's shoes by the sound of it.

A few minutes and the door opened again and then closed with a quiet click.

"I hope this is important." The voice speaking Belgium-accented French seemed to come from the man who had arrived first. It sounded like Dumont, whom Malcolm had met a handful of times. "It's more dangerous meeting now than ever."

"I have a delivery for you." The second man had a deeper voice and sounded older. He too spoke Belgian-accented French. Something in his voice teased at Malcolm's memory. "To Paris by the usual channels."

"How the hell can you think of usual channels at a time like this?"

"We haven't got time to hide or grieve or suffer from qualms." From the soft thud and creak, the second man had dropped into a chair. "We proceed as usual."

"I tell you it's dangerous."

"It's more dangerous to panic." A rustle of fabric as though the second man had leaned back in his chair.

"We can't go on as if everything's normal," Dumont insisted. "We have to talk."

"About what?"

"Rannoch's asking questions. Along with another man. Davenport. Depending on what La Fleur told them—"

"La Fleur couldn't have told them much, or they'd be asking very different questions." The second man gave a low laugh. A laugh that struck a chord in Malcolm's memory. The card room at a score of entertainments in Brussels this spring. A portly man with keen eyes and a ready smile.

Good God. Dumont's confederate was the Comte de Vedrin. The man who had held Julia Ashton's gaming debts. As coincidences it strained belief. But if it wasn't a coincidence—

"Everything's changed." From the sound of footsteps, Dumont was pacing. "Without the Silver Hawk—"

"Don't use that as an excuse," Vedrin said. "The Silver Hawk was clever but not irreplaceable."

"We can't—"

"Don't forget I made the Silver Hawk." Vedrin's controlled voice wielded sudden force. "I can make another."

"Agents like that don't fall into your lap every day."

"True. It's a sad loss."

A long silence. Dumont had gone still. "What the devil happened last night?" he demanded. "Why was the Silver Hawk there? Was that your doing?"

"No." A short, clipped word.

Dumont began pacing again. "We know *we* weren't behind the ambush. We know the British weren't behind it—"

"Do we?"

"If so, they'd have been shooting at their own people."

"A point."

"So who the hell was doing the shooting?" Dumont demanded. "And who were they shooting at?"

"I'd give a great deal to know."

"Is it true?" Dumont sounded as though he'd moved closer to the other man. "That the Silver Hawk was ordered to kill Malcolm Rannoch?"

An unusually long silence. "I assume so."

Malcolm felt the jolt of tension that ran through his wife.

"Why?" Dumont demanded. "He's only one agent—"

"One very clever agent."

"Still just one man. Why?"

Another, longer silence. "I don't know."

"But if you didn't give the order who did?" Dumont persisted. "You ran the Silver Hawk."

"I spotted the Silver Hawk," Vedrin said. "I arranged her recruitment. But I didn't run her. She was handled outside the network."

"The ambush at the château." Dumont's voice quickened with

interest. "Do you think it was an attempt to kill Rannoch? Do you think the Silver Hawk set it up?"

"And got caught in her own trap? She was usually cleverer than that."

"She was a woman."

"Your point being?" Vedrin's voice held an undertone of amusement. "In my experience, women make better agents. They're usually more cautious and often more devious than men."

Dumont gave a short laugh. "She was devious all right. Deceiving her husband and—"

"Don't you dare judge her. It was her job. A job she did exceedingly well."

"I only meant she had to have been under a great deal of strain. She could have made a mistake—"

"She could. But Julia Ashton was an exceedingly clever woman."

ᘒ 22 ᘒ

Wednesday, 14 June–Thursday, 15 June

Suzanne was too good an agent to draw breath, but Malcolm could feel the shock that ran through her. Similar to the wave of shock that coursed through him.

"Clever or not, she's dead," Dumont said.

"And we have to pick up the pieces. The next few days are likely to prove crucial." The chair creaked as though Vedrin had got to his feet. "I suggest you take the package I brought and return to the theatre before our absence is noted."

The door opened and closed. A few minutes later, a second set of footsteps crossed the room and the door creaked open and shut again. Training held them all still behind the curtains for another three minutes. At last, of one accord they pushed the curtains aside and stepped into the room.

Davenport's face was white. Malcolm put a hand on the other man's arm. "Sit down."

"I'm not going to collapse." Davenport's voice shook with barely leashed rage. "God in heaven——"

"She was in debt to Vedrin," Malcolm said. "Who I'm sure deliberately played on her weakness for cards."

Davenport pulled away from Malcolm and strode across the room. "Anthony Chase paid off her debts."

"Vedrin must not have told him the full extent. He didn't want to be paid back, he wanted an agent. An agent who was a British officer's wife."

Davenport stared at the girandoles on a candle sconce, as though the answer to his sister-in-law's behavior lay in the play of light on the crystals. "Julia of all people. The least likely spy I can imagine."

"It's the least likely prospects who make the best agents." Suzanne's hands curled round a chairback. She had cause to know what a good agent a decorous wife could make, but her eyes, usually so clear and level, were wide with shock.

"Julia was—" Davenport shook his head. "Her greatest dilemma seemed to be selecting a bonnet. I'm not sure she was even certain who was at war with whom on the Continent. Or that she cared."

"That was four years ago," Malcolm said. "A great deal can change."

Davenport slammed his hand down on the polished surface of a pier table. "I'm a fool. I didn't have the faintest understanding of my wife. How can I claim to have understood her sister?"

"The longer I'm in this business, the less I feel I understand anyone," Malcolm said.

"You're too modest, Rannoch." Davenport rubbed his hand. "From what I've seen you're damnably acute."

"We can all be deceived." Malcolm poured a glass of cognac and gave it to Davenport.

Davenport stared at the glass, then took a long swallow.

"She was obviously very good at what she did," Suzanne said. "Vedrin and Dumont had a great deal of respect for her."

"Billy just now told me that he'd found Julia going through his pockets the last time they were together," Malcolm said. "I should have guessed—"

"At least now their affair makes sense. And her attempt to seduce Lord Uxbridge." Suzanne dropped into a chair. "The French wanted an inside source in the Allied army. They had her try Uxbridge first, probably because she knew him and he has a reputation as a ladies' man. When that didn't work, she turned her attentions to the Prince of Orange. With more success."

Davenport's fingers curled round the glass. "Bastards." He cast a quick glance at Malcolm and Suzanne. "Yes, I know, it's terribly conventional to worry about my sister-in-law being defiled, but the thought of someone blackmailing Julia to—"

"I know," Malcolm said. "I'd like to throttle them myself. Though we'd be fools to think our own side hasn't done as much."

"And Anthony Chase?" Suzanne rested her elbow on the table, her chin in her hand. "Did the French arrange that as well? Or did she fall in love as Chase claimed?"

Davenport took a sip of cognac. "If the French were behind it, you'd think they'd have found someone more powerful than Chase for her to seduce."

"When she wrote to Lady Cordelia that it had got beyond her control—that was probably when she was ordered to kill Malcolm," Suzanne said. "One thing to pass on the odd bit of information. Another to commit murder."

"You sound very sure," Davenport said.

Suzanne met his gaze. "I'm putting myself in her position."

"So she wrote the letter to her sister in a panic, perhaps just after she was given the order." Malcolm leaned against the table. "Then she realized involving her sister would only make matters worse. So she wrote the second letter, telling Lady Cordelia it had all been a fancy and not to worry. Only Lady Cordelia had already set sail for Belgium."

"She said she feared for her life," Suzanne said. "A threat from her handlers if she didn't follow through on her orders?"

"Probably." Davenport's mouth tightened. "It's odd. I'm not feeling particularly confident of my skills at judging people. But from Ashton's response last night to the news of Julia's death— even after he learned of her affair with the Prince of Orange—I'd swear he'd have forgiven the debts. And yet she was so afraid of telling him the truth that instead she became a French spy."

Malcolm turned his head to regard Davenport. "Are you suggesting that she had other reasons for becoming a French spy?"

"Or other reasons for fearing Ashton. Perhaps he wasn't quite the besotted husband he seemed last night."

Malcolm regarded Davenport for a moment, weighing the wisdom of adding further fuel to an already-explosive situation. "That appears to be true. Fitzroy told me just now that he happened upon Ashton and Violet Chase embracing in the garden last night."

Davenport clunked his glass down on the pier table. "Ashton's a better actor than I credited."

Suzanne was frowning. "Sarah Lennox told me she saw Violet Chase in the retiring room and that Violet seemed to be lying about where she'd been."

Davenport gave a bitter nod of acknowledgment. "So the seemingly grieving widower who was shocked at his wife's affair was engaged in a liaison with his former almost fiancée. Whose brother was having an affair with Julia Ashton. I never could keep up with Cordelia's set."

"It doesn't necessarily mean Captain Ashton isn't grieving," Suzanne said. "Or that he wasn't shocked at Lady Julia's affair. Gentlemen—some gentlemen—are quite capable of carrying on liaisons while expecting their wives to remain faithful. Though I don't think either of you is in that category."

"You flatter me, Mrs. Rannoch," Davenport said.

"Honest observation, Colonel Davenport."

"Not so shocking for the beau monde perhaps," Malcolm said. "But the Ashtons had a reputation for being different. If Lady Julia was acting a part, so was Ashton apparently."

"As an unmarried woman, Violet Chase was at far more risk in a love affair than Lady Julia or other married women," Suzanne said.

"And if Ashton decided he'd made a mistake three years ago, that it was Violet he wanted to be married to—" Davenport's fingers curled round his brandy glass.

"It gives them both motives," Malcolm agreed. "But I still think it's more likely Lady Julia's death is connected to her work as a spy."

"Her second letter to Lady Cordelia implies she'd decided on a way out of her predicament," Suzanne said. "Which may have meant she'd decided to go forward with killing Malcolm."

Malcolm shook his head. "It's—"

"A fact, darling, however inexplicable. We have Dumont's and Vedrin's word for it now."

"If Julia set up the ambush she should have had the wit not to run out in front of the bullets," Davenport said. "Not to mention one would think she wouldn't have made a rendezvous with the Prince of Orange at the same time."

"True." Suzanne frowned. "It makes more sense that the ambushers were trying to kill Lady Julia. And that whoever was behind the ambush sent the letter to the Prince of Orange so he wouldn't be there. Her French handlers, who decided she'd become too much of a liability? Perhaps she did refuse to kill Malcolm."

"Perhaps," Davenport said. "On the other hand, if anyone on our side learned she was a French spy they'd be in the devil of a fix. Imagine the ripples of scandal if it got out that the Prince of Orange was sleeping with a French agent who happened to be a British officer's wife. Much easier to tidy up the whole thing if Julia simply died."

Malcolm cast a sideways look at him.

"It's been done before," Davenport said. "Don't deny it."

"I won't attempt to. But if the British were behind the ambush, I like to think they'd have had enough respect for our abilities not to have us investigate."

"Wellington and Stuart might not have even known about it," Davenport pointed out. "British intelligence is positively byzantine."

"If Anthony Chase had learned that the woman he was ready to throw everything over for was not only the Prince of Orange's mistress but was a French spy—" Suzanne shook her head.

"Quite," Malcolm said, his voice grim.

"The attacks on you didn't stop with Lady Julia's death," Suzanne added. "So this mysterious person who was running the Silver Hawk is still intent on his mission."

"His inexplicable mission," Malcolm said. "Addison's tailing Dumont, and I have someone on Vedrin as well. We need to make a late appearance at Lady Conyngham's party."

Davenport raised his brows.

"Because that's where we'll find Wellington," Malcolm said.

Wellington stared from Malcolm to Davenport to Suzanne. They were in a small salon in Lady Conyngham's elegant Brussels house. "You're sure?"

"Unless Vedrin and Dumont were engaged in a very elaborate charade," Malcolm said. "Which stretches the bounds of belief even in this business."

"Good God." Wellington exchanged a look with Stuart, who was in the salon with them. "Julia Ashton was—"

"It's never wise to underestimate a woman, Your Grace," Suzanne said.

"As you've taught me, my dear." Wellington spared her a brief smile, though the worry didn't leave his eyes. "But you're extraordinary."

"Evidently Lady Julia was as well," Malcolm said.

"That's one word for it. Damnation." Wellington scowled at a gilt candelabrum. "The prince has returned to his Headquarters at Braine-le-Comte, but he'll be back tomorrow for the Duchess of Richmond's ball. He's to dine with me. We need to discover what he may have told Lady Julia." He looked at Malcolm. "You talk to him. He's more likely to admit his indiscretions to you."

"Of course," Malcolm said. "You think the ball will go forward tomorrow night?"

"We can't move until we're sure where the French attack is coming from. Meanwhile we need to keep things as normal as possible in Brussels."

"We'll need to learn what Ashton may have told his wife as well," Stuart said.

Wellington nodded. "Davenport, he's your brother-in-law. You have—"

"Something in common?" Davenport said, his dry voice more taut than usual. "Both being betrayed by Brooke sisters?"

"He's likeliest to talk to you," Wellington said. "Take Rannoch with you. You have men following both Dumont and Vedrin?"

Malcolm nodded.

"We'll have to take Dumont and the other soldiers in the spy ring in before we march. And do something about Vedrin."

"That may create diplomatic complications," Stuart said. "He's well connected, and it will be his word against Rannoch's and Davenport's. And Henri Rivaux's, but if we use Rivaux his friends will know he's betrayed them."

"Deal with it," Wellington said. "If—"

He was interrupted by a knock at the door from one of Lady Conyngham's footmen. "Your pardon, Your Grace. But there's a man asking for Monsieur Rannoch. A Monsieur Addison."

Wellington flicked a glance at Malcolm. "Show him in."

A few minutes later, the footman ushered Addison in through a side door. He wore a dark coat, breeches, and boots for his night of tailing, but as he stepped into the candlelight Suzanne saw dark patches of blood glistening on the fabric of his coat. She ran toward him. "Addison, you're—"

"I'm all right, madam." Addison gave her a faint smile. His fair hair, usually combed smooth, fell over his face. "It isn't my blood."

"Whose is it?" Malcolm asked.

"Monsieur Dumont's." Addison drew a breath. He looked as though he'd been running. "I was tailing him, keeping a safe distance back. He was set upon by thieves and knifed in the street. I ran forward, but by the time I reached him they'd run off and Dumont was dead. Once I'd ascertained I could do nothing for him, I went through his pockets." He glanced down at the bloodstains on his clothes, then reached into one of his pockets and pulled out a cloth-wrapped bundle. "All I found was this."

They all crowded round as Malcolm unwrapped the bundle.

Something sparkled in the candlelight. Inside the cloth was a sapphire-and-diamond necklace.

"This must be what Vedrin gave Dumont," Davenport said.

"What—?" Stuart asked.

"Funding, I suspect," Malcolm said. "They were smuggling jewels out of Brussels to support Bonaparte."

Wellington stared down at the glittering necklace. "So Johnny

Ashton's wife was helping supply funds to Napoleon Bonaparte. Funds which Bonaparte is even now using to march against us. We're about to fight an emperor, and now we're embroiled in a damned imperial scandal."

Malcolm stared at the candelabrum on the writing table in their bedchamber as he struck a flint to steel and each taper flared to life in turn. "Poor Lady Julia. Damnable to have done that to her."

"She made a choice." Suzanne dropped her shawl and reticule on the dressing table and began to peel off her gloves. The night's revelations pounded in her head.

Malcolm cast a quick glance at her as he set down the tinderbox. "You're usually more sympathetic with another woman."

Suzanne tugged at a glove. It had caught on her wedding ring. "Lady Julia was in a difficult situation. But she had choices. She could have told her husband the truth."

"One wonders why she didn't." Malcolm began to undo the buttons on his coat.

Suzanne watched her husband for a moment. Past choices gnawed at her mind. "She did no more than we've done. Just for the opposite side."

"We chose this life." He stripped off the coat, with a force that would no doubt horrify Addison, and flung it over the wing-back chair.

"It's not as though you've never recruited an agent," Suzanne pointed out.

"Recruited. Not blackmailed. Though God knows—"

In his eyes, she could see the ghosts of farmers, prostitutes, soldiers, and priests who had lost their lives in the Peninsula as British agents. "Guilt is a singularly useless emotion, darling." God knows she said as much to herself often enough. She pulled the glove from her fingertips. "Lady Julia may have been blackmailed into her work, but she obviously had an aptitude for it. Surprisingly so for an untrained agent."

"Are you suggesting this goes back farther than Brussels?"

"No, that doesn't make a great deal of sense." She dropped the glove beside her scarf and reticule, frowning at the tangle of ivory silk, embroidered silver net, and beaded champagne satin. "Perhaps Lady Julia found she enjoyed the chance to be more than the perfect wife."

He shot a look at her. "You identify with her."

"Hardly." She swallowed, tasting bitter dregs. "I'd never claim to be a perfect wife."

"You know very well what people think about you." The smile faded from his eyes. "But Lady Julia was—"

"Betraying her husband rather than working with him?" Suzanne kept her gaze steady on her husband's face as she dropped the second glove on the dressing table. "All couples are different, darling. We already knew she was able to betray John Ashton in some ways."

"The question is which came first. We don't know that any of her love affairs began before the spying." Malcolm stared at his shirt cuff as he unfastened it.

"Apparently this all began because she didn't want her husband to know about her gambling debts. So she cared what he thought."

"Or she was afraid of him." Malcolm undid the other shirt cuff. "If she knew he was having an affair with Violet Chase—"

"That might have made her angry," Suzanne said. "Or hurt. But it wouldn't have made her fear him."

"If she suspected he wanted to find a way out of their marriage—"

Suzanne stared through the candlelight at him. "Is this my husband the rationalist talking? Darling, are you suggesting Julia Ashton wrote to her sister that she was afraid because she'd learned her husband was plotting to kill her so he could marry Violet Chase?"

"No. Maybe." He scraped a hand through his hair. "I'm trying to come up with a thesis that fits the facts. And yet I can't help thinking—"

"What?"

He crossed to the dressing table. "The look on Ashton's face last night when he learned about Lady Julia's affair with the Prince of Orange. Whoever betrayed whom first, I'd swear he was in genuine torment." He reached out and pulled her abruptly into his arms.

"Malcolm—" Suzanne said, half a laugh, half a gasp of surprise.

He took her face between his hands. She could feel his fingers trembling. "How by all that's holy did I wind up with you?"

Her breath caught in her throat. "I ask myself the same thing every day, darling."

"You made the best of a difficult bargain."

She kissed him, because she didn't trust herself to speak.

The sun beat down on the cobblestones. Suzanne's chemise clung to her skin and the lace of her mantilla seemed to be plastered to her neck and shoulders. At least it wasn't as heavy as a cloak. And it let her blend in with the other Bruxellois hurrying along the street. She stopped to buy oranges from a street-seller and put them in the basket she carried over her arm, a matron doing her marketing. She turned down a side street, keeping her pace steady.

The shade offered by the close-set buildings was a welcome relief. Laundry flapped overhead in the faint breeze. The side street was empty, but she continued her slow pace and pulled her shopping list from her basket. One never knew who might be watching from an overhanging window.

Near the gilded magnificence of the Place Royale, she went down a flight of stone steps to the Rue d'Isabelle, thrown into shadows by the taller buildings that crowded round it, nodded at a woman watering the flowers in her window box, stopped to pet a cat dozing in the sun, and then turned down a narrow alley. Even in the middle of the afternoon, little sun leached between the close-set buildings in the medieval part of the city. She pulled a key from the bottom of her basket and unlocked the third door. She pushed it open and stepped into a close passage that smelled faintly of damp. Down the passage, up the splintery flight of stairs. At the stair head, she gave a thrush's call. An answering call sounded from behind the first door. Suzanne drew a breath and turned the door handle.

Raoul O'Roarke was sitting on a ladder-back chair at a small table, turning the pages of *Le Moniteur,* as impeccably dressed as he had been at the opera last night, though he wore a pale gray coat, pantaloons, and Hessians. He got to his feet at her entrance. "What is it? You know it's risky—"

"This couldn't wait." She threw her basket on the narrow cot against the wall. "Why the hell didn't you tell me that Julia Ashton was one of ours?"

❧ 23 ❧

Raoul stared at her, frozen in rare shock. *"Querida—"*
"Don't you dare." She closed the distance between them.
"Whose idea was it to kill Malcolm?"

He reached for her hands. "For God's sake, you can't—"

Suzanne jerked her hands from his grip and seized the lapels of
his coat. "We're talking about my husband."

"Give me a moment to catch up. I'm not as quick as I once was.
You're saying Julia Ashton was a French spy?"

"Don't you dare pretend you didn't know."

"I'm not pretending."

"You bastard." She could feel the hot, close air clawing at her
skin. "I knew you didn't tell me everything, but to keep me in the
dark about this—"

"Suzanne." He took her shoulders in a hard clasp. "I didn't
know. I didn't have the least suspicion. I swear it."

She looked into his gray eyes, familiar yet elusive. She could almost always tell when he was lying. Almost. "You can't expect me
to believe—"

"You know what a web intelligence is. On the British side as
well as ours." His gaze held her own, calm and steady. "No one
knows every agent."

"You—"

"Even me. I'm good, but I'm not that good. Use your head, *querida*. If I had known, don't you think I'd have told you after Julia Ashton died? For fear of what you might uncover in the investigation?"

"I didn't tell you I was investigating."

"First you credit me with omniscience, then you treat me like a blind fool. Do you imagine I didn't know Malcolm was investigating Lady Julia's death? And that of course you were helping him?"

She released a breath. "I concede the point."

"Progress." His grip slid from her shoulders to her arms. He drew her over to the cot and pulled up the ladder-back chair beside her. "Tell me what you know."

She recounted what they'd uncovered about Julia Ashton's work for the French as the Silver Hawk.

"Dangerous to create an agent through blackmail," Raoul said. "Messy, and they tend to be unreliable."

"According to Vedrin she was run by someone getting orders directly from Paris. That person ordered her to kill Malcolm." She scanned Raoul's face again, lean, fine boned, elusive.

He returned her gaze, his own unexpectedly open. "Do you really think I'd be capable of killing Malcolm? I've known him since he was a boy, even if we did end up on opposite sides."

"Since when have you been one to let friendship stand in your way?"

He watched her in silence for a moment. "Do you think I'd be capable of killing him knowing what he's come to mean to you?"

"Not lightly." She kept her gaze locked on his. "But if you thought it important enough—"

He gave an odd, twisted smile. "There are some things you still don't know about me, *querida*."

"You're right. I don't know how far you'll go."

"Or where I'll stop." He leaned toward her, hands on his knees. "Consider it practically then. You're of much more use to me as the wife of Malcolm Rannoch, diplomat and British agent, than you would be as a widow."

She flinched at the word "widow." "Who would want to kill Malcolm?"

"I don't know." For a moment, she'd swear she saw unbanked rage in Raoul's eyes.

The air seemed to have grown even warmer since she entered the room, heavy with the promise of rain. She tugged her mantilla from her head. "Is it true?" She stripped off her gloves. "That the French have crossed the frontier?"

His gaze flickered over her face as though it were enemy terrain.

"Dear God." She stared at the only person in the world to whom she'd told the unvarnished truth since she was fifteen. "You don't trust me."

"It's not a question of trust. You know as well as I do it makes no sense to reveal non-essential information."

"Three years ago you'd have told me."

"Three years ago you weren't the wife of a British agent."

"Whom I married on your orders to spy for France."

"My suggestion, not my orders." Raoul sat back in his chair and crossed his legs. "I recall quite distinctly telling you you'd have to decide for yourself."

She glanced away, fingers locked on her elbows. It seemed a world away, but she could vividly recall that meeting, in a garret room in Lisbon not unlike this one, the bite of late November sharp in the air. The British diplomat she'd met on a mission had unexpectedly proposed to her, thinking she'd been left alone and penniless when her parents were killed in the war. She'd gone to Raoul to ask what to do. She'd been startled, aware of the dangers and opportunities, intrigued by the challenge.

She hadn't had the least idea what she was getting into.

"It was also before you fell in love with him," Raoul said in a quiet voice.

Suzanne met the gaze of her former lover. "You think I've gone soft."

"I think you're under unbearable strain. It isn't just Malcolm. It's Somerset and March and Gordon and Canning and all the others you talk about. They've become your friends. Believe me, I know. All those years in Spain pretending I was allied with the British. I formed friendships myself. With people who are my friends to this day. Who haven't the least idea of my true loyalties. But I was never as deeply immersed in British diplomatic and military circles as you are."

She closed her arms over her chest. "I managed in Vienna. I knew how I felt about Malcolm then."

"But reporting on the deliberations in Vienna, with so many different sides and with just about everyone dealing in intelligence, was quite different from passing on Wellington's plans in the buildup to armed conflict. With your friends—and the husband you love—on the opposite side."

Her fingers dug deeper into her arms. "It doesn't change what I believe in. It doesn't change the fact that I think Bonaparte's return is the best hope we have for retaining some trace of liberty, equality, and fraternity. If I didn't, do you think I'd have done what I've done? Lied to my husband, deceived my friends, made a mockery of every vow I've ever sworn—"

"No." His gaze moved over her face. "I don't expect you to believe this, but I trust you as much as I've ever trusted anyone."

For a moment she was fifteen again, the angry, defiant girl whose father had raised her on Paine and Locke and Beaumarchais, who had seen her father and sister killed by British soldiers, who had been left broken and alone in a strange city. The girl Raoul O'Roarke had found in a brothel, restored to a sense of purpose, trained as an agent. She'd been playing a part for so long she sometimes forgot who she really was. But somewhere beneath the silk and goffered linen and canvas stays of Mrs. Malcolm Rannoch, the core of that girl remained. A girl who would put her cause ahead of all else.

She remembered March and Fitzroy the previous night. Cheerful, loyal, about to charge off to a battle she was doing everything in her power to ensure they lost. "I am getting soft."

"You're better than you ever were. I'm only afraid you'll break your health."

"I'm fine." She met his gaze. "If Julia Ashton was being run from Paris, that means someone in Paris wants Malcolm dead."

"So it does." His mouth turned grim.

"Why?"

"I don't know."

"You wouldn't tell me if you did know."

"Perhaps not. But as it happens, I truly haven't the least idea. God knows the British would feel your husband's absence. But it would hardly turn the tide of the war."

"You sound like Malcolm. He's refusing to take the whole thing seriously."

"*Querida*—" He reached out and gripped her hand. "I'll learn what I can. My word on it."

His promise was ridiculously warming. "Thank you. And Julia Ashton?"

"I have every faith that you and Malcolm can discover who killed her. And I've heard excellent reports of Harry Davenport."

"No matter where the investigation takes us?"

"I trust you to be careful."

She picked up her gloves and drew them through her fingers. The bars of light coming through the high window glinted off her wedding band. "Harry Davenport's wife hurt him so much I doubt he'll ever be able to trust again. When I think of what I've done to Malcolm—"

"There are different kinds of betrayal," Raoul said.

She looked up, conscious of the pressure of his gaze. "You never asked me to seduce a powerful man after I married Malcolm. A Lord Uxbridge or a Prince of Orange."

"No."

"I could have discovered useful information. I did often enough before I married Malcolm." And, if she was honest with herself, at times she'd enjoyed the challenge.

A muscle flexed beside his mouth. He'd always been calmly matter-of-fact about the missions she embarked on that could involve seduction. "It was different after you married Malcolm."

"Why? It's all part of the job, that's what you told me. You've done the same yourself."

"Very true. But for all my roles, I've never played the part of a loyal spouse."

"Played."

"You could have lost Malcolm's trust and any information you can get from him. And you could have destroyed your marriage."

She gave a short laugh.

"However it began, your marriage is a very real thing."

"A real thing built on lies and deceit."

"You told me once that though he might not know your true name, Malcolm knew you as no one else ever had. Even me."

She remembered that conversation keenly. Fresh from her first visit to Britain as Malcolm's wife. Still reeling from the wondrous, painful realization that she'd fallen in love with the man she'd married. For days together she'd been determined to stop spying. She'd even contemplated telling her husband the truth. She'd told Raoul as much when she'd met him in secret on the way to Vienna for the Congress. To be fair, he'd replied that she'd have to do as she saw fit. Had he seen how it would be even then? Because when she'd reached Vienna it had been all too clear how things stood. The powers that be—including Britain's foreign secretary, Lord Castlereagh—were determined to turn back the clock to the ancien régime. To get rid of every reform made in Europe for the past twenty-five years. To stifle all dissent for fear of revolution. That wasn't the world she wanted her son to grow up in.

And so while her husband, who by no means wanted such a world himself, had performed his duties as an attaché and argued with Castlereagh over the port, she'd gone on passing information to Raoul. And when Napoleon Bonaparte escaped from Elba, she'd been aware of a mingled rush of fear and hope.

She picked up her mantilla and gloves and got to her feet. "I should get back. Malcolm has gone with Harry Davenport to talk to John Ashton."

Raoul got to his feet as well. "One way or another it will all be over soon."

She flung the mantilla over her shoulders. "I'm supposed to find that comforting?"

"No. But it will let you move forward."

She froze in the midst of drawing on her gloves and studied his face. His cheekbones were white, his mouth taut with strain. And his eyes—"You're terrified."

"My dear. How could I not be?" He took her ungloved hand and lifted it to his lips with a formality that carried tenderness but no echo of a lover. "Are you going to be all right?"

She pulled her hand from his clasp and tugged on her second glove. "What would you do if I said I wasn't?"

"Get you out of here."

She jerked her mantilla over her shoulders. "Even you aren't so omnipotent."

"Trust me, if necessary I'd arrange it."

"I'll manage. I'm not a fool."

"You're human. Something we forget at our peril." He hesitated, as though perhaps about to say something more. "Be careful, *querida*."

"I always am." She picked up her basket. "You trained me well."

John Ashton stared from Malcolm to Davenport. "This is a damnable time to be making jokes, Rannoch."

"I'm afraid it's no joke," Malcolm said. "I'm sorry, Ashton."

"No." Ashton spun away and took a turn round the Headquarters sitting room where they were closeted. "For God's sake I knew my own wife." He gave a rough laugh. "God, that's rich. Yes, she deceived me with another man. But Julia wouldn't—"

"I'm afraid there's no doubt," Malcolm said.

Ashton stared at him with eyes like glass blasted by a shell. "She can't have known what she was doing."

"Vedrin was blackmailing her," Malcolm said. "She was in an impossible situation."

"But she could have told me."

"Why didn't she?" Davenport, leaning against the wall, spoke with the quiet of an assassin about to slide a knife from the scabbard.

"I don't know." Ashton ran a hand over his hair. "We quarreled over her debts early in our marriage. But I settled everything up."

"And if you'd found out she was in debt again?"

"I'd have been angry, but I wouldn't—"

"Wouldn't what?" Davenport asked, with the same deceptive quiet.

"My God." Ashton stared at him. "You think I—What? That I'd have beat her if she'd told me? Thrown her from the house? What kind of monster do you think I am?"

"I don't think anything yet, Ashton," Davenport said. "Insufficient data. But the evidence suggests Julia was afraid of you."

"Damn you—" Ashton lunged across the room and smashed his fist into Davenport's jaw. Davenport tumbled to the floorboards.

Malcolm ran forward. Davenport waved him off and pushed himself up on one elbow. "You have a right to be in a temper, Ashton."

"I don't hit women. I'd never have hurt Julia."

"It's difficult to know what one might do in a temper." Davenport got to his feet, wincing at the pressure on his bad arm. "I've surprised myself with my own behavior on more than one occasion."

"You think—" Ashton stared at him, as though the full extent of the nightmare was dawning on him. "You think I was behind Julia's death."

"I think a man who learned his wife had not only betrayed him with a lover but had betrayed the country for which he risked his life would be under considerable strain."

Ashton flinched at hearing his wife's crimes put into words. "But I didn't know."

"So you said."

"But you're not sure." Ashton's gaze flickered from Davenport to Malcolm.

"We can't be," Malcolm said. "What might you have told your wife that she could have passed along to the French?"

"Nothing. I didn't discuss my work with her. Julia seemed to have no interest in it." His eyes darkened, a man sifting through his memories and twisting every one to see it in a new light. "If she was spying for the French wouldn't she have tried to draw me out?"

"Perhaps she didn't want to make you suspicious with changed behavior." Malcolm watched Ashton for a moment. "Could she have known about your involvement with Violet Chase?"

"My what?" Ashton's eyes widened, but Malcolm caught a flash of guilt in their depths.

"You and Miss Chase were seen embracing in the garden at Stuart's ball," Malcolm said.

Ashton drew a shuddering breath. "Oh, dear God. I should have known."

24

Suzanne slipped through a side door to the shop of Madame Longé, the dressmaker who was one of her best sources in Brussels. She returned her basket to the back of a cupboard in the storeroom, removed her mantilla and gloves, and donned the chip straw hat and gauze scarf in which she had left the Rue Ducale. It took her three tries to fasten the satin ribbons into anything approaching a bow, but by the time she was tugging on the second of her threadnet gloves her hands had very nearly stopped shaking.

Ridiculous. She had been a spy for nearly six years. She had been lying to her husband from the day they met. She had confronted the fact that she loved him and made the decision that it didn't change what she believed in. She had perfected the art of keeping her life in neat boxes and laughing in defiance at the risk that the boxes might come tumbling down about her ears. She had learned to sip champagne and eat lobster patties and ignore the bitter aftertaste of betrayal.

It shouldn't be different now. She couldn't afford to let it be different. She drew a breath that shuddered against her corset laces, tugged the ribbons on her hat tighter, and stepped into the front of the shop. After stopping to collect the new gown of pearl-beaded silver gauze over ivory satin that she'd ordered for the Duchess of

Richmond's ball, she swept out the front door, a lady of fashion who had spent the morning at a fitting.

In the Rue Ducale, Valentin informed her that Lady Cordelia Davenport had called with a young lady and that they were waiting for her in the garden.

Stepping through the French window into the garden, Suzanne saw that the young lady was very young indeed. Not yet four by the look of it. She was crouched on the flagstones with Colin, lining up his lead soldiers. Cordelia and Blanca sat at the wrought-iron table watching the children.

"You must be Livia," Suzanne said.

Livia Davenport got to her feet and curtsied. She had blond hair, several shades paler than her mother's, and her mother's blue eyes and heart-shaped face. Whoever Livia's father might be, she bore little resemblance to him.

"I'm sorry." Cordelia got to her feet as Suzanne came toward her. "Livia was reluctant to see me leave without her. I had to tell her yesterday that her aunt Julia died, and though I've tried to say nothing about the coming battle, I think she understands something is about to happen."

"Children always seem to." Suzanne looked at her son. He and Livia had returned to lining up the lead soldiers in a bed of lavender. Suzanne recalled Colin flinging his arms round Fitzroy Somerset's legs three days before. Colin thought of Fitzroy and March and Canning and Gordon as uncles. In the Peninsula Colin had been too young to understand when friends died. That wouldn't be true of this battle.

But the sight of her son steadied her. One couldn't break down round children, so one simply didn't. "I'm glad you brought her. It's good for Colin to have a friend to play with."

Cordelia's gaze moved over Suzanne's face. "Are the rumors true? That Bonaparte's finally crossed the frontier?"

"It seems so."

Beneath the brim of her willow shavings bonnet Cordelia's face drained of color. Suzanne put a hand on the other woman's arm and pressed her into one of the wrought-iron chairs.

"I'll get some lemonade," Blanca said, darting a quick glance between the women. She moved toward the house, stopping to admire Colin and Livia's efforts with the soldiers.

"I'm sorry," Cordelia said. "I didn't mean to be such a fool."

Suzanne dropped into a chair across from her. "It still may come to nothing."

"Spoken like a diplomatic wife." Cordelia glanced at her daughter for a moment, then turned her gaze back to Suzanne. "It's odd. I knew I might see Harry when I was in Paris last year, but he was off on a mission. By design, I've often thought."

"And you weren't sure whether you were relieved or sorry?"

Cordelia's mouth twisted. "Perhaps. Going to Paris was an act of recklessness. But then I've always been known for my reckless behavior. And of course I knew I might see him in Brussels. On the journey across the Channel and the drive from Ostend every moment I wasn't worrying about Julia, I was imaging my meeting with Harry. Playing out every possible scenario. I was so worried about seeing him again, I never considered that this might be the last time I saw him at all."

"Malcolm isn't a soldier, but I feel a knot of panic whenever he goes off on a mission."

"You're very kind, Mrs. Rannoch. You're sympathizing without pointing out that Harry's been in danger the better part of these past four years and I've made no attempt to see him. To all practical purposes he's not even my husband."

"I wouldn't dream of suggesting anything of the sort."

"Because you're too tactful."

"Because I've seen you and Colonel Davenport together enough to know that whatever is between you it isn't nothing."

Cordelia glanced at her daughter again. A smile twisted her lips. "We lived together for a year. I'm not entirely heartless. I somehow always thought—" She shook her head. "I'm not sure what I thought. Except that it wouldn't end like this. One got used to it during the war, of course. The constant knowledge that people one knew were in danger. The moment of terror when the casualty lists came out. But somehow it still seemed distant. I suppose you grew accustomed to it, living in the Peninsula."

"I don't think one ever grows accustomed to it." Particularly when one was working for the opposite side from one's husband and his friends. "But perhaps one learns to manage the fear." Suzanne looked at Cordelia for a moment. "Your husband has been in battle many times. As has Major Chase."

Cordelia's shoulders jerked, but she met Suzanne's gaze squarely. "George has a wife. He isn't mine to worry about."

"That doesn't necessarily stop anyone from worrying."

Memories shot through Cordelia's gaze. "I talked to George last night. About Julia. But—" Despite the afternoon heat, she rubbed her arms, bare between her gloves and the puffed muslin sleeves of her gown. "I told him what we had would have turned to ashes sooner or later. I still believe it."

"But you can't be sure."

Cordelia stared down at her gloved fingers digging into the flesh of her arms. "A part of me will always be the sixteen-year-old who fell in love with him over the Christmas punch bowl."

For a moment Suzanne saw Raoul, when she had left him just now, and then when she, too, had been sixteen. Already hardened and cynical yet desperate for something to believe in. Whatever else he had done, he would always be the man who had restored her to a sense of purpose. "A first love is always a first love," she said.

Cordelia studied her for a moment but didn't ask the obvious question. "Of all the damnable times to be wallowing in my own past." She swallowed and folded her hands in her lap. "You learned something yesterday."

"Yes."

"But you can't tell me. I understand. I didn't come here to wheedle or beg."

"There's one thing I can tell you. That I'd like your help with." Suzanne recounted Sarah Lennox's story about Violet Chase and then Fitzroy Somerset's account of finding Violet and John Ashton embracing in the garden at Stuart's ball. She phrased this last carefully, for she knew Cordelia was fond of her brother-in-law.

Cordelia squeezed her eyes shut. "Damnation. I thought Johnny was prevaricating about something when we talked about Julia, but I never suspected—"

"It was clear yesterday that Miss Chase still cares for him."

"But I'd swear Johnny—" Cordelia shook her head. "After what I've learned in the past two days, I shouldn't be surprised by any revelation."

"Will you go with me to talk to Miss Chase?"

"You think Violet will tell me the truth?"

"I think you'll have the best chance of determining how much truth there is in whatever story she gives us."

The footman at the Chase house informed Suzanne and Cordelia that Miss Chase had taken the children to the park. Suzanne and Cordelia proceeded thither and found Violet on one of the gravel walks with her niece and nephew and a nursemaid.

Violet was bent over her nephew, a boy of about eighteen months, helping pull a wooden horse along the gravel. An unusual image for the stylish Violet Chase. She went still when she looked up to see Suzanne and Cordelia approaching. Then Violet murmured something to her nephew and the nurse who was pushing a baby carriage. "Cordelia. Mrs. Rannoch." Violet walked forward. "I didn't expect to see you again so soon."

"It's good to get the children out-of-doors," Suzanne said.

Violet glanced at her nephew and the baby. "Tony has been trying to convince Jane to go to Antwerp. Jane's been refusing in unusually sharp tones. All the while I think they're really arguing about something else entirely. I decided to take the children and escape the house."

"Sensible," Cordelia said.

Violet pushed a ringlet, damp from perspiration in the heat, beneath the brim of her leghorn bonnet. "Tony seems to think we're really in for fighting this time, but I saw Georgy Lennox a quarter hour ago, and she says Lord Hill assured them the talk of imminent battle is unfounded. I suppose it's a good thing I had my maid lay out my dress for her mother's ball tonight."

"If Mrs. Chase goes to Antwerp will you go with her?" Suzanne asked.

"Of course not." Violet straightened her shoulders. "If there is a battle, both my brothers will be in it."

"Not to mention Johnny," Cordelia said.

Violet lifted her chin. "I'm still fond of him."

Cordelia returned her gaze. "I've been so focused on what Julia was doing the night of Stuart's ball, I've quite forgot about other people and what they might have seen. Sarah Lennox told Mrs. Rannoch she found you in some distress that night."

Fear shot into Violet's eyes. She opened her mouth as though to deny Lady Sarah's report, then spun away and stared at the refreshment pavilion, toward which the nurse was being pulled by young Master Chase. "I should have known Sarah couldn't keep her mouth shut."

Cordelia touched her friend's shoulder. "Violet—"

Violet jerked away from Cordelia's touch. "I told Sarah what happened. Eddy Featherstonaugh made himself disagreeable in the garden. I'm not as used to those things as you are."

"Point taken," Cordelia said.

"But you don't believe me."

"Sarah didn't."

"Sarah Lennox is a—Oh, what's the use." Violet flung up her hands. "You want to know what I was doing. We none of us seem to be able to have secrets anymore."

"Anything anyone may have seen that night could be important," Suzanne said.

"Isn't it obvious?" Violet returned. "I slipped out of the ballroom, stole a horse from Stuart's stables, rode to the Château de Vere, and shot Julia."

"Very funny," Cordelia said.

"So you don't think I'm capable of it?"

"I don't think you'd have ridden all that way in a ball dress."

"I might if I'd been determined enough. But I—" Violet's brows drew together.

"Vi—" Cordelia touched her arm again.

Violet scowled at the crowd round the refreshment pavilion, but this time she didn't pull away. "If you must know, I saw Julia slip out of the ballroom. Not knowing she was engaged in more than one illicit liaison, I was sure she was going to meet Tony. I was going to confront them. I thought perhaps that would shame her into ending the affair."

Cordelia shot a quick glance at Suzanne. They'd been prepared for Violet not to tell them about her tryst with John Ashton, but they hadn't expected more revelations about Julia. "And—?" Cordelia asked.

Violet folded her arms across her chest. "I followed her into the garden. She did meet Tony. By the yew hedge."

Suzanne exchanged a quick look with Cordelia. "Did you confront them?"

Violet stirred a fallen leaf with the toe of her Roman sandal. "I was going to. But once I got close enough to hear what they were saying, it seemed more awkward than I expected. And they weren't in each other's arms. They were quarreling."

"What about?" Suzanne asked, keeping her voice steady and gentle. If this was a story, it was a surprisingly detailed one.

Violet frowned as though still puzzled by the memory. "I think Julia was trying to break off the affair. At one point Tony seized her arms, and I heard him say, 'It can't end so easily. Surely you realize that.' Julia pulled away and said, 'You can't ask such a thing of me.' I thought perhaps she'd actually taken our conversation to heart. If she was ending things, the last thing I wanted was to interrupt. Then they moved farther away, and I couldn't hear what they were saying. Finally Tony flung away from her and stalked back into the ballroom."

"And Julia?" Cordelia asked.

"She ran across the garden toward the wall. I suddenly didn't want her to see me. If she'd been angry at me, she might have taken Tony back out of spite. As it was, I suppose she went off to her rendezvous with the Prince of Orange."

"She went off to her death," Cordelia said.

Violet bit her lip, but her eyes were defiant. "I know what you're thinking. About Tony being angry at her. That's why I didn't tell you this yesterday. But I followed him back into the ballroom, and he was in the ballroom the rest of the night." She looked between Suzanne and Cordelia. "I swear I overheard them."

"I'm not questioning that," Suzanne said. "It's just that we heard a different story about your being in the garden from another source. Who saw you with Captain Ashton."

Violet's face drained of color, as though she had stumbled into a nightmare. "Oh, poison. I should have known."

❧ 25 ❧

"Oh, dear God." John Ashton looked from Malcolm to Davenport, eyes dark, mouth white. "I should have known."

"That you'd be caught?" Davenport asked.

"Yes. No. It wasn't like that. You can't think Violet—I would never—"

"Do you deny you were in the garden with her at the ball?" Davenport said.

"No." Guilt settled over Ashton's features. He stared straight at them, as though forcing himself to confront his sins. "Violet and I—we were once practically betrothed. Davenport will remember. I didn't serve her a very good turn when I married Julia. There was some unpleasantness."

"Tony Chase planted you a facer at Boodle's," Malcolm said.

"Yes. In retrospect I deserved it." Memories shot through Ashton's gaze. He swallowed. "But at the ball I found myself standing beside Violet. I asked her to dance. To my surprise she agreed. We talked about inconsequential things. Safe topics. But for a moment it was as though it was three years ago and life was infinitely simpler." Ashton took a quick turn about the room. "After the dance we walked out onto the terrace and into the garden. I think we were still both caught in the spell of the past. I know I was." For a moment that spell showed in his eyes. "I didn't intend—Things hadn't been as easy as they might between Julia and me of late. With my duties and the constant round of entertainments we often only seemed to see each other in passing and when we did—" He shook his head. "We'd had a stupid quarrel two days before when I suggested she take our son and return to England. That was the most emotion there'd been between us in weeks."

"And so that evening with Miss Chase you found yourself wondering if you'd married the wrong girl," Davenport said.

"No. That is—Truth to tell, I didn't think at all." Ashton met Davenport's hard stare, his own gaze wracked with torment. "You mustn't think any dishonor attaches to Miss Chase. I should have known better—And then, only a short time later, to learn that Julia was dead—"

"And you were a free man," Davenport murmured.

Ashton lurched toward him. "Damn it, Davenport—"

Malcolm moved to intervene. But Ashton drew a rough breath, as though forcing the lid down on his anger. "You're doing what you need to do. What you have to do to learn who killed Julia and why. And by God I want you to discover that."

"Oh, poison." Violet looked from Suzanne to Cordelia. "I should have known."

"Interesting," Cordelia said. "I thought you'd deny it."

Violet flung up her lavender-kid-gloved hands. "What's the good of denying anything? Mrs. Rannoch and her husband seem to have an uncanny knack for uncovering uncomfortable secrets." She drew a breath. "I really did overhear Julia and Tony. Telling you that seemed the lesser of two evils. That was after Johnny and I—After we went into the garden."

"I know Johnny still means a great deal to you," Cordelia said. "It's not surprising that you—"

Violet gave a dry laugh. "You think Johnny and I were having an affair? Sorry to disappoint you, Cordy, it's not nearly so scandalous. But you're right that I never got over him. And suddenly there's no guarantee who'll be alive in a few weeks. Or even days." The fear that they all lived with welled up in her eyes. "Which is why I blatantly put myself in Johnny's way at the ball. So he more or less had to ask me to dance. And then after the dance, I said I was overcome by the heat and could we go out into the garden. Most gentlemen would see that as the invitation it was, but Johnny's far too honorable. I don't think anyone could have been more surprised than he was when I practically flung myself into his arms."

"Apparently he didn't push you away," Cordelia said, her voice surprisingly gentle.

"No." Violet glanced to the side, as though the memory was too private to share. "I think for a moment we were both caught up in the past. And perhaps Johnny wasn't as happy with Julia as everyone liked to believe." Her gaze moved back to Cordelia. "But *he'd* never have betrayed *her*."

Malcolm and Davenport found Lieutenant-Colonel the Hon. Sir Alexander Gordon lounging in a straight-back chair in the outer office at Headquarters, playing backgammon with Colonel Canning. Wellington's aides-de-camp had a tendency to lounge about when they weren't galloping hell for leather to deliver messages in seemingly impossible amounts of times.

"Back already?" Gordon asked as Malcolm and Davenport entered the room. "I thought you lot were supposed to be figuring out what the devil the French are up to so the rest of us can figure out when we're supposed to go charging into the cannon's mouth."

Malcolm grinned. He'd been one year behind Gordon at Harrow and had worked with his elder brother, Lord Aberdeen, in the diplomatic corps. "We're doing our best. Could we have a word, Gordon?"

"Good Lord." Gordon pushed back his chair. "I seem to be important all of a sudden."

Fitzroy, as usual working away at dispatches, lifted his head. "Don't give Gordon any ideas. He'll be insufferable."

"He's insufferable already," Canning said. "Don't forget you owed me twenty pounds when we left off, Gordon."

"You wound me," Gordon said, hand on his heart. "I never forget a debt."

"Hmph," Canning said.

Gordon accompanied Malcolm and Davenport into the same antechamber in which they'd spoken with John Ashton. "What's so serious?" he asked. "Aside from the fact that we're about to go off to the worst battle of our lives."

Malcolm closed the door and leaned against it. "March mentioned last night that you were gone from Stuart's ball for over an hour."

Gordon gave a visible start. He was a clever man, but he didn't have an agent's skills at dissembling. He flung himself into a chair with a grin that was a shade too deliberate. "Good God. Surely you don't think I had something to do with Julia Ashton's death? She was a lovely lady, but—Oh, sorry, Davenport. I forget she was your sister-in-law. My condolences."

"Thank you," Davenport said. "We're interested in anything unusual that happened at the ball and anything anyone might have seen."

"Wish I could help, but I didn't see anything."

"Where did you go?" Davenport asked.

Gordon shifted in his chair. "Look, I know these are extraordinary circumstances, but as it happens I went to see a lady. Who happens to have a jealous husband. And her husband's Belgian, so the duke wouldn't like it. Stirring up trouble with the locals. Went straight there and came straight back. Didn't see Lady Julia or anyone else. So I'm afraid I can't help you, much as I'd like to be at the heart of the drama. If—"

"Damn it, Gordon," Malcolm said.

"What?"

"From the time we were at Harrow, it's meant one thing when you shift in your chair like that."

"What?"

"That you're lying."

Gordon pushed himself to his feet. "That's a damned nasty accusation."

"And whenever anyone calls you on it, you get all huffy."

Gordon grimaced. "You're a good fellow, Malcolm, but you've

always been too clever for your own good. Not everyone is as devious as your spy friends."

Malcolm crossed to Gordon's side. "Where did you really go the night of the ball?"

"I told you." Gordon straightened his shoulders, as though waiting to confront an enemy charge. "Take me before the duke. I'll say the same."

Malcolm looked into the gaze of his school friend. "Then you'd be lying to him as well."

"Malcolm thought Captain Chase was lying about something," Suzanne said, as she and Cordelia settled themselves back at the wrought-iron table in the garden in the Rue Ducale. "This could explain it."

"But was he lying because he couldn't bear to admit Julia had broken with him?" Cordelia asked. "Or because he feared her breaking with him would cast suspicion on him? Or—?" She glanced at Colin and Livia, now giving the lead soldiers a ride round the garden in Colin's wooden wagon. "I never did believe Julia could really be planning to run off with Tony, whatever Tony claimed. Whatever George told me last night." She threw her gloves on the table. "And then there's Johnny and Violet."

"Do you believe Miss Chase's account?"

"I'm inclined to. But perhaps it's only because for some reason I cling to the idea that Johnny wouldn't have betrayed Julia. I suppose I need to believe someone I know is incapable of betrayal. Besides you and Mr. Rannoch."

Suzanne's fingernail caught on the threadnet of her own glove. "There are as many types of betrayal as there are people to commit it. If—"

The click of the French window interrupted her. Suzanne looked round, expecting Blanca, who had gone inside for more lemonade. Instead her husband and Cordelia's stepped into the garden.

"I'm glad you're here, Lady Cordelia," Malcolm said, walking forward quickly. "We—"

He broke off. Beside him, Harry Davenport had gone absolutely still. His gaze was fixed not on his wife but on young Livia, tugging at the wagon that had got stuck on a flagstone.

As though aware of his regard, Livia glanced up and studied him with wide blue eyes.

"Colonel 'Port." Colin ran over to fling his arms round Davenport's boots.

"How do you do, old chap." Davenport bent down to ruffle Colin's hair. His face was nearly as pale as the points of his shirt.

Livia stood studying the new arrival.

Cordelia took a step toward her daughter, then checked herself. She and Davenport both went still, frozen in an agony of uncertainty.

Confronting an inevitable moment that plainly neither of them was ready for.

❧ 26 ❧

Suzanne felt the tension between Harry and Cordelia Davenport like a physical force in the air. Her own heartbeat seemed to have stilled. Malcolm was standing as though holding every muscle in check.

"You must be Livia." Davenport crouched down to her level, keeping one hand on Colin's shoulder. "My name is Harry. I haven't been in England for a long time." He paused, as though desperately seeking the right words. Or perhaps any words. "Not since before you were born, which is a great pity. I'm"—he hesitated for a few seconds that stretched like an eternity—"I'm your papa."

Cordelia's shoulders tensed, but she stayed where she was.

Livia continued to regard Davenport. Her gaze moved over him, as though he were a creature from a storybook suddenly come to life. "You're a soldier."

"So I am." Davenport kept his voice level, but Suzanne suspected if she were close enough she'd be able to see the pulse beating beneath his skin. "That's why I've been away from England."

Livia shifted her weight from one foot to the other. "Mummy told me. She says you're very brave."

Davenport was still pale as bleached linen, but his mouth twisted in a half smile. "Your mother can exaggerate."

"What's 'xaggerate?" Colin asked.

"Telling stories that go a bit beyond the truth. And in this case make me seem a good deal better than I am."

Cordelia opened her mouth, then bit back the words.

"I've seen a picture of you," Livia said. "In our house. In London. When you were a little boy. You look different now."

"It's been a very long time since I was a little boy."

Livia nodded. "I turned three in January."

"And I didn't send you a present. I have a great deal to make up for."

Livia dragged the toe of her black kid slipper over the flagstones. "Mummy says you're very busy."

Davenport's mouth relaxed into a smile, this one less bitter. "I don't think that's much of an excuse for not sending presents, do you?"

Livia considered this and shook her head vigorously. Then her face went solemn. "We came to Brussels to see Aunt Julia. Did you know her?"

The smile fled from Davenport's eyes. "Yes. She was a very lovely lady."

Livia's eyes fixed round and serious on his face. "She's dead."

"I know. I'm very sorry for it."

"Uncle Johnny was crying when we saw him yesterday, though he tried not to let us see. I don't think Robbie understands."

"Robbie isn't as grown-up as you. He's lucky to have you for a cousin."

Livia studied Davenport a few moments longer, then walked up to him, put her hand on his shoulder, and pressed a kiss to his cheek.

If Davenport had gone still before, Suzanne thought now his heart might well have stopped beating altogether. "Thank you," he said. "I'm honored."

Livia laughed. She had a warm, tinkling, infectious laugh. Suzanne suspected Cordelia had sounded much the same before life intervened.

Colin looked round at the adults, who had all gone silent again. "I'm hungry."

Malcolm stepped forward and took his son's hand. "Tell you what, old chap. Why don't Mummy and I take you and Livia to the kitchen and find you some lemonade and cookies."

Livia took Suzanne's hand with great readiness, but she cast a glance over her shoulder at her newfound father. Cordelia watched the tableau, eyes wide with something like wonder, a line of worry between her brows.

"Your cheeks are damp," Malcolm told Suzanne, when they were in the kitchen, the children settled at the deal table with their refreshments.

Suzanne put a hand to her face. "It's going to rain. There's an uncommon amount of moisture in the air."

"Quite," said her husband.

Cordelia watched the French window close behind her daughter and the Rannoch family. She was conscious of the heat of the sun through her muslin gown, the pressure of her bonnet ribbons against her skin, the damp in the air that warned of rain in the coming days. She forced her gaze to her husband, who had got to his feet but was still standing rooted to the spot where he had met Livia. "I'm sorry," she said. "I should have been prepared for this."

"Some things one can't prepare for." Harry's voice was even, but she didn't think she'd ever seen him so pale. "Though it might have been best if we had a chance to consult. I didn't know—It seemed—That is, she was bound to hear someone refer to me as her father."

"Harry, no." She took two steps toward him. Her legs felt stiff and unsteady under her. "I'm immeasurably grateful—It's just that I didn't mean to force her on you."

"You didn't. I was the one who introduced myself."

"You were put in a difficult position. I didn't mean you to have to—"

"What did you think I would do? Acknowledge her to the world but deny her to her face? I didn't think your opinion of me was quite so low."

"No, of course not. But I thought—That is, it seemed it wasn't so much that you had acknowledged her as that you—"

"Ignored the whole matter? How could I, when you were polite enough to write to tell me you were pregnant?"

The memory of that letter rushed over her in a wash of shame. "I thought you deserved to know. I thought you deserved a chance—"

"To repudiate your child?"

"Stop putting words in my mouth, Harry. I'm very grateful to you for doing as much as you have for Livia. I didn't want to make it worse."

"The world knows her as my daughter. It would be a bit difficult for her not to do so as well."

"Harry—" A thousand thoughts tumbled in her head and froze on her lips. "I need to sit down. Surely you do as well, unless you're quite inhuman."

"To own the truth, I've never in my life come so near to fainting."

Cordelia dropped down on one of the wrought-iron chairs at the table. The metal was warm from the sun. "I have talked to Livia about you," she said.

Harry moved to a chair opposite her. "Said that I'm brave." He gave an unexpected grin. "You can be a shocking liar, Cordy."

"Undoubtedly. But in this case I think I was telling the unvarnished truth."

"Doing it much too brown, my girl." He crossed one booted foot over the other. "I suppose the picture of me you've shown her is the one that hangs on the stair wall? Where I look like I'm bored or going to be sick or both. As I remember it was both."

"It's the only likeness I have of you. Livia was asking questions."

"About me?"

"Children do."

"She's—" Harry hesitated. "She's an engaging child."

"Thank you. That is—I can hardly take credit for it."

"On the contrary. I had a miserable enough childhood to know the look of a child who enjoys the opposite."

She looked at him across the table, not quite sure she'd heard aright. "Thank you. I'm not used to compliments on my parenting."

"Perhaps because a number of people don't recognize good parenting when they see it." He leaned back in his chair. "Why did you name her Livia?"

"The historical Livia was a strong woman," she said, picking her way through a conversational thicket set with mines and mantraps. "And I've always liked the Julio-Claudians. I thought they were your favorites."

"So they are. But I never thought of you as a classicist."

"We used to have some quite entertaining discussions as I recall." She remembered, with a vividness that surprised her, coming home from a ball or the theatre to find him at work in the library. Peering over his shoulder at what he was writing, pouring them each a glass of brandy, dropping into a chair and debating the finer points of a bit of translation or details regarding an historical personage. Once or twice she'd thought she might have had a more entertaining evening at home with him than if she'd gone out.

For a moment she thought she saw the same memories in his eyes. Then his gaze went closed, the way it did. "But it was never one of your chief interests," he said.

That wasn't strictly true. She'd been good at languages and fascinated by history as a child. She'd done lessons with George and Tony before they went to Eton and later helped them when they were home for holidays. But for her the allure of books had always fought with the tug of society. "If you mean I liked going out, it's true. But after you left I found myself with time in the evenings. I read some of the books you left in the library."

"Not invited out as much as you used to be?"

She met his gaze. "I may have sunk to a lower level, but I still don't lack for entertainment."

"I'm sorry," he said, "that was unpardonable—"

"Livia was sick as a baby. I spent a number of nights at home with her."

He cast a quick glance toward the house. "Is she—"

"She's perfectly sturdy now."

His gaze continued fastened on the French windows. "Cordy—" He sounded like a man who'd spent days without water.

She drew a ragged breath. The air felt unbearably hot against her skin. "I'm honestly not sure, Harry. I'm sorry."

He met her gaze and to her surprise gave a twisted smile. "I don't suppose it really matters, does it?"

"Of course it matters. How could it not?"

"Would it change anything between us if we knew we'd made a child one of the nights we spent together? Instead of you doing so with George? We'd still be the same people. George would still be the same person. And Livia's herself, not the sum of whoever may be her parents."

"That's generous of you."

"It's a statement of fact."

Silence settled over the table. Not as uncomfortable as some of the silences between them, yet the pressure of the air hurt her lungs.

"We both made choices," Harry said. "God knows I've spent enough time these past four years rethinking my every action since I met you. But in the end we have to live with the consequences of the choices."

"You're very wise all of a sudden."

"Don't place any reliance upon it lasting."

"Harry—" She sought for the right words from an infinity of possible bad choices. "When I married you I didn't intend—"

"To be unfaithful?"

She nodded. "I thought we could rub along. I never pretended—"

"To be in love with me. No, you were refreshingly honest. I was the one who was fool enough to think I could be happy with you on any terms. God knows what I was thinking. Except men in love don't tend to think much at all."

Even in the early days of their marriage, he'd rarely used the word "love." For some reason it made the breath catch in her throat. "Why?" she asked.

"Why what?"

"Why did you fall in love with me?"

"Do you really have to ask why a man would fall in love with you, Cordy?"

"It would take more than a pretty face to catch your interest."

He gave a short laugh. "You do me too much credit."

"I don't think so."

He was silent for a moment, his gaze on the toe of his boot. "You have a knack for seizing life that I never had myself, Cordelia. And—"

"What?"

He scraped his foot over the gravel. "There were times I looked into your eyes and thought I saw an echo of my own loneliness."

For some reason, her throat went tight. "I was never lonely."

"No?" He looked up. His gaze lingered on her face. "My mistake then. It wouldn't be the only thing I was wrong about when it came to you."

She gripped her hands together. "Couples have managed quite handily on less than we had."

"I think perhaps—" He broke off.

"What?" she asked.

"Perhaps it's easier when the force of feelings is less. As you should know."

"George." His name hung in the garden between them.

"The love of your life returned to England."

Her mouth went dry. "I thought he was."

"Thought?"

She hunched her shoulders. "At the time I thought what George and I felt for each other excused anything. But I don't know that I believe in love at all anymore."

"Then perhaps we've got round to the same way of thinking."

Her gaze flew to his face. "I don't think I've ever properly said I'm sorry. There's no way to say it that sounds remotely adequate. But for what it's worth, I am."

"Cordelia—" Harry stared at her across the table for a long moment. When he at last spoke, she wasn't sure his words were what he had originally intended to say. "Did you have any idea Julia was a French spy?"

❧ 27 ❧

Suzanne accompanied her husband back into the garden, to find Cordelia staring across the table at her husband, with a smashed look that suggested utter shock.

"I've told her," Davenport said. "Sorry, Rannoch. One of my quixotic moments."

"On the contrary." Malcolm pulled out a chair for Suzanne. "I'd welcome Lady Cordelia's opinion."

"Dear God." Cordelia put a hand to her face.

Suzanne reached across the table to touch Cordelia's arm. "It must seem completely incredible."

"On the one hand it does. And yet—It makes sense of so much. Her two letters to me. Her affair with the Prince of Orange. But how could she—"

"A typical mistake of an elder sibling," Malcolm said.

"Refusing to think one's younger sibling can do wrong?"

"Refusing to think one's younger sibling can take initiative. I'm the eldest myself."

"Yes, I suppose I do tend to see Julia as my little sister." Cordelia pushed herself to her feet with sudden force. "Those bastards. To play upon her weakness, to force her to betray her country, to send her into a man's bed—I've never been one to hate the French, but I could kill the men who drove her to this. Why the devil didn't she tell Johnny?"

"Why indeed?" Davenport said.

Cordelia spun toward him. "You think there's some reason she didn't?"

"I think it's odd."

"Why didn't she tell me? I'd have pawned every jewel I possessed—"

"Cordy." Davenport got to his feet in a swift move and went to her side. "Don't be so foolish as to blame yourself. You'll make me regret telling you."

"Damn it, Harry. She was my responsibility."

"She was a grown woman who made her own choices. I know you well enough to know you'd never make anyone else responsible for your choices."

"She was my sister." Cordelia pressed her hands to her face. A choked sob spilled between her fingers.

To Suzanne's amazement, Davenport put his arms round his wife and pulled her against him. To her even greater amazement, Cordelia drew a shuddering breath, then turned in her husband's arms and clutched the fabric of his coat. Her knuckles were white against the dark blue fabric.

"Life is hard enough," Davenport said into Cordelia's hair. "Don't make it worse."

Cordelia lifted her head from his shoulder and gave a crooked smile. "Of all the people to be offering me comfort."

"I know what it is to feel regret. And I know just how corrosive regret can be."

She wiped a hand across her eyes, smearing the blacking on her lashes. "I know my sister. I seem to be saying that a lot lately. But Julia could have applied to Johnny or me for the funds. There has to be more to it."

"Ashton says he and Violet Chase just exchanged the one kiss," Malcolm said. "And that it was all his fault."

"So does Violet." Cordelia moved back to the table and dropped into her chair. "Save that she says she was the one who initiated it."

"Lady Julia might have had reasons other than blackmail for becoming a spy." Even as she spoke, Suzanne wondered at her own daring. But years in the intelligence world had taught her that telling the unvarnished truth was often the safest course.

"Are you suggesting my sister became a committed Bonapartist?" Cordelia asked.

"A committed Republican perhaps," Malcolm said. "One can understand the impulse to one committed to the rights of man. I've been accused of my sympathies tilting too far in that direction myself."

Suzanne forced a smile to her lips.

"But you haven't spied against your country," Cordelia said.

"Unless Rannoch's a very clever agent indeed." Davenport joined his wife and the others at the table.

Cordelia shook her head. "My sister was one of the least political people I knew."

"She could have had more personal reasons." Malcolm leaned back in his chair. "How she felt about her spymaster for instance."

Suzanne met her husband's gaze. "You think her spymaster was her lover?"

"It's certainly one way to create an agent."

Suzanne frowned in genuine consideration. For all Raoul had been and still was to her, it wouldn't have been enough in her case. "Love" hadn't been a word in her vocabulary. She'd been driven by her beliefs and if she'd admitted to feelings they'd been something she'd tucked in round the edges. A part of her bristled at the suggestion that a woman would blacken her soul simply for the love of a man. Yet she couldn't deny the possibility.

"It seems Julia ended things with Anthony Chase at Stuart's ball." Suzanne related the scene Violet Chase had described overhearing.

"If Julia's spymaster put her up to the liaison with Tony—" Cordelia said.

"He probably also ordered her to end it," Suzanne said. "Though on the brink of war, you'd think intelligence from an officer would be helpful."

"Perhaps they were worried Tony Chase was growing suspicious," Davenport said. "He still has one of the best motives to have got rid of Julia."

"If her spymaster was afraid Julia had revealed information to Chase, he might have decided Julia was a liability," Malcolm said.

"I'd very much like to find out who this spymaster is," Suzanne said. "Given that he wants my husband dead."

Amazing how often she could speak the unvarnished truth. Even when talking about French spies.

Malcolm loosed his hands on the reins, letting Perdita lengthen her stride. He cast a sideways glance at Davenport in the leafy shadows of the trees that overhung the Allée Verte. "It can't have been easy."

Davenport's gaze was fixed on the soldiers and civilians cantering or trotting on the path ahead. "Given what I've been through these past four years, do you really think an encounter with a three-and-a-half-year-old would unsettle me?"

"Yes," Malcolm said.

Davenport gave a grin that didn't quite hide the conflict in his eyes. "Caught. I don't think I knew what sheer terror was until I looked across your garden at a small person some three feet tall. French cuirassiers are nothing to it."

In quick succession, Malcolm remembered sitting beside Suzanne's bed, holding the basin of hot water, his cold terror at her pain-wracked face, the wonder of the moment he first glimpsed Colin's head, the wash of fear and amazement when Geoffrey Blackwell placed the baby in his arms. "I remember the terror vividly."

Davenport studied two red-coated hussars from the King's German Legion cantering toward them. "My case is hardly the same as yours."

Davenport couldn't possibly know how similar the circumstances of their paternity were. Malcolm swallowed a welling of memories. "She's your daughter," he said. "You acknowledged her as such. You introduced yourself as her father. Whatever existed before today, you now have a bond that will never go away."

He meant it as both a reassurance and a warning. As much as he thought of what Davenport had done in the garden, he would do worse damage if he then walked away from young Livia.

Davenport nodded, eyes on the rays of sunlight that slanted through the trees. "I still remember when I received Cordelia's letter saying she was pregnant. I told myself it didn't mean anything. But my hands were shaking so badly I couldn't pour myself a glass of whisky. To own the truth, I thought I was doing something magnanimous by allowing Livia to be considered my own. I never thought about *her*. That she'd expect more from a father than his name."

It was perhaps the longest speech Malcolm had ever heard Davenport make about anything remotely personal. "Perhaps you thought you'd done enough given the circumstances."

"Livia wasn't responsible for the circumstances. I should have written the occasional letter. Sent gifts at her birthday and Christmas. Not left it entirely up to Cordy to create a father out of made-up stories and a bad portrait of me at the age of twelve."

"And now?" Malcolm asked.

Davenport nodded at Lady Charlotte Greville and her daughter, a girl of about twelve, passing them in a phaeton. "I didn't see much of my own parents when they were alive, not that they set an example of connubial bliss. I spent school holidays with my uncle, who left me to my own devices while he pursued the pleasures of town. I escaped into the library. I thought I was rather lucky. No ties meant no risk of being disappointed."

"I spent a good deal of my childhood in the library as well," Malcolm said. "My wife would tell you it's where I'd still spend much of my time if her efforts or the call of duty didn't pull me out." He hesitated, but Davenport had confided so much, more seemed to be required. "My brother and sister and I were in Scotland most of the time, my parents in London. Though they spent little time together. My mother died when I was nineteen."

He broke off, because much as he was coming to trust Davenport, there were things he wasn't prepared to talk about. Particularly not after last autumn's events in Vienna. "It didn't exactly leave me with a favorable view of matrimony," he said instead. "For years I thought I'd never marry at all. I was convinced I'd be a disaster at it. I warned Suzanne of as much when I proposed."

"She saw beyond it."

"She was in difficult circumstances, or I'd never have dared take the risk. I still wonder sometimes if I was fair to her."

Davenport edged his horse to the side as three officers from the Royal Horse Artillery approached, riding abreast. "I gave scant consideration to Cordelia's feelings when I offered for her. The damnable thing about thinking one is immune to love is that one loses all perspective when one tumbles into it. Or what one thinks is love."

Malcolm shot a sideways glance at him. "Thinks?"

"I'm dead to all feeling, remember?"

"I don't think one can ever really be dead to all feeling, much as one might wish to be." Malcolm shifted his grip on the reins. "As I said, I was terrified when Colin was born. With so poor an example, I was sure I'd make a damnable parent."

Davenport grimaced. "I don't think I have the makings of a good father. But I'll do my best. After all, Cordy appears to be a more than passable mother, which I wouldn't have expected."

"People can surprise you."

"So they can. If—"

Davenport broke off as they at last caught sight of Anthony Chase, bent forward over the neck of a blood mare, galloping hell for leather down the allée. He passed them, then wheeled round and rode back at them, the horse's hooves pounding against the path. He drew up short a few feet off. Sweat gleamed on the mare's sides and his own forehead.

"What the devil?" He looked from Malcolm to Davenport. "Don't tell me you have more questions. Couldn't you make sense of it the first time?"

"New facts require new questions." Malcolm tightened the reins on Perdita, made restive by the energetic mare. "You didn't tell us the woman for whom you were planning to abandon all for love had broken off your liaison only hours before she was killed."

The mare danced sideways as Tony's hands jerked on the reins. "Who told you that?"

"Your sister." Davenport edged his own horse to the side, as though to box Tony in. "She followed you into the garden to confront Lady Julia."

"Damnation." Tony loosed a hand from the reins and dug his fingers into his hair. "Violet never did know when to stay out of things."

"For what it's worth, she tried to avoid telling us," Malcolm said. "She wanted to protect you."

"She did a damn poor job of it, didn't she?"

"So it's true?" Davenport said.

Tony's mouth tightened. "I loved Julia. I'd have given my life for her. I was going to give up the life I had for her. That's true."

"But she felt differently," Malcolm said.

Tony fingered the reins. "It never occurred to me. That one could love someone so completely and not see that the feeling wasn't returned. Or not want to see it."

"Hell, isn't it?" Davenport said in a voice not entirely devoid of sympathy.

"Was that why you lied to us?" Malcolm asked Anthony Chase. "Because you couldn't bear to admit you'd been wrong about her?"

"No." Tony gave a short laugh. "God knows it was hard to believe, but Julia drove home the reality."

"Why then?"

Tony drew a harsh breath, then released it, as though making a decision. "Because I was protecting my brother."

❧ 28 ❧

Davenport exchanged a quick look with Malcolm. "What does George have to do with it?"

"Everything," Tony Chase said. "He's the reason Julia broke with me."

"He talked Lady Julia into ending the affair?" Malcolm asked.

"You could say so." Tony's hands clenched on the reins. "Inasmuch as he wanted her for himself."

"George was having an affair with Julia?" For once Davenport's voice was stripped of all irony.

Tony shot a hard look at him. "Surely you didn't think your wife was the only woman my brother dallied with? Two sisters. If he'd married them it would be considered incest."

"Lady Julia told you she was breaking with you because she'd fallen in love with your brother?" Malcolm said.

"I already knew." Tony edged his horse down the allée. Malcolm and Davenport followed. "I saw them together earlier in the evening. In one of the antechambers. In each other's arms."

"And then?" Malcolm asked, voice neutral. "She broke with you?"

"I confronted her. She didn't deny the affair. She didn't deny anything. She looked"—Tony spurred his horse to a faster speed—"pitying."

"That can't have been easy to take."

"I told her I was damned if I'd share her with my brother. She said of course this was the end between us. That was when I lost my head. I said it couldn't end this way. My God, it couldn't have all been lies."

"Love can be real without being lasting," Malcolm said, then wondered why he felt compelled to offer Anthony Chase any sympathy.

"You must have been furious," Davenport said.

Tony pulled his horse up and stared at Davenport. "You think I was somehow behind her death? Even if I could have arranged it so quickly, it wasn't Julia I wanted to kill. It was George."

"Did you confront him?" Malcolm asked.

"With Julia dead there seemed no point." Tony shook his head. "I don't know what possessed him."

"Jealousy?" Malcolm suggested.

"Of me?" Tony Chase gave a short laugh. "God knows we've always been rivals the way brothers are. But I never thought he'd serve me such a turn. We always—"

"Kept your hands off each other's women?" Davenport asked.

"Yes. No. Damn it, a man doesn't—" Tony glanced at Davenport. "You should know. How it feels to realize the woman one loves is sharing another man's bed."

"So I do." Davenport fixed Tony Chase with a hard stare. "It's the closest I've ever come to wanting to commit murder."

Cordelia hugged her arms round herself, fingers digging into her elbows. As though she could shock herself back into reality. "God help me. I didn't know my own sister."

"You didn't know one aspect of her." Suzanne Rannoch reached for the teapot. They had retreated to the salon, and Suzanne had ordered tea. She might not be an Englishwoman by birth, but she seemed to have adopted the British belief that tea soothed all troubles.

"An aspect that overshadows all else."

"Yes, I can see how it would seem that way. Oh, dear, how silly of me." Suzanne reached for a napkin to blot up the tea she'd spattered on the silver tray.

"You don't think it does overshadow all else?"

"I think your sister was a complex woman with complex motives. The fact that she was a French spy doesn't change the fact that she was your sister. Or that she cared for you."

"How can you know that?"

"Because I've seen your memories of her."

"I'm questioning every one of those memories." Cordelia glanced out the window. Livia and Colin were once again playing in the garden under the watchful eye of Suzanne's companion, Blanca. "And in my preoccupation with Julia I was woefully unprepared for introducing Livia to Harry."

"You've spent years apart from Colonel Davenport." Suzanne held out a cup of tea.

"But I knew I might encounter him in Brussels." Cordelia returned to the table and accepted the cup. "I was so preoccupied with how I would deal with him, I failed wholly to think about Livia. Of all the things I should have discussed with Harry, that was the most vital."

"It sounds as though you did discuss it, if a bit late."

Cordelia dropped onto one of the sofas beside Suzanne. "Harry was—I had no right to expect him to be so generous."

"What did you expect him to do?"

"God knows. At first I was simply relieved he left us in peace. Then guilt set in." Cordelia turned her head to look at Suzanne, shame and defiance roiling within her. "The truth is, I'm not sure who my daughter's father is."

"I assumed as much."

Cordelia stared at Suzanne Rannoch, startled by the matter-of-fact tone as much as the words.

"Given the timing of your affair with George Chase. Unless you and Colonel Davenport—"

"Had stopped sharing a bed? No, it wasn't that tidy." Cordelia took a quick swallow of tea. It scalded her mouth. "I don't understand why he was so kind."

"Perhaps because he realizes none of this is Livia's fault."

"Harry has the devil of a tongue, but he's a good man." Cordelia reached for the milk jug and splashed some milk into her tea. "Far better than I deserved."

"But not, I imagine, an easy man to know."

Cordelia gave a short laugh. "No."

"I know a bit about that."

Cordelia studied Suzanne Rannoch. "You and your husband seem almost to be able to read each other's thoughts."

Suzanne gave a rueful smile. "It wasn't always that way. When we married we were quite literally little more than strangers. Even now when it comes to some things—" She shook her head.

Cordelia saw Malcolm Rannoch's face—polite, pleasant, and as guarded as though he wore armor. "I don't imagine Mr. Rannoch shares his feelings easily."

"No. It's difficult for him," Suzanne said. "He never meant to marry until he found himself coming to my rescue. Marriage is a damnable invasion of privacy."

Cordelia nearly choked on a sip of tea. "What an odd way of thinking of it."

"Two independent people suddenly forced to share a house—or in our case cramped lodgings. It was weeks before Malcolm and I managed not to have my scent bottle and powder and rouge pot and his shaving things crowding each other off the dressing table."

"Harry and I always had plenty of space." Perhaps too much. It had felt as though they'd rattled about in their stylish house on Hill Street. Even though she'd chosen the watered silk wall hangings and mahogany furniture, it had never really seemed like home. As though they were playing at being grown-ups. "But I still remember how odd it was to look at him over the breakfast things. To realize I owed him some account of how I was spending my day. Though to be fair Harry always let me go my own way."

"More perhaps than you wanted?"

Cordelia shrugged. "At the time I thought it was fortunate, as it was quite awkward spending as much time together as we did. But there were moments when I wondered why he'd married me at all."

Suzanne reached for her own tea and took a sip. "So you tried to get his attention?"

Cordelia shook her head. "It's too easy to excuse my behavior as a cry for my husband's attention. I wanted George. I thought our love was powerful enough nothing could or should stand in its way. I told myself Harry couldn't be happy married to a woman who didn't love him, but the truth is I was appallingly blind to how I hurt him."

Suzanne leaned forward to pour milk into her own teacup. "I don't think it's possible to be married without hurting the other person at some point."

"You're a fine one to talk."

Suzanne looked up, silver teaspoon clutched between her fingers. "What?"

"Whatever you may think you've done to Mr. Rannoch—putting together an unfortunate seating arrangement, failing to charm one of his diplomatic colleagues—it can hardly compare to what I've done to Harry."

Suzanne stared at the polished silver spoon as she stirred the milk into her tea. "There are all different types of betrayal. And whatever Malcolm and I have, it's been hard won. I don't think—"

She broke off at a rap on the door. A moment later, Valentin stepped into the room to say that Mrs. Anthony Chase had called.

Harry scowled down the allée as Anthony Chase galloped off. Careless and heedless even in his grief. Or at least his supposed grief. "Damn the man."

"I own to feeling distinctly little sympathy for him," Rannoch said, "despite his claims to have lost the only woman he ever really loved. Or perhaps because of them."

"Quite. But it wasn't Tony I was thinking of."

"George? You had little enough cause to like him before this."

"And yet I thought—" Harry broke off. He felt the pressure of Rannoch's gaze on him, but the other man said nothing. Harry shifted his grip on the reins. "I thought he loved Cordy. Somewhere beneath the anger and guilt perhaps a part of me thought he deserved her because he was the love of her life. If it wasn't for that—"

"You wouldn't have left?"

Harry gave a wry grimace, though the pain of that last scene with Cordelia sliced through him, sharp as a fresh sword cut. "I was scarcely in a fit state to judge coherently. Like a callow young idiot, I wanted nothing more than to die, but I wasn't quite brave enough to do it for myself. And yet—I hate to think of a woman who was even remotely my wife throwing herself away on a man like that."

"I wouldn't have thought it of him," Rannoch said.

"You thought he had too much honor?" Harry asked with a short laugh.

"Of a sort. The Chase brothers strike me as the type who can seduce at liberty but think it's a violation of the code to go after their brother's women."

"Evidently even that was doing them too much credit."

"The personalities involved aside, it doesn't make a great deal of sense," Rannoch said. "I always thought it odd that the French put Lady Julia up to her liaison with Anthony Chase. For them then to have her form a liaison with his brother, when neither of them has any particular knowledge—"

"That we know of."

Rannoch shot a look at him. "True. If—"

A bullet whistled out of the trees and shot past Harry straight toward Malcolm Rannoch.

❧ 29 ❧

Jane Chase came into Suzanne Rannoch's salon quickly. The Pomona green ribbons on Jane's straw bonnet looked as though they'd been hastily tied, Cordelia noted, and didn't match the turquoise sash of her muslin gown. "Forgive me, Mrs. Rannoch. But I thought this should be said at once. Cordelia, I'm glad you're here."

"Please sit down, Mrs. Chase," Suzanne said.

Jane dropped into a chair but sat bolt upright, plucking at the sprigged muslin of her skirt. Suzanne poured a cup of tea, stirred in two lumps of sugar, and pressed it into Jane's hand. Jane took a quick sip, sloshing tea into the saucer. "Impossible now to think I once believed Tony loved me."

"I think he did," Cordelia said, an image sharp in her memory of Tony stumbling through the quadrille with unwonted awkwardness, unable to take his eyes off Jane. "As much as Tony is capable of loving anyone."

Jane's gloved fingers tightened round the rose-flowered porcelain of her teacup. "But he wouldn't have married me if I hadn't had a tidy fortune."

"That's true of a number of couples. I wouldn't have married Harry if he hadn't had a tidy fortune."

"You weren't in love with Harry."

"No." Cordelia's cup rattled in her fingers. "True enough."

Jane took a careful sip of tea, then set down her cup and saucer as though she feared she'd smash them to bits. "He did seem genuinely to care for me at first. Perhaps he even intended to be faithful." She smoothed her lemon-kid-gloved hands over her skirt, pressing the muslin taut. "I was so sure I wasn't the sort of silly girl to fall victim to infatuation, the way my younger sisters were always doing. I thought I could tell the difference between that and love."

"You hadn't known Tony since he was a boy," Cordelia said. Though she herself hadn't precisely done better with George. "Besides, as I said, I think he did love you. Just—"

"Not enough for it to last?" For all the weary bitterness in her voice, Jane's gaze held the pain of a wound that was far from healed.

"I'm not sure Tony is capable of being in love and having it last," Cordelia said. "In my more cynical moments, I'm not sure any of us is."

Jane locked her hands together, the kid taut across her knuckles. "And yet love can persist. Beyond all reason. It can blind one to horrors that should be obvious."

She pushed herself to her feet and moved to the window with quick, jerky steps. "Three nights ago—the night before Stuart's ball, the night before Julia died—the nurse woke me because my little boy was fretful." She looked over her shoulder at Suzanne and Cordelia. "I think the children can sense something is going on, for all we try to keep to their usual routine."

"I've seen the same with Livia," Cordelia said.

"I went in to sit with Jamie. I told him a nonsense story, stayed with him until he went back to sleep." Jane plucked at her sash. "On my way back to my bedchamber, I heard voices in the hall below."

She hesitated. Cordelia had the oddest sense her friend was standing on the edge of a precipice, still unsure whether or not to step forward and tumble into the abyss. "The first voice belonged to my husband. The other was a man's voice I didn't recognize. I caught a glimpse of them down the stairwell, but all I could see of this man was a dark coat and hair that looked dark as well. At least it didn't gleam in the candlelight the way Tony's did."

She paused again, one foot in the abyss. Her last chance to jump back. "The only words I could make out were the man saying, 'Everything is set,'" she said in a rush, "and Tony saying something about 'you will receive payment.'"

Cordelia swallowed, tasting unexpected bitterness. Somehow despite all the revelations, she hadn't thought it possible.

Suzanne Rannoch sat very still. "That could refer to a number of things."

"So it could," Jane said, face pale, eyes filled with the agony of uncertainty. "But—"

"But Lady Julia's death the next night made you wonder."

"How could I not?" The words tore from Jane's lips. "Especially when we learned her death wasn't accidental."

"You knew that the first time we spoke," Suzanne said. "Why come to us now?"

"Because my first instinct was to protect Tony. Until I realized I couldn't live with myself." Jane locked her hands together, as though to still the thoughts roiling inside her. "I need to know the truth, Mrs. Rannoch. But I'm not brave enough to seek it myself."

Malcolm Rannoch's horse bolted down the allée. Harry set his heels to his own horse and cantered after. But even as he set off, Rannoch got his horse under control, pulling up on the reins and circling round. "I'm all right," he called to Harry, clutching his shoulder. "Go after him."

Harry turned his horse toward the trees that bordered the path. He'd had Claudius with him in Spain. The horse responded at once, crashing through brush, dodging between the trees.

Another shot whistled between the branches. Harry ducked and caught sight of a man in a dark coat lowering his rifle. He touched his heels to Claudius again. The shooter set off at a gallop. Harry urged Claudius to a faster speed. He cut between two trees and had to pull up abruptly at the sight of a bramble hedge, too close to jump.

The shooter was beyond his reach. He returned to the allée to find Rannoch on his feet, breathing hard but examining something he held between two fingers.

"A rifle bullet," he said, looking up at Harry.

"I saw him," Harry said. "He got off another shot, then he bolted." He ran an appraising gaze over Rannoch. "You were hit?"

"It grazed my shoulder. Hardly worth mentioning."

"I doubt your wife will agree."

Rannoch gave a wry grin. "Before we face her, we need to tell the duke."

Wellington set down his wineglass as Malcolm and Davenport stepped into the Headquarters dining room where the duke was dining with his staff and the Prince of Orange. "Good God, Rannoch, did you let the French get to you again?"

"I'm afraid so, sir. I seem to have lost my touch since the Peninsula."

Canning gave an appreciative laugh. Alexander Gordon avoided Malcolm's gaze.

Wellington peered at Malcolm through the late-afternoon light that streamed through the dining parlor windows. "What was it this time, swords or a pistol?"

"A rifle. In the Allée Verte."

"Good God." Fitzroy's knife clattered to his plate.

The Prince of Orange looked from Malcolm to Wellington. "*Pardonnez-moi?* Someone is trying to kill Malcolm? Why?"

"It seems to have something to do with your mistress's death," Davenport said.

The prince's face drained of color. Canning and Gordon exchanged glances. Fitzroy cast a questioning look at Malcolm.

Wellington waved a hand toward two empty chairs. "Sit down. Drink some wine. You look as though you could do with it." He continued cutting into his mutton. "We've had some interesting news. The prince reports that the Prussians have been driven from Binche and that he himself heard gunfire round Charleroi, which confirms the news I've had from Ziethen and Blücher. It appears the French have attacked the Prussians south of the Sambre."

Davenport poured himself a glass of wine, his hand not faltering. "Do we march?"

"Not yet." Wellington took a bite of mutton. "I've ordered the divisions to concentrate, but I'm still afraid the gunfire round Charleroi is a feint. The French could just as easily advance to the west, through Mons or Tournai. If I were Bonaparte I'd attack from the west and cut us off from the North Sea and our supply lines. As well as our evacuation route. Bonaparte's no fool. I'm waiting for intelligence from Grant. What the devil's keeping him, Davenport?"

"I don't know, sir. Having been commanded elsewhere."

"Hrmph." Wellington turned to Fitzroy, Gordon, Canning, and the rest of his staff. "Take your plates into the outer office. The prince and I need a word with Rannoch and Davenport in private."

The prince was still frowning. "Was someone trying to kill Malcolm at the château two nights ago?" he asked as Wellington's staff withdrew. "And Julia was caught in the cross fire?"

"It may be more complicated." Malcolm reached for the glass of wine Davenport had poured for him and took a sip, controlling the instinctive wince at the pain that shot through his arm. He glanced at Wellington. Wellington gave a crisp nod.

"It appears Lady Julia was not simply a disinterested observer in events in Brussels this spring," Malcolm said.

"Of course not," Billy said. "She was a...a British officer's wife."

"Quite. But she had her own loyalties that were rather more complicated." Malcolm looked directly into his friend's eyes, recalling John Ashton's shock at the news. "Lady Julia was giving information to the French."

"Julia was—?" The prince shook his head. "No, it's not possible."

"I'm afraid the evidence is incontrovertible." Malcolm leaned forward. "Think, Billy. You said last night that you had found her going through the pockets of your coat."

"But—" Billy's eyes went wide with horror as disbelief gave way to sick certainty. *"Mon Dieu."*

"What could she have learned?" Wellington asked, in a soft voice that held the force of a sword cut.

"Nothing."

"Billy," Malcolm said.

The prince put a hand to his neckcloth. "There was a note from Rebecque about the disposition of the troops round Braine-le-Comte. If I'd known—"

"No sense refining upon it now." Wellington set down his wineglass, sloshing the Burgundy. "Our friend Vedrin gave his minder the slip before we could bring him in and seems to have gone to earth. There's little to be done on any front until we receive more news. We'd best prepare for the ball."

The prince stared at him. "You mean—"

"To forestall panic as long as possible. Once rumors get about we'll have every Bonapartist in the city setting off fireworks."

The prince winced but met the duke's gaze. "And you think the Dutch-Belgian soldiers will desert."

"I think it's entirely possible they will if they think the battle is lost before it begins. Besides, I need to speak to a number of my officers, and the ball is where I'll find most every British officer of rank. Rannoch, you'd best get home and let your wife patch you up or you won't be presentable." He took a sip of wine. "And more to the point, Suzanne won't forgive me."

Suzanne snipped off a length of linen. "You've always been good at adapting your thesis as new data emerges, darling. I trust you've now abandoned your claim that no one could be trying to kill you?"

"It is becoming a bit indefensible."

Suzanne tied the ends of the bandage, willing her fingers to be steady. "It's a good thing you aren't a soldier. Neither one of your arms is going to be of much use."

"I still managed to ride."

She swallowed the fear that threatened to choke her. "I've seen you manage to ride with a broken arm and a bullet in your side."

"So you should know this is nothing. I'm more interested in what we learned from Anthony Chase before the shooting started."

"What?" Cordelia asked. She was sitting beside Suzanne on one of the salon sofas, handing her items from her medical supply box. Malcolm looked at Davenport.

"Cordy—" Davenport looked into his wife's eyes. "Tony claims Julia broke with him because she was having an affair with George."

Cordelia stared at him for the length of a half-dozen heartbeats. Then she flung back her head and gave a shout of bitter laughter. "Oh, dear God."

"It doesn't surprise you?"

"That George would have an affair with my sister? We know he's capable of betraying his marriage."

"But he—"

"Loved me?" Cordelia shook her head. "I told you, I don't believe in love anymore." She frowned. "Why would the French want Julia to spy on George?"

"I don't know." Malcolm drew his shirt up over his bandaged shoulder.

"So this is why—" Cordelia pushed herself to her feet and paced the length of the salon, flounced muslin skirts whipping about her legs. "Julia broke with Tony because she was having an affair with George."

"And Tony learned of it apparently," Davenport said. "That forced the issue."

"Tony must have been furious," Cordelia said. "And he's a rifleman."

"Anyone could have hired someone to fire those shots in the allée," Malcolm said. "Even if Tony Chase was behind it, I doubt he actually did the shooting."

"No, but—" Cordelia exchanged a look with Suzanne, then told Malcolm and Davenport about Jane Chase's account of her husband's visitor the night before the ball.

Malcolm's brows drew together. "Anthony Chase says he didn't learn of the affair until he saw his brother and Lady Julia together at the ball."

"Says," Davenport murmured.

Malcolm was looking at Suzanne. "Mrs. Chase must be very angry at her husband."

"Jane Chase is terrified of what her husband might be capable of, afraid she doesn't know him, and sick at the thought that she loves him despite it all," Suzanne said. "She wants to know the truth."

"Which could break her heart."

Suzanne rubbed her arms. "So could not knowing."

Malcolm exchanged a look with Davenport. "It appears we need to talk to both Chase brothers at the ball tonight."

Cordelia drew a breath. Suzanne saw Davenport's gaze go to his wife's face. Whatever she might claim, Cordelia's feelings for George Chase were far more complicated than cynical indifference.

Cordelia forced a smile to her lips. "It appears the next step for all of us is to dress for the ball."

❧ 30 ❧

Swags of crimson, gold, and black, the Royal colors of the Netherlands, veiled the rose trellis wallpaper in the Duchess of Richmond's ballroom. Ribbons and flowers garlanded the pillars. The younger Lennoxes had thrown open the windows that ran along one side of the room, letting in a welcome breeze to stir the hot, heavy air. Cool moonlight blended on the parquet floor with warmer light from the brilliant chandeliers. The flames of dozens of branches of candles shimmered in the dark glass of the French windows and the brightly polished gilt-edged mirrors. The strains of a waltz rose above the clink of glasses and buzz of brittle talk. But Suzanne had the oddest sense the delicate atmosphere could shatter as easily as one could break a champagne glass with a silver spoon.

"There are so many dignitaries present, from so many countries," Georgiana Lennox said. "It's quite a chore keeping precedence straight."

"Just like Vienna," Aline murmured.

Indeed the profusion of medals, braid, and gold and silver lace glittering in the candlelight called to mind scenes at the Congress, as did the perfume, beeswax, and sweat vying with the sweet aroma from the banks of roses and lilies that decorated the room.

But the two hundred some guests crowding Georgiana's mother's ballroom were a small crowd compared to the thousand and more Prince and Princess Metternich had entertained at their villa.

"It looks splendid," Suzanne said.

Georgiana gave a smile slightly strained about the edges. "You'd never guess my sisters use this room as a schoolroom, would you? Or that we've been known to play battledore and shuttlecock in here." She scanned the crowd. "I do wish Wellington would come."

"He may have ordered the army ready to march," Aline said, "but he obviously isn't in a panic. Half his officers are here."

"But there's a distinct dearth of Dutch-Belgians." Georgiana tugged at a loose thread in her sleeve. "None of General Perponcher's officers has put in an appearance."

"Lord Hill is saying everything that is reassuring." Suzanne scanned the soldiers thronging the floor with ladies in gauzy, ribbon-trimmed gowns in a hothouse of colors—-lilac, rose, Pomona green, jonquil, cerulean blue. Her gaze settled on a man in Belgian uniform. Good God. Surely that handsome face with the slanting cheekbones belonged to General de la Bédoyère, who had taken his regiment over to Napoleon and was now one of his aides-de-camp. La Bédoyère met her gaze for the briefest moment, a reckless glint in his eyes, then continued to glance round the room.

Aline pulled her lace shawl closer about her shoulders despite the heat in the room. "Georgy's right, Perponcher's officers not being here is worrying."

Georgiana shot a surprised look at her. "You're always so calm, Allie."

"Calm?" Aline's voice turned unwontedly sharp. "My insides are roiling about, and for once I don't think it's anything to do with the baby."

"But—"

"My husband's a military doctor, Georgy. That means he'll be near the front. Which does rather strain one's savoir faire."

Suzanne put an arm round Aline and squeezed her shoulders.

With everything else going on these past days, she'd quite failed to think about what her young cousin was going through. "Geoff's been through countless battles."

"And he'll be in much less danger than the soldiers. I know." Aline's shoulders were taut beneath Suzanne's arm. "But somehow it doesn't help."

Georgiana flicked her fan open and then closed. "The Prince of Orange gave this to me," she said, fingering the amber sticks. "So odd to think of him commanding troops. I can't help—"

"If one ignores the smell of nervousness in the air and half the conversation, it could almost be a normal evening." Cordelia emerged from the crowd to stand beside them. Though Suzanne knew just how little time her friend had had to tend to her toilette, she was as dramatic as always in jet-beaded gossamer net over cream-colored silk.

"Define normal," Aline said.

"There's the rub. If—" Cordelia broke off as a tall, sandy-haired man in a colonel's uniform came toward them. Colonel Peregrine Waterford. Suzanne had met him in the Peninsula and seen him once or twice in Brussels.

Waterford greeted all the women, but his gaze lingered on Cordelia, hot with memories. "I was hoping I could persuade you to dance." His voice was a bit slurred, as though he'd been dipping too deep into the Richmonds' excellent champagne.

Cordelia's answering smile was as distant as it was polite. "Thank you, Colonel, but I won't dance tonight. My sister died only two days ago."

Embarrassment shot through the colonel's eyes. He murmured an apology and his condolences on her loss, then quickly took himself off.

"How ill-mannered," Georgiana said. "I'm sorry, Cordelia."

"I'm the one who should apologize, Georgy. Your mother wouldn't thank me for letting you so close to one of my scandals."

"Oh, stuff." Georgiana gave a quick flick of her fan. A great deal had changed in her attitude toward Cordelia since Stuart's ball two days ago. "Scandal seems quite irrelevant now."

"Scandal is sadly never irrelevant. And the past seems to be always with us. Oh, good, here's someone who should know something. Lord Uxbridge." Cordelia held out her hand to the cavalry commander, who was walking toward them. "Do tell us you have news."

"I'm afraid not." Uxbridge bowed over her hand. "But surely you don't think all the officers would have leave to be here were the situation really dire?"

"Yes," Cordelia said, "if Wellington wanted people to believe the situation less dire than it is."

Uxbridge threw back his head and laughed. "Touché. It's a pity you couldn't have joined the cavalry, Cordy. I could have made something of you."

"It's just so hard not knowing," Georgiana said. "Three of my brothers are in the army, as is Mrs. Blackwell's husband."

"And my husband," Cordelia said.

Georgiana cast a quick glance at her. "I'm sorry. I didn't think—"

"Quite understandable. But Harry is my husband and the father of my daughter, and as it happens his fate is a matter of some concern to me."

Uxbridge looked at her, brows drawing together. "Cordelia—"

"Lord Uxbridge." Cordelia put her hands on his shoulders with the familiarity of an old friend. "Tell us the truth."

Uxbridge smiled down at her. "The truth, my dear Cordelia, is that I know little more than you."

"But you rather think Wellington should have told you more, as second in command."

"You never heard me say so, Cordy."

Cordelia laughed.

Georgiana shivered. "How can you laugh at a time like this?"

Cordelia smiled at the younger woman and put an arm round her. "My dear Georgy. It's difficult to see what else we can do."

"Spoken like a soldier's wife," Uxbridge said. He smiled as he spoke, but Suzanne caught a flicker in his gaze. She suspected he was thinking of his own wife, home in England with their children, and the chances that she'd find herself a widow.

The waltz on the dance floor had come to an end. A wail cut the air that took Suzanne back to the previous summer. Dunmykel,

Malcolm's family estate in Perthshire. Granite cliffs, the tang of salt water, clean pine-scented air, and the unmistakable sound of bagpipes. Kilted sergeants and privates from the 92nd Foot and the 42nd Royal Highlanders marched into the room. The candlelight gleamed off their white sporrans and the brilliant tartans that trailed over their shoulders.

The crowd drew back and broke into applause. "Mama wanted to show off Highland dances," Georgiana murmured. Her mother was a daughter of the Duke of Gordon. "She did so want the evening to be memorable." Georgiana bit her lip, for the evening was almost bound to be memorable for reasons that had nothing to do with the entertainment.

Yet when crossed swords glinted on the parquet floor and the Highlanders danced over them to the wail of the pipes, it was almost enough to drive out thoughts of the coming battle. Except that those swords looked all too lethal.

Suzanne felt a light touch at her waist as the sword dance gave way to a strathspey. "I could almost imagine I'm home," Malcolm murmured.

She twisted her head round to glimpse an ache of longing in her husband's eyes. She'd seen last summer how much Dunmykel meant to him. Even after their visit she didn't understand the reasons for his self-imposed exile from his home and family. A homesickness he would never admit to was sharp in his gaze now. With a chill, she realized he was wondering if he'd ever see Dunmykel again.

She caught his hand in her own and squeezed it hard. He smiled at her. "You're missing the show."

She turned back to the dancers. Their legs, clad in red-checkered stockings, seemed to move ever faster. The sound of the pipes swirled through the candle-warmed air and bounced off the ballroom ceiling. Incredible to think that these musicians and dancers would soon be marching off to battle. On her husband's side. And against her own.

The performance came to an end to a burst of applause. Georgiana was pulled onto the dance floor by her friend Lord Hay, and

Lord Uxbridge's attention was claimed by his sister, Lady Caroline Capel. Geoffrey Blackwell came up to join them.

"I hear Suzanne's been patching you up," he said, running an appraising gaze over Malcolm.

"Quite ably. Your expertise needs to be saved for the serious work."

"There'll be plenty of that soon enough, I fear."

Aline slipped her arm through her husband's.

Geoffrey looked down at her. "I'm a—"

"Doctor. I know. I'm very fortunate compared to Lady Cordelia, whose husband is actually a soldier."

"There's enough worry to go round," Cordelia said. "Though nothing to be gained by dwelling on it."

"Men like Davenport who've been wounded once tend to be careful," Geoffrey said.

"Thank you, Dr. Blackwell, that's most reassuring even if you just made it up."

"Rubbish, I don't have time for reassurances," Geoffrey said. "My wife could tell you that."

"I'm afraid the sad truth is that wives can't stop worrying," Cordelia said. "A side effect of being left behind."

Aline tightened her grip on her husband's arm. "At least I knew what I was getting into when I married you. Just like Suzanne."

Malcolm gave a wry grimace. "I'm afraid Suzanne hadn't the least idea what she was getting into when she married me. Fortunately for me, or she'd never have said yes." He squeezed Suzanne's arm and moved off. Suzanne knew full well where he was going, and from the tension that ran through Cordelia, she guessed the other woman did as well.

They'd both seen his gaze fall on George Chase.

George Chase stood on the edge of the dance floor with a fair-haired woman in a lavender gown.

"Chase?" Malcolm said. "Could I have a word with you?"

George gave a frown, quickly banished, and touched the woman on the arm. "I'm sorry, darling. We'll have that dance in a bit."

Malcolm led the way out of the ballroom and across the passage to the Duke of Richmond's study. Davenport was already there, perched on the edge of the desk. George paused on the threshold.

"Sorry," Davenport said. "I told Rannoch it would be better if he talked to you alone, but he insisted."

"It's quite all right," George said, walking forward. "We're both adults."

Davenport got to his feet. "Good of you to say so, considering I didn't act much like one last night."

George Chase looked between Davenport and Malcolm, who was leaning against the closed door. "I assume this is about Julia." He hesitated a moment. "I don't know if Cordelia's told you I knew about her affair with Tony. I tried to talk him out of it. Unsuccessfully, I'm afraid."

"Yet in the end you did put an end to it," Malcolm said. "By having an affair with her yourself."

"What—" George stared at him with an expression that in other circumstances might have been comical.

"Tony told us," Davenport said. "He saw you with Julia at Stuart's ball. He confronted her about it in the garden later in the evening, and they quarreled. Your sister overheard them."

"Violet overheard them—Oh, dear God." George dropped into a chair and put his hands over his face. "Look, I can quite see how it would seem this way to you—"

"You're denying the affair?" Malcolm said.

George pushed himself to his feet and strode across the room. "What a bloody mess."

"I can understand you'd find it awkward to admit to seducing Cordelia's sister," Davenport said. "Rather ruins the love story. If it's any consolation, Cordelia now claims she doesn't believe in love at all."

"For God's sake, Davenport, shut up." George rounded on him. "I don't care what the devil Cordelia says, she'll always be—"

"Yes?" Davenport asked.

George glanced away. "That's beside the point. But if you have any understanding at all of what Cordelia means to me, you must know I'd never have taken Julia to my bed."

"I've long since ceased thinking I know anything when it comes to you, Chase. Or to my wife."

George swallowed. "I deserve that. I deserve that you don't think I have a shred of honor. In your shoes I wouldn't believe my claim. But it's true."

"Your brother saw you and Julia together," Davenport said.

George paced to the desk and drummed his fingers on its top. "I found Julia in the passage during the ball. She was obviously distressed. She confessed to me about the affair with Tony. I was comforting her. I had my arm round her at one point. I can only guess Tony saw that and misinterpreted."

"Lady Julia didn't deny the affair with you when your brother confronted her," Malcolm said.

George looked up with a grimace. "I think she was looking for an excuse to break with Tony. She was obviously tormented about the affair. Concerned for what it was doing to her husband, to her child. Concerned, too, that my brother wouldn't take her leaving him lightly."

"Yes, everyone seems to agree that Tony is the jealous type," Davenport said. "However incapable he may be of fidelity himself."

George glanced between Malcolm and Davenport. "Oh no. Tony is jealous, but you can't think—"

"What?" Davenport asked.

George drew a breath, as though even now he could not quite say it. "That Tony arranged Julia's death somehow?"

"We're still gathering information," Malcolm said. "For what it's worth, your brother says he didn't tell us about your affair with Julia because he was protecting you."

"Why—" A look of bitter realization crossed George's face. "Of course. Because as her lover I'd have a motive to have been behind her death. Poor Tony. This would be funny if it weren't so tragic."

"Did Lady Julia say anything to you that night that would give any clue as to why she was killed?" Malcolm asked.

Chase took another turn about the room. "She said she'd got herself in a dreadful mess. That she'd done Johnny an appalling wrong. That she couldn't think how she could ever have considered leaving her child. But all the risks she saw were to her marriage and family, not to her person." He looked from Malcolm to Davenport. "Look, if there isn't more I can tell you—I'd like a last dance with my wife."

Malcolm moved away from the door. "Of course."

He stared at the door as it closed behind George Chase, then turned to Davenport.

"A plausible story," Davenport said in an expressionless voice. "Save that it hardly fits with Julia the French agent."

"Unless she was playing some sort of game with George Chase." Malcolm cast another frowning glance at the door. "I'm oddly inclined to believe Major Chase when he denies the affair."

"But?" Davenport asked.

"But I'm quite sure he's lying about something."

❧ 31 ❧

"May I persuade you to dance, Mrs. Rannoch?"

It was Raoul O'Roarke and from the look in his eyes he had information.

Suzanne stepped into his arms and into the movement of the waltz. She hadn't known how to waltz when she first became his agent. He'd taught her. As well as teaching her how to pick a lock and decode a document and wield a dagger and pistol. It had seemed so simple then. A cause, a belief, an enemy to defeat. A clear vision that came before all else.

The clasp of his fingers, the touch of his hand on her back, the smell of his shaving soap were at once familiar and alien. Taking her back to a time when she had been a different person. A person who didn't understand the meaning of betrayal.

"You look charming," he said, as they glided about the room in the promenade that began the dance.

"I feel the way I did when I was first pregnant with Colin."

"Uncertain?"

"Ill."

"Good."

"Good?" she said as they began to circle the floor.

He adjusted his clasp on her hand, holding her a very correct distance away from him. "One of the best ways not to break is to admit you're on the edge of breaking."

She fixed her gaze on the top jet button on his waistcoat. "I don't break."

"You've never been through this before. We none of us have."

She forced her gaze to his face. "I assume you learned something or you wouldn't have asked me to dance."

He swung her forward, holding her facing away from him. "I haven't been able to discover who was running Julia Ashton," he murmured into her ear.

She drew a breath of frustration. "So we know no more than—"

"But apparently the order to kill Malcolm had something to do with Truxhillo." He drew their hands overhead as she twirled to the side.

Fortunately the dance required her to keep her gaze locked on his. "In Spain?"

"So I would imagine."

"But why is it important?"

He didn't shake his head, which might have drawn attention from the other dancers, but she could read the equivalent in his eyes. "I don't know. I was hoping you might. Or Malcolm might."

"How the devil am I supposed to—"

"You've managed more complicated scenarios."

She was silent for a measure of music. "Malcolm hasn't said so in so many words, but I know the minute the army marches he'll be off on some errand."

Raoul twirled her forward and then back to face him. "Yes, I imagine he will."

"Do you have any instructions for me?"

"Only to keep your eye out for useful information. And to look after yourself." For a moment she caught something in his gaze that she'd never seen before. An ache that she'd almost have called regret. But he merely said, "I'll let you know if I learn more about Julia Ashton."

"Thank you." She twirled under his arm. "I could swear I

caught a glimpse of la Bédoyère earlier in the evening. In Belgian uniform."

"So did I. He told me he had an ambition to shake Wellington's hand. Young fool."

"I could imagine you doing the same."

Raoul gave a faint smile. "Possibly."

They circled the floor in silence. She kept her gaze fixed on the deceptively simple folds of his cravat.

"I might have asked you to dance anyway, you know," Raoul said. "Giving way to impulse. You're not the only one who's unsure about what tomorrow may hold."

She looked up into his eyes. "But you'll be in Brussels."

"I'll be where I'm needed most. Like your husband."

Malcolm walked up to a knot of green-jacketed riflemen. "Could I have a word with you, Chase?"

Anthony Chase stared at him for a moment, then gave a curt nod and followed Malcolm to the French windows. They stood in the open frame of one of the windows, the cooler air from the garden washing over them. "Thank you," Malcolm said.

Tony gave a bleak smile. "I want to find out what happened to Julia. However things ended between us, I—What else do you have to ask me about?"

"The man who was seen going into your house late the night before the ball," Malcolm said. It was the story he and Davenport had agreed would serve best. Neither wanted to tell Tony his wife had betrayed him if they could help it.

Shock reverberated through Tony's eyes. "What makes you think—"

"There are informants all over Brussels. I understand you'd engaged this man's services. I'm not entirely clear what for."

Tony grimaced. "God, what a bloody farce. It's as though events are conspiring to make you waste time on me."

"The sooner I have an answer, the sooner I can sort out what's important."

"If you must know, I'd been concerned about Julia. Something had seemed different the last few days. I was as jealous as only a man desperately in love can be. So I—" His mouth twisted with self-derision. "I hired a man to follow her."

"What did he report to you?"

"Nothing. He didn't start his work until the day of the ball, and he didn't see her leave Stuart's. He was the first person I went to after she died. Bloody useless." Tony stared at Malcolm for a moment, his face half lit by the warm candlelight, half washed by cool moonlight. "I saw you leave the ballroom with my brother."

Malcolm settled his shoulders against the window frame. "He denies that Lady Julia was his mistress."

"But Julia said—"

"Your brother thinks she was using that as an excuse to end her affair with you."

Tony's brows drew together. "Do you believe him?"

"I'm not sure," Malcolm said.

Suzanne stared up at Raoul as they circled automatically in the pattern of the waltz. She'd been used to him facing danger in the Peninsula, but somehow she hadn't expected it here. "But you're—"

"Willing to do whatever it takes."

A knot of panic tightened round her throat. "You can't—"

A burst of applause near the door cut into her words. The musicians stopped playing. She turned to the doorway, knowing whom she'd see there. The Duke of Wellington stood surrounded by a crowd of blue-coated staff officers. Georgiana ran off the dance floor to him, dragging Lord Hay by the hand. "Do put an end to the suspense," she said, her voice carrying clearly in the suddenly still room. "Are the rumors true?"

Wellington looked down at her. His gaze softened with paternal tenderness, but his voice was crisp and direct. "Yes, they are true; we are off tomorrow."

A hum spread through the ballroom as the words were repeated over and over. Raoul's hand closed at Suzanne's waist. "It's nothing we didn't already know."

"No," she said, forcing the breath from her lungs.

The dancers still on the floor broke apart, seeking out spouses and sweethearts, children and parents. Suzanne saw Sarah Lennox anxiously scanning the room, no doubt looking for General Maitland. The Duchess of Richmond's gaze darted from Lord March, her eldest son, to Lord John and fifteen-year-old Lord William. Several officers were hurrying toward the door, stopping to make brief farewells. Aline, who had been dancing with Lord March, ran across the floor to her husband and Malcolm. Suzanne met Malcolm's gaze for a moment. She almost ran to him, but that would be silly. They were not heedless young lovers, and he'd say goodbye before he went anywhere.

The musicians began playing again. Even as some moved toward the door, couples swept back onto the floor, scarlet-coated arms close round pale frocks, eyes locked on each other, heedless of propriety and the watchful eyes of mothers. Or husbands.

Cordelia slipped through the crowd to Suzanne's side, dodging past a young lieutenant and a girl in pink, who were clutching each other's hands, and a plumed lady of an age to have soldier sons, face buried in a handkerchief. "We knew it was happening," Cordelia said. "But somehow it didn't seem real until now. Oh, forgive me," she added, catching sight of Raoul.

Suzanne performed the introduction.

"I know your husband, Lady Cordelia," Raoul said. "Naturally you're concerned for him."

Cordelia looked at him for a moment. "Thank you for understanding."

"Your husband is an impressive man," Raoul said. Which, Suzanne knew, was the unvarnished truth. She'd more than once heard Raoul comment, with mingled admiration and frustration, on Harry Davenport's brilliance as an intelligence officer.

"It's odd," Cordelia said, when Raoul had moved off. "Half the people I meet here know more about Harry's life in the past four years than I do. I'd never have thought that Harry—"

"Was the sort for adventure? Malcolm would say intelligence work isn't about adventure, it's about analyzing data and calculating odds."

"So analyzing the Punic wars is good training for analyzing French troop movement?"

"Precisely. Malcolm read history at Baliol."

"Some of the best conversations Harry and I had were about classical history." Cordelia cast a quick glance round the ballroom, a swirl of noise and color. "I wish—"

"Cordy." Violet Chase ran up to them and gripped Cordelia's arm. One puffed sleeve of sapphire gauze slipped from her shoulder and a ringlet had fallen loose from its pearl pins. "Where's Johnny? Is he here?"

"He didn't intend to be," Cordelia said, "and I doubt he'd have changed his mind."

Violet squeezed her eyes shut. "Dear God. I can't not say good-bye."

"Violet—"

"Don't you see?" Violet tightened her grip on Cordelia's arm. "I daresay he despises me after I flung myself at him in the garden two nights ago, but pride doesn't matter anymore. I don't even care how he feels about me. I can't imagine he feels very much. But I need to tell him how I feel about him. Before it's too late."

"I'm sorry, Vi." Cordelia squeezed her friend's hands.

Violet drew a shuddering breath. "He's never going to get over Julia, is he?"

"I don't know about never, but it's going to take time. Whatever he's learned about her, she was his wife."

"Damn Julia." Violet's eyes darkened to indigo. "Despite everything she did I can't think about her without feeling guilty."

"About Johnny? Vi, I wouldn't—"

"Not just about Johnny." Violet hesitated a moment, then looked from Cordelia to Suzanne. Her lips trembled, but her gaze was steady with determination. "The night of Stuart's ball Tony didn't go home with Jane and me. He said he was meeting some of his fellow officers at a café."

"He followed John Ashton home," Suzanne said. "He was concerned about Lady Julia. He learned she'd been killed from one of the servants. I think he spent the rest of the night in a tavern."

Violet gave a quick, jerky nod. "That wasn't why I told you. Tony saw Jane and me to our carriage. When he handed me into the carriage I glanced down and—" She cast a quick glance to either side, then looked back at Suzanne and Cordelia. The strains of the waltz and the buzz of excited talk echoed in the silence. "There was a stain on his sleeve. I think it was blood."

❦ 32 ❦

Suzanne looked into Violet Chase's bright, fierce gaze. She recognized the guilt she saw there all too well. "It was very brave of you to tell us that."

Violet lifted her chin. "It was an appalling betrayal of my brother. But we're none of us going to have any peace if we don't learn what happened to Julia. Johnny especially. And somehow— After hating her for years, I can't stop feeling I owe her the truth."

"Thank you, Vi," Cordelia said.

"I'm a fool." Violet tugged her sleeve up over her shoulder. "There could be other ways Tony got blood on his sleeve."

"So there could," Suzanne said.

Violet gave a quick nod and then looked at Cordelia. "If you see Johnny, tell him—Tell him I'll be thinking of him."

"Dear God," Cordelia said when Violet moved off. Her lip rouge and eye blacking stood out against her pale face.

"She's right," Suzanne said. "There could be another explanation."

"For the blood and for what Jane overheard?"

"One thing I've learned being married to an intelligence officer is to be wary of the obvious explanation."

"But—" Cordelia broke off as their husbands slipped through the crowd to join them.

"What's happened?" Davenport asked, scanning his wife's face. "Isn't Wellington's news enough?"

"It would take more than Bonaparte marching to make you go so white."

Cordelia swallowed. "Violet told us she saw blood on Tony's sleeve the night of the ball."

Davenport's gaze jerked round the room.

"Tony Chase told me he'd engaged the man his wife heard him with to follow Julia," Malcolm said. "He gave me the man's name and direction. If we ask him about the blood I'm sure he'll have an equally plausible story. Just like Gordon did for slipping away from the ball."

"Gordon had no motive to kill Julia," Davenport said. "Whereas we have more evidence against Anthony Chase by the hour."

Suzanne pictured Alexander Gordon's cheerful, mocking face and considered the hints of steel she'd glimpsed beneath his carefree façade. "Gordon is one of Wellington's most trusted aides-decamp," she pointed out.

Malcolm stared at her. "My God, Suzette."

Davenport looked between them. "You think Wellington ordered Gordon to deal with Julia?" His voice had the taut quality of a rope pulled to the point of breaking.

"And then had us investigate?" Malcolm shook his head. "I'd like to think he has more respect for us. Not to mention a greater sense of honor."

"I'd have agreed with you when Julia was merely the Prince of Orange's mistress," Davenport said. "But if Wellington had learned she was a French spy, I'd say all bets are off. Codes of honor tend not to apply to spies. As we both have cause to know."

"It still wouldn't make sense for Gordon to have been working with Tony Chase. Who's the one we have the evidence against."

"Unless it was Tony who figured out his mistress was a French spy and went to Wellington," Davenport said, still scanning the room.

"Harry." Cordelia put a hand on her husband's arm.

"What?"

"The procession's about to form for supper."

"And?"

She curled her black-gloved fingers round his arm. "You won't solve anything by causing an incident right this moment. And I need you to escort me."

He cast a surprised look at her. "It isn't fashionable for husbands and wives to sit together."

She tightened her grip on his arm. "Don't be difficult."

"Malcolm," Suzanne said, under cover of the hum of conversation as the company began to move toward the passage to the hall, "does Truxhillo mean anything to you?"

"In Spain? Why?"

"Supposedly it has to do with why the Silver Hawk's employer wants you dead."

He cast a surprised glance at her. "How do you know?"

"My dressmaker's assistant," Suzanne said, her prepared story easy on her lips. "I asked her for information, and she said she'd see what she could learn. She smuggled me a message just now with one of the footmen. She has a number of clients with French sympathies. She couldn't or wouldn't say from whom she heard it, but her intelligence has been good before."

Malcolm frowned. "A British expeditionary force on their way to rendezvous with some *guerrilleros* were ambushed by a French patrol near Truxhillo in early '11. They fought off superior numbers. It was where Anthony Chase first distinguished himself."

"Captain Chase?" Suzanne tried to fit this in with what Raoul had told her.

"He was only a lieutenant then. The captain and half the men were killed, but Chase rallied the survivors and led them to victory."

"How odd. Do you think—"

She broke off at a stir of movement near the doorway. An officer, dressed for riding, not dancing, his hair damp with sweat, pushed his way through the crowd. Lieutenant Webster, she realized, Lady Holland's son from her first marriage. He handed a paper to the Prince of Orange, who was standing with Wellington, Lady Charlotte Greville, and the Duchess of Richmond by the ballroom door. The prince glanced at the paper without much concern and then held it out, unopened, to Wellington.

"Billy," Malcolm murmured. "You need to learn to read dispatches."

Wellington slit open the dispatch and scanned it quickly. His face remained impassive, but tension shot through his shoulders. "Webster," he said, "four horses to the Prince of Orange's carriage."

Wellington issued more low-voiced instructions, then turned to the Duchess of Richmond with an easy smile and went to take Georgiana's arm to lead her in to supper. The company proceeded down the passage and across the hall to the dining room. Royal Dutch red, black, and gold veiled the walls here as well. White linen, polished silver, and sparkling crystal gleamed on the tables. Champagne bottles stood cooling in silver buckets. A world of elegance and artifice, far removed from the battlefield.

But Suzanne had barely dropped into her chair when the Prince of Orange hurried into the room, pushed his way between the linen-covered tables, and began to whisper to Wellington. They conversed for some minutes, their words unintelligible, while the rest of the company stared at their wineglasses and silverware in taut silence.

"I have no fresh orders to give," Wellington said at last. His lowered tones gave way to a voice meant to carry. "I advise Your Royal Highness to go back to your quarters and to bed."

The prince regarded him in surprise, then nodded, straightened up, and made his way from the room at a more dignified pace. Wellington smiled and said something to Georgiana that made her laugh.

Davenport took a sip of wine. "Might as well enjoy a good meal. God knows when we'll get another."

Cordelia looked at him for a moment but merely picked up her wineglass. "Wellington's the only one in the room who's still managing to act as though this is a social occasion," she observed a few moments later. The duke was sitting between Georgiana and his Brussels flirt, Lady Frances Webster. He had given Georgiana a miniature that she exclaimed over. He was smiling and laughing in response.

"He's an excellent actor," Malcolm said. "Excuse me." He got to his feet and conferred briefly with the Prince of Orange near the door.

"The dispatch Webster brought was from Rebecque at Braine-le-Comte," he said when he returned to their table. "Written at ten this evening and reporting that the French under Grouchy have attacked the Prussians at Sombreffe."

"Are they still fighting?" Davenport asked.

"No, the Prussians have fallen back to Fleurus. But before he could follow Wellington's order to return to Braine-le-Comte, Billy received another dispatch from Rebecque, this one written at ten-thirty, half an hour after the one Webster brought. Apparently having taken Charleroi, more French troops under Marshal Ney have pushed up the central *chaussée* to the crossroads at Quatre Bras. Ney and some French cavalry engaged Prince Bernhard and the Nassau troops at Frasnes."

Davenport frowned. "I thought Prince Bernhard was at Genappe."

"Apparently he moved forward. Ney didn't have enough forces to pursue the engagement. He's bivouacked for the night. Rebecque and Perponcher decided to ignore Wellington's orders and send Perponcher's second division to Quatre Bras to support Prince Bernhard."

Suzanne cast a glance at the duke. "For once I suspect Wellington doesn't mind his orders being disregarded."

Cordelia frowned. "Caro mentioned going through Quatre Bras on a picnic last month. It's almost directly south of Brussels, isn't it? So Wellington must have been wrong about the real attack coming from the west—"

"Yes, it looks as though the French are attacking from the south," Davenport finished for her. "To separate us from the Prussians. Grouchy's attacked the Prussians, and Ney's keeping us from going to their aid. Clever man, Boney."

Suzanne said nothing. If that was true and Wellington had only just realized it, the French had gained valuable time. She didn't dare risk a glance round the supper room for Raoul. She wondered how much he knew.

As the company picked at their food, rumors about the contents of the Prince of Orange's message spread through the room. Suzanne avoided the impulse to look at Raoul and see how he was taking things. She wondered if Malcolm would leave Brussels tonight or if they'd have until tomorrow before someone sent him on an errand.

Though some had already left the ball and some, like Fitzroy and Harriet Somerset, weren't present at all, the tables were crowded. Lord Uxbridge attempted to keep up a convivial mood, toasting the Richmonds' fifteen-year-old son, Lord William Lennox (his arm in a sling and a bandage on his head from his recent riding accident), and some of the other junior officers who were standing round the sideboard due to the lack of space.

When the meal came to an end, the spell that had held the company under some semblance of illusion that they were at an ordinary ball well and truly broke. Malcolm was claimed by Stuart, Davenport by Colonel Canning. Raoul met Suzanne's gaze briefly across the supper room. It was, she knew, the only good-bye they would have.

By the time Suzanne and Cordelia stepped back into the hall it was a scene of chaos. Soldiers calling for their horses; girls darting across the floor, tripping over their skirts, shouting the names of their beloveds; parents scanning the crowd for sons. The musicians had begun to play again in the ballroom, but the strains of the waltz vied with the call of bugles and the shrill song of fifes from outside. A broken champagne glass scrunched under Suzanne's satin slipper. By the dining room door a young captain stood holding the hands of a girl in orange blossom crêpe. A little farther off a girl in pink muslin had sunk to the floor, weeping into her hands. Suzanne felt Cordelia go still beside her.

A man in a rifleman's uniform brushed past them, a girl in white on his arm. Suzanne suppressed a start at the sight of those finely molded features. Then she forced her gaze away. The ghosts of her past seemed irrelevant in the chaos of the present.

"Suzanne." Georgiana touched her arm. "I'm going to help

March pack up his things." She glanced toward the ballroom. "I can't believe people are so heartless as to still be dancing."

Cordelia drew a harsh breath. "I wouldn't be too hard on them. It may be their last chance."

"Malcolm. Glad I found you." Stuart gripped Malcolm's arm, his face uncharacteristically grim. He jerked his head toward the Duke of Richmond's study. Malcolm followed the ambassador into the room to find Wellington and the Duke of Richmond already there, amid the ranks of books and the smell of old leather and dusty paper. Richmond was spreading a map out on the desk.

"Napoleon has humbugged me by God!" Wellington glanced at the door as Malcolm and Stuart stepped into the room. "He has gained twenty-four hours' march on me. And separated us from the Prussians."

"What do you intend doing?" the Duke of Richmond asked. He was a soldier himself, in command of the reserves in Brussels. Three of his sons were in the army, and Malcolm knew Richmond himself had been displeased not to receive an appointment on Wellington's staff.

Wellington moved to the desk and stared down at the map. "I have ordered the army to concentrate at Quatre Bras, but we shan't stop him there, and if so," he said, pressing his thumb down on the map, "I must fight him *here*."

Malcolm moved to the duke's side to see what he was pointing at. Wellington's thumbnail rested on a small village called Waterloo.

❧ 33 ❧

Jane Chase paused on the staircase. Women pushed past her, fastening the ties on cloaks they'd retrieved from upstairs, pausing to scan the hall below with anxious eyes, hurrying forward and calling the names of lovers, husbands, sons, brothers. The hall was a sea of red and green and blue coats and pale gowns as soldiers took their leave. The front door banged open and shut every few moments as someone new departed, letting in a blast from the bugles calling the soldiers to march.

Jane had already said one tearful good-bye, but now she was looking for her husband. She hadn't seen him since supper and then across the room. He'd had a pretty girl in blue on his left and a pretty girl in yellow on his right. Jane wasn't sure of their names, though she thought one had been one of the Lennox daughters. Truth to tell Jane had avoided Tony as much as possible all afternoon and evening. Guilt bit her in the throat whenever she looked at him.

But now reality had hit with the force of a cannonball. The reality that her husband would soon be gone. And that there was no guarantee she'd ever see him again.

"Jane." Tony appeared at the base of the stairs. "Thank God, I've been looking for you. I'm afraid I'm going to have to leave at once."

She ran down the steps and seized his hands. He returned her clasp, a look of faint surprise on his face.

"Tony, I—"

He put his finger to her lips. "I'm sorry, Janie. There's no time to say it all now."

For a moment they were standing in the ballroom of her parents' London house, a quadrille playing in the background, the scent of hyacinths in the air, the world fading away round them. She was a girl again, robbed of her customary irony, struck by the wonder of having found love—that thing she had always laughed at—and having found someone who loved her.

Betraying tears sprang to her eyes at the memories. She reached up and pushed his hair back from his forehead. "I'm sorry, too, Tony."

He grimaced. "Don't, Janie, there's no sense—" He tightened his grip on her hands and pulled her closer. "I love you, Jane."

A flash of bitterness shot through her. "If that was true, you wouldn't—"

"Whatever I've done, it has nothing to do with you, my darling." He stooped his head toward her, then hesitated.

She closed the distance between them and lifted her lips to his. "Whatever happens, Tony, remember I loved you. More than anything."

"Cordelia."

Cordelia turned round at the sound of her name, hoping it was Harry. She hadn't seen him since supper. Officers were streaming out the door, and she realized he might well have left without saying good-bye. Why should he after all? Whatever they'd shared in the last two days was set against four years of being strangers.

She turned to find not Harry but her brother-in-law crossing the hall toward her. "Johnny." She moved through the crowd and took his hands. "I didn't know you were here." He was dressed for riding, she saw, not dancing.

"I came to find you." He returned the clasp of her hands with a convulsive clench. "I thought the duchess would understand in the circumstances. I'm off to my regiment. Are you staying?"

"At the ball? Not much longer, but—"

"In Brussels."

"Where else would I be?"

She thought he might be going to try to talk her out of it, but he nodded with evident relief. "Robbie's nurse is a sensible girl, but I was wondering—"

"Of course, they can both come to me. I should have suggested it myself."

"Thank you." His fingers tightened over her hands. "I didn't realize how quickly events would unfold."

"None of us did." Cordelia hugged him. He clutched her for a moment, a drowning man grasping onto a spar.

"Johnny, listen." She drew back and took his face between her hands. "You don't have anything to prove. It isn't your job to make up for Julia's faults. Just come back alive to your son."

He drew a rough breath, but she saw his eyes focus with welcome clarity. He nodded and kissed her cheek.

"Johnny." The cry rose above the voices round them. Violet Chase rushed forward in a stir of sapphire gauze. For a moment Cordelia thought she'd fling herself at Johnny, but she stopped a few feet off. "I was afraid you weren't here."

Johnny blinked at her as though she'd stumbled in from another world. "I came to find Cordy. To talk to her about Robbie."

"Of course." Violet drew a breath. "Johnny, I'm so sorry. About Julia. About everything. I was afraid I'd never have a chance to say so."

He met her gaze. Cordelia felt the reverberations in the air—echoes stretching from the night he'd danced with Julia at Emily Cowper's to whatever had passed between them at Stuart's ball.

"Thank you," Johnny said.

Violet swallowed, put out her hand, but checked herself before she touched him. "Be careful."

Johnny managed a faint smile. "As careful as a man can be with bullets flying about."

Violet's fingers twisted in the folds of her skirt. "There are people who'd be very distressed if anything happened to you."

To Cordelia's surprise, Johnny took Violet's hand and pressed it. "It's kind of you to say so."

Violet gave an unexpected smile. "Rubbish. You know perfectly well I'm not in the least kind. It's just that—What's happened tonight has a way of making so many things seem absurdly trivial, doesn't it?"

Johnny met her gaze, his own surprisingly steady. "Yes, I suppose in a way it does." He hesitated. "Vi—"

She flung her arms round him, as though they were still the children who played on the banks of the stream between their parents' estates, and hugged him hard. "Take care, Johnny."

"Rannoch." Davenport fell in beside Malcolm outside the door of the duke's study. "What did Hookey have to say?"

"That Bonaparte has humbugged him. He's gained a day's march on us and separated us from the Prussians."

Davenport grimaced. "Exile apparently hasn't dulled Boney's brilliance. It looks as though I'm back to being a staff officer. I'm off to Fleurus with a message. I don't know if I'll get back to Brussels before the fighting starts. Tony Chase—"

"I'll talk to him." Malcolm nearly said more, but he wasn't quite ready to share the suspicions roiling in his head. "You need to find Lady Cordelia and make your farewells."

Two cavalry officers pushed past them. A girl in blue ran up and seized one by the arm. Davenport glanced at them for a moment, then turned his gaze back to Malcolm. "Look, Rannoch." His voice was clipped. "I know Cordelia. I've no illusions she'll go home or even to Antwerp."

"I shouldn't think so. Suzanne wouldn't, either."

A smile of acknowledgment tugged at Davenport's mouth. "And Wellington wouldn't thank me for considering defeat. But I have a healthy respect for Napoleon Bonaparte. Should the unthinkable happen—"

Malcolm gripped his friend's shoulder. He had many acquaintances but few friends. He realized Davenport had become one of them. "I'll make sure Lady Cordelia and your daughter get to safety. My word on it."

Davenport met his gaze, for once with no hint of mockery. "Thank you."

Davenport strode off in search of his wife. Malcolm spared a brief thought for what it would be like to say farewell to Suzanne with such a nightmare of estrangement between them. Then he pushed the thought to where personal thoughts had to go at times like these and glanced round the chaos of the hall for Anthony Chase. Soldiers pushed past; white-gloved fingers clutched scarlet-coated arms; shouts for horses and calls to husbands, wives, sweethearts, children, parents cut the air. Malcolm saw a flash of green and a bright gold head near the front door and pushed his way through the crowd, only to find it was a lieutenant in the 95th rather than Chase.

He turned back toward the ballroom and saw a familiar face. "March. Are you off?"

"When I've seen my parents," Lord March said. "Georgy helped me pack."

"You haven't seen Tony Chase by any chance, have you?"

"Not since supper, I think. Probably slipped off to say good-bye to his latest mistress." March grimaced with distaste. "I've always thought Jane Chase deserved better."

"I won't argue with you there. Though one can't deny Chase's bravery at Truxhillo."

"No, though if you ask me half of his success was the French being so bloody incompetent."

"I was in Andalusia at the time," Malcolm said. "I think the accounts I've heard were rather exaggerated."

March frowned. "It's odd. Tony Chase asked me about that."

"About the accounts being exaggerated?"

"Where you were at the time, of all things. Seemed to think you were on a mission near Truxhillo."

Malcolm felt his pulse quicken. "When was this?"

"Fortnight or so ago. Wellington's ball for Blücher perhaps? One of the endless round of parties we've been attending. The days have a way of running together."

Malcolm gripped the other man's arm. "Thank you, March. Look after yourself."

"Always do, old fellow."

Malcolm scanned the hall for Tony Chase again. Finding him had suddenly become a matter of pressing urgency.

Geoffrey Blackwell caught sight of Suzanne, the silver gauze and ivory satin of her gown shimmering in the candlelight. She was just inside the door to the ballroom, a gloved arm round Sarah Lennox, who was visibly holding back tears. Suzanne seemed as self-assured as always, but he knew her senses were keyed to wherever Malcolm was. Geoffrey slipped through the crowd, his dark coat making him feel invisible in the sea of red and blue and rifleman's green.

He touched Suzanne's arm as Lady Sarah moved off with one of her sisters. "I'm off tonight. I want to make sure I have a makeshift surgery established before there are any casualties." He hesitated, searching for words that would say what was required without being excessive. "Suzanne—"

"Of course Allie should come to us. I'll welcome the company. And of course should we need to leave, we'll take her with us."

"That's the Suzanne I know. Not afraid to admit the possibility of defeat."

"It would be foolish to do so. Not that I'm suggesting it's likely."

"No. You're much too sensible. Thank you, my dear." He cast a glance round the ballroom, wondering how many of the young men clutching sweethearts' hands or hugging parents would be lying on stretchers by this time tomorrow. Or already dead. "Whatever happens, wounded are bound to be brought into Brussels. You saw enough in the Peninsula to know what lies ahead. It will be like nothing Allie's ever seen."

"Allie has a good head on her shoulders. She'll cope."

Geoffrey controlled an inward flinch. "For a lifelong bachelor, I picked a damnable time to get married."

"Nonsense. You got married because you fell in love with Aline. Of all the insane reasons people marry that's the most sensible I can imagine."

Geoffrey smiled, though something still twisted sharp inside him. If anything happened to him, he'd be leaving Aline to raise their child alone. "My dear Suzanne. Who would have thought war would turn you into a romantic?"

"Geoff." Aline slipped through the crowd to stand beside them. Her ash-brown hair was coming free from its pins and slithering round her face. She smiled at him with determination. "Are you off?"

He looked at her for a moment, memorizing the arc of her brows, the steady brightness of her wide, dark eyes, the sweet, ironic curve of her mouth. "As soon as I found you to say good-bye."

"Right. Well then." She looked up at him. In five months of marriage, despite a number of surprisingly intense private moments, she'd never done more than take his arm in public. Now she stepped forward, reached up, and kissed him full on the lips. "We'll be waiting for you. Both of us."

"Harry." Cordelia skidded over fallen roses and shards of broken champagne glasses on the hall floor. "Thank God. I was afraid you'd left."

"Cordy." He was standing by the base of the stairs, drawing on his gloves. She thought, inconsequentially, that he must have had them off since supper. Absurd the way one's mind worked at such moments. "You're staying in Brussels?" he asked.

"Don't try to argue me out of—"

He gave a faint smile. "I wouldn't dream of it. This is no time to waste one's breath. But in the event it becomes necessary, Rannoch can help you get back to England."

She nodded, swallowing her surprise.

Harry continued pulling on his gloves. "Should I—In the event I don't see you again, my man of business has all the necessary documents. Alford-Smith in St. Albans Lane. There's a portion for you and everything else is in trust for Livia with you as trustee. Neither of you should want for anything."

She stared at him. It was as though she was looking at a stranger, and yet she sensed he had never spoken so genuinely. "Harry—I didn't expect—"

He tugged the second glove smooth. "What did you think I'd do? Support you and Livia in life and abandon you in death?"

"No, of course not. But I wish you wouldn't talk about—"

"Merely taking precautions. I've lived through a tiresome number of battles, I daresay I shall live through this one."

Beneath his easy tone and cool gaze something belied his words. She looked at him for a moment, every nerve stretched taut beneath her skin. This could be the last time she would ever see him. She reached up and curled her gloved fingers behind his neck.

He stiffened beneath her touch. "Cordy—"

"I have no right to ask you to come back to me, Harry. But for God's sake, please come back." She drew his head down and pressed her mouth to his.

For a moment he went completely still. Then his arms closed about her, as though he would meld her to him. His mouth tasted of wine. His hair was soft beneath her gloved fingers, his hands taut and urgent through the net and silk of her gown, his mouth desperate yet oddly tender against her own.

When he raised his head, his eyes were like dark glass. He stared down at her with the wonder and fear of a man who has stepped into an alien world. "I'm sorry. I didn't—"

She put her hand against the side of his face. Her fingers trembled. "Thank you. That is, I didn't mean to—"

He seized her hand and pressed it to his lips with a fervor equal to his kiss. "Tell Livia—"

"You can tell her yourself when you come back."

He gave a twisted smile. "Look after yourself, Cordy."

She swallowed. "That's one thing I've always been good at."

* * *

"Suzette." Malcolm emerged out of the crowd at her side. "Have you seen Anthony Chase?"

"He was by the stairs with Jane a quarter hour or so ago. I think he must have left."

"Damnation."

"Malcolm?" Suzanne scanned her husband's face. "What is it?"

"I think Chase is a French spy."

❧ 34 ❧

Suzanne stared at her husband, not sure she had heard him aright. Shouted names and bugle calls and the lilt of the waltz swirled about them. Just behind Malcolm, a red-coated lieutenant was taking leave of his parents. "You think—"

"Truxhillo. Supposedly the reason the Silver Hawk's master wants me dead. Also the moment that made Anthony Chase a hero. Against remarkable odds. But what if it was designed to make him a hero? What if the French set it up because Chase was one of theirs?"

Suzanne sought frantically through her knowledge from Raoul for anything that would support or refute this. Fortunately or not, nothing did. "There's no proof—"

"None except that it makes the puzzle pieces fall into place. Tony Chase didn't try to rescue Julia from the Comte de Vedrin, he and Vedrin recruited her."

"And wanted her to kill you? Because he was afraid you knew Truxhillo was a setup?"

"March just told me that only a fortnight ago Anthony Chase asked him where I was during the Truxhillo attack. He seemed to think I was on a mission nearby. Which I wasn't. But apparently Tony thought I had knowledge of what happened at Truxhillo."

"As did the Silver Hawk's spymaster."

"The whole deathless love affair Tony has been telling us about, the love affair that didn't fit with any of the other facts we know about Lady Julia. It never existed."

The sound of sobbing cut the air. The lieutenant's mother had burst into tears as her son departed. Her husband put his arm round her. Suzanne frowned, fragments of information shifting in her head in light of Malcolm's theory. "When Violet heard Julia and Tony fighting at Stuart's ball. Tony told Julia she couldn't just walk away. He didn't meant the love affair—"

"He meant her work for him. Quite." Malcolm squeezed her hand, his gaze roaming over the ballroom. "I have to find Wellington."

"Cordelia." Caro caught her arm. "Have you heard?"

"It would have been difficult not to."

"I've already sent word back to the house for them to start packing. We can leave for Antwerp at dawn."

Cordelia stared at her friend. "You want to leave?"

"For God's sake, Cordy, there's about to be a battle." Caro's fingers tightened on her arm. "The French could be in Brussels tomorrow."

"For shame, Caro, Wellington wouldn't thank you for even considering the possibility of defeat."

"Cordy—"

"Besides, the fighting's sure to last a few days at least."

A blast of night air rushed into the hall as a trio of infantry officers went out the door. One paused to look over his shoulder at a girl in a white frock with pink ribbons who stood with her gaze glued to his face.

"Cordelia." Caro seized her hands. "I know I'm not the most practical person. Being in Brussels at all was flirting with disaster, which is what I've done all my life. But even I can tell that staying here would be madness."

"Since when have you steered clear of madness?"

"Since now." Caro cast a quick glance round the hall, beginning to empty of soldiers. The girl in white had begun to weep. A fair-haired girl in lavender ran to comfort her.

Cordelia hugged Caroline. "It's all right, Caro. I understand. You should go to Antwerp. But I need to stay."

"Why?" Caro's wide eyes skimmed over her face. "Because of Julia? You can't think you can learn the truth with battle about to break out."

"This may be a better time than ever. But it's not just Julia."

"George? Cordy, for God's sake—"

"Not George." Cordelia realized she hadn't seen him since supper and had felt no impulse to look for him. "Of that I assure you. He's Annabel's to worry about."

A young dragoon lieutenant pushed past them, clutching a lady's white kid glove as though it were a talisman. Caro scanned Cordelia's face with anxious eyes. "Harry? If you're doing this because you think you can repay some debt to Harry—"

"No." Cordelia felt an odd sort of smile break across her face. "Not a debt."

"What then?"

"I'm not sure."

"You can wait for him in Antwerp. God knows I'm worried about my brother Fred, but—"

Cordelia gave her friend another hug. "We'll be fine, Caro."

Caro clung to her for a moment, then drew back and studied her face. "You look happy."

Cordelia shook her head. "Not happy—who could be happy in the midst of all this? But perhaps—"

"What?" Caro's voice was sharp with concern.

"Perhaps things seem possible now that once didn't."

"Oh, Cordy." Caro's voice held wonder, worry, and something else that might have been envy. "You could so easily be burned."

"Of course. But when is that not true of anything that matters?"

Wellington stared at Malcolm, fingers frozen on the ties of his evening cloak. "You're telling me one of my officers is a French spy?"

"I'm telling you I suspect he is."

"Damn it, Rannoch, we're marching off to war. Where is he?"

"Off to his regiment. Presumably."
Wellington jerked the cords closed. "Find him. And deal with it."

A few couples were still waltzing in the ballroom. Cordelia found Suzanne beside a gilded table that held a porcelain bowl of wilting roses and a brace of candles dripping wax onto the marble tabletop.

"Did you find Harry?" Suzanne asked.

"He's just left. You're staying in Brussels?"

"Of course."

Cordelia smiled, more relieved than she would care to admit to know she would have her friend to rely upon in what was to come. "I knew you could be depended upon. Livia and I will be at the Hôtel d'Angleterre."

"Lady Caroline's leaving?"

"Along with half the expatriates in Brussels. I can't quarrel with her. But I feel compelled to stay."

"Of course. But not in an hôtel. You and Livia must come to us."

Cordelia shook her head. "That isn't why I told you—"

"I know that. But it's the logical solution."

"It's not just Livia and me. I've told Johnny I'll take Robbie and his nurse in."

"Aline's coming to us as well. We have plenty of room." Suzanne touched Cordelia's arm. "You'll be doing me a great favor. Malcolm is bound to be off on an errand, and God knows when he'll be back. I'll be going mad with worry, and I suspect you will as well."

Cordelia looked at her for a moment, a dozen polite denials trembling on her lips. Then she said simply, "Thank you."

"Splendid. I daresay—" Suzanne broke off as a tall, fair-haired man in a colonel's uniform brushed past them.

The colonel went stock-still, his gaze locked on Suzanne's. "Suz—Mrs. Rannoch."

"Colonel Radley." Suzanne's voice was as icy as Cordelia had ever heard it. She turned to Cordelia and performed a quick introduction.

Radley inclined his head. He had an elegantly boned face and a self-assured blue gaze that implied he was quite aware of how handsome he was. But that confident gaze shifted over Suzanne as though she was a cipher he could not solve. "I'm off to join my regiment. Are you staying in Brussels?"

"Of course," Suzanne said. "My husband's here."

"Your devotion continues to be remarkable." Radley regarded Suzanne a moment longer, half-speculative, half-challenging. Then he nodded and moved off.

Cordelia adjusted the folds of her Grecian scarf. Suzanne Rannoch was a surprising woman, but Cordelia had never thought to find her friend playing out the equivalent of her own scene with Peregrine Waterford.

"I knew Frederick Radley in the Peninsula," Suzanne said. "Before I married Malcolm." She gave a faint smile and looked directly into Cordelia's eyes. "You aren't the only one with ghosts, Cordy."

Suzanne studied Malcolm's face. "You're not going home to change?"

He shook his head. "There's no time. Richmond's lending me a horse. I need to find Anthony Chase or at the very least warn his commanding officer. It's not precisely a message I can trust to someone else."

Beside them, a dragoon was pulling a flower from a girl's gold ringlets, while a fresh-faced young Foot Guard lifted a dark-haired girl's hand to his lips. Suzanne's hands closed on her husband's arms. "Be careful."

A smile pulled at his mouth, the familiar, maddening smile he employed when going into danger without her. "I'm only delivering a message."

"You're looking for a man who means to kill you."

"He won't try to do it himself."

"You don't know what he'll attempt if he's driven to desperation."

He gripped her shoulders. "I'll try to be back tomorrow. I think it will be a day or so before anything decisive occurs."

She leaned into him and put her mouth to his. His arms closed round her with the force of everything he couldn't put into words. Bugle calls sounded in the distance. The French had gained valuable time. Something sang within her at the knowledge, and yet at the same time her heart twisted at the danger her husband faced.

He drew back and set his hands on her shoulders. "Should the news not be good, you should have plenty of time to get to Antwerp. I'll find you there. Or back in England if necessary."

She gave a quick nod. "Cordelia is coming to stay with me. Allie as well."

"Good." He hesitated a moment, then added, "There are still papers in the compartment in the bottom of my dispatch box. Where I told you to look when we were in Vienna. Travel documents, letters for Aunt Frances and David. And for you and Colin."

A chill shot through the gauze and satin of her gown. "Malcolm—"

"In our line of work, it's always wise to be prepared."

She had letters for him and Colin as well, but Raoul had them in safekeeping. One in case she died and took her secrets to the grave, one in case she died and Malcolm had already learned the truth of her work. Since she'd married and become a mother she feared death as never before, but even more she feared a future in which she was gone and her husband and son hated her.

She reached up and kissed Malcolm again, branding him with a memory meant to survive whatever was to come.

❧ 35 ❧

Friday, 16 June

Suzanne changed into her nightdress but knew sleep would elude her. Outside her window booted feet thudded, iron wheels groaned, horses whinnied, and their hoofs beat a quick tattoo against the cobblestones. Drums and bugles and fifes sounded in the distance. Doors banged open and shut, accompanied by calls of farewell.

She lit the tapers on her escritoire and wrote out everything she had learned at the ball, in code, for Raoul, in case there was information he wasn't aware of. The need to be meticulous, to remember numbers and names and geographic positions, steadied her. Until she found herself staring down at the black ink marks. Acts of betrayal against Malcolm and Harry Davenport and Fitzroy Somerset and countless others turned to neat strokes of the pen.

She saw Frederick Radley in the Duchess of Richmond's ballroom, looking at her with the same arrogance as when she'd seduced him on a mission nearly three years ago.

Radley had nearly trapped her in Vienna. She'd been forced to tell Malcolm a version of the truth of her relationship with him. And Malcolm had believed her without question. It hadn't made the least difference to him that his wife had had a lover before she married him.

Droplets of ink spattered from her pen onto the paper. Her fingers were shaking. Her whole body seemed to be shaking. She dropped the pen and hugged her arms round herself. Stupid, stupid, stupid. It was no different now from how it had ever been. She tried to conjure memories of Lord Castlereagh and Prince Metternich in Vienna, their cool, bloodless voices inexorably arguing the need to turn the clock back on every reform made in the past twenty-five years.

One could form friendships with the other side. One could fall in love with someone on the other side. It didn't change the sides.

She reached for the pen again, just as she heard a door banging below. She grabbed her dressing gown and ran onto the landing, struggling into the folds of satin and lace.

Addison stood in the hall below, bareheaded and mud spattered. Blanca was already running down the stairs.

"I'm sorry, madam," he said as Suzanne followed Blanca down the stairs. "I'm scarcely fit for the house."

"Nonsense, but you must be exhausted and starving. Come into the kitchen, and we'll get you something to eat. You've just missed Malcolm. He left from the ball. You must have passed him on the road."

"Very likely. It was difficult enough to keep to the road in the chaos, let alone see the faces of passersby."

"There's blood on your coat," Blanca said, seizing his arm. It had long been plain to Suzanne that her maid had feelings for Malcolm's valet that went beyond friendship, but she'd never been able to determine how far matters had progressed between them.

Addison gave the ghost of a smile. "It isn't mine."

While Blanca heated soup, Addison sat at the deal table in the kitchen with Suzanne, sipped from a glass of whisky she'd given him, and recounted what he'd learned. "I was with one of the Belgian picquets at Quatre Bras at about five when French lancers attacked them. Light cavalry soon joined in. But the Belgians stood firm and fought them off. They deserve better than the way people have been talking about them."

Blanca snorted. "That's the British. You'd think no one else had ever learned how to hold a musket." Blanca had seen a good deal of the British army in Spain and the respect—or lack of it—with which they viewed her Spanish compatriots.

Addison cast a quick smile of acknowledgment at her, then turned back to Suzanne. "The French fell back to Frasnes. But they'll attack again in the morning. And from what I saw, the Belgians will be badly outnumbered if our reinforcements don't get to them in time. A Belgian private told me even with reinforcements they only have about seven thousand men and eight guns and the French must have twenty thousand."

The words reverberated in Suzanne's head, wonderful and terrible. "Wellington's ordered the army to march," she said. "They'll be there soon."

Addison took a sip of whisky, holding the glass in both hands. "I only hope it's soon enough."

She stayed in the kitchen a quarter hour longer, then went back upstairs because Blanca and Addison deserved their privacy. And because she had work to do. Because really there was no choice in the matter. She hadn't come this far to turn her back on her cause and her comrades now.

The village of Quatre Bras stood at a crossroads. One road led north from Charleroi, which was now in French hands, to Brussels. The other was the link between Wellington's troops in the west and Marshal Blücher's Prussians in the east. Take the crossroads and one could separate the British and the Prussians. Which would give the French a chance at victory.

She dipped her pen back in the inkpot, her hand now steady. With decision came a certain calm, even if something felt numb and dead inside her. She turned Addison's information into neat lines of code, sealed the paper with red wax pressed with a plain button, and then put a pelisse of indigo sarcenet on over her nightdress and laced on a pair of half boots. The house was quiet. She wondered if Blanca had gone to share Addison's bed. She hoped she had. She slipped out through the French windows to the garden and found her way by memory through the gate to the mews. Shouts, booted feet marching, the clip-clop of horse hoofs, the scrape of wheels, the call of bugles, the shrill music of fifes, the beating of drums still filled the air. The red-orange glow of torches pierced the pre-dawn darkness. She cut across a larger street and passed a group of infantrymen, but they merely nodded at her, assuming she was going to or from saying farewell to a lover or husband.

Philippe Valery opened the door of his lodgings off the Rue de Laeken and stared at her with wide blue eyes. "You shouldn't have come, madame. It's too dangerous."

"There's no time for the usual precautions. And just about everyone in Brussels has other concerns tonight." She slipped into his room and pulled the sealed paper from her sleeve. "Can you get this to Raoul? It's important."

Philippe gave a quick nod. Despite the hour, he was fully dressed. In the greasy light of the single tallow candle Suzanne noted a pack on the floor by the door. "I'm off in any case," he said, his thin face taut with excitement. "I'm going to join the army."

Suzanne put out her hand. "Philippe, no. Your work is here."

"Not once the fighting actually starts. Things will be decided before our information can be of use. I don't want to be on the sidelines." He fumbled in his pocket. "Can you take this in case anything happens to me? For Anne-Marie."

Suzanne hugged him. She'd known his father in the Peninsula. He'd been one of her ablest contacts until he died at the battle of Fuentes de Oñoro. She'd met Philippe's mother in Paris a year ago when the Allies invaded and Napoleon was sent to Elba. Madame Valery passed messages for the Bonapartists herself and was proud of her son. It was her face Suzanne saw as she embraced Philippe. He was seventeen. Only fifteen years older than Colin.

"We shall have a great victory, madame," Philippe said. "You'll see."

Had her own eyes ever had that look of shining certainty? Suzanne hugged him again and smoothed his fair hair as though he were her son. If the French marched into Brussels in triumph, she wouldn't be there to see it. She'd be fleeing to her husband's country. Hopefully with her husband.

* * *

Malcolm tightened his arm round the throat of the man he had just taken prisoner in the Forest of Soignies. "Who sent you?"

His captive went silent and still. Precisely what Malcolm would have done in the same situation.

"Why were you following me?"

"You?" English, a north London accent. "I wasn't following you."

Progress. Though surprising. "What the hell are you doing here if you weren't following me?"

Silence. The wood was shadowy and still about them, though the tramp of feet sounded in the distance.

"Look." Malcolm pressed his pistol closer to the man's side. "We're in the midst of a war now. Gentlemen's niceties tend to go by the wayside." An argument that might work if the man didn't have a good sense of Malcolm's character.

Silence again.

"Did the Silver Hawk send you?" Malcolm asked.

"The who?" the man asked, voice sharp with surprise.

"The—"

Booted feet crunched through underbrush. An improbable sound split the air. Someone whistling Papageno's bird catcher's aria. Malcolm went still, but the whistling broke off abruptly. "Who goes there?" a voice with a distinct Scots accent demanded.

Malcolm drew back into the shadows, maintaining his hold on his quarry.

The boots thudded closer. "See here—Good Lord, Rannoch?"

"MacDermid," Malcolm said. "Fancy meeting you here."

Major Hamish MacDermid peered at Malcolm in the pre-dawn light. "What the devil are you up to?"

"Interrogating a suspect."

MacDermid shifted his position, staring at the man in Malcolm's grip. "Good God. It's Watkins."

"You know this man?"

"Should think so. He's Chase's batman."

"This man is Anthony Chase's batman?"

"Not Tony's. George's."

The man in Malcolm's grip drew a breath. "Mr. Rannoch. Perhaps it would be best if we spoke."

"Excellent idea. That's been my suggestion all along." Malcolm released his grip on Watkins's throat and spun him round, keeping the pistol leveled at his chest. "Major George Chase sent you to follow me?"

"Not you, sir." Watkins drew a breath as though unsure what to say. His gaze slid sideways to MacDermid, then back to Malcolm. He released his breath. "Major Chase had me looking for Captain Tony."

Raoul O'Roarke swung down from his horse at French Headquarters at Charleroi. The mare's sides heaved and her coat was damp with sweat from the hard ride. Raoul patted her neck, turned the reins over to a sentry, and made his way to Napoleon's tent (even now it grated on Raoul's Republican convictions to think of him as the emperor).

Raoul could feel the crackle of Suzanne's message inside the cuff of his shirt. She'd done well. Amazingly well, though he knew just how much it had cost her. He'd been right to put his faith in her. He pictured the girl he'd first met in the brothel in Léon, the almost feral wariness in the way she held herself, the fierce line of her jaw, the burning eyes, the quick, biting wit. She'd changed a great deal. But the core of that girl remained.

General Flahaut, aide-de-camp to Napoleon, ducked out of the tent, tugging his coat on over a stained shirt and crumpled cravat. His well-cut features were drawn with exhaustion and blue shadows showed beneath his eyes.

"I have a message for him," Raoul said.

"He's asleep," Flahaut said. "As I was."

"I have intelligence from Quatre Bras. The Allies only have a battery of eight guns and no more than seven thousand men. If you move now, you can take the crossroads easily."

"It's the middle of the night."

"It's the middle of a war."

"Look, O'Roarke. We've been marching and fighting since two

in the morning yesterday. Fifteen hours without respite or refreshment and more than that for the forward troops. Our men are dropping from exhaustion. Not to mention that they're spread from Marchienne to Fleurus."

"I was at a ball in Brussels last night with Wellington. He ordered his troops to march. He'll have reinforcements at Quatre Bras by afternoon. You have a very small window in which to gain a crucial advantage. Damn it, man, this could decide the campaign."

Flahaut shook his head. "It will be up to Ney, God help him. He's been given command of the left wing. He's barely had time to settle in. He doesn't yet know the strength of his regiments. Or the names of their generals, let alone their colonels. Or how many men actually kept up with the march and got here. He and the emperor were closeted until two."

Raoul took a step forward, fueled by the frustration of past missed opportunities. "For God's sake—"

"Yes, yes, I'll give them the message."

"Thank you." Raoul stepped back and surveyed the younger man. In the distance, he could hear the sound of someone cleaning a musket. "Flahaut—"

"Yes?" Flahaut turned back from the tent, voice sagging with fatigue. "What else?"

"Have a care, *mon ami.*"

"I wouldn't have survived this long had I not learned to do so."

"Your father will be impossible to live with should anything happen to you."

Flahaut grimaced. He would know Raoul meant not the late Comte de Flahaut, his legal father, but the man most assumed to have fathered him. Prince Talleyrand, once foreign minister to Napoleon Bonaparte, now foreign minister to Louis XVIII. While Flahaut fought to restore Napoleon, Talleyrand was in Vienna representing the Royalist government. "I don't think he'll ever forgive me for returning to the emperor."

"He's your father," Raoul said. "He'll forgive you."

"I had to follow the dictates of my conscience. Besides, it could mean a great deal for—"

"For you and Hortense," Raoul concluded for him. Flahaut was the longtime lover of Hortense Bonaparte, Josephine's daughter, Napoleon's stepdaughter, and the unhappy wife of Napoleon's younger brother Louis.

Flahaut drew a rough breath. "Yes." He studied Raoul for a moment. "How's Suzanne Lescaut? That is, she's Suzanne Rannoch now, isn't she?"

"As well as can be expected in the circumstances. She's in Brussels with her husband."

"Good God."

"Feeling the pull of competing loyalties."

"But she's still—"

"My agent? Yes. I owe the information I just gave you to her." Flahaut smiled. "Brilliant as ever."

"And still loyal. Also very much in love with her husband."

Flahaut's dark brows drew together. "That can't be easy for you."

Raoul swallowed, throat raw. "In some ways I think it was inevitable. She was never mine to hold."

Flahaut's gaze shifted over his face. "That doesn't make the feelings go away."

Memories Raoul did his best to suppress shot unbidden through his mind. Her hair soft between his fingers. The reckless light in her eyes when she returned from a successful mission. The warmth of her body, relaxed in sleep as she never was in waking, curled against his own. "No. It doesn't."

"I haven't forgot the great service Suzanne did Hortense and me. I never shall forget it. Nor will Hortense." Flahaut stared at the sentry lights in the distance. "It's odd, in the midst of everything, how one can form friendships. And how those friendships can matter in the face of all else."

"There are times," said Raoul, committed heart and soul to his cause for above thirty years, "when I think those friendships are the only thing that matters. Go carefully, *mon ami*."

Malcolm pushed open the door of a sitting room in the abbey that served as Lord Uxbridge's Headquarters at Ninove. The smell of wine filled the air. Several open bottles stood on the floor. One of Uxbridge's staff was sprawled in a chair, asleep or half-asleep. Two were playing chess by the light of a lamp. George Chase sat hunched over a sheet of writing paper. "I need to speak to you, Chase," Malcolm said, as a cross fire of surprised gazes shot over him.

George pushed himself to his feet. "Rannoch. What the devil—"

"It's about your brother."

Concern and something that might have been fear flashed through George's eyes. He gave a curt nod and led the way to an adjoining anteroom. "I just got here," he said, as he lit a brace of candles. "Uxbridge hasn't arrived yet. I think Wellington gave him orders for us to march to Enghien, but at the moment I'm not sure of anything." He struck a spark to the last taper. "What are you doing here, Rannoch?"

"Thought I'd escort Watkins back. We had an unexpected encounter. Took a bit of time to straighten things out, but it seems we were both on the same mission."

"What—"

"Following your brother."

"You were following Tony?" George dropped the tinderbox to clatter on the table. "Why?"

"I could ask you the same question."

"Damn it, Rannoch. We're in the middle of a war."

"The start actually. But yes, I'd have thought you'd have other things on your mind."

"I needed to get a message to Tony." George stared at him in the wash of candlelight. Outside the abbey's leaded glass windows, the sky was lightening to pale charcoal. "Why were you looking for him?"

"On Wellington's orders. Do you know why he isn't with his regiment?"

"No, but you have to admit it's chaos out there—"

There was, regrettably, no time for finesse. "Chase." Malcolm set his shoulders to the door. Thuds and curses came from outside the abbey where a group of soldiers were trying to right an officer's carriage that had tumbled into a ditch. "How long have you known your brother is working for the French?"

The candlelight jumped in George Chase's eyes. "By God, Rannoch, I could call you out for that."

"But somehow I don't think you will."

George's mouth tightened. "While we're getting ready to fight and die, you're indulging some crazy fantasy—"

"Tony was working for the French. He was running Julia Ashton. If you were working with him, I'll learn the truth sooner or later. If you weren't, the sooner we share information the better. It may be your only chance to save your sorry brother."

"Damnation." George's hands closed behind him on the edge of the table. "How the hell did you work that out?"

"Piecing together facts. Am I right?"

George drew a long breath, as though weighing words and options. "Infernally so. Except that Tony wasn't running Julia. I was."

✎ 36 ✎

The sound of shattered crystal echoed through the anteroom. The soldiers trying to right the coach outside must have dropped one of the officer's trunks. Malcolm stared at George Chase. Either the man had just admitted to being a French spy, or—"Are you saying Julia was a double?"

George regarded him with a gaze that seemed to have a keener edge than it had a few moments before. "We're on the same side, Rannoch. We're both in intelligence. You know as well as I do agents don't know each other's names. Almost no one knew about my work. Julia didn't until she came to me with her dilemma."

"When your brother tried to blackmail her into spying for the French."

Pain and anger twisted in George's eyes. "Damnable to have done that to her. Julia could scarcely believe it. She'd known Tony her whole life."

"Did you already know your brother was working for the French?"

George's gaze slid to the side. "I—"

"Suspected?"

He gave a curt nod. "But didn't want to believe it. Tony is— Whatever else he is, he's my brother. Even after Julia came to me there was no proof."

"So you persuaded her to be a double?"

"Actually it was Julia's idea." George scraped a hand through his hair. "At first I said it was impossible. Agents need training. She wasn't fit for it."

Malcolm, thinking of his own wife, suppressed a smile. When they married, Suzanne had taken to intelligence work as though she'd been trained for it her whole life.

George gave a wry smile. "Julia nearly took my head off. She said she was tired of being the perfect wife. That this was her chance to make a difference."

It sounded so like Suzanne that Malcolm nearly laughed. At the same time a chill ran through him. So many agents met Julia Ashton's fate, one way or another.

George strode across the room and leaned against the wall between two of the windows. The gray dawn light turned his face into something gaunt and stark. "God help me, I agreed. I needed to keep tabs on Tony. I wanted to find out what he was doing, without—"

"Turning him in for treason."

George met Malcolm's gaze squarely. "Can you blame me?"

"No. I have a brother myself." Who would even now be preparing to go into battle. Edgar hadn't been at the Duchess of Richmond's ball. When had he last seen him? Wellington's ball for Blücher? No, the cavalry review a few days later. At neither event had they exchanged more than a few words. "Who knew about Julia's work for you?"

George hesitated a moment. Outside, wheels spun through dirt and men groaned as they tried to push the carriage from the ditch. "Carfax. I report to him directly."

"So do I." Malcolm grimaced, thinking of the unofficial chief of British intelligence. Carfax was the father of his best friend, David Mallinson, but not an easy man to know. "Not the first time he's failed to share information."

George moved to a chest in the corner. A bottle stood atop it. He splashed brandy into two glasses and handed one to Malcolm. "It seemed safe enough. Tony wasn't asking Julia to do anything dangerous."

Malcolm's fingers tightened round his glass. "He asked her to seduce Lord Uxbridge. And then the Prince of Orange."

George flinched, his hand halfway to his lips. "I didn't know. Not at first. She'd entered into the affair with the prince before I realized."

"But you didn't call things off."

"No." George turned his glass in his hand. His mouth twisted with a self-hatred Malcolm knew all too well. "Tell me you've never used sex to get information."

Malcolm thought of Rachel Garnier. "A point."

"But it's different when it's someone you know."

"Not in theory, as I keep saying." Malcolm took a sip of brandy. "Did Carfax know?"

George swallowed. "He knew about Julia working for me as a double with the French. He didn't know Tony was her contact. He doesn't know I suspect Tony at all. I told myself I was waiting to gather conclusive proof."

"And Lady Julia's affair with the Prince of Orange?"

"Carfax insisted Julia go on with the affair. He said anything else would compromise the mission. Besides, he—"

"Found it useful to have an inside source with the Prince of Orange."

George gave a bitter smile. "Does that surprise you?"

"No. It's damnably like Carfax." Malcolm pictured his spymaster, giving him a mocking look over the rim of his spectacles. "Knowing all the other things he hasn't caviled at, I don't know why I'd think he'd cavil at that." He took a sip of brandy. "Was Julia having an affair with your brother?"

"She said not, and I'm inclined to believe her. I think the affair was Tony's invention to explain his association with her."

"Your sister found a love letter he was writing to her. A code?"

"I suspect so."

"A clever way to disguise it. So Julia got information from Slender Billy and passed it along to you. You sent reports to Carfax and told Lady Julia what it was safe for her to tell your brother."

"Yes." George tossed down a swallow of brandy. "I imagine you and I use the same courier system to report to Carfax."

Shouts of victory indicated the soldiers had righted the over-turned carriage. "What else did Lady Julia do?" Malcolm asked.

"There was a group of Belgian Bonapartists she and Tony were working with. The Comte de Vedrin was their leader. They were passing gold and jewels along to Paris. Thanks to Julia we were able to intercept quite a bit of it. Julia surprised me. I didn't think she'd take to intelligence so well. It was as though she came alive once she started."

Malcolm took a measured sip of brandy. "Your brother ordered her to kill me."

George went still. Outside, closer than the overturned carriage, a soldier was cleaning his gun. The sound of the ramrod scraping the barrel echoed through the still air. "I didn't realize you knew," George said.

"I may have been shockingly slow to put the pieces together, but I haven't entirely lost my investigative abilities."

George's jaw tightened. "I didn't know what to make of it. Why on earth should Tony—"

"Possibly care about me."

George frowned into his brandy glass. "I couldn't see the con-nection. Tony wouldn't tell Julia why. Do you know?"

"Apparently it was something to do with Truxhillo."

"But—"

"I think Truxhillo may have been set up by the French to prove your brother's heroism."

"Good God." George stared at him across the anteroom. "You think Tony was working for the French in the Peninsula?"

"Do you have proof he wasn't? He's become an important agent. He reports straight to Paris."

George's fingers tightened round his glass. "So you knew Trux-hillo was a setup?"

"No. That's what's odd. If I'm right, something had given Tony the idea that I knew and could expose him. What did Julia do when your brother demanded that she arrange my death?"

"She was in a panic. She said she hadn't bargained on this. I told her to pretend to go along with Tony, that we could make sure nothing actually happened to you, but she got more and more worried."

"And the night of Stuart's ball she told Tony she was stopping her work for him. That's what your sister overheard."

"I'm afraid so. Julia had come to me earlier in the evening, very distressed about her work, though she said nothing about stopping. I comforted her. Tony may have seen us. Or her supposed affair with me may have been another invention of his."

Malcolm studied George Chase's face, etched with guilt, yet with the hardness of a seasoned agent who'd learned to live with his choices. "So you weren't having an affair with Julia."

"Good God no. She was Cordelia's sister."

"And that put her off-limits."

"Yes." The single word spoke volumes about how George Chase still felt about Cordelia Davenport.

"So you don't think your brother knew Julia was working with you?"

George stared at him, gaze wracked by demons that would never rest. "Dear God I hope not."

"But you can't be sure."

George tossed back the last of his brandy. "No."

The sound of a cork popping split the night air. The soldiers must have liberated some of the officer's champagne. "What happened at the Château de Vere?" Malcolm asked.

"You were the one who was there, Rannoch." Questions shot through George's eyes, the sort of questions that would probably haunt his sleep for the rest of his life. "Do you think Tony set up the ambush?"

"To kill me? Or Julia? Or both of us? I think it's possible."

George looked him full in the face and nodded, a soldier owning up to dereliction of duty. "I should have told you the whole after Julia died. I told myself I should wait for orders from Carfax about revealing Julia's work for us. That you could handle anything Tony tried. But the truth is I was stalling for time. Because I still couldn't bring myself—"

"To turn in your brother."

George nodded. "I kept thinking if I could keep Tony from doing mischief through the battle, once things were decided—"

"Tony's tried to kill me twice in the last two days."

Shock flared in George's eyes. "I didn't know. I didn't think—"

"Fatal mistake to underestimate one's younger sibling."

A muscle tensed in George's jaw. "I deserve anything you may do to me."

"Anything I might do to you wouldn't solve our present problems. Your traitor brother, who may be responsible for Julia Ashton's death, is running loose on the eve of battle."

Livia Davenport held tight to her mother's hand and stared round the entrance hall in the Rue Ducale. Colin raced forward over the black and white marble tiles, came to a skidding halt, and bowed as Suzanne had taught him. "Welcome."

Livia grinned, then let go her mother's hand and curtsied with equal formality. "It's like having a brother. Brothers." She glanced over her shoulder at her cousin Robbie, held in his nurse's arms. Robbie wriggled to get down and ran over to the other children.

"Robbie, this is Master Colin Rannoch," Cordelia said. "And his mama, Mrs. Rannoch."

"Is your papa a soldier, too?" Robbie asked Colin.

Colin shook his head. "But he went away last night."

"My papa's a soldier," Livia said.

Robbie swung his gaze to her. "You don't have a papa."

"Yes, I do. I met him yesterday."

Robbie frowned, puzzling this out, then turned back to Colin. "I don't have a mama now."

"Where is she?" Colin asked.

"She's dead," Robbie said with a matter-of-factness that tore at Suzanne's chest.

Colin cast an anxious glance at Suzanne.

"I know you must miss her dreadfully, Master Ashton," Suzanne said. "We're very glad you can be here with us. Let's go up and see your rooms, shall we?"

When the children were settled in the nursery with Livia's and

Robbie's nurses, examining Colin's toys, Suzanne took Cordelia down to the salon where she'd had coffee sent in.

"It's good to see them playing." Cordelia rubbed her arms. "I keep waiting for it to hit Robbie that Julia's gone. Then I'm afraid it has and he didn't see her enough for it to matter as it should."

"Your sister was—"

"Restless. She thought she knew what she wanted when we were girls. But once she had it, it didn't make her happy. Then she wasn't sure what to do with herself. Sometimes I'm afraid having Robbie was like ticking off one more item on a list of things she was supposed to do. Whereas for me—" Cordelia shook her head. "Motherhood was a distinct surprise."

"It was for me as well," Suzanne said, and then bit her tongue, her instinct to confide warring with every dictate of a trained agent.

Cordelia looked at her for a moment, the supposedly perfect wife who presumably would have been eager to give her husband children. Suzanne couldn't be sure what Cordelia saw, but she had a dismaying fear that her carefully constructed defenses had slipped.

But instead of asking questions, Cordelia glanced out the window into the garden. "Livia's been talking about Harry ever since yesterday."

"That's good surely."

"Yes, but I can't help worrying she's met him only to—"

"Cordelia." Suzanne went to the other woman's side, biting back the obvious platitudes. "Even if she never sees him again, it's better for her to have the one good memory."

Cordelia nodded. The gaze she lifted to Suzanne held unimagined horrors. "I can't bear the thought that last night was the last time I'll see him. So commonplace. I'm sure women all over the city are saying that this morning."

"Which doesn't make it any less real."

"Lowering to realize I'm just like everyone else. I've always prided myself on being an original."

"War provides a sad amount of commonality."

The door opened to admit Aline, who came into the room with a determined step. "Valentin took my bags up. I told him there was no need to bother you. The streets were so quiet on the way here. Now the bugles and fifes and marching have stopped I could almost imagine it was a hideous nightmare. If Brussels weren't so eerily empty." She dropped down on the sofa and reached for the coffeepot. "I don't think I slept a wink."

"Nor did I." Cordelia moved to the sofa. "Do pour me out a cup as well."

Aline filled three cups, letting loose the rich aroma of the coffee. "The Comtesse de Ribaucourt is organizing ladies to prepare lint this afternoon. I thought it might be good to feel one was doing something useful."

"I never saw myself as the lint-scraping sort," Cordelia said, "but I quite agree."

Aline gulped down a sip of coffee. "People keep saying one can't admit the possibility of defeat. But whichever way the battle goes, there are going to be wounded."

Suzanne reached for her own coffee and took a fortifying sip. That was what she had told herself for years. People died in war. Different people might die because of her actions, but people would die regardless.

"Suzanne?" Aline said. "Are you all right?"

"Yes, love. Just a bit—"

"Overwhelmed," Cordelia concluded for her. "Commonplace or not, it's overwhelming."

"I wish I'd paid more attention when Geoff was patching people up. At the moment those skills seem infinitely more useful than solving quadratic equations." Aline pushed herself to her feet. "Damn. I did so want to avoid this."

"War?" Cordelia asked.

"Caring about people." Aline strode to the window and stood staring out at the garden. "Oh, I've always cared about my family in the detached way our family does. But for years I thought I was above personal relationships. Or not worthy of them. Or something. Numbers always seemed so much safer. It wasn't until last night I realized how very right I was."

"Would you go back?" Cordelia asked. "Would you change any of it if you could?"

Aline turned round and shook her head at once. "Of course not." Her hand went to her stomach. "I can't imagine my life without Geoff. Or the baby, even though the baby still scarcely seems real half the time."

Cordelia nodded and took a sip of coffee. "If you wouldn't change anything, then you're more fortunate than most. How soon can we start scraping lint?"

Georgiana Lennox looked up from a length of linen fixed to a board in her lap. "The bugles and drums and everything made it hard to sleep. Not that I could have in any case. But now the quiet is almost worse. At least when we can hear we have some sense of what's going on."

"Whereas the quiet encourages our worst imaginings," Cordelia said.

"Precisely." Georgiana scraped her knife over the linen. "Harriet Somerset has gone to Antwerp. So has Lady De Lancey. She said Sir William insisted. I suppose as quartermaster general he's all too well aware of what could go wrong. Papa has post-horses in our stable. Wellington promised to send word if it's necessary to leave. Of course publicly he can't admit the possibility, but privately he has to be practical."

"Even in the worst-case scenario," Suzanne said, "it would take the French a day or so to reach Brussels." How odd she was calling that the worst-case scenario.

Georgiana nodded with determination. "If only—"

She broke off as the door of the salon opened to admit Lady Frances Webster.

"Lady Frances!" exclaimed the younger Miss Ord. "Surely you've had news."

"I can't imagine why you would think so," Lady Frances said with a smile. She was known to be at the least the Duke of Wellington's flirt, possibly more.

Miss Ord closed her mouth in confusion. Her sister touched her arm.

Lady Frances might not have Cordelia's or Caroline Lamb's reputation, but she was no stranger to scandal. Suzanne had heard from more than one person about Frances Webster's flirtation with Lord Byron and that the poet had actually given her a lock of his hair. With the aplomb of one used to navigating difficult social waters, Lady Frances moved away from those ladies more likely to gossip and sank down in a chair by Suzanne, Aline, Cordelia, and Georgiana, settling her skirts with care. She was seven months pregnant, though that had done nothing to reduce the gossip. "In truth the duke has promised to send word if necessary," she said, "as I'm sure he has to your family, Georgy. But so far I've heard nothing. Which I take as a good sign." She reached for a length of linen. "The duke would approve that none of you has left."

"Personally I find the French less daunting than being stuck on the road to Antwerp," Aline said. "Though perhaps you'd best not repeat that to the duke."

Lady Frances gave one of her lovely, artless smiles. "Nearly everyone who's left in Brussels seems to be here," she said, scanning the room.

It was of course an exaggeration, but in Lady Frances and Georgiana's world—not to mention Cordelia's and Aline's and Malcolm's—"everyone" had a different meaning.

Lady Frances's gaze fell upon Violet and Jane Chase, sharing a settee across the room. "I remember Mrs. Chase saying good-bye to her husband at your mother's ball, Georgy. Very affecting. They're old friends of your family, I believe, Lady Cordelia?"

"We all grew up together in Derbyshire."

"I thought I remembered that. Though I didn't get the impression Mrs. Chase and your late sister were the best of friends."

Cordelia's fingers jerked on her knife, cutting through the linen she was scraping. "What makes you think that, Lady Frances?"

"I heard them quarreling at Stuart's ball. I came round a bend in the passage, and they went quiet all of a sudden, but it was clear it wasn't a pleasant conversation."

Aline cast a sharp look between Cordelia and Suzanne.

"Did you hear anything to indicate what they were quarreling about?" Suzanne asked.

Lady Frances's delicate brows drew together. "It sounded as though Julia was saying something about 'not worth throwing your life away.' Of course I felt hopelessly awkward and was trying to pretend I hadn't heard anything at all. It was the oddest thing, though."

"What?" Cordelia said in a tight voice.

Lady Frances tucked a pale blond ringlet behind her ear. "Lady Julia had a red mark on her face. I had the distinct suspicion that Mrs. Chase had actually struck her." Lady Frances looked up and met Cordelia's tense gaze. "Oh, dear. That would have been just before your poor sister was killed. But surely you can't think—No, it's too absurd. Mrs. Chase couldn't possibly have anything to do with that horrid business."

"Of course not," Cordelia said. "Do you have any more linen, Aline?"

ᶒᶄ 37 ᶄᶒ

Cordelia pulled the door of the nursery to with more force than was necessary. She and Suzanne had looked in on the children upon their return from the Comtesse de Ribaucourt's. "Julia seems to have quarreled with everyone the night she was killed."

"One can certainly imagine her quarreling with Jane Chase," Suzanne said. "And I can see Mrs. Chase being reluctant to tell us. Save that—"

"Jane's confided so much else to us," Cordelia said. "Including her suspicions that Tony was behind Julia's death. What was so terrible about her quarrel with Julia that made it worse than that?"

"Her quarrel with Julia could cast suspicion on her rather than her husband," Suzanne said.

Cordelia drew a sharp breath. "Why on earth would Julia have been telling Jane not to throw her life away? Could Jane have been contemplating leaving Tony? In that case—"

She broke off at the sound of carriage wheels rattling to a stop directly below. They ran to the window to see that a post chaise had pulled up before the house.

"That must be the only carriage to come *into* Brussels today," Cordelia said.

The door opened before the coachman had let down the steps.

A tall man with strongly marked features and smooth, dark uncovered hair sprang down, quickly followed by a slightly less tall man with pale skin and wavy brown hair showing beneath the curling brim of a beaver hat.

"Good heavens," Suzanne said. She spun round, pausing to scoop up Colin, who had run out of the nursery and was tugging at her skirts, and hurried down the stairs and across the hall to the front door. She pushed it open, ignoring Valentin, to find David Mallinson, Viscount Worsley, and Simon Tanner on the front steps.

"Suzie." A grin broke across Simon's angular face. "You're a sight for sore eyes. You see, David, I told you she wouldn't have turned craven and fled to Antwerp."

Suzanne nearly laughed from the sheer relief of seeing familiar, friendly faces. Still holding Colin, she leaned forward to hug first Simon, then David.

Colin surveyed them with a serious gaze.

"Good day, young chap," Simon said. "I don't suppose you remember us. It's been nearly a year."

"Your uncle Simon and your uncle David," Suzanne said. "Two of Daddy's best and oldest friends."

Colin shook hands solemnly.

"David! Simon!" Aline came running down the hall like the schoolgirl she had been not so very long ago and hugged both men.

"Mrs. Blackwell." David spun her round. "I haven't seen you since you've become a married woman."

"I'm precisely the same. Save that I'm going to have a baby."

"And this is Lady Cordelia Davenport." Suzanne turned to Cordelia, who had followed her down the stairs. "She and her daughter are staying with us, as is Aline."

"David and I've known each other since we were in the nursery," Cordelia said, shaking David's hand. "Mr. Tanner, we met once at Carfax Court years ago. I've enjoyed many of your plays."

Simon grinned. "You're a diplomat, Lady Cordelia."

"And you and David are either exceedingly brave or exceedingly foolhardy to be traveling into Brussels today of all days."

"As it happens my father sent us," David said. "With messages for Malcolm."

David's father was Lord Carfax, unofficial head of British intelligence. It wasn't unusual for him to send messages to Malcolm, but David was an unusual choice of messenger. "I'm afraid Malcolm is off on an errand," Suzanne said.

"Leaving you alone?" David's brows rose.

"Not for the first or last time. And it's not as though there's a great deal he could do if the French do come marching through." A cannonade rumbled through the air to punctuate her words. "Miles off," she said in a brisk voice. "Let's get your bags unloaded and then come into the salon for some refreshment."

"The line of carriages going out of Brussels was worse than the crush outside a Mayfair ball," Simon said a quarter hour later, relaxing into a corner of one of the sofas with a glass of sherry. "Of course we galloped briskly through, even if we did get some odd looks at some of the posting houses. Not to mention stories to rival any fiction I could devise. According to some accounts the French were already in Brussels."

David leaned forward, face drawn. "Have you had any news?"

"Not since last night." Suzanne quickly brought the two men up to date on what they knew, with Cordelia and Aline filling in bits and pieces.

"Nothing to do but wait," Aline concluded.

"Damnable." Simon took a quick sip of sherry. "Whatever I thought of the war in the first place."

Cordelia cast a quick glance at him.

"Some of us argued strenuously that there were other ways to deal with Bonaparte," he said. "David did so quite eloquently in the House, to his father's horror."

David shook his head. "Even the prime minister had his doubts at first. But that's all changed."

"I rather think my husband might agree with you about there being other ways," Cordelia said. "But nobody asked him, as he'd be quick to point out."

"It's done now," David said. "We can but hope for victory."

Suzanne took a sip of sherry.

Another cannonade shook the windows of the salon. Aline flinched. Cordelia squeezed her hand.

"I'm so sorry about your sister, Cordelia," David said.

"You know?" Cordelia's sherry glass tilted in her fingers.

David exchanged a glance with Simon. "We stopped at an inn in Ghent to change horses and learned of it from a party of British who had fled Brussels. I was never more shocked. I still remember Julia playing with Amelia."

A smile shot across Cordelia's face, then faded. "Damnable to remember and think of what happened to them both."

Suzanne felt as though she'd stumbled into a play in the midst of the third act. A not unfamiliar sensation with her husband's friends. She might only have known Cordelia for two days, but of course Cordelia and David and Malcolm had all grown up in the small, interconnected world of the British ton.

"Amelia Beckwith was my father's ward," David said in response to the confusion in her gaze. "The daughter of an army friend. Father was a soldier before he succeeded to the earldom."

Suzanne nodded. It was, she knew, how Lord Carfax had come to work in intelligence. As a younger son he'd gone into the army. He'd kept his unofficial position as head of British intelligence operations after he succeeded to the earldom when his nephew and elder brother died in quick succession.

"Amelia's father was killed in India in 1805," David said. "Her mother had died in childbirth, so Father became her guardian. She came to live with us when she was twelve."

"She was just Julia's age," Cordelia said. "They met that summer at a party the Duchess of Devonshire gave at Chatsworth for the younger set."

"I think Amy liked having a friend who was outside our family," David said. "She felt the contrast of her position with my sisters'."

"She wasn't from a wellborn family?" Suzanne asked.

David flushed. Talking about social position discomfited him. "Not particularly."

"More to the point she didn't have any dowry to speak of," Simon said, his voice unusually grim.

"Yes," David said. "It made marriage more challenging for her."

Cordelia took a sip of sherry. "She never lacked for dancing partners, but marriage proposals were more problematic. A damnable predicament. Of course Julia and I didn't have any dowry to speak of, either, but at least we had the Brooke name."

"Bel never mentioned her." Suzanne had become good friends with David's sister Isobel when she and Malcolm had visited Britain the previous summer.

"No. We tend not to. It's not a happy story." David stared into his sherry glass as though looking into unwelcome memories. "Amelia drowned in the lake at Carfax Court four and a half years ago. She was seventeen." He hesitated, as though perhaps about to say more, but bit back whatever it was.

"I remember how devastated Julia was," Cordelia said. "One doesn't expect to lose one's friends at seventeen." She drew a sharp breath.

Aline met her gaze. "Unless they're marching off to battle."

Blanca did up the last string on Suzanne's gown. "I never can get used to dressing for dinner with the world tumbling to pieces about us."

"It's the British stiff upper lip." Suzanne smoothed her tulle-edged rose sarcenet skirt. She remembered putting on silk and pearls and sitting down to dinner with Wellington on the eve of the battle of Toulouse.

"Are you all right?" Blanca asked.

Suzanne turned round and smiled into her friend's concerned gaze. "As right as I can be."

"If we lose—"

"Who do you mean by 'we'?"

"That's not funny."

"I wasn't necessarily trying to be funny."

Blanca rubbed her arms. "Addison's worried. He actually admitted it to me, which he never does. All I could think to do was put my arms round him. I was nearly sick all over his coat."

Suzanne took Blanca's hand and squeezed it, though her own stomach was twisted into knots. "We'll get through this."

"You always say that."

"We always do."

Blanca shook her head. "Mr. Rannoch's off in the midst of it, and you know—"

Suzanne drew a sharp breath. Beneath the ruching on her bodice and the busk of her stays, guilt sliced into her chest. "I know Malcolm is doing what he considers his duty. And I know I'm doing the same. And that we could neither of us live with ourselves if we did anything different."

She pulled on her gloves, gave Blanca a quick hug, and made her way downstairs to the salon. The swish of beaded satin greeted her. Cordelia was pacing the length of the room.

"Sorry." She turned to Suzanne with a smile. "I can't seem to sit still."

Suzanne closed the door. "I know the feeling."

"Thank God we have David and Mr. Tanner to provide some distraction. I can see why Mr. Rannoch prizes them both as friends."

Suzanne perched on the curved arm of one of the sofas. Somehow she couldn't bring herself to sit properly. "Malcolm and David met at Harrow, and then they met Simon at Oxford. They were all in a production of *Henry IV Part I*. As Malcolm tells it they used to sit about in coffeehouses giving speeches on the ills of the world and how to correct them."

"I wish I could have heard them."

"So do I."

Cordelia perched on the other arm of the sofa. "David and Mr. Tanner share rooms?"

"In the Albany."

Cordelia nodded and didn't say more. It wasn't unusual for two young bachelors to share lodgings, but from the look on Cordelia's face Suzanne suspected she understood that David and Simon's relationship was more complicated. They were, in fact, more truly intimate than most married couples Suzanne knew. Arguably more so than she and Malcolm. For one thing, they had chosen to share their lives rather than being thrown together by circumstances and a war. And then there was the fact that neither was spying on the other. They had a comfortably settled relationship, overshadowed, Suzanne knew, by the fact that as heir to an earldom David was expected to marry and produce a son.

"I envy them," Cordelia said.

"Envy?"

"They're so wonderfully at ease in each other's presence." Cordelia plucked at the moss green satin of her skirt. "I can't imagine feeling so sure of another person."

David and Simon came into the room a few moments later, and though their shoulders didn't even brush and they moved at once to opposite ends of the room, Suzanne had to agree with Cordelia's assessment. The intimacy between them was as tangible as the warmth of the candles.

Aline followed them, tugging at her primrose satin sash. They moved into the dining room and made a strained pretense of conversation through dinner. At length Cordelia tossed down the last of her wine and pushed back her chair. "I can't take it anymore. I'm going to walk on the ramparts. Anyone care to come?"

In the end, they all did. A welcome breeze stirred the air on Brussels's stone ramparts. The cannonade was louder here, breaking the air like thunderclaps, but in a way it was easier. "It feels as though we're closer to it," Aline said as a burst of sound died in the distance. "And that makes it seem as though we can make a difference. Nonsensical."

Others had left their homes to walk the ramparts in the warm night air. They stopped several times to exchange greetings with acquaintances or to share news or the lack of it. Suzanne caught sight of a familiar figure gripping the moss-covered stone wall up ahead, bareheaded, clutching a shawl over a gauzy white gown.

"Mademoiselle Garnier," she called.

Rachel Garnier looked round, smiled, but hesitated to come forward. Suzanne moved to her side and introduced her to the others. Rachel exchanged greetings with a cautious smile and fell into step beside them. "Is Monsieur Rannoch with the army?" she asked.

Suzanne nodded. "Since last night."

Rachel plucked at her shawl with nervous fingers. "Le Paon d'Or isn't doing much of a business tonight. Obviously."

"You must be concerned for Monsieur Rivaux." The understanding between Rachel and the young Belgian lieutenant had obviously gone far beyond an exchange of services.

Rachel kept her gaze fixed on the stones ahead. "Henri came to see me last night before he left. He made a ridiculously romantic speech."

"These circumstances do tend to bring out declarations."

Rachel shook her head, stirring loose strands of hair about her face. "He doesn't understand—"

"Or perhaps he understands all too well," Suzanne said. Six years ago, before she became Raoul O'Roarke's agent, she'd been no different from Rachel. Save that the brothel where she'd been employed had been far less elegant than Le Paon d'Or. "Love can grow in unlikely places."

Rachel turned to look her full in the face. "I gave up believing in love by the time I was sixteen, Madame Rannoch."

"So did I," Suzanne said. For a moment, the cheap wine they'd drunk in the brothel in Léon was bitter in her throat. "But as with so many decisions one makes when one's young, I was wrong."

Rachel's brows drew together. "If—"

She went still, as did the others up ahead. The wind whistled against the stone and stirred the branches of the elm trees along the ramparts, suddenly loud in the stillness.

"It's stopped," Cordelia said, hugging her shawl about her. "Whatever's happened, it's over for tonight."

They turned and walked back in the warm, still night air. Rachel stayed with them part of the way to the Rue Ducale, then turned and waved good-bye. Her expression seemed a shade less grim than when they had met on the ramparts.

Valentin opened the door in the Rue Ducale, a grin on his face. Suzanne saw why when she stepped into the hall. A tall figure appeared in the library doorway, in his shirtsleeves, a whisky glass in one hand.

Suzanne ran down the marble-tiled floor and flung her arms round her husband. Malcolm's arms closed round her with gratifying force. When she pulled back enough to lift her face to his, he kissed her full on the lips, heedless of the others in the hall. Quite unlike her undemonstrative husband. But then nothing seemed to be the way it had been any longer. Half the whisky spilled over both of them.

She drew back at last, breathless, torn between a desire to laugh and to cry.

"I should go away more often," Malcolm said with a grin, though his fingers trembled where he still held her. "I told you I was just delivering a message."

"Liar." She took his hand and drew him down the hall. "Look who's joined us."

Malcolm went forward to embrace his two friends. "I should have known you were madmen enough to journey into a war zone. Glad to see age isn't rendering us too staid."

He turned to Aline and Cordelia. "Geoff's fine. I left him stitching up a wound in a young private's collarbone while giving instructions about how to set an arm and bring down an attack of wound fever."

Aline scarcely moved a muscle, but her breath shuddered through the hall.

"I saw Davenport about nine," Malcolm said to Cordelia. "A musket ball grazed his cheek, but otherwise he was unhurt."

Cordelia squeezed her eyes shut for a moment. "Thank you."

"I didn't see Ashton or George Chase, but most of the British cavalry missed the fighting."

They removed to the library, where Simon took it upon himself to refill Malcolm's glass and pour whisky for the others.

"The fighting didn't begin until about three," Malcolm said. "God knows why. If Ney had attacked sooner, we'd have been in a pretty plight."

Suzanne, who had been in the midst of taking a sip of whisky, choked and then swallowed with determination.

"When the fighting started most of our troops still hadn't arrived. Apparently the orders got muddled. But they were there by three-thirty or so and fought amazingly well after having just marched. A number of officers fought in their ball dress."

"So we prevailed?" David asked, his face taut.

"We seemed to be prevailing when I left. We were outnumbered much of the day. The Highlanders—some of the same fellows who danced at the ball last night—took a savage beating. Picton came up in relief and the Brunswickers and Van Merlen's cavalry. A few Dutch-Belgians have gone over to the French, but most have stayed loyal to the Allies."

"What about the Prussians?" Aline asked. "They haven't been able to join Wellington's forces?"

"No, they're about seven miles to the east at Ligny fighting Bonaparte himself. Wellington managed to ride over and confer with Blücher this morning before the fighting started, but it will be the devil's own work to maintain communication between the two armies."

Suzanne's nails bit into her palms. "You're going back."

"Technically it's up to the staff to maintain communication, but practically I think I can be of help."

"You seem to have been very close to the fighting," Simon said.

"Oh, I kept a healthy distance. I'm just good at synthesizing reports."

Aline went up to her room soon after, pleading the exhaustion of pregnancy. Cordelia looked from Malcolm to David and Simon. "Shall I leave as well?"

"No, if you're up to it, I'd prefer it if you stayed. You're already well in the middle of this." Malcolm glanced at David. "Your father sent you, didn't he?"

David swallowed. "Malcolm—"

"Whatever your message, you can deliver it in front of Suzanne and Cordelia. And Simon. We're in the midst of an investigation, and your father's news may have bearing on it."

David turned his whisky glass in his hand, gaze on the pale gold liquid.

"I'm not involved in the investigation," Simon said. "Would you feel better if I left?"

David's mouth relaxed into a reluctant smile. "Don't be an idiot." He reached inside his coat and drew out a sealed paper. "Father gave me this for you, Malcolm. I'm to tell you—Father thinks the French are intercepting your communications to him."

❧ 38 ❧

Suzanne's whisky glass tilted in her fingers. She tightened her grip, so hard she nearly snapped the stem. *Don't forget to breathe.* She could hear Raoul's voice in her ear. *That's the key to preserving one's equilibrium.*

Malcolm took the paper David was holding out to him. "Did your father say why he thought our communications were compromised?"

"Something to do with Upper Wimpole Street. Is that a code for something?"

Malcolm frowned at the paper. "It's the address where a French spy ring was meeting in London."

Suzanne choked down another sip of whisky.

Malcolm opened Carfax's letter and glanced through it, then moved to the desk and reached for ink and paper. "Drink some more whisky. It will take a bit of time to decode this. Suzette, get the David Hume."

It was a book code. Suzanne read out from the appropriate page in the volume of David Hume, her voice eerily calm to her own ears as she helped Malcolm decode the message. A message, she well knew, that might lead directly back to her. Her palms were damp, but her voice remained steady. Never had she so valued her early acting training.

When the letter was transformed to plaintext, Malcolm frowned at it but didn't seem overly surprised.

"Well?" Simon asked. "Was it worth our rushing into a war zone?"

"Most definitely, though as it happens I'd already worked some of it out on my own. With the disruption to our courier system, Carfax decided it was important I know about one of his double agents. Who has since been murdered."

Cordelia clunked her glass down. "Do you mean—"

Malcolm crossed the room and dropped down beside Cordelia. "I've learned a number of things in the past twenty-four hours. It wasn't the Comte de Vedrin who tried to blackmail your sister into spying for the French. It was Tony Chase."

Cordelia's eyes went wide and still in her pale face. "Dear God."

"And so Julia went to Tony's brother. Who, unbeknownst to me, is in intelligence himself, reporting directly to Lord Carfax. Julia wasn't spying for the French. She was spying for us and reporting to George."

"And George"—Cordelia squeezed her eyes shut—"had my sister whoring herself to the Prince of Orange to get information."

"Intelligence is a dirty business. As George reminded me only hours ago." Malcolm looked at Simon and David, then back at Cordelia. "With your permission—"

"Oh yes," she said. "Of course. They already know so much."

Malcolm quickly brought David and Simon up to date on the investigation into Julia Ashton's death, with Suzanne filling in bits and pieces. Cordelia sipped her whisky in silence, her fingers white-knuckled round the glass.

"You know what I find the greatest relief?" she said. "Not that my sister wasn't a traitor. That she wasn't fool enough to contemplate leaving her husband and child and running off with Tony Chase."

"I can understand that," Malcolm said.

David was frowning. "So Anthony Chase wants you dead?"

"Apparently. Presumably because he thinks I understand what really happened at Truxhillo. Which I don't."

"And the ambush that killed Lady Julia," Simon said. "Were they shooting at you? Or at Lady Julia?"

"We still don't know."

Cordelia hunched forward, shivering. "I didn't think I had any illusions about Tony. I always knew he was selfish and arrogant. But I never—"

Suzanne moved to the sofa beside Cordelia and dropped an arm round her. "You grew up with him."

"I don't know why that should make a difference."

"But it does."

Cordelia swallowed. "Yes."

"Where's Anthony Chase now?" David asked.

Malcolm turned his whisky glass in his hand. "That would seem to be the question. I spent the better part of today looking for him."

Cordelia rubbed her hand over her eyes. "You think he's joined the French?"

"Perhaps. I'm more worried he's still here to make difficulties for the British."

"I'm more worried he hasn't given up on killing you," Suzanne said. She could breathe again now the message had been decoded, but she knew that wasn't the end of it. Her blood seemed to have frozen and no amount of whisky could warm her.

David shook his head. "God in heaven—"

Malcolm gave him a crooked grin. "It's all right. After a few years of living our life, you get used to insanity."

Cordelia was frowning into her whisky glass. "I couldn't understand Julia's fancying herself head over heels in love with Tony. But I can understand this. Feeling the need to find something to do with oneself."

"And that makes it easier?" Suzanne asked.

"I don't know that it should," Cordelia said. "But it does."

David looked at Malcolm. "What does Upper Wimpole Street have to do with all this?"

"About a fortnight ago I sent your father information about a French spy ring operating there. But apparently they'd all flown the coop before Carfax could take them into custody. He thinks the only way they could have known to flee is if someone intercepted our communications and passed along a warning." Malcolm glanced down at the plaintext of Carfax's message again. "Your father also says he counts upon my discretion involving the family matter he mentioned, and that he hopes we can speak further after Bonaparte is dispatched. Do you know what he's talking about?"

David's brows rose. "You don't?"

"Not in the least."

David gave a slow nod. "More proof the French are intercepting your communications perhaps. Father wrote to you over a month since."

"About?"

David looked from Suzanne to Cordelia to Simon. Apparently even his lover wasn't privy to this particular piece of information.

"Do you want us to leave?" Suzanne asked.

David hesitated a moment, then shook his head. "An old instinct to protect family secrets. But it's foolish to hold back when we've confided so much. In fact, we were talking about it earlier today." He drew a breath. "It's Amelia. Father's taken it into his head her death wasn't an accident."

Cordelia gasped. Simon went very still.

"What makes Carfax suddenly suspect that?" Malcolm asked.

"One of the gardeners at Carfax Court fell ill recently. On his deathbed he confessed to his wife that he'd seen Amelia arguing with a man by the lake the day she died."

"Did he say why he'd kept quiet about it?"

David shook his head. "One suspects money was involved, though the man's widow claims to have found no evidence of it. Father thought—He knows how ably you investigated Princess Tatiana's murder in Vienna last autumn. He wants you to look into Amy's death."

"David," Simon said in a voice like rope pulled to the breaking point.

David cast a quick glance at his lover.

Simon was staring at David with dawning horror on his face. "All this happened a month since?"

"I would have—" David's fingers curled inward. "I'd have told you, but it was...a family matter."

Simon returned David's gaze for a long moment. "Quite."

"Simon—"

Simon sat back in his chair, his knuckles white round his whisky glass. "You know I try to stay out of matters involving your family. But in this case, it might have saved time if you'd told me."

David's brows drew together, dark slashes against his pale skin. "I don't see—"

"What do you know about Amy's death, Simon?" Malcolm asked.

Simon took a deliberate sip of whisky. "I wasn't at Carfax Court or Carfax House in London a great deal, but I was there enough to get to know Amelia."

David's family turned a blind eye to David's relationship with Simon, keeping up the pretense that they were friends who shared rooms, though Suzanne knew Lord Carfax was increasingly eager for David to marry and produce an heir.

"There was a certain sympathy between Amelia and me," Simon continued. "We both knew what it was to be outsiders in that world."

Simon's father, the son of a wealthy brewer from Northumberland, had gone off to Paris to paint and married an artist's model, Simon's mother. After they both died, the ten-year-old Simon had been sent back to England, to a family that didn't know what to make of him and packed him off to Westminster and then Oxford. He'd always had a comfortable fortune, but he was an outsider in David's aristocratic world and his Radical politics rendered him even more so. It was one of the reasons Suzanne had felt an instant kinship with him.

"So we'd talk," Simon said. "About inconsequential things usually, but we got in the habit of turning to each other when we felt particularly out in the cold. Turn of phrase," he added, in response to a look from David. "That winter—God, there's no easy way to say this." He met David's gaze across the library. "The day before she died, Amelia had confided to me that she was expecting a child."

David went as still as a sculpture carved in ice. For seconds together he simply stared at Simon. When he spoke at last, he seemed to have difficulty forcing the words from his throat. "And you never—"

"I told her I was sure there was a way out of her predicament." Simon pushed himself to his feet but checked himself, accepting the fire in David's gaze like a duelist taking a pistol shot. "I thought I had a bit of time. I was trying to figure out how to tell you, if there was a way we could get her away for long enough without your parents knowing, how we could manage things if she wanted to keep the child. I was walking across the grounds looking for you the next day so I could tell you, when the gardener's boy came running with her body in his arms."

"And then?" David stared at his lover, a pulse beating in his jaw.

"It never occurred to me that anyone had done her harm. But I feared she might have taken her own life." Simon swallowed, his gaze fixed on David's face. "I was going to tell you when we were alone that night, and then I realized—what the hell good would it have done?"

"What good would it have done for me to know the truth about my foster sister's death?" David's voice shook with disbelief. "If I'd known what she'd been going through—"

"That's just it. It was too late for you to protect her. All knowing her plight would have done is make you torture yourself. You might even have tried to find her lover—"

"Damned right, I would have," said David, who rarely swore in the presence of ladies.

"To what end?"

"So I could make the bastard pay."

"Yes, that's what I was afraid of. You might even have been mad enough to challenge him to a duel."

"I—" David, as opposed in theory to dueling as Malcolm was, opened his mouth to deny this, then went silent.

"Precisely," Simon said. "As reform-minded as you are you're still an English gentleman. Forgive me if I had no desire to see the man I love breaking the law and risking his life."

David kept his gaze on Simon. There might have been no one

else in the room. David didn't even seem to notice that Simon had alluded directly to their relationship, something that in the general course of things neither of them did in front of others. "If you'd told me even a few hours sooner—"

"Don't you think I haven't said that to myself every day for the past four and a half years?"

David drew a harsh breath. "She didn't give you any clue to who it was?"

"No."

"Damn it, Simon, you can't think I'd challenge the man to a duel now."

"I'm not entirely convinced of it. But as it happens, she truly didn't tell me."

David looked at Cordelia. "Do you think Amelia confided in your sister?"

"Julia never mentioned anything about it to me. But—" Cordelia looked at Malcolm. "Do you think this is really all coincidence? Lord Carfax became suspicious that Julia's childhood friend was murdered. And shortly afterwards Julia was killed herself."

"Which of your friends was in Derbyshire in the winter of 1810 to 1811?" Malcolm asked.

Cordelia swallowed. "All of them. George and Tony both were home on leave, and Johnny was there."

"Did Amelia seem particularly close to any of them?"

Cordelia shook her head. "Not that I remember. I was only in Derbyshire for a short time myself. Harry and I went to a house party in the Lake District. Truth to tell, George had just come back to England, and I was trying to avoid him. Much good it did me."

Malcolm nodded. "I was at Carfax Court myself briefly that winter, but I can't say I was aware of any particular sympathy between Amelia and anyone." He looked at David and Simon. Both shook their heads.

"I've gone over all my memories of that winter time and time again," Simon said. "If—"

A rumbling sound interrupted him. Carriages moving over cobblestones. Shouts quickly followed from the street outside. Without so much as exchanging glances, they all ran into the hall and out into the street. People spilled from the houses on either side of the street, some in nightclothes, some clutching glasses of wine or handfuls of cards. Shouts and questions in English and French cut the air. At last Suzanne made out that supposedly an artillery train had just retreated through the city, the British were in retreat, and the French were within a half hour's march.

She shook her head, sure it couldn't be over so simply. Though a part of her hoped against hope that it was.

"I think the artillery was going to the front," Malcolm said. "Wellington wouldn't retreat so easily."

Suzanne knew the duke well enough to realize that was all too true.

Malcolm turned back toward the house while their neighbors continued to argue. Cordelia moved to Suzanne's side. David and Simon followed, walking a few feet apart, the distance between them palpable.

"We'll get no more intelligence tonight," Malcolm said as they stepped into the hall.

Cordelia cast a glance at David and Simon, then moved toward the stairs. "I don't know that I can sleep, but I suppose we should try."

They all took candles and climbed the stairs. On the landing, they murmured subdued good nights. David and Simon hadn't so much as met each other's gaze. "Cordelia," Malcolm said softly, when he and Suzanne and Cordelia were alone on the first-floor landing.

Cordelia looked at him in inquiry over the flame of her candle.

"George says Julia worked for him, but they weren't lovers."

Cordelia returned Malcolm's gaze for a long moment and inclined her head. "Thank you. Though oddly, I find that it doesn't matter very much anymore."

"I hope David and Simon talk," Suzanne said to Malcolm in the privacy of their bedchamber.

"I doubt they will." Malcolm set his candle on the chest of drawers. "David's the sort who shuts down instead of fighting."

"There's a reason you're such good friends. You're much alike." Suzanne used her candle to light the tapers on her dressing table. "Did you know Amelia Beckwith?"

"A bit. But in those days I was even more inclined to retreat to the library with a book than I am now. I certainly never guessed—" He shrugged out of his coat, the same black evening coat he'd worn to the Duchess of Richmond's ball, and stared at the dusty superfine with drawn brows.

Suzanne peeled off her gloves and dropped them on the dressing table. "Cordelia's right. The connection to Julia is suspiciously coincidental."

"So it is." Malcolm tugged at his crumpled cravat. "And if Julia Ashton's killer is the person who intercepted messages between Carfax and me it narrows the field."

Suzanne froze in the midst of removing her pearl earrings. "You think Tony Chase was intercepting your communications with Carfax?"

"Possibly." Malcolm began to unbutton his stained ivory brocade waistcoat. "But George Chase is the one who knew Carfax's courier system."

"Tony Chase could have learned about the courier system from his brother somehow."

"He could. Or I could have been wrong to believe George's denials that he's working for the French as well."

Suzanne dropped the second earring in its velvet-lined compartment beside the first, biting back all the objections she couldn't possibly make. "Damn George for not telling you Tony was trying to kill you."

Malcolm shrugged out of his waistcoat, wincing at the pull on the wound in his side. "I'm not feeling particularly charitable toward him myself. But I think I do understand."

Suzanne's fingers froze on the silver filigree clasp of her necklace. "Are you saying you'd protect Edgar, even at the risk of someone else's life?"

"No. At least I hope not. But I can understand the impulse. And then there's—" He broke off, frowning at the shirt cuff he'd been unfastening.

"Fitz." Suzanne carefully aligned the pearl necklace against the black velvet in her jewelry box. Fitzwilliam Vaughn, Malcolm's friend and fellow attaché from Vienna, was now on a mission in India. Talking about him at all was like touching a half-healed wound.

"Difficult not to make the comparison." Malcolm tugged the button free. "I need to find Tony Chase. For a whole host of reasons."

Suzanne crossed the room to her husband. "I can't believe you can actually stay the night."

Malcolm pulled his shirt over his head with tired fingers. Someone, she was pleased to see, probably Geoffrey Blackwell, had changed his bandages. "I'm scarcely fit for anything else."

Her gaze moved over the hollow of his throat, the angle of his shoulders, the lean lines of muscle picked out by the candlelight. "Not anything?"

His eyes widened in genuine surprise. "Suzette—"

"If there ever was a time to take pleasure where we can find it—" She took his face between her hands and covered his mouth with her own. When the pull of competing loyalties threatened to tear her in two, she'd always been able to find solace in his arms. A communication that bridged all differences and drove out treacherous thoughts. Once, when she'd feared Malcolm would never let down the barriers that kept them apart, she'd thought this was the only sort of knowledge she'd ever have of him. Even now it was the easiest way to reach him. And the only way she knew to drive the demons from her mind.

His arms closed tight round her, but she felt his moment of hesitation, as though he feared to take advantage of her humor. She deepened the kiss and sank her fingers into his hair, leaving no doubt of what she wanted. When his lips moved to her cheek, she heard the edge of desperation in his breath. The desperation of a man who wonders if he's making love to his wife for the last time.

His fingers shook as he lifted her in his arms and moved to the bed. She pulled him down to her and surrendered to welcome oblivion. Later she even slept for a time, curled against his chest, one hand clasping his own, his heartbeat steady beneath her ear.

A cry jerked her from her sleep. Malcolm was already on his feet, pulling on his dressing gown and pushing up the window. She scrambled into her own dressing gown and ran to his side. She could make out the words now. *"Les français sont ici! Les français sont ici!"*

❧ 39 ❧

Saturday, 17 June

Suzanne leaned out the window beside Malcolm. In the street below, a man banged on their door, shouted his message about the French, then ran down the street to do the same at the next house. The street was full of people again, in varying states of déshabille, some milling about, some carrying paintings, chairs, chests, and small tables down to their cellars.

"'Rumor doth double, like voice and echo, the numbers of the feared.'" Malcolm closed the window and gave her a quick kiss.

They found Cordelia and David in the hall with Valentin and the maids. "Blanca's in the nursery," Cordelia said, her arm round Brigitte, one of the maids, a girl of fifteen. "The children seem to have slept through it, thank goodness."

Aline came hurrying through the green baize door from the kitchen. "Simon's making coffee, and he says there'll be toast and eggs in a quarter hour."

"I'll see what I can learn from Stuart," Malcolm said.

He returned from Stuart's by the time they had finished Simon's impromptu breakfast. "Some Belgian troops ran from the battlefield apparently," he said, dropping into a chair at the breakfast table and accepting a cup of coffee from Suzanne. "Their cavalry galloped through the city early this morning and set off a panic. The roads to Antwerp are more clogged than they were yesterday."

"Good thing we're planning to sit tight." Simon spread marmalade on a piece of toast. He and David had barely made eye contact all morning.

Malcolm pushed back his chair a short time later. "Stuart will keep you apprised of news." He hesitated. "Casualties from Quatre Bras are sure to reach the city today."

Suzanne nodded. "That will keep us busy."

She persuaded him to let her change his bandages before he left and was relieved to see both wounds were healing cleanly. She went out into the street with him and saw him swing himself up onto Perdita. She touched her fingers to the horse's neck. "Take care of each other." Perdita nuzzled her hair in response.

Malcolm bent down from the saddle to give her a quick, hard kiss. It was as though they both feared that this time a more prolonged farewell was tempting fate. Not that either of them believed in fate.

David left the house shortly after Malcolm saying he was going to see what news he could discover. The ladies were going to walk round to the Comtesse de Ribaucourt's again. Cordelia and Aline went to put on their bonnets. Suzanne lingered downstairs and followed Simon into the study. She found him standing by the windows. The lines of his back showed taut against the glazing. The light from the window glanced off his whitened knuckles.

"I know it's still morning, but you look as though you could do with a drink," she said, moving to the table with the decanters.

"A drink won't solve this." Simon turned round and leaned against the windowsill.

"No, but it can dull the edges of the pain. Trust me, I know."

"You're a fine one to talk. Do you and Malcolm ever fight?"

She splashed sherry into two glasses. "It's not so much what we say as what goes unsaid."

He gave a wintry smile. "That sounds like Malcolm."

She crossed to him and put one of the glasses in his hand. "It's amazing what one can get through."

He curled his fingers round the etched glass and stared down into the sherry. "I don't think David will ever forgive me."

"One doesn't forgive precisely. One gets past things."

He took a swallow of sherry. "So cynical, Lady?"

"So realistic, Lord. I've been married two and a half years. You've been with David longer than that."

"And we've got past a lot. But this is family. And duty. And honor. Everything that makes David what he is."

And Malcolm. Last autumn in Vienna when she confessed about her relationship with Frederick Radley, Malcolm had got past the revelation that she wasn't the sexual innocent he'd thought her to be when they'd married with surprising ease. What she'd told him was a series of half-truths, but she still hadn't thought his feelings for her would survive it. "People can surprise you."

"So they can. But everyone has their breaking point. David's a brilliant man, a humanist, an idealist, a reformer. But he's also an English gentleman to his core."

A chill coursed through her. However much Malcolm had surprised her last autumn, she couldn't expect his feelings for her would survive greater revelations. He loved her, which she'd never thought possible, but his love was predicated on his not knowing the truth of who she was.

She forced a sip of sherry down her throat. "Mr. Darcy."

Simon raised his brows.

"Do you remember when I first read *Pride and Prejudice*? You'd sent it to Malcolm in Lisbon. I hadn't even met you yet, but I wrote to you after I read the book. I said Malcolm reminded me of Mr. Darcy in some ways, and you wrote back that you felt the same about David. That inbred sense of duty and responsibility. Appealing. But damnably difficult to live with."

Simon swirled the sherry in his glass. "I always knew David's family loyalty would come between us. I just didn't think it would be like this."

For a moment, Lord Carfax was such a tangible force in the room he might have been present. Suzanne touched Simon's arm. "We're none of us thinking very rationally right now."

"I've replayed my decisions about Amelia every day for the past four and a half years. If I had to do it again, I'd tell David of her plight immediately. But I still don't think I'd tell him after she died. Protecting him. Perhaps protecting myself." He took another swallow of sherry. "No apology is going to wipe away what I did."

Suzanne slid her arm round him. "Give it time. You and David have more between you than most couples I know."

"But then the more one cares, the more power one has to hurt." Simon looked down at her. "Are you all right?"

"Of course."

"Liar. You must be a stone lighter than when I saw you in England last summer. And you were thin then."

"It's the wretched heat." She drew a breath. "Malcolm is out there looking for a man who's trying to kill him." And who was spying for her side.

Simon put his own arm round her and she leaned against him, grateful beyond measure for simple human warmth.

"You back, Malcolm?" Colonel Canning, his dark blue aide-de-camp's frock coat creased, his collar stained, edged his horse toward Malcolm's own. "Thought you'd returned to Brussels."

"I did."

"Crazy devil." Canning cast a glance round the fields of Quatre Bras. Bloodstains showed against the trampled corn. Bodies sprawled where they had fallen yesterday. A sickening number of kilted Highlanders and cuirassiers in burnished breastplates lay about the walled farm of Quatre Bras at the center of the crossroads. Soldiers who had survived the battle sipped tea from tin cups or cleaned their weapons, waiting for their battalions to be called to march. "Don't you know when you're well out of it?"

"I do. I got a night in a soft bed."

"And returned in time to see our retreat." Canning grimaced as the soldiers whose battalion had just been called fell into place, marching north toward Mont-Saint-Jean, to keep in contact with their Prussian allies.

"Tactical withdrawal."

"That's the spirit. Hookey would be proud of you." Canning

cast a glance at Wellington, lying on his cloak on the grass not far off, a newspaper spread over his face. "He was laughing over some gossip from the London papers not long ago."

"Which goes miles toward keeping up morale." Fitzroy Somerset pulled up beside them. "You might not think it to look round, but the withdrawal's actually going quite smoothly." He cast a glance at the sky where inky black clouds had begun to mass. "And so far the rain's held off."

Malcolm glanced toward Frasnes, where he'd heard Ney had withdrawn for the night. "Have the French given you any trouble?"

"No, they've been strangely silent. Though the more of our men march, the more nervous the remaining ones get. There are that many fewer to face a French attack if it does come."

Canning cast a glance at Fitzroy, then leaned toward Malcolm. "I say, Rannoch, what the devil's happened between you and Gordon? I could tell something was up when you and Davenport spoke to him at Headquarters—God, was it only the day before yesterday? And when I said something about you last night he got an odd look on his face."

Fitzroy's fair brows drew together. After all, he'd been there when March told Malcolm about Gordon slipping away from Stuart's ball.

"Just a tedious bit of investigation," Malcolm said. "Nothing lasting." At least, he profoundly hoped that was the case. Suzanne's comment that Gordon was the sort of man Wellington might have employed to deal with Julia Ashton lingered uncomfortably in his memory.

Concern drew at Canning's good-natured face. For all he had gone through in the Peninsular War, Malcolm doubted it had ever occurred to Canning that his friends could be on anything but the side of truth and honor. "I just hate to see you not friends. Not given what we may be facing tomorrow."

"So do I." Malcolm looked from Canning to Fitzroy. "You haven't seen George Chase by any chance, have you?"

"He's probably with Uxbridge," Fitzroy said. "The cavalry's got orders to cover the retreat."

Canning regarded Malcolm for a moment. "Is this to do with Julia Ashton's death?"

"What makes you think that?" Malcolm asked.

"You have that look you get when the game's afoot." Canning leaned forward in the saddle again. "Does George Chase have anything to do with Julia Ashton? Besides the fact that he was her sister's lover?"

"Do you have reason to think he does?" Malcolm asked, his pulse quickening.

"No. But if you do—" Canning fingered his reins. "I went out into the garden at Stuart's ball. Not long before all that fuss about Wellington and Stuart and Slender Billy leaving the ballroom. I saw Chase and his brother coming in through the garden gate."

Fitzroy, quick to see the implications, drew a sharp breath.

Malcolm stared into Canning's open, cheerful face. "You saw George and Anthony Chase coming through the garden gate together at Stuart's ball?"

"Yes, I told you—"

"Why in God's name didn't you say something sooner?"

"I didn't think anything of it. All sorts of people must have been in and out of the house that night. But if there's any chance George Chase has anything to do with Lady Julia's death—"

"Quite," Malcolm said.

A tearful Georgiana Lennox greeted Suzanne, Cordelia, and Aline at the Comtesse de Ribaucourt's. "The Duke of Brunswick has been killed. I said good-bye to him at Mama's ball only the night before last. And—" She bit her lip and put her hands over her eyes. "Lord Hay."

"Oh, Georgy." Suzanne hugged her friend. The bright-eyed young ensign had been a favorite waltzing partner of Georgiana's. Suzanne had wondered if in time he'd become something more.

Georgiana hiccoughed. "I keep seeing him that night. After we found out the troops were to march. He wanted me to dance, and I was cross because he was so excited to be going off to war. I can't believe that was the last time I'll ever speak to him." She dashed a hand across her eyes.

"No time for tears, Georgy." Cordelia put her hands on the younger girl's shoulders. "The streets will be full of wounded before long. We have work to do."

Georgiana swallowed and gave a quick nod. Cordelia squeezed her shoulders.

"Mrs. Rannoch."

Suzanne turned round at the anxious voice to see Violet Chase hurrying toward them.

"I wondered if you'd heard—" Violet stopped, fingering a fold of her blue-sprigged skirt. "I thought perhaps your husband had come back to Brussels last night."

"Malcolm said most of the British cavalry weren't involved in the fighting yesterday," Suzanne said. "So George should have been out of danger. As should Captain Ashton. I'm afraid we don't know about Tony."

Violet drew a gasping breath. "Thank you."

Georgiana looked after Violet as she returned to Jane, who was sitting bolt upright on a settee. "When we heard about the Highlanders being cut to pieces yesterday poor Mrs. Chase went quite pale. Which I thought odd, as her husband's in the 95th and Major Chase is on Lord Uxbridge's staff. I suppose they must have friends among the Highlanders."

Suzanne looked at Jane Chase, scraping lint with methodical fingers and numb eyes. Lady Frances Webster's comments the previous day—God, had it only been a day?—about Jane Chase's apparent quarrel with Julia echoed through her mind. With a host of new implications.

They left the comtesse's, armed with scissors and lint and flasks of water and brandy, and nearly tripped over wounded soldiers as they stepped from the house. The sun beat down on the cobblestones, loosing the smell of blood and dirt from crusted uniforms. The wounded lay everywhere. Some had walked the more than twenty miles from Quatre Bras and dropped where they stood. Others had been brought into the city in carts and wagons. Suzanne had nursed the wounded in the Peninsula. Geoffrey Blackwell had taught her to dig out bullets and stitch wounds and more times than she cared to remember she'd closed the eyes of the dead. But never had she seen casualties on this scale.

Cordelia, who would have no such past history, worked beside her with brisk determination, as did Aline. The morning's panic was gone from the streets. Bruxellois and British expatriates worked side by side, as though present need had pushed their fears to the background.

In the chaos, it was an easy matter for Suzanne to slip off and make her way to Madame Longé's. Wounded men lay on the floor of the dressmaker's, and Madame Longé and her assistants were cutting bolts of pristine muslin into bandages. Their sympathies might be Bonapartist, but that did not stop them from doing what they could for the wounded. Lucille, the seamstress who was Suzanne's chief contact, scrambled to her feet and hurried to Suzanne's side.

Suzanne put a message for Raoul into Lucille's hand. "I don't know when he'll be back in Brussels." Or if, but that was something she wouldn't let herself think about. "But I know he'll check here. This is important."

Lucille nodded. "I'll make sure he gets it, madame."

"Thank you." Suzanne squeezed Lucille's hand and returned to the street where she and Cordelia and Aline were working, armed with a pile of fresh bandages.

Early in the afternoon—at least she guessed it was so, though she'd rather lost track of time—she returned to the Comtesse de Ribaucourt's for more water and saw a familiar figure outside the door. Rachel Garnier's hair was drawn back in a simple knot and she wore a gray muslin round gown, but her face was unmistakable.

"Madame Rannoch," she said, coming toward Suzanne. "Are you going inside? Could you see if they have any lint to spare? I've quite run out."

"Of course. Come in with me. You can sit for a moment."

Rachel shook her head. "I hardly think I'd be well received."

They might be at war, but the divide between a prostitute and a lady of fashion was greater than that between the British and the

French. Suzanne bit back an hysterical laugh at the thought of what the comtesse would think should she know of Suzanne's own past. She had been an outsider when she married Malcolm, an émigrée war bride who had snagged a wealthy husband. Slowly she was coming to be accepted in Malcolm's world. But they would shun her in an instant if they had the least idea of her true origins. And there were times when she thought it wasn't her work for the French that would be the most shocking to Malcolm's friends.

She went inside and returned quickly, flasks of water replenished and more rolls of lint gathered up for Rachel. Rachel smiled in gratitude. "Is Monsieur Rannoch still with the army?"

Suzanne nodded. "He returned to Brussels last night, but he's gone back." She scanned Rachel's tense face. "Have you had news of Lieutenant Rivaux?"

Rachel shook her head and made a show of tucking the lint beneath her arm. "There's no reason for anyone to let me know. I don't have any right to be concerned."

"Concern isn't a matter of rights."

Rachel gave a faint smile. "Concern isn't supposed to be something I have time for. But yes, I am. Terribly."

Over Rachel's shoulder Suzanne saw another familiar figure coming down the street. Jane Chase.

"Mrs. Rannoch." Jane's face was drained of color and her cambric morning dress was caked with dirt about the hem and splashed with blood, but then that was true of Suzanne and Rachel and everyone else tending the wounded.

Suzanne introduced Rachel. Jane shook hands with no appearance of shock. Either she didn't know who Rachel was or she was more unconventional than Suzanne had at first supposed.

"I came in search of more brandy," Jane said.

"I'll go in with you," Suzanne offered.

Jane faltered climbing the steps to the door. Suzanne took her arm and steered her past the footman into the front salon. "Sit down for a moment." She pressed Jane into a chair. "You look ready to drop."

It was true, though her reasons for asking Jane to sit were hardly disinterested. But then what did she ever do that was wholly disinterested?

Suzanne poured a cup of the tea the comtesse had set out and put it into Jane's hand. "In truth I've been wanting to speak with you."

Jane took an automatic sip and looked at Suzanne with confused eyes.

"Lady Frances Webster heard you quarreling with Julia Ashton at Stuart's ball."

Jane's eyes narrowed. She wasn't quite as ready to drop as she appeared. "I passed Julia in the passage outside one of the salons, but we merely exchanged greetings. Lady Frances must have been mistaken."

"And then today Georgy Lennox said you went quite pale at the news about the Highlanders."

Jane's fingers tightened round the teacup. "The news was dreadful. So many of the soldiers who danced for us at the duchess's ball are dead."

"It's horrible. But Georgy didn't mention anyone else going pale. Are you close to anyone in the regiment?"

"No, of course not, but—"

"Because when I put the two things together, the oddest thought occurred to me." Suzanne looked into Jane Chase's hazel eyes. "Mrs. Chase, do you have a lover among the Highlanders?"

❧ 40 ❧

The cup tumbled from Jane Chase's fingers, spattering tea over her already-stained skirt and shattering into shards of rose and gold porcelain on the carpet. Jane stared down at the wreckage as though looking into hell, then raised her gaze to Suzanne's face. "How in God's name do you do it?"

"Putting puzzle pieces together. And then shifting the puzzle to look at it in a different way."

Jane put her hands over her face.

"I must say after what your husband put you through, I'm rather relieved at the thought you had a lover," Suzanne said.

Jane gave a harsh laugh. "I never meant—I had mad revenge thoughts when I first realized Tony had strayed, but they soon faded. I thought I was better than he was. Ironic, isn't it?"

"Not in the least, considering I suspect you cared for your lover more than Captain Chase cared for any of his."

"Then I met Will. Captain William Flemming. At a review last month. Violet was overcome by the heat, and he offered to fetch us lemonade." She drew a strained breath, though for a moment remembered happiness flashed in her eyes. "He looked at me as though I was a woman. More than that. He looked at me as though I was a person, which is an even rarer thing."

"Infinitely," Suzanne said, thinking of Malcolm.

Jane's fingers twisted in the folds of her skirt. "It was completely mad, yet in Brussels these past few weeks one didn't think of the future. Despite everything hanging over us, I think I was the happiest I've been in years." She stared down at the broken cup. "If it wasn't for Will perhaps I'd have taken the children back to England."

"It does no good to refine upon the past. Or to blame yourself."

"And yet despite it all—" Jane hugged her arms round herself. "I thought Tony couldn't hurt me more, but the affair with Julia Ashton did hurt. And when I said good-bye to him at the duchess's ball—Mrs. Rannoch, does it sound utterly mad to love two men at once in entirely different ways?"

Suzanne remembered her wash of panic at the thought of Raoul going off to battle. "No. Merely hellishly uncomfortable."

Jane stared at her hands. "I don't think Tony knew. Knows. I don't think it ever even occurred to him it was possible."

"Men can be so damnably obtuse." Or in Malcolm's case hearteningly naïve in his faith in humanity, not to mention in his wife. "But Lady Julia learned of it."

"I'm still not sure how. Will and I wrote to each other occasionally, but we were careful." Jane drew a shuddering breath. "At Stuart's ball, I danced with Will—Tony didn't even notice of course—and I was overcome by how utterly impossible our liaison was. Julia found me in tears. She told me she'd ended things with Tony and that she'd have thought I had the wit to know things weren't always what they appeared. I mumbled something. Then Julia took me by the shoulders and said—" Jane's eyes went dark not with guilt but with anger.

"What?" Suzanne asked in a gentle voice.

"She said I was a fool to think it could possibly be worth it to throw away my husband and children for an idle fancy."

"That must have been galling."

"For a moment I was struck dumb." Jane pushed herself to her feet. "When I was able to speak, I said how dared she of all people offer me advice and especially advice of that sort. Julia said it was precisely because of her own mistakes that she understood what I was risking. She seemed so serious that for a moment I actually found myself nodding my head. Then the full, horrid absurdity struck me. And so I struck her."

"I can understand the impulse."

"I shouldn't have let myself sink to that level. But in that moment—" Jane shook her head, mouth drawn into a taut line. "All my anger at everything that's happened since my marriage was focused on Julia."

Jane spun away, suppressed violence in the snap of her skirts and the taut line of her shoulders. Before Suzanne could respond, the front door opened and Sarah and Georgiana Lennox's voices sounded in the hall. Jane hurried to join them, and Suzanne knew she had pushed her as far as she could for now. Suzanne spoke briefly with the Lennox sisters, who were pale and drawn at what they had seen but determined. They were the daughters and sisters of soldiers.

A few minutes later they all left the house armed with fresh supplies and separated to return to where they'd been working. Jane Chase had recovered her equanimity remarkably well. Suzanne struggled to rearrange the puzzle pieces in light of this new information. The depth of Jane's anger at Julia was plain, and however blatant Tony Chase's philandering, a woman stood to lose far more than her husband if her love affair was discovered. But it was difficult to imagine Jane having the resources and the time to arrange the ambush. Although—

"Madame Rannoch." It was Lucille, hurrying down the street toward her. "I was hoping I could find you. I thought you'd want to know. Your friend stopped by the shop. She said she'll be at home this afternoon."

Suzanne drew a breath of relief, while at the same time tension shot through her. Raoul was alive. And what she had to discuss with him could shake her world to the core.

Cordelia snipped off a length of linen and knotted her bandage. "There. I'm afraid I've mangled it horribly. Thank you for being so forbearing."

"On the contrary, ma'am." The Highland sergeant was pale and a sheen of sweat showed on his forehead, but he spoke in a cheerful voice. "I've known more than one surgeon with hands that were less steady."

"You're very kind." Cordelia pulled a flask of water from her pocket. "Were many of your comrades killed?"

His eyes, a pale, clear blue, darkened at the memories. "Only five of us were left standing."

Cordelia shivered as she uncorked the flask. "I saw some of your comrades dance at the Duchess of Richmond's ball." She slid her arm beneath his shoulders and lifted him to take a sip of water. "It seems horrid now that we all stood about applauding entertainment right before you marched off to battle." Betraying tears sprang to her eyes as she eased him back down on the cobblestones. She adjusted the folded coat that formed a makeshift pillow.

"Is your husband in the army, ma'am?"

She nodded, eyes on the frayed wool of the coat.

"He's a lucky man to have you to come back to."

Cordelia choked, torn between a laugh and a sob. She could only hope that having her in Brussels didn't make Harry less eager to return.

Today was entirely beyond her experience. In her childhood, even minor scrapes and bruises had been tended to by the nursery maids. The closest she'd come to actually dealing with an injury was when Julia had fallen and banged her knee. Cordelia had run ahead to alert their nurse while George carried Julia back to the house. Since Livia's birth, Cordelia had learned to cope with scraped knees and runny noses and the occasional cut finger. But nothing like this. When they'd first stepped into the street from the comtesse's, she'd nearly doubled over and been sick on the cobblestones.

Suzanne Rannoch's fingers had closed round her wrist in an iron grip that was somehow reassuring. Suzanne was so amazingly calm. Snipping bandages, bathing wounds and packing them with lint, even stitching cuts and digging out bullets with no laudanum to keep the men from screaming. Cordelia couldn't hope for a quarter of Suzanne's sangfroid, but she could at least copy some of it. And somehow, though the smells and cries were still there, they had become part of her accepted reality. It was not that the horror had lessened, simply that it was difficult to imagine anything else. There was something almost commonplace about going through the motions of bathing wounds, cleaning out bits of cloth and debris from torn flesh, snipping bandages, wiping foreheads, offering sips of water, judging which wounds she could treat herself and when it was necessary to summon one of the Belgian doctors moving tirelessly among the wounded.

The first time she had looked up from fumbling with a flask of brandy to see the young private she was treating staring back at her with the fixed glassiness of death, she'd nearly been sick again. For a moment she'd been thrown back four nights to Stuart's ball, looking down at Julia's lifeless body. But now closing the eyes of the dead was another accepted part of her reality.

"Cordelia." The sound of her name stopped her as she turned from putting the sergeant into the care of two young boys who were going to help him back to his billet. It was Violet Chase, side curls plastered to her forehead and cheeks, India muslin gown spattered with gray and black and red, sash lost somewhere along the way. "Do you have any more lint?" Violet asked. "I was on my way back to the comtesse's to ask for some."

Cordelia handed her a packet of lint. Violet took it but hesitated a moment, glancing round the street. Wounded men lined either side. "Do you remember the time Tony hit George in the head with a cricket ball? I think that's the most blood I've ever seen. Until today."

Cordelia nodded. "You look as though you're bearing up."

"No alternative."

"Collapse and have hysterics."

"Too tiresome. And there'd be no one to listen."

Cordelia smiled at her childhood friend. "How's Jane?"

"Working feverishly. So's Annabel. I shall have to take back every time I ever called her missish."

Cordelia gave a twisted smile. "I knew that when Annabel put up with everything George and I put her through."

Violet fingered a fold of her skirt. "Why does it take something so dreadful happening for one to realize what's important?"

"My dear Violet, if we were more rational creatures, life would be much simpler. But perhaps less interesting. Here now, don't cry." Cordelia flung her arms round her friend as Violet gave a choked sob. They clung together as they hadn't since they were in the schoolroom. Before Julia and Johnny, George and Harry, and all the circumstances that had put distance between them.

At length Violet drew back, rubbing her eyes. "I'll do now. I didn't mean to be a watering pot."

Cordelia smiled. "What are old friends for?"

Violet nodded, turned away, then looked back over her shoulder. "Cordy? Do you think I could possibly manage to be a passable wife?"

"I think there's always been very little you couldn't do with enough determination."

A smile broke across Violet's face. Then she bit her lip, no doubt at the fear that she'd never get the chance to put Cordelia's words to the test.

George Chase stared at Malcolm through the pelting rain that dripped from the overhanging branches. "Now you think I'm a double agent?" he demanded in a furious whisper.

Malcolm kept his hands steady on the reins. French lancers had come up at the end of the British withdrawal from Quatre Bras, so he hadn't been able to seek out George for some time. He had found George at last delivering a message to the cavalry protecting the long column from French pursuit as the Allied army fell back to maintain communications with the Prussians. At Malcolm's suggestion, he and George had withdrawn to a copse of trees that bordered the road. George had been ready enough to talk, but at Malcolm's questions anger flared in his eyes, swift as the lightning that broke the sky.

"Information you had access to fell into French hands," Malcolm said in response to George's question.

George cast a quick glance toward the road, but the relentless torrent of rain, the thud of boots slogging through the mud, and the jangle of bridles and neighing of horses provided better cover than stone walls. "I was hardly the only one who had access to it."

"And you slipped out of Stuart's ball in company with your brother the night Lady Julia was killed."

"That's what makes you think I'm working for the French?"

"Given that your brother is, it's not a surprising conclusion." Someone fired off a pistol not far away. The French kept dancing close to the column but pulled back as soon as the Allied cavalry threatened engagement. "As I calculate it, you and Tony would have had time to set up the ambush that killed Lady Julia. Or possibly to have ridden to the château and killed her yourselves."

George pulled his horse to the side as a burst of rainwater broke through the leaves above. From the distance came the sound of round shot thudding into the mud. "The explanation is much more prosaic. Tony confronted me about seeing me with Julia earlier in the evening. We went out into the garden and then into the mews so no one would hear us."

"You told me he didn't speak to you about seeing you with Lady Julia."

George passed a weary hand over his face. "Because I knew the more I said the more it would lead to just this type of question."

"Did you tell him you knew Julia was his agent?"

"No, of course not. I was still protecting her cover. And my own."

It was barely plausible. Plausible enough that Malcolm knew he wouldn't be able to shake George Chase. So he fell back on his next best option and switched tacks without pausing to give George time to reflect. "You visited Carfax House quite a bit growing up. It's not surprising you ended up working for Carfax."

A Congreve rocket, set off by Major Whinyates's troop, exploded in the distance with a hiss. It had probably fallen wide of its mark, as rockets usually did. Hopefully at least it had scared the French and hadn't fallen on any of the Allies. George adjusted his grip on the reins. "I suppose you could put it that way. Carfax suggested the arrangement when I bought my commission."

"You knew David before I did. And his sisters. And Amelia Beckwith."

"Carfax's ward?" Through the leafy shadows, George's face betrayed remembered sadness but no present fear. "Yes, of course. Terrible what happened to her."

"And I suppose your brother knew her as well."

"We were all invited to Carfax House entertainments."

Malcolm kept his gaze steady on George's face. For all his open, friendly demeanor, George, like him, was trained to deception. "Do you think there's any possibility Amelia was more than an acquaintance to your brother?"

Seemingly genuine bewilderment shot through George's gaze. "What are you suggesting?"

"It seems Amelia may have had a lover just before she died."

George drew a breath. "What on earth does that have to do with Julia's death?"

"I'm not entirely sure yet. But Amelia and Julia were friends. Julia might have known the lover's identity."

The horror of hitherto-unforeseen possibilities filled George's eyes. "And you think this lover—"

"It's too early to think anything."

A crack of lightning cut the sky, followed by the roar of thunder. George stared through the trees at the blur of red that was the slowly moving Allied column. "If Amelia had a lover it wasn't Tony."

"You sound very sure."

George shot a look at Malcolm. "It wasn't me, either."

"Who was it?"

"I never said—"

"You didn't need to."

George tugged at his high-standing collar. "Look, Rannoch—"

"Was it John Ashton?"

"Johnny?" George gave a harsh laugh, louder than anything he had said. "Rather reassuring that even you can bark up the wrong tree."

"Who then? If you want me to find Julia's killer, you don't want me wasting my time."

George stared at him for a moment. Another pistol fired in the distance. Three shots answered it. "I'm actually surprised you didn't know. He's more your friend than mine. He used to visit Carfax Court when he was at school in England."

"Who?"

George hesitated a moment, as though he still feared to put it into words. In the column, someone was singing "Ahé Marmont," a favorite song from the Peninsula. "His Royal Highness the Prince of Orange."

❧ 41 ❧

Suzanne slammed shut the door to the room in the alley off the Rue d'Isabelle. "Damn it, Raoul, we're in trouble. I should have known this would happen. We should have had a plan—"

"*Querida.*" He caught her wrists in both hands. "Calm down. Things always go wrong. We can always fix them. What's happened?"

"Carfax figured out there's an information leak."

He released his breath. "For God's sake, *querida*, Carfax is a spymaster. He has to know he probably has a dozen information leaks."

"It was the raid on the Comte de Lisle's group in London. I knew warning them was dangerous."

"Are you saying you wish we hadn't?"

"No, of course not. But Carfax figured out we must have intercepted his communications to be able to warn them, and now Malcolm thinks George Chase is the leak—"

"Well, then."

Suzanne jerked her hands free of his grip. "He thinks an innocent man is a double agent."

Raoul folded his arms across his chest. "Malcolm is a sensible man. He'll sort it out. And I imagine Major Chase can take care of himself."

"It's playing merry hell with the investigation into Julia Ashton's death. And I'm lying to Malcolm."

Raoul regarded her in silence.

It was several seconds before she realized the full idiocy of what she'd said. She put her hands to her face. "Oh, my God."

"When you're playing a role for a long time it can seem real," Raoul said, his voice gentle. "Or perhaps in this case it would be more accurate to say it becomes real."

"I've lied to Malcolm every day of our marriage. I lie to him by omission every moment we spend together. I don't know why lying about the investigation should seem worse."

"Perhaps because it feels more personal."

"When we investigated Princess Tatiana's murder in Vienna we worked as a team. It was—" She rubbed her arms. "Rather wonderful."

"You obviously complement each other well."

"But this is different. Julia Ashton was a French spy; her death is mired in intelligence operations." She pressed her fingers to her forehead. Her temples were throbbing. "I committed a great sin against Malcolm when I married him. Before I married him. Before I properly knew him. Knowing him—loving him—doesn't change the sin."

"Not in theory. But it makes it damnably more difficult in practice."

She groaned and dropped into the ladder-back chair. "I didn't come here to wallow in my guilt. What do we do?"

Raoul moved to the cot. "I expect George Chase will be able to convince Malcolm he isn't a double agent."

"Which will force Malcolm to look for the leak elsewhere."

"He has a lot to distract him now. And a wide field when he does look." Raoul dropped down on the edge of the cot. "You're the last person in the world he'd suspect, *querida*."

Her fingers dug into the muslin of her skirt. "I know. That's what makes it so awful." She swallowed hard, forcing down everything roiling inside her. She'd done it for two and a half years; she could go on doing it.

"Suzanne—" Raoul leaned toward her, then winced, his hand going to his side.

She sprang to her feet. "You're hurt."

"Only a scratch." He put out a hand to forestall her. "I was liaisoning with some Belgians who'd made overtures about deserting, and I ran into a British patrol."

"Let me see." She reached for his arm.

He caught her wrist. "A competent doctor cleaned it thoroughly and put a nice bandage on it."

"Which doesn't mean it isn't festering." She dropped down beside him on the cot. "Take off your shirt. Don't turn prim; it isn't anything I haven't seen before. And I've seen countless British and Belgian soldiers in worse states of undress today."

He grimaced and tugged at his cravat. "I thought you'd have been nursing the wounded."

She drew an uneven breath, seeing the men lying in the street, thinking of the French who'd put them there. Whom she'd helped put them there.

"It's war," Raoul said, unbuttoning his waistcoat. "People are going to be killed and wounded. Once they're wounded one helps where one can."

"And sends them back to fight against one's own side."

"And holds on to one's humanity." He dragged his shirt over his head. "Besides, I think this is all going to be decided one way or another before the wounded heal."

"Have you got any lint?"

He didn't, but she found a bottle of brandy and an old shirt. This room wasn't Raoul's official residence in Brussels, but he kept it stocked with supplies. She tore the shirt into strips. When he protested, she said, "You can get another shirt. We can't get another you if you develop wound fever."

Raoul gave a wry grimace that changed to a gasp as she peeled back the dressing. The wound was long but not very deep. It was oozing, but the blood was clean red, with no sign of infection. She gave another sigh of relief, her mind filled with vivid memories of a week when he'd lain feverish in a mud hut in the Spanish mountains.

"You got Philippe's message?" she asked, dousing a strip of shirt with brandy.

"Yes. That was adroitly done. I got to Headquarters early on the sixteenth. Bonaparte was asleep, but I spoke to Flahaut. He promised to deliver the message."

"And then?"

Raoul grimaced again and not, she thought, because she was pressing the brandy-soaked cloth to his wound. "God knows. If the message had been heeded properly, Ney could have taken Quatre Bras before the Allies were able to reinforce it, and then we could have marched on to Brussels."

"I kept thinking of that yesterday whenever a fresh rumor spread."

"Instead Ney delayed and delayed, waiting for orders that were unconscionably late and damnably unclear when they finally arrived. It was three o'clock before he finally hurled Reille's corps at Quatre Bras. Late enough the Allies could hold out for reinforcements."

Raoul's voice shook with rage. Suzanne touched his shoulder.

"Ney thought Napoleon's reserves would reinforce his attack, but instead Bonaparte decided to concentrate his troops assisting Grouchy with the Prussians to the east."

"When did he let Ney know?"

"He didn't."

She pulled a fragment of matted dressing from Raoul's wound. Raoul, brooding on the idiocies of yesterday, scarcely seemed to notice. "I heard d'Erlon's corps spent yesterday riding back and forth," she said.

"On top of everything else. D'Erlon kept getting contradictory orders from Napoleon and Ney." More than anything else, Raoul hated stupidity.

Suzanne touched his shoulder again. He gave her a brief smile. "There's nothing to be gained repining on it now."

Another of Raoul's maxims that she'd learned was vital to holding on to one's sanity. "Do we have a chance?" she asked.

"If Bonaparte can keep the Allied army and the Prussians separated—yes. Not everything's gone our way, but not everything's gone theirs, either."

"How's Flahaut?" She pictured the handsome comte whom she'd met when she assisted his mistress, Hortense Bonaparte, in concealing her pregnancy and the birth of her child three and a half years ago. She'd admired his loyalty to Hortense throughout the ordeal.

"Exhausted. Worried Talleyrand will never forgive him."

Suzanne smiled at the thought of the French foreign minister whom she'd last seen in Vienna. "He will. Talleyrand's a number of things, but he doesn't forget he's a father. And if anyone understands about changing sides he should." She pressed a pad of clean cloth over the wound.

Raoul winced. "I'm not sure how much weight the pull of loyalty and ideals holds with Prince Talleyrand."

"No, but after our time in Vienna, I think he understands the pull of love rather better than I'd have guessed."

Raoul raised his brows.

"Dorothée," Suzanne said, seeing her friend, Talleyrand's niece-by-marriage, who had been his hostess in Vienna. She used a long strip cut from the shirt to secure the fresh dressing.

"Poor devil."

"He'll live." She went to the chest of drawers for another clean shirt.

Raoul looked up at her. "Did you learn anything more about Truxhillo?"

Her fingers stilled on the shirt. Anthony Chase was a French agent and therefore properly Raoul's loyalties should lie with him.

"You don't trust me," Raoul said. It wasn't an accusation or a reproach, merely a statement of fact.

She clenched the folds of linen. "It's not—"

"That simple?" He gave a faint, self-mocking smile. "No, it never is."

She held out the shirt, scanning his face as though she could read clues there to how much she could trust him. Which was absurd. As well as she knew him, she knew full well she didn't have the key to who he was. He knew her equally well, and that probably gave him an edge in deception.

But as Prince Adam Czartoryski had said to Malcolm last autumn in the midst of the treachery of the Congress of Vienna, one had to trust someone. She gave Raoul the shirt and her trust. "Captain Anthony Chase was a French agent."

Raoul's brows rose. "Interesting. He was running Julia Ashton?"

She helped him pull the shirt over his head. "He thought he was."

"Thought?" Raoul's head emerged from folds of linen.

"Julia was a double."

"Good God." For the second time in the past three days she had the rare experience of seeing genuine surprise on Raoul's face.

She told him about Tony and Truxhillo and about George running Julia. "So George was getting information from Julia," she concluded. "And Julia was feeding false information to Tony."

"Typical. All that fuss to set up Anthony Chase as a hero so he'd make a good agent and they didn't pick someone with a keener understanding."

Suzanne leaned forward, resting her chin on her hands. "According to his sister, Anthony Chase had blood on his coat the night of Stuart's ball. He has the perfect motive to have set up the ambush. He wanted Malcolm gone, and Julia was threatening to stop working for him."

"Have you discovered why?"

"Why what?"

"Why Lady Julia suddenly wanted to stop working for Captain Chase. And more importantly for his brother."

"I can only assume her self-disgust got the better of her. It's ugly work being a double agent. She may not have been betraying her husband through treason, but she was betraying him with other men." The one betrayal Suzanne had managed not to commit.

"All of which she'd been doing for some time. As you should know better than anyone, one can go along as one is for an amazing amount of time. It takes some sort of shock to change things."

Suzanne's nails curled into her palms. She'd had a shock of that sort the previous summer, when she'd looked at Malcolm on a stretch of Perthshire beach and realized she loved him. But in the end even that hadn't been enough to shake her from her purpose. What would it have taken to jolt Lady Julia out of her course of action?

"You identify with her," Raoul said.

Suzanne bit back an instinctive protest. "I suppose I can't help but do so in a way. A woman close to my age, playing the intelligence game. Lying to her husband." She sat back on the cot. "Her little boy is staying with us. He's adorable. Just about Colin's age. His father is off risking his life, and he's going to grow up without a mother." She met Raoul's gaze. "It changes one, having children."

He was silent for the length of a heartbeat. "So I would think."

"I hate what was done to her. I hate that she was a pawn."

"You're a lot of things, but you'll never be a pawn, *querida*."

A mirthless laugh escaped her lips. "Can't we all be pawns in the right circumstances? It depends on who controls the board." She pushed herself to her feet. "Carfax also sent Malcolm a personal message about his ward's death. A message that disappeared entirely. Malcolm naturally thinks the same person who warned the Comte de Lisle intercepted Carfax's message, but I know I didn't take it. There's no chance George Chase really is a double agent, is there?"

"I've heard nothing to suggest it, but anything's possible. I didn't know about his brother, or Lady Julia."

"Will you—"

"I'll make inquiries. Of course."

"Thank you." Suzanne twisted her wedding band round her finger, feeling the marks of the date engraved on the inside. "Philippe told me he was going to join the army."

"He told me as well. I'm not surprised."

"He's a boy."

"A number of boys will die tomorrow on both sides. As they did in the Peninsula."

Suzanne hugged her arms round herself. "Perhaps I see it differently now I have a son."

Raoul got to his feet as well and regarded her for a moment. "If the battle goes our way"—his voice caught slightly on the word "our"—"if the day goes to the French, you should go to Antwerp. Wellington may have to fall back and let Napoleon have Brussels."

"That's precisely what Malcolm said." She gave the ghost of a smile that hurt her face.

"Sensible advice. It won't be as bad in Brussels as the British fear, but you could find yourself detained. Depending upon what happens next, you may need to set sail for England."

"Again, that's what Malcolm said. He left me travel documents. David Mallinson and Simon Tanner are here. They'll travel with us. I have Aline to see to as well and Cordelia Davenport."

Raoul nodded. "Should you not be able to get out of Brussels for some reason, you can send word to me."

She shook her head. "No. It's too dangerous."

He scanned her face and gave a slow nod, understanding her meaning. She wouldn't run any risk of Malcolm learning the truth about her work for the French. "I understand," he said in a gentle voice. "Just remember it's an option, in some unforeseen eventuality."

A chill coursed through her. "You mean if Malcolm is killed." She had always prided herself on thinking through every scenario, but this was something she hadn't let herself contemplate. Would she go to England, an alien land and so long the enemy, and bring her son up as a British gentleman? Would she turn her back on everything and take Colin to France?

"I'm only letting you know you have options," Raoul said.

"Even should the battle go to Napoleon, the British won't give up easily."

"No, but the alliance could fall apart. That's what we have to hope for."

A restored Napoleon. Malcolm would have to go back to Britain, at least for a time, but ultimately he could be sent to the French imperial court as a diplomat. She felt a crazy desire to laugh at the thought. If he survived. They'd been playing the same game for so long, it was difficult to imagine the rules changing so completely.

"Should I not come back, you can rely on Villon," Raoul said in the same calm voice.

Her gaze flew to his face.

"Only thinking through every eventuality." He touched his fingers to her cheek. "Take care of yourself, *querida*."

❧ 42 ❧

"Cordelia."

Cordelia looked up from tying a bandage round the arm of a rifleman to see the broad shoulders and classical features of Lord Eglinton. Sweat gleamed on his forehead. He wore one of his beautifully cut coats, though his cravat looked to have been tied with unwonted haste and his dark hair was uncovered.

"Thank God," Eglinton said. "I've been looking all over the city for you. I've managed to secure a carriage and pair. At the cost of six months' income, but well worth it. I can convey you and Livia to Antwerp."

Cordelia sat back on her heels and met Eglinton's earnest gaze. They'd had a very agreeable liaison in Paris last summer that had stretched into the early autumn. "Thank you, Teddy. But I have no intention of leaving."

"For God's sake, Cordy." Eglinton knelt opposite her, heedless of the effect of the dirty cobblestones on his biscuit-colored pantaloons. "I'm not asking anything of you. I just want you to be safe. Look round you. You can't stay here."

Cordelia knotted off the ends of the bandage and smiled at the rifleman, who was trying to pretend to be deaf. "I'm well able to take care of myself. I always have been."

Eglinton shook his head. "You're a madwoman."

"But then you've always known that, haven't you? Perhaps you'd help me get this gentleman to his billet before you leave?"

Eglinton half-carried the man to his billet and made one more effort to remonstrate with her. She kissed his cheek and gave him a quick hug, then knelt to peel back a matted makeshift dressing from the leg of a Belgian corporal. She was so focused on the tasks at hand that she scarcely noticed when the sky clouded over, save that the heat of the sun wasn't quite so unbearable. Then she saw a bright flash and heard a rumble she at first thought was another cannonade. She felt a spatter of damp on the back of her neck and the next thing she knew the clouds let loose a torrent.

She was closing the eyes of a fair-haired boy with a gaping wound in his side when Suzanne ran up to her, soaking wet, her hair half tumbled from its pins and plastered to her face, the bloodstains on her cream-colored gown turned to spreading pink by the damp. "Come back to the Rue Ducale. I've just sent Aline home. David and Simon have filled the house with wounded, and we won't be much good to anyone if we come down with pneumonia."

Cordelia managed a shaky smile and tucked the letter the fair-haired boy had given her for his sweetheart into the bodice of her gown.

Suzanne opened the front door in the Rue Ducale without bothering to ring for Valentin. The smells of blood, sweat, and brandy filled the air. The black and white marble floor, pristine and gleaming this morning, was now lined with pallets on which lay wounded men. In addition to the chandelier, a variety of lamps and candles lent illumination against the stormy sky.

Livia was holding a flask of water up to a gray-haired man with a bandage round his head, while Robbie and Colin knelt on either side of a pale-faced man, propped up against pillows, who was creating a boat out of paper for them.

Blanca looked up from packing a Highland private's chest wound with lint. "The children are less frightened when they know what's happening."

Livia capped the flask and ran over to Cordelia. "You got all wet. Blanca said you were taking care of hurt soldiers."

Cordelia nodded. She didn't trust herself to speak. She knelt down and hugged her daughter, heedless of her damp and soiled gown. Livia wrapped her arms tight round her.

"Is my papa hurt?" Livia asked when Cordelia at last released her.

"Not the last we heard," Cordelia said in a steady voice.

Livia nodded. "And Uncle Johnny?" She glanced at Robbie.

"The last we heard he was all right, too."

"But they could both be dead, couldn't they?" Livia said in a matter-of-fact voice, eyes wide and anxious.

"Darling—" Cordelia forced down every easy reassurance that sprang to her lips. She put her hands on Livia's shoulders. "We don't know. But as many men as have been wounded and killed, there are many more who are unhurt."

Livia nodded again. "I said I hated the French, but Uncle Simon said there are lots of French soldiers who are hurt, too."

Cordelia met Simon Tanner's gaze. He had just emerged from the kitchen with a tray of hot broth. He gave a faint smile. "An excellent point," she said. "War is quite beastly for everyone."

Livia went to sit beside Colin and Robbie, who were sailing the paper boat in a river of the soldier's blankets. David came in through the front door, his coat soaked, his hat gone, his hair streaming water. He carried an armful of lint and brandy and laudanum, which he relinquished to Blanca. Cordelia, Suzanne, and Simon met him by the base of the stairs.

"Is there any news?" Suzanne was the first to speak.

David nodded, eyes grave. "Apparently the Allied army is retreating."

Cordelia sucked in her breath.

"They'd have to," Suzanne said. "The Prussians had to fall back this morning, and Wellington needs to maintain communications with Blücher."

"Yes," David said, "I thought the same myself. But it seems to have renewed the panic in the city. I was stopped half a dozen times on my way back from the chemist's and asked if I had horses to sell. And offered a more outrageous sum each time."

"Rather a waste that you already have a fortune," Simon murmured. He glanced round the group. "You'd all best get out of your wet clothes. We don't have any spare hands to tend chills. I sent Aline up the moment she came in. I think we've used up most of the brandy and whisky cleaning wounds, but there's still plenty of wine."

Suzanne knocked on Cordelia's door ten minutes or so later. "I thought you might need help with your gown. Your maid's downstairs helping Blanca."

"Thank you," Cordelia said. She was reaching over her shoulders, struggling to do up the strings. She'd thought the Pomona green sarcenet was one of her easier dresses to put on, but her fingers wouldn't seem to cooperate. "How did you manage?" she asked, as Suzanne stepped into the room in pomegranate crêpe over a white satin slip, her hair neatly pinned.

"Years of practice. And learning to order gowns that fasten easily. I haven't always had a maid and Blanca's often occupied elsewhere." She did up Cordelia's strings with deft fingers.

Cordelia picked up her silver-backed brush from the dressing table and dragged it through her hair. Or tried to. Her fingers were still shaking. She dropped down on the dressing table bench, hunched over. "I'm sorry. I don't know what's come over me."

"It's often that way." Suzanne perched on the edge of the bed. "The reality doesn't sink in until one has the leisure to think. That's kept me from going mad more than once."

For all her composure, the looking glass showed that Suzanne's eyes were filled with ghosts. Cordelia spun round on the dressing table bench. "What you must have been through—Even after today I can scarcely imagine it. I must seem a dreadful watering pot."

"Today was enough to shake anyone. And I don't think one ever grows wholly inured to it. At least I hope not. The first time I helped Geoffrey Blackwell I threw up all over the man he was trying to operate on."

The stories Cordelia had heard about the war in the Peninsula, always something vague and distant, suddenly seemed so real they sent a chill through her. She knew little about Suzanne's past, but she'd heard her family had died in the war. "You nursed the wounded in Spain."

"Malcolm and I were following the army during the push across the frontier into France. I did what I could. One learns to cope. You would."

"I don't know. George didn't think I could even cope in genteel poverty, and I have a horrible feeling he was right."

"You've coped with scandal and being a social outcast."

Cordelia turned back to the mirror and pulled her hair up with a sharp twist. "I didn't have much choice."

"Precisely."

Cordelia reached for a handful of pins and jammed them haphazardly into her hair. "Self-preservation as much as anything else."

"As I said." Suzanne got to her feet and moved to the dressing table. She took the hairpins and arranged Cordelia's hair with gentle fingers. "It's harder, knowing one's husband is out there, wondering if the same could be happening to him."

Cordelia shuddered. "What a damnable time to realize it."

"What?"

Cordelia drew in and released her breath. Her lungs hurt. "That I'd be utterly devastated if anything happened to Harry."

Suzanne smoothed a wave of hair over Cordelia's forehead. "It can rather sneak up on one."

"What?"

"Loving one's husband."

Cordelia looked up at her friend with a dozen unvoiced questions about the Rannochs' marriage.

Suzanne returned her gaze. "Malcolm's and my marriage didn't precisely have a conventional start."

Cordelia studied her for a moment. "Mine did. There's nothing more conventional than marrying for money."

Suzanne dropped down on the dressing table bench beside her. "When I first met Colonel Davenport in the Peninsula it was clear that he was a difficult man to know. And bitterly unhappy. I didn't understand why until I met you."

"Because of how miserable I made him?"

"Because he was desperately in love with you."

"Was."

"That sort of feeling doesn't go away. Not from what I've observed these past few days."

Cordelia pushed herself to her feet. "I was caught up in the romance of the moment. All those tearful good-byes and the waltz playing for God's sake. For a moment I turned into some sort of heroine. The same one who rose to the occasion today. When it's over, I daresay I shall go back to being just as selfish and heedless as before."

"I doubt it." Suzanne got to her feet as well. "For one thing, I don't think you were nearly so selfish or heedless as you make out." She reached for the door handle and paused for a moment, her fingers curled round the polished brass. "And for another, I don't think any of us is going to emerge from this unchanged."

An hour or so later, attired in dry clothes, the children tucked into bed, the wounded settled as best as possible for the night, they sat down to a makeshift dinner in the dining room. Rain still pounded on the roof and spilled from the eaves.

"It's going to be a damned muddy battlefield," Simon murmured, refilling the glasses of Bordeaux.

Amazing how hungry she was now she had time to think of it. But then, Cordelia realized, she hadn't eaten anything since breakfast. They were in the midst of devouring vegetable soup and bread when a commotion in the hall had them all on their feet with a celerity that belied their attempts at composure. They hurried into the hall to find Malcolm Rannoch standing between the rows of pallets, dripping water onto the marble tiles. Another man stood behind him. Harry.

Air flooded her lungs as though she'd been holding her breath for hours without realizing it.

Suzanne ran forward, took her husband's hands, and lifted her face for his kiss. Cordelia remained where she was, because she didn't have any right to do otherwise.

"Colonel Davenport." Suzanne held out her hand. "I'm so glad to see you safe. You both must want to go upstairs and put on dry things. We have food in the dining room."

Cordelia met Harry's gaze as he moved to the stairs. He still wore his ball dress from the night before last, the once brilliant white pantaloons gray with mud, the coat and fringed sash crusted with dirt and blood. She wondered how much of it was his. She smiled, a little uncertain. He returned the smile, though his eyes were tired. His face was gray with exhaustion, and he moved stiffly.

The men came into the dining room ten minutes later, attired in dry clothes, Harry in garments borrowed from Malcolm. Suzanne introduced him to David and Simon, whom he had met years ago in Derbyshire.

As they all moved to the dining table, Cordelia touched her husband's arm, unsure if it was an invasion. It had been one thing to kiss him in the heightened atmosphere of the ball. It was another now, with the cold, prosaic horror of battle all round them. Harry looked down at her for a moment, his gaze unreadable, then squeezed her fingers.

Suzanne served Malcolm and Harry Davenport, since the servants were all either tending the wounded or snatching much-needed rest. Both men took several bites in silence. At length, Davenport tossed down a deep draught of Bordeaux and said, "Wellington's forces are bivouacked near Mont-Saint-Jean for the night."

"They *have* retreated," Aline said. "It must be more than ten miles."

"No help for it." Davenport dipped his spoon into his soup. "The Prussians are at Wavre, and Wellington needs to keep the armies close."

"He was right when he looked at the map in the Duke of Richmond's study," Malcolm said. "Mont-Saint-Jean is just south of Waterloo. It looks as though that's where the fighting will be."

"There definitely will be a battle tomorrow?" Suzanne asked.

Her husband's mouth tightened. "Without question."

"At least the ground will be better at Waterloo," Davenport said. "The corn at Quatre Bras was high as a man's head. The infantry could scarcely see the French till they were on top of them, and it was the devil's own work for the cavalry. Thank God Rebecque and Perponcher had moved Perponcher's troops the night before, or I don't think we'd have got out of it."

"Did Slender Billy take his command?" Suzanne asked. "I didn't even think to ask last night."

Malcolm grimaced. "I think Billy was in a temper over Picton taking orders directly from Wellington and cutting him out of the line of command. Picton had Halkett's brigade deployed in square to support his own division and the Brunswickers. Billy ordered them instead to form line for more firepower. When Halkett protested that that would leave them dangerously exposed to cavalry, Billy said there was no French cavalry for miles."

"Was it very bad?" Suzanne asked.

Malcolm snatched up his wineglass and took a long swallow. "The French cavalry hiding in the folds of ground opposite must have had scouts watching for us to make just such a mistake. They came thundering down on Halkett's brigade." His fingers tightened round the stem of his glass. "The Sixty-ninth lost its colors and God knows how many men lost their lives."

"Not your fault." Suzanne touched his hand.

"No, of course not. I'm not even a soldier, thank God."

Davenport gave a short laugh. "But you're blaming yourself."

"Billy needs guidance."

"You aren't the one who placed him in command," Davenport said.

Malcolm grimaced. "The wonders of royalty."

"Enough to make one yearn for the Bonapartists," Simon murmured.

Suzanne kept her gaze fixed on the bloodred wine in her glass.

"Grant reached Quatre Bras in the middle of the day yesterday," Davenport said. "It turns out he did send word to Wellington about Bonaparte's attack coming through Charleroi. Early on the fifteenth. But General Dörnberg intercepted the message and sent it back saying he didn't believe a word of it. That in fact it convinced him to the contrary. That Bonaparte's attack would come from the west."

David stared at him across the table. "Good God."

"One could almost believe Dörnberg's been a French agent all these years," Malcolm said. "But I think the truth is he's just woefully incompetent."

Suzanne considered this for a moment. Dörnberg, once a colonel in Jerome Bonaparte's army, had deserted and joined the British two years ago. Quite clever if he'd been a double agent all this time, waiting for the right moment to wreak havoc on the British. Just the sort of thing Raoul might have planned. Could Dörnberg's witlessness these past two years all be part of an elaborate pose?

Cordelia took a sip of wine. "One wonders how Dörnberg ever got to be a general."

"If he were the only incompetent man ever to rise to general, the army would be very fortunate," Davenport said.

No, Suzanne decided. On the whole it was probably too much to think that Dörnberg had been maintaining a pose.

"Some French lancers got into Genappe during our retreat today and Uxbridge sent Life Guards to engage them." Davenport looked at Cordelia. "Ashton was among their number. He came through it unscathed, though the lot of them got caked in mud."

Cordelia smiled, relief evident in her face. "I daresay they got some joshing for caring about a bit of mud on their uniforms."

Davenport gave a genuine grin. "It was a splendid opportunity for the Peninsular veterans to laugh at Hyde Park soldiers."

Malcolm pushed back his chair. "We should be off. We have to stop by Davenport's lodgings and get him a proper uniform. With your permission, Suzette, we'll raid the kitchen. Rations are in short supply."

Suzanne found her husband a quarter hour later throwing things into a knapsack in their bedchamber. "You're planning to be gone for some days."

"Only trying to be prepared for every eventuality." He gave her a quick smile. "You're pale as parchment. Have you managed to sleep?"

"Enough." She moved into the room and sat on the edge of the bed. "Darling, in the midst of all this I have news. About the investigation." She told him about her talk with Jane Chase.

Malcolm froze in the midst of putting a shirt into the knapsack. "Good God."

"It gives Jane Chase all the more reason to have been furious with Lady Julia. Though I find it hard to imagine her arranging the ambush."

Malcolm stuffed the shirt into the knapsack. "You could."

"An excellent point." She smiled, though she was not entirely joking, and she knew he hadn't been, either. "We shouldn't underestimate her."

He crossed to the chest of drawers and picked up his shaving kit. "I have information as well. According to Canning, George and Tony Chase slipped out of Stuart's ball together. George claims they only went as far as the mews to have a confrontation about Lady Julia. Just as he claims not to be a double agent."

Suzanne swallowed, her talk with Raoul sharp in her mind. "Malcolm—"

"And I learned the identity of Amelia Beckwith's lover."

She drew in her breath. "Who?"

Malcolm threw the shaving kit into the knapsack. "Slender Billy."

Her hand closed hard on the bedpost. "Dear God. Of course. Billy was in England all those years. He stayed at Carfax Court?"

"Numerous times. I was often there as well. But I was—"

"Hiding out in the library. Where else would you be?"

"Until I met you." He gave her a brief, warming smile. "George Chase says he saw Billy and Amy slip off together more than once. And that Julia is the one who told him about the affair."

"It was an affair? That is, they were—"

"George seemed to think so. And Amelia told Simon she was pregnant."

Suzanne leaned forward, still reeling from this news. "Do you seriously think Billy—"

"Would be capable of murder?" Malcolm frowned into the

knapsack. "I think anyone's probably capable of murder if pushed in the right way. It's hard for me to imagine Billy killing a girl he loved, but if he lost his temper—"

"If Lady Julia knew about the affair, and then something made her think Billy could have had something to do with Miss Beckwith's death—-"

"Billy would have had a motive to get rid of Lady Julia." Malcolm tugged the knapsack closed, yanking on the strings. "But we're getting ahead of ourselves. We still have Tony Chase slipping out of the ball and returning with blood on his coat. Not to mention whatever George Chase was doing. But I need to talk to Billy. Meanwhile I don't want David to know a word of this. I sympathize with Simon's fears. The last thing I want to see is my best friend challenging the Crown Prince of the Netherlands to a duel."

"You're going to talk to Billy when you go back tonight?"

Malcolm shook his head. "I daren't risk upsetting him before the battle. It will have to wait. I still need to find Tony. I suspect he may be with the French."

Suzanne pushed herself to her feet and fixed her husband with a hard stare. "You're going to pursue Tony Chase behind French lines in the middle of a battle."

"It wouldn't be the first time I've gone behind French lines."

"Not in circumstances like these. If you're caught—" A spy would receive none of the consideration of a prisoner of war. He'd be either tortured or shot on sight.

"Then it's a good thing I have no intention of being caught."

She caught him by the lapels of his coat, the nightmare she'd lived with for two and a half years sharp before her eyes. That Malcolm would die at French hands.

"Sweetheart." He looked down at her with a smile that tore at her heart. "Such a lack of faith in my abilities."

She tightened her grip. "This isn't a game, Malcolm."

"My darling, of course it's a game. It always has been. With life-and-death stakes."

Only she could know how very true his words were. She kissed him, as though she were exacting a promise.

* * *

Cordelia saw Harry cast a glance upstairs. She touched his arm. "Do you want to see her?"

His gaze jerked to her face. "I don't want to wake her."

"It won't be dreadful if you do." She took his hand and drew him to the stairs. They were on the half landing before she realized this was the first time she'd held his hand in four years.

Livia was curled on her side in the bed in Cordelia's room, her arm wrapped tight round her stuffed cat Portia. Harry stopped just inside the door and stood staring at her in the glow of the tin-shaded night-light. Her chest rose rhythmically beneath the blankets. He took a cautious step forward.

Livia stirred. "Mummy?" She rolled onto her back and blinked up at Harry. From the look on Harry's face, Cordelia was sure Livia had given him one of her smiles. "Daddy. Is the war over?"

"Not yet, I'm afraid." Harry walked up to the bed. "I was able to come back to Brussels for a few hours. I'm sorry I woke you."

"I'm glad." Livia sat up, making the covers slither and the bed creak. "You didn't say good-bye when you left the first time."

"No, I couldn't." Harry sat down on the edge of the bed. He seemed to be moving with great care, as though he was afraid to put a foot wrong. "I had to leave right away, you see."

Livia pushed herself up against the pillows. "I hate wars."

"So do I."

"There are lots of hurt men downstairs. Mummy and Aunt Suzanne and the others are taking care of them."

"Your mother's being very brave. So are you."

Livia wrinkled her nose, the way she did when she was puzzling something out. "What else could we do?"

"That's what I mean, sweetheart."

Livia considered this a moment longer, then stretched up her arms to him. Harry leaned forward, his arms encircling her, and pressed a kiss to the top of her head. A lump rose in Cordelia's throat. The next thing she knew, her cheeks were damp.

"You're good at this," she said to Harry outside in the passage.

He gave her a crooked grin, but his eyes were veiled. Whatever he felt, he wasn't ready to share it with her. "Liar."

"You know what to say so naturally. It's taken me years."

She could hear voices in the hall downstairs, Malcolm's and David's and then Suzanne's. This was her last moment alone with her husband. She gripped his arms. "I suppose it's pointless to tell you to take care of yourself."

"On the contrary. I always do. I trust you'll do the same."

"Self-preservation has always been one of my chief talents. Should worse come to worst, I doubt the French would be any harder to deal with than the London scandalmongers."

He gave the ghost of a smile, then stooped his head and brushed his mouth over hers. The fevered farewells of the Duchess of Richmond's ball were a thing of the past. Somehow they seemed wrong here, with death below and waiting outside Brussels.

He stepped back with a quick, almost embarrassed smile. She echoed the smile, equally awkward. They returned downstairs without further speech.

The Rannochs, too, seemed to have already said their good-byes. Malcolm hugged Aline, clasped David and Simon by the hand, swung up onto his horse, and bent to give Suzanne a brief kiss. Harry merely turned to give Cordelia a last smile. She lifted her hand in farewell.

Then she stood still and watched him ride off, imprinting on her mind what might be her last glimpse of her husband.

∾ 43 ∾

Cordelia managed to put on her nightdress, splash her face with water, and clean her teeth. Then she tossed and turned for what felt like hours but proved to have been barely one hour when she finally gave it up, swung her feet to the floor, and looked at the clock on the mantel. Livia was breathing deeply, her face burrowed into Portia's fur. Cordelia smoothed the covers over her daughter, pulled on her dressing gown, and slipped into the passage.

She could see light from the hall below. As she made her way down the stairs, she heard a faint murmur and a fretful moan, of the sort Livia made when she was feverish. A lamp and two branches of candles burned in the hall, casting a warm glow on the black and white tiles and the sheets and blankets thrown over the wounded. Suzanne Rannoch knelt beside one of the pallets, smoothing the hair of a young Belgian private.

Cordelia knelt opposite her but said nothing until the private had drifted into sleep. Suzanne sat back on her heels and wiped a hand across her face. "Thank goodness he can sleep. It's quite eluded me."

"Me too." Cordelia glanced round the hall and saw that a sheet was pulled over the face of one of the men.

"Robbins, the ensign from the Ninety-fifth. He died about half an hour ago," Suzanne said in a calm voice. "It seemed unfeeling somehow to put him out in the street."

Cordelia found she was shaking. Suzanne touched her arm. "Come into the kitchen. I'll make tea."

There was something surreal about the prosaic sight of the black iron range, the comforting glow of the coals, Suzanne filling the kettle with water and spooning tea out of a blue enamel tin. Like her nurse years ago, in a faraway world where she and Julia and Tony and George and Violet and Johnny had sat grouped round the table, exhausted from a day's adventure but safe and secure in the warmth of home.

The whistling of the kettle cut through her reverie. "You'd think I could hate the French," she said. "But who's fighting whom almost seems irrelevant."

An odd sort of tension shot through Suzanne's back. "So I've found." She splashed boiling water over the tea leaves, letting loose a cloud of fragrant steam.

"If the hall were full of wounded French I suspect I'd be doing precisely the same."

Suzanne plopped the lid back on the teapot. "Once they're wounded, one does what one can." She set the teapot on the table, filled a bowl with sugar from another tin and a jug with milk from a cooler in the adjoining scullery.

"You're very at home in the kitchen," Cordelia said.

Suzanne smiled as she set out cups and saucers. "We lived in cramped lodgings when I first married Malcolm, with only Blanca and Addison to help us. And there are times when I've made tea over a campfire in the open air."

"We started out with a full complement of everything when we returned from our wedding journey." Cordelia glanced down at her hands and the gold of her wedding band, remembering how odd it had first felt to wear it. The wedding journey itself, looking at Roman ruins in the north of England, had been pleasanter than she anticipated. Tramping about looking for potsherds had been surprising fun and had given them something to talk about. The conversations over dinner had grown a bit strained, but the nights, while not without their awkwardness, had been unexpectedly compelling. Almost disturbingly so. And then they'd returned to London and stepped into the cold formality of the house in Hill Street, the staff of eight drawn up to greet them, awaiting her orders. "But I felt rather as if we were playing at being married."

Suzanne dropped into a chair opposite her. "The first few months I felt as though I was"—she hesitated—"playing a part." She picked up the teapot and filled the cups. "I think Malcolm found it dreadfully hard to remember there was someone to wonder if he was coming home to dinner or to worry if he suddenly went off on a mission."

Cordelia curled her hands round her teacup. Despite the warmth of the night, she was chilled. "Saying good-bye to Harry tonight, I felt—"

"What?" Suzanne asked.

"Like a wife."

"Not a bad way to feel."

Cordelia lifted the cup to her lips and blew on the steam. "I think it may be the first time I've felt like a wife in the five years of my marriage."

"It's odd what can bring the feeling home." Suzanne splashed milk into her tea and stirred it with precise strokes. "I think the first time I felt like a wife was sitting by a camp bed where Malcolm lay wounded. We'd been married three months. It occurred to me that I could lose him. A sense of loss cut right through me, though I wasn't sure precisely what it was I had."

Cordelia forced down a sip of tea. It scalded her throat. "I may never see Harry again."

"I may never see Malcolm again. Though it's hardly the first time that's been true of either of them."

"When Harry was in the Peninsula I was braced for news of his death with every battle. What it would mean to be a widow. What it would be like to know there was no chance he'd ever forgive me. Not that I ever thought he'd forgive me in any case."

"People can surprise you."

Cordelia shook her head. "It's one thing to make promises at a time like this. It's another to live with them. And I'm not the easiest person to live with in any case."

"I don't imagine Colonel Davenport is, either."

"No." Cordelia turned her cup between her hands. "Though in some ways—He always let me go my own way. And he was never dull."

"And Major Chase?"

Cordelia choked on a sip of tea. "Of course I don't want anything to happen to George. But what was between us is over."

"Are you sure?"

Cordelia stared into her cooling tea, forcing honesty on herself. "As much as one ever fully gets over a first love."

Suzanne's eyes darkened with unvoiced memories. "That's the devil of it, isn't it?"

"Malcolm. Davenport." Fitzroy Somerset, as usual, was bent over a pile of paperwork by the light of a single, guttering candle in the inn at Waterloo that served as Wellington's temporary Headquarters. "Have you brought food?"

"And wine." Malcolm pulled a bottle out from under his sodden greatcoat and set it on the gateleg table. Davenport did likewise. "Where's the duke?"

"Asleep. I hope. I'm to call him between two and three so he can write letters. He's been waiting all evening for news from Blücher."

"Still nothing?" Davenport asked.

Fitzroy shook his head. "But Müffling continues to insist Blücher can and will support us tomorrow. So much depends on it." A rare frown creased Fitzroy's face.

"Have a glass of wine." Malcolm, having extracted the cork from one of the bottles, splashed wine into a glass and held it out to Fitzroy. "For once you almost look worried. Which is enough to send your friends into a panic."

Fitzroy grinned and accepted the glass.

Malcolm stripped off his greatcoat. "I sent your message on to Harriet in Antwerp. Suzette had seen the Duchess of Richmond, who had word that Harriet's well, as is the baby."

Fitzroy smiled. "Thanks." He took a sip of wine. "The duke's marked out a position at Mont-Saint-Jean. He would have preferred the ground on the opposite ridge at La Belle Alliance, but De Lancey thought it too extended. The emperor's taken up the ground at La Belle Alliance. Boney had his batteries fire off some shots to try to smoke out our position, and some of our lads had the bad sense to fire back and give themselves away."

"And so the duke's in a temper?" Davenport picked up a glass of wine.

"He was. He's calmed down a bit. Or he's so busy he's forgot he was angry."

"You back, Malcolm?" Canning strolled into the room, yawning. "Still don't have the wit to see when you're well out of it?"

Malcolm took a sip of wine. "Can't stand the thought of you lot having all the fun."

"Ha. You don't believe that for a moment. I've heard you talk about war. Pour me a glass of that wine, will you? The beds are too damned hard for sleeping."

Alexander Gordon followed Canning into the room. "Is that wine? Always said you were a good man, Malcolm. For a diplomat." He spoke in a cheerful voice. Their quarrel over why he had left Stuart's ball might never have been. He moved to the table and accepted a glass of wine from Malcolm. "Lord, will the rain never let up? This is going to be the slowest battle ever, with all of us slogging through the mud."

Fitzroy looked up from his paperwork. "There's still time for it to dry out."

Gordon dropped into a chair with his glass of wine. "You're a damned optimist, Somerset."

"If by that you mean I'm not given to exaggerated flights of fancy, I'll concede the point." Fitzroy held a lump of red sealing wax over his candle.

"You wrote to Harriet that we and the Prussians had repulsed the French."

Fitzroy dripped the melting wax onto his folded letter. "The French didn't overrun us."

"What would you call our retreat today?" Gordon asked. "Advancing backward?"

Fitzroy pressed a seal into the wax. "When you're married, Gordon, you'll understand."

"Malcolm is married." Canning looked up from his wine to come to Gordon's defense. "You wouldn't catch him telling such a farrago to Suzanne."

Gordon snorted. "Suzanne wouldn't believe it."

"Suzanne's lived through battles before," Fitzroy said. "Though she always had nerves of steel as I recall," he added, looking at Malcolm. "Even when you first brought her to Lisbon."

"She'd already been through a great deal," Malcolm said. Even more, he had learned last autumn in Vienna, than he had at first supposed.

Gordon stretched his feet out toward the fire. "I miss Spain. Battle seemed friendlier in Spain."

"By the way," Canning said, "I saw Harry Smith earlier. With Lambert's brigade from Ghent and not long before that from America."

"Is Juana with him?" Malcolm asked. Juana Smith, like Suzanne, was a Spanish war bride.

"Yes, though he's sending her to Brussels in the morning."

Davenport, who had been leaning against the wall, moved toward Fitzroy. "Could I beg a sheet of writing paper?"

"Certainly. Ink as well."

Davenport took the paper and ink and retired to a chair in the corner by the fireplace.

The door opened again, letting in a gust of wind, a hail of raindrops, and Geoffrey Blackwell. "Damnable weather. It's all I can do to keep my instruments clean."

"Sit down by the fire." Canning got up to offer Blackwell his chair.

"No, no." Blackwell waved a hand. "I may have nearly thirty years on you, Canning, but I'm not quite decrepit. Besides, have to get back to my patients. I have a good half dozen who'll pull through if we can stave off wound fever. Only came to see if Malcolm was back."

"Allie's holding up well," Malcolm said.

Blackwell met his gaze and colored slightly. "Thank you."

"David and Simon are in Brussels. They and Suzanne and Allie and Cordelia have the house full of wounded soldiers. You trained Suzette and Allie well."

Blackwell gave a crisp nod. "Glad to hear it. God knows there must be need enough of nursing in Brussels."

Davenport crossed to Malcolm and held out a folded piece of paper. "Would you mind keeping this and giving it to Cordelia? In the event I don't return."

Malcolm met his gaze for a moment. Davenport's expression was as armored as ever, but his blue eyes looked as though they could be smashed with a word. "Of course," Malcolm said, and tucked the letter into his pocket.

"Thank you." Davenport was silent for a moment. "It's a damnable thing to find, on the eve of what's probably going to be the worst battle in which one's ever participated, that on the whole one would prefer not to die."

"I can think of another Harry who couldn't sleep before a battle against the French. He came through well enough."

Davenport grinned. " 'Fraid I'm not up to a St. Crispin's Day speech."

"I don't think it's much Wellington's style, either."

By the fireplace, Gordon let out a laugh.

"You're impossible," Canning said. "I don't know why your friends put up with you."

"My fellow staff officers don't have any choice."

"You have friends outside the staff. In fact, it's disgusting how many friends you have."

"Most of them don't have any choice, either. Campbell and Flemming grew up with me—"

"Will Flemming?" Malcolm asked.

For a moment Gordon went still. Then he gave a deliberate smile, a trifle too broad. "Yes, he and Jack Campbell and I grew up on neighboring estates. Those are the friends one can never get rid of, don't you know."

"Quite." Malcolm stared at Gordon. Between them Gordon and Canning had given him a new piece of the puzzle. He reached for his greatcoat—still damp, but at least it would keep the rain off the rest of his clothes—and moved to the door.

"Where are you off to?" Davenport asked.

"To have a talk with George Chase."

Lord Uxbridge and his staff were quartered in a whitewashed cottage on Waterloo's single street. Malcolm wouldn't go so far as to wake George Chase the night before a battle, but he rather suspected Uxbridge's staff, like Wellington's, would find sleep eluded them. Sure enough, he entered a parlor choked with tobacco smoke and the smell of wet wool to find a group of Uxbridge's officers lounging on chairs and the floor, sharing cigarillos and red wine by the flickering firelight.

He was greeted with jokes about civilians who didn't know when they were well out of it, pleas for the latest news from Brussels, and an offer of wine. He laughed off the jokes, answered the questions as best he could, and declined the wine. "Actually, I was hoping for a word with you, Chase."

George Chase met his gaze without flinching, his face pale even in the red-orange glow of the fire. "Of course." He pushed himself to his feet. "Shall we go outside?"

To the accompaniment of much ribbing about fools who couldn't stay out of the rain, Malcolm and George went out beneath the overhang of the roof. Rain dripped relentlessly from the roof and splashed against the cobblestones. The glow of candles and fires showed in the windows of the houses and thatched cottages where fortunate generals and their staffs were quartered. Few were sleeping tonight.

George dug his shoulder into the wall. "Uxbridge called on Wellington and asked him what the plans for tomorrow were. Said he thought he ought to know as second in command. Apparently Wellington told him Bonaparte had not confided his plans in him and as Wellington's plans depend on Boney's, he couldn't possibly tell Uxbridge what they were. Added some nonsense about them both doing their duty." George scanned Malcolm's face. "But I don't think you asked me out here to discuss battle strategy. Have you found Tony?"

"No. But I think I'm beginning to piece the picture together."
Malcolm folded his arms across his chest. "When you and Tony
left Stuart's ball did you meet Alexander Gordon and Will Flemming?"

George stared at him. "How the hell do you do it?"

"Your brother fought a duel with Will Flemming the night of
Stuart's ball."

George glanced to the side, then swung his gaze back to Malcolm. "They were—Damn it, Rannoch, I'll kill you if you reveal
this, but Flemming had formed a liaison with my sister-in-law."

"Hardly shocking given the way your brother carried on."

"It's not—"

"Not the same? No, that's true. Your sister-in-law had license to
break her vows by your brother's betrayal. Your brother had no
such excuse."

"Rannoch, will you stop it with your damned Radical—"

"I don't see what's so radical about—"

"So says the man with the perfect marriage and the wife who
will never stray."

Malcolm leaned back, resting his hands against the rough
whitewashed wall. "Gordon was Flemming's second, I presume.
Were you your brother's?"

"Obviously."

"You were the second in a duel—a violation of the law and
Wellington's orders—for your brother, whom you knew to be a
French spy?"

George cast a quick glance about at the word "spy." "This had
nothing to do with that. It was an affair of honor. My brother asked
me to act for him. What was I supposed to do?"

"Refuse?"

"I couldn't let Tony know I was on to him. Besides—"

"You thought this sort of honor went deeper than betraying
one's country?"

"It's not the same—One doesn't refuse when a friend asks such
a thing of one. Let alone a brother."

"I think I'd refuse if Edgar asked me to be his second," Malcolm said, though in point of fact he had fought one duel himself,

much as he abhorred the practice. One duel in which he had not been the challenger.

"Spare me your damned moralizing. You're a gentleman. You know how these things work. Or you should."

"Regrettably."

"Well then." A crack of lightning illumined George's face. His well-cut features looked unusually hard.

"Why fight the duel during the ball?" Malcolm asked over the answering roar of thunder. "As the second, you must have arranged it."

"Wellington and most of the senior staff would be at the ball and out of the way. Gordon and I reasoned it was as safe a time as any. If we could slip out and return quietly, no one would know we'd been gone."

"You were counting on your brother not actually killing Flemming?"

"I'd been impressing upon him that honor could be satisfied simply by the meeting itself. I prayed I'd been successful."

"Where did you go?"

George drew a breath. Nearby a horse whinnied. "The park. Empty at that hour. We had a surgeon present of course."

"And then?"

"Tony had a restless glitter in his eye. I was terrified of what he might do. It's not just possessiveness. I think he does love Jane. In his way."

" 'Love' is perhaps the most bastardized word in the English language. Go on."

"Tony shot wide. Deliberately, I suspect. I think Flemming was trying to shoot wide as well, but his hand was shaking badly—he'd been drinking. He ended up winging Tony."

"Hence the blood on your brother's coat."

"Quite." George drew a weary sigh. The rough, methodical scrape of a sword being sharpened against stone sounded from inside the house. "The surgeon patched him up, and we all went back to the ball. Flemming and Gordon and the surgeon can vouch for Tony's and my whereabouts."

"Our investigation into Lady Julia's death would have been speeded along considerably if you'd told me this to begin with."

"For God's sake, Rannoch, I couldn't have told you my brother had been fighting a duel over his wife's infidelity. You must see that."

"You're protecting your traitor brother from being accused of dueling?"

"I'm protecting my sister-in-law's reputation, you damned idiot."

"I'll do everything I can to keep Mrs. Chase out of this."

George looked at him for a moment and gave a curt nod. "Thank you."

Alexander Gordon met Malcolm's gaze when he stepped back into the parlor in Wellington's Headquarters.

"You're an idiot, Gordon," Malcolm said.

Gordon's face relaxed into a grin. "Oh, well. That's not exactly a new revelation."

Fitzroy lifted a paper from the table at which he was working. "A lieutenant in the Fifty-second delivered this for you a quarter hour since, Malcolm. Said he had it from a villager."

Malcolm took the paper and recognized the handwriting of one of his best sources within the French army, a cook in a regiment of lancers.

"Important?" Canning asked.

"Probably. It's in code." And had no doubt passed through so many hands that it would be impossible to trace it back to its source. Malcolm took the paper over to the corner where Davenport had left the ink and paper he'd used earlier and decoded the brief message.

He looked up to find Davenport watching him.

Malcolm folded the letter and the plaintext and tucked the papers into his cuff. "It appears I know where to find Anthony Chase."

❧ 44 ❧

Sunday, 18 June

"What the hell—"
"I wouldn't advise you to move, Chase. You have a sensitive part of your anatomy exposed." Malcolm had surprised Anthony Chase when Chase stumbled into the trees near where he'd bivouacked to relieve himself. Malcolm had one arm clamped round Chase's shoulders and a pistol held to his head.

"*Rannoch?* What the devil are you doing here?"

"I could ask you the same."

Tony was silent for a moment. A pre-dawn glow spilled through the overhanging branches. A breeze rustled through the trees, but there was no sound of humans within earshot. "I would think that would be obvious to a man in your profession. I'm on a mission."

"For which army?"

Tony was silent, but Malcolm felt the tension that ran through him.

"I know," Malcolm said. "Your brother knows."

"How the devil—"

"Lady Julia was betraying you with your brother."

"Julia wasn't my mistress."

"Apparently she wasn't your brother's, either. But she was spying on you for him."

Tangible shock ran through Tony's body. "She—No. It's not possible."

"She was the perfect agent because people underestimated her. Including you. She never was your creature. She was George's from the beginning."

"You can't prove—"

"Give it up, Chase." Malcolm kept the pistol steady against Tony's temple. "You're working for the French. Your brother knew. Lady Julia knew. Now I know as well."

"And you came here to drag me back to face justice?" Tony's harsh laugh echoed through the trees. "I'll be most interested to see how you attempt to carry that off."

"I have no such delusions. I can't stop you from fighting for the French. And I'm not much interested in doing so. One soldier won't turn the tide of battle. But I can warn you that if you attempt to come back to the Allies as an agent provocateur, you'll be arrested for treason."

"Point taken."

Malcolm studied the back of Tony's head. The matted blond hair, the arrogant angle at which he carried himself even now. "If you'd learned Julia was a double I imagine it would have made you exceedingly angry."

"I didn't know."

"So you say."

"You think I'm that good an actor?"

"Possibly. I'm still not decided about quite what you are, Chase. What gave you the idea that I knew about Truxhillo?"

"George told me," Tony said without hesitation. "Didn't realize what a favor he was doing me."

Malcolm frowned, going over his conversations with George Chase.

"And so of course I did want you dead," Tony continued. "But as it happens I couldn't have ridden to the château and shot at all of you. I was otherwise engaged."

"Fighting a duel with your wife's lover."

Tony jerked against his hold. "How the devil—"

"Your brother told me."

"Damn George."

"But that wouldn't have prevented you from arranging for someone else to ambush us at the château and kill Lady Julia."

"I didn't—"

Tony didn't get any further. Malcolm flung him to the muddy ground and put a foot on his back. As Tony tried to struggle up, Malcolm dealt him a blow to the head with the butt of his pistol. Tony subsided into the mud and fallen leaves, unconscious.

Raoul O'Roarke scanned the field in the pale gathering light. Mist hovered over the ground, but the day promised to be clear and hot.

"The ground's still too wet," Flahaut said beside him. "We're going to have to delay."

Raoul glanced round at the soldiers cleaning their weapons, sipping coffee, tramping their feet against the damp ground. One could almost smell the eagerness for battle running through the men. "They're going to get impatient."

"Can't be helped." Flahaut's face was drawn with tension. Today would decide whether he was branded a traitor or crowned as a hero who might have a chance for a life with the woman he loved. "We can't get the guns into position in this mud, and the men wouldn't be able to move fast enough."

Raoul nodded. His gaze focused on a figure in the distance. It looked like—Raoul lifted his spyglass. Good God. Malcolm Rannoch was a madman. Not but what Raoul hadn't been behind enemy lines often enough himself. But he could do so in the guise of an ally. And he didn't have a wife and son to think of. At least not who were dependent on him.

"What is it?" Flahaut asked.

"Nothing," Raoul said, lowering the spyglass. "Nothing at all."

"Malcolm." The voice called out across the street as Malcolm rode back into the village of Waterloo. He turned to see the Prince of Orange standing before the house that had been his quarters for the night, drawing on his gloves.

Malcolm swung down from Perdita and walked toward Billy.

The rain had let up and a dawn glow battled the mist, but the ground was still a sea of ankle-deep mud.

Billy walked forward, grinning. "I knew you'd be back."

"On a day like today, where else could I be, sir?"

"That's the spirit." Billy met Malcolm in the midst of the street, mud squelching round their boots. Gold braid glittered on Billy's uniform jacket in the fitful light, but above his stiff, high-standing black collar, his face was the face of an uncertain undergraduate. "Somehow I didn't quite believe today would actually come. Facing Bonaparte. After two days ago—"

"Don't think about two days ago." Malcolm gripped Billy by the shoulders. "All that matters is today. One moment at a time."

Billy swallowed. "But I don't know—"

Malcolm had a clear memory of teaching Billy to hold a cricket bat on the lawn at Carfax Court. He looked into the eager, anxious gaze. The gaze of his boyhood friend. The gaze of the man who might be a killer. He pushed all questions about Amelia Beckwith and Julia Ashton to the back of his mind and said the words that needed to be said. "You'll do splendidly, sir."

Harry held his restive horse in check and ran his gaze over Malcolm Rannoch as they waited in the street for the duke's staff to assemble. The duke and his aides had been breakfasting by the time Rannoch returned to Waterloo, so they'd had no chance for private conversation until now. "Well?" Harry asked Rannoch.

"Nothing conclusive."

"For God's sake, Rannoch, this isn't my first engagement. I won't be distracted. But if I'm going to die, I'd like to have as many pieces of the puzzle as possible in my possession."

"I confess I feel much the same." Rannoch told him about Tony Chase's duel with Will Flemming.

Harry shook his head. "Damned fools. So our obvious suspect has an alibi."

"He could still have set up the ambush."

"But much of the evidence against him and against George is explained away."

"There's still Billy." Rannoch's gaze drifted down the street. The Prince of Orange was conferring with March and Rebecque. Harry noted the concern in Rannoch's eyes. Concern and, beneath it, fear. "You're fond of him," he said.

Rannoch's mouth tightened. "He isn't the first murder suspect I've been fond of."

Malcolm was far from the only civilian to ride out with the Duke of Wellington. In addition to his staff, the Prince of Orange, and Lord Uxbridge, Wellington was accompanied by a diplomatic corps including Pozzo di Borgo, who was Corsican but represented Tsar Alexander of Russia, Spanish General Alava, the Austrian representative Baron Vincent, and Prussian Baron von Müffling. Wellington, in white buckskin breeches and tasseled top boots, the gold knotted sash of a Spanish field marshal showing beneath his blue coat, might have been setting out on a fox hunt. Malcolm, who knew the value of costume and disguise, could appreciate that everything from Wellington's polished, casual dress to his easy manner was part of his campaign tactics.

As they rode toward the troops, two men on horseback approached them. "Good God," murmured Alexander Gordon, who was riding beside Malcolm. "It's Richmond."

It was indeed his grace the Duke of Richmond, whom Malcolm had last seen in his study at the ball, poring over the map as Wellington pointed at the village of Waterloo. Beside the duke rode his fifteen-year-old son, Lord William, his arm in a sling and a bandage on his head. Malcolm recalled Uxbridge toasting William and the other junior officers at the Richmond ball.

"William has come to present himself for duty," Richmond informed Wellington.

Wellington cast a glance at the young lieutenant. "Nonsense. William, you ought to be in bed. Duke, you have no business here."

Richmond's reply was carried away on the wind, but he appeared to be arguing with his friend Wellington. He and William continued to ride alongside Wellington's cortège, and when they did move off it was toward General Picton's division rather than back to Brussels.

Malcolm turned his head to see a tall figure in the short-tailed blue jacket and red-plumed shako of the light dragoons riding toward him. Even before the rider was close enough for Malcolm to make out his features or his captain's insignia, his posture was unmistakable. Malcolm's throat tightened, and he breathed a small sigh of relief. He hadn't consciously let himself think it, but he'd been dreading the prospect that he might never see his brother again.

"Malcolm." Edgar reined in beside him. "I was hoping I could find you."

"You knew I'd be here?"

"I know you, brother mine." A shadow crossed Edgar's normally sunny face. Since their mother's death, they didn't know each other as well as they once had. Then he gave one of his careless grins. "Have a care, will you? You're the only brother I've got."

Malcolm felt his own face relax into a smile. "I could say the same to you. And I'm only observing."

"Ha. You may be able to run intellectual rings round me, Malcolm, but I'm not quite so naïve." Edgar glanced toward Picton's division. "Couldn't believe it when I saw Richmond and young William."

"Family honor," Malcolm said.

Edgar turned his gaze back to him. "At least if anything happens to either of us we know it won't affect Father overmuch." He said it matter-of-factly, because matter-of-fact was what they'd come to be when it came to their father, out of sheer survival instinct.

"Quite," Malcolm said. For a moment, the name of their mother, who would have cared, hung between them, tightening the air with past questions and past guilt.

Edgar gathered up his reins. "Give my love to Suzanne and Colin if I don't come back. And to Gelly."

"Likewise," Malcolm said. Gisèle was their seventeen-year-old sister, home in England with Aline's mother. He looked into Edgar's eyes, the eyes of his boyhood confidant and first friend, and for a moment understood precisely why George Chase hadn't turned Tony in. His throat went tight with all the things he couldn't say. He clapped his brother on the arm. "Go carefully, Edgar."

Edgar's gloved fingers closed over Malcolm's own. "You too."

Malcolm watched his brother ride out of view. Mist hung over the fields, mixed with smoke from the Allied cooking fires and those of the French on the opposite ridge. Steam rose from cheap tea brewed in iron kettles. The smell of clay pipes and officers' cigars mingled with the stench of wool still sodden from the night's rain. Shots split the air as soldiers fired their guns to clean them.

"Waste of ammunition," Davenport said to Malcolm. "It's going to be a long day."

And it had yet to properly begin. A breeze gusted over what would be the battlefield, stirring the corn, cutting through the curtain of mist. Wellington had taken up a position before the small village of Mont-Saint-Jean. Fitzroy had said that the duke would have preferred the position across the field at the inn of La Belle Alliance, which Bonaparte occupied, but the Allied position had its advantages. Wellington had seen the ground when he was in Brussels the previous year. Malcolm remembered the duke mentioning the slope of the land to the north, which would allow him to keep most of his troops out of sight of an enemy across the field.

To the left stood the fortified farm La Haye Sainte, with whitewashed walls and a blue-tiled roof that gleamed where the sunlight broke the mist, and still farther to the left the twin farms of Papelotte and La Haye. To the right, in a small valley hidden by cornfields, was Hougoumont, a pretty, walled château surrounded by a wood and a hedged orchard. Both Hougoumont and La Haye Sainte had been garrisoned with Allied soldiers.

The ground before them sloped down to a valley, through which the road to Charleroi ran, then rose to the ridge on which stood La Belle Alliance. On this ridge, the French army had begun to deploy. An elegant, masterful pageant. Malcolm lifted his spyglass. Lancers with white-plumed *shapkas* on their heads, chasseurs with plumes of scarlet and green, hussars, dragoons, cuirassiers, and carabiniers, and the Imperial Guard in their scarlet-faced blue coats. Gunners adjusted the positions of their weapons. Pennants snapped in the breeze and gold eagles caught the sun as it battled the mist.

"Sweet Jesus," Davenport murmured.

"Bonaparte understands the value of theatre," Malcolm said.

"Unless he's also a master of illusion, there are a bloody lot of them. I hope to God the Prussians get here."

Malcolm cast a glance along the Allied lines. "We happy few."

"Shakespeare was a genius, but he'd never been on a battlefield. Do you know what you're in for, Rannoch?"

"I've seen battles before," Malcolm said, scenes from the Peninsula fresh in his mind. "But I don't think any of us has seen anything like what's about to unfold."

Cheers went up among the French troops as a figure on a gray horse galloped into their midst.

"Boney," Davenport said. "Odd to think I've never seen him before."

Malcolm handed his spyglass to Davenport. Bonaparte wore the undress uniform of a colonel in the Imperial Guard and a bicorne hat without cockades. Wellington, too, wore casual dress for battle, though his buckskins and blue coat were more in the style of a gentleman out for a morning's ride. He wore four cockades on his own bicorne, for Britain, Spain, Portugal, and the Netherlands.

Even without a spyglass, the cheers of the French troops for Bonaparte were evident. In response Wellington rode among his own troops, at a sedate trot rather than Bonaparte's gallop. The duke was greeted with respectful nods but no cheering.

Alexander Gordon pulled up beside Malcolm and Davenport. "Uxbridge has ordered sherry for his staff so they can toast today's fox."

"Fox hunting always struck me as a bloody business," Davenport said. "And a damned waste. My sympathies go to the fox."

Gordon shot an amused glance at him and held out a paper. "Well, while you're feeling sympathetic toward Boney, you can take this to Picton. Wellington's orders."

Davenport wheeled his horse round but turned back to Mal-

colm before he rode off. "I don't say this often, but it's been a pleasure working with you, Malcolm."

Malcolm reached between the horses to clasp the other man's
hand. "Likewise, Harry."

Gordon cast a glance after Davenport as he galloped off. "Odd
devil. But a brave one." He turned his gaze to Malcolm. "We all
right, Rannoch?"

"Really, Gordon. Arranging a duel in the middle of a ball?"

Gordon flushed. "Flemming's one of my oldest friends. One
doesn't refuse such a request from a friend. Besides, no one was
badly hurt. If Will hadn't been drinking he wouldn't have winged
Tony Chase at all." His gaze moved to the field stretching before
them and the French on the opposite ridge. "Seems like child's
play compared to today."

"It gives both Chase brothers an alibi."

Gordon met his gaze, a soldier not shirking rebuke. "I couldn't
tell you, Malcolm. It was a confidence."

Malcolm reached out and gripped his friend's arm. "It's all right,
Sandy. I do understand."

Gordon's face relaxed, though doubt still lurked in his eyes.
"If—"

As Gordon spoke, the roar of guns cracked open the summer
morning.

It had begun.

Suzanne was kneeling on the hall floor, spooning gruel to
Christophe, the young Belgian private, when the sound of guns
thundered through the house. Strangely not as loud as the noise
two days ago from Quatre Bras, which was farther from Brussels,
but still enough to shake the windows in their frames and set the
crystals in the chandelier tinkling.

"It's started," Christophe said.

"Yes." Suzanne kept her fingers steady on the spoon. The hall
clock showed that it was just before eleven-thirty. Across the hall,
Cordelia was applying fresh fomentations to Angus, the Highland
sergeant. Aline was bathing the face of Higgins, an infantry corpo-

ral. Both women went still and met Suzanne's gaze for a moment. Suzanne gave them the most encouraging smile she could muster. Aline grinned with determination. Cordelia gave an ironic smile. Suzanne looked back at Christophe. "It's started, but it will be a long time before it ends."

"I should be there."

"Nonsense. You did more than enough at Quatre Bras. You have to let others have their turn."

He gave a weak smile. "You're kind, Madame Rannoch."

"I'm practical. Have some more broth."

David and Simon came through the front door a few minutes later. They had gone to arrange burial for the soldier who had died during the night. Suzanne, Cordelia, and Aline met them by the door. They had long since given up having a footman answer the door. The servants were all helping care for the wounded, either in the house or in the streets.

"Any news?" Aline asked.

"Wild rumors," David said. "No news."

"Save that apparently some wealthy Bruxellois are preparing a banquet to welcome the victorious emperor and his officers," Simon added. "Meanwhile, some of their compatriots are fleeing for Antwerp. People are lined up trying to get passports from Colonel Jones. Poor devil may be thinking it would have been less arduous to take the field than to be left in Brussels as military commander."

"And more wounded are being brought in," David said.

"Or limping in. We found one man who fell at Quatre Bras two days ago." Anger sharpened Simon's usually ironic voice. "He crawled out of the mud yesterday and walked twenty-some miles to Brussels. It's a miracle he survived. We got him to his billet."

David looked at Suzanne. "We thought we'd take one of the carriages and drive toward Waterloo. We can bring back what men we can and see if we can learn any news."

"Of course."

David and Simon left the house, shoulder to shoulder. They worked together seamlessly in the face of necessity, yet she could still feel the distance between them. As though the air between them was empty where before it had pulsed with a tangible connection. How much could be lost so quickly.

Stuart stopped by an hour or so later. "All those years in Lisbon," he said, glancing round the hall, "I don't think I ever realized quite how fortunate we were to be so removed from the battlefield." He squeezed her arm. "You're doing a capital job, which doesn't surprise me in the least."

"Thank you," Suzanne said, oddly touched. Stuart had come to be almost like family in the years she'd been Malcolm's wife. For some reason, seeing anyone she was close to these past few days made her want to burst into tears.

Stuart took her arm and steered her into the privacy of the study, where no soldiers were quartered. "I received a dispatch from Wellington at seven this morning. Basically instructing me to guard against panic." He regarded her with a faint smile. "You aren't panicked, I take it?"

"After all these years don't you know me?"

The smile deepened to a grin. "Quite right." His face turned serious. "We need to be ready to move the British civilians and our allies out of Brussels should things go against us. Wellington may have to fall back and leave Brussels to the French. Are you prepared to move quickly if necessary?"

She nodded. "Malcolm left travel documents and we have horses ready in the stables. I have the necessary items packed."

"Good girl. I've talked to Capellen"—Baron van der Capellen was the secretary of state of the Netherlands—"and he's issued a proclamation designed to be reassuring. I daresay it will be some time before we hear anything more. I haven't had any news from Malcolm. I suspect you haven't, either?"

She shook her head.

"Yes, well, I wouldn't have expected to. Don't believe everything you hear today. Rumors are thick as molasses already."

"My dear sir," Suzanne said, firmly ignoring the fear that was twisting her stomach into knots, "by now you should know me well enough to realize I'm a healthy skeptic about everything."

"You're one in a million, Suzanne. If there were more women like you, I wouldn't be a bachelor."

"If you were less fond of flirting you wouldn't be a bachelor."

He grinned. "You have a point. One would never have guessed it was Malcolm who had the makings of an ideal husband. But then you make it look easy."

She nearly did cry then. It was only all her years of training that preserved her self-command.

❧ 45 ❧

B lack smoke swirled through the remnants of mist. The French guns sounded, the Allied cannon thundered back. Most of the French fire focused on the château of Hougoumont. Harry, sent with a message from Wellington, who was directing the battle over the château personally, to the Prince of Orange, who had command of the troops involved, drew Claudius up on the ridge above the château at an angle that gave him a good view of the scene below. French and Hanoverians clashed in the wood south of the château. Howitzer shells rained down from the Allied ridge, but the French pushed on. Through the thick smoke, Harry saw that some of the French were already scaling the walls and attempting to drag British muskets out of the loopholes the British had cut in the stone.

"Do you think the battle hangs on this?" A Dutch-Belgian lieutenant pulled up beside Harry.

"Not necessarily, but if the French take the château they'll be in a damned good position to fire on us." Davenport turned and then started as he recognized the thin, intent face of the lieutenant he had last seen at Le Paon d'Or with Rachel Garnier. "Rivaux."

"Colonel Davenport." Henri Rivaux sketched a salute. "The prince has sent me with a message for the duke."

"I'm bringing a message from the duke to the prince." Harry

ran his gaze over Rivaux. His shoulders were straight, his hands steady on the reins, but his face was as pale as linen fresh from the laundry basket. "Your first battle?"

"Is it that obvious?"

"Not in the least. When did you last see your lady in Brussels?"

"Rachel? Just before we marched." Rivaux gave a brief smile. "Thank you. For asking. For calling her that. For understanding—"

"What she means to you?" Harry prided himself on having little use for love, but he vividly recalled the way Rivaux's gaze had clung to Rachel's face. It had taken Harry back to the ballroom at Devonshire House five years ago. His first glimpse of Cordelia's brilliant, discontented face, and the start of a longing that tore at the soul. "If there's any good that comes of war, I think perhaps it's that it makes us understand what's important."

Rivaux nodded. "How true. If—Good God."

Below them, French infantry had pushed through the northern gates of the château. Five men in the uniform of the Coldstream Guard fell against the gates, pressing them closed against the force of more French who would pour through. The gates shuddered. The French pressed forward, the guards pushed back, while inside the French who had already broken through battled the Allied defenders. At last, the gates slammed closed.

"Pity the poor French bastards left inside," Harry said.

Rivaux, who had been a spy among French sympathizers, grimaced. Then he gathered up the reins and gave a quick salute. "I must be off. My compliments to you, Colonel Davenport."

"And mine to you." Harry returned the salute.

Rivaux galloped toward Wellington's position. A few moments later, a howitzer shell fell short of its mark and slammed into Rivaux's horse.

Horse and rider tumbled to the ground. Harry touched his heels to Claudius and galloped forward. Rivaux's horse had had its front legs blown off at the knees. Its chest was a pulpy mess. Harry swung down from the saddle, cast a quick glance at the horse, and put a bullet through the poor animal's head. Then he bent over Rivaux. A fragment had struck the lieutenant in the chest and another in the head. His eyes were closed, but as Harry bent over him they blinked open. "Davenport. Silly. Must—"

"I'll take your message. After I get you behind the lines."

Rivaux struggled to draw a breath. "Can't—"

"Don't be a damned idiot, Rivaux." Harry lifted the young lieutenant in his arms as gently as he could, but Rivaux sucked in his breath. By the time Harry levered him over Claudius, Rivaux seemed to have fainted, which was probably a mercy. Harry swung into the saddle and touched his heels to Claudius.

His quickest route took him to the Prince of Orange, whom he found with March and Rebecque beside him. "I've a message for you, sir," Harry said. "And one of your men who needs attending to."

"Good God!" the prince exclaimed. "Poor Rivaux. Is he—"

"He will be if he doesn't receive attention quickly."

March had already set about issuing orders. As two soldiers lifted Rivaux from the saddle, he opened his eyes and looked at Davenport. "Tell Rachel—"

"My dear fellow, I daresay you'll see her before I do." Harry took Rivaux's hand and pressed it between his own. Then he looked into Rivaux's eyes, making no attempt to maintain his usual ironic defenses. "But should the need arise you have my word on it. I'll tell her precisely how you feel."

"You can't know—"

"Oh, but I do." An image of the twenty-year-old Cordelia hung vivid in his mind. For once, he didn't try to banish it. "Love's a remarkably universal emotion."

Raoul O'Roarke reined in his restive horse, sweat dripping from his forehead, and muttered a curse. The damned assault on Hougoumont, intended as a diversion, had sucked up far too many French troops. They should have taken the château within the first hour. It was now almost half past one, nearly two hours since the assault on Hougoumont had begun. Jerome Bonaparte, Napoleon's youngest brother, was leading a ferocious fight, but he was pulling precious resources away from the rest of the battle.

Raoul had spent the time supervising the placement of a battery of guns—twelve-pounders and eight-pounders and horse artillery—in front of d'Erlon's infantry divisions. Now, with a crashing rumble, a renewed cannonade thundered across the valley. The cannonballs should have ricocheted over the crest of the opposite ridge and reached the Allied soldiers sheltering behind it, but they fell into the mud. The poor Dutch-Belgian devils at the front of the Allied lines were cut to pieces, but most of the Allied army remained safely behind the reverse slope of the ridge or the thick hedges that bordered it.

Though the assault of the guns was less effective than it should have been, the French infantry began to advance in columns. Save that instead of the narrow columns that Raoul had seen prove ruinously ineffective against British infantry, d'Erlon spread his men into shallower, wider columns that were closer to line formation yet still deeper than the Allied lines they faced. "Clever," Raoul murmured to Flahaut, who had pulled up beside him. "The British muskets cut our columns to pieces in the Peninsula."

Drumbeats and voices raised in "The Marseillaise" echoed across the valley. Flahaut scanned the mass of advancing French. "They look as though they're going to sweep right over the British and Dutch-Belgians."

Raoul frowned at the Allied ridge. It wasn't like Wellington to sit this quietly and let the enemy overwhelm him. "I wouldn't cry victory yet. 'That island of England breeds very valiant creatures,' " he added in English rather than the French they'd been speaking.

"Must you start quoting now of all times, O'Roarke?"

"It's rather apt. Wellington's sure to have a counter-measure up his sleeve."

"I wouldn't doubt it." Flahaut gathered up the reins, then looked back over his shoulder. "O'Roarke," he said, over the roar of cannon fire and blare of martial music.

Raoul looked into the younger man's eyes, dark with fear and uncertainty. "If I live through this and you don't, of course I'll tell Hortense. Not that she doesn't know already."

"Thank you." A smile crossed Flahaut's smoke-blackened, blood-smeared face. He regarded Raoul for a moment, eyes narrowed against the smoke and the glare of the sun. "What about Suzanne?"

Raoul drew a breath. His neckcloth seemed to have tightened round his throat. "Tell her that I have every confidence she'll make the right decisions."

Flahaut looked at him a moment longer, then saluted and rode off. Raoul turned his gaze to the opposite ridge. Quiot's left brigade had success at the walled farm of La Haye Sainte, driving back the King's German Legion troops in the orchard. His right brigade drove Prince Bernhard's Saxe-Weimar brigade from the twin farms of Papelotte and La Haye and pushed the 95th from the sandpit opposite La Haye Sainte. A Dutch-Belgian light brigade either withdrew or fled.

But Wellington had indeed had a counter-measure up his sleeve. Squadron after squadron of Allied heavy cavalry charged down the slope. The French cavalry met them near La Haye Sainte. The French cuirassiers should have been able to hold them, but the Allied cavalry were fresh and ready for blood after missing the fighting at Quatre Bras. The French cavalry broke in confusion before the Allied charge. Much of the infantry followed suit in a tangle of fallen men and blood-spattered ground.

Raoul spurred his horse forward from his station at the gun battery, calling to the retreating soldiers to rally and re-form. His cries fell on deaf ears. Formations dissolved, men ran away, others stood their ground and hacked wildly at the onrushing Allied soldiers only to be mowed down by the tide. The eagles of the 45th and 105th glittered in the hands of Allied soldiers, drunk on their success.

Raoul waited for the British cavalry to rally and draw back. But the Scots Greys instead pounded on across the valley. Good God, the madmen. They would be slaughtered.

The thunder of hooves shook the ground. Cries of "92nd" and "Scotland forever" carried on the breeze over the screams and groans and neighing of horses as the Allied cavalry fell beneath the blows of the French cuirassiers and lancers who had been sent up as reinforcements. For a moment Raoul could almost smell the salt breeze off Dunmykel Bay in Perthshire.

More Allied cavalry pounded after. Life Guards and King's Dragoons judging by the helmets and crests. They slammed against Travers's cuirassiers, British swords smashing against French breastplates. Raoul drew in his breath. Dear heaven, was that Lord Uxbridge leading the Household Cavalry? Why the devil hadn't the cavalry commander remained behind to direct the reserves?

The breeze carried the sickly-sweet smell of fresh blood. Buglers sounded the rally, but by then the British cavalry were tired, scattered, and deep in enemy lines. Raoul drew his sword as the British swept over the French guns. Instinct took over, honed through the Revolution, the United Irish Uprising, the Peninsular War. He cut, parried, slashed, dispatching soldier after soldier.

He ran his sword through the throat of a dragoon, pulled it clear, and wheeled his horse round to parry an attack from a hussar lieutenant. He dispatched the hussar with a cut to the chest, then nearly fell from the saddle as his horse stumbled. He looked down to see that his horse had tripped over the body of a French private. He found himself staring into the dead blue eyes of Philippe Valery.

Later, when the numbness wore off, he would feel grief. If he survived.

Someone touched his arm. He spun round in the saddle, sword raised.

"O'Roarke." Flahaut grabbed him by the arm. "Pull back. The British are trapped."

French lancers and hussars filled the valley, cutting the British cavalry off from their lines. The British cavalry circled in disarray. One colonel, both his arms shot off, gripped his horse's reins between his teeth. French swords and lances hacked and stabbed those who tried to ride back to their own lines. Raoul saw Sir William Ponsonby, with whom he had shared a glass of champagne at the Duchess of Richmond's ball, fall to a lance thrust.

"Christ," Flahaut said. "Only a handful of them can have survived."

Raoul wiped his hand across his face and realized he'd smeared blood over his forehead. "They took two eagles. And more than a dozen of our guns are disabled."

"Are you saying the fight went to them?"

Raoul tugged a handkerchief from his pocket and dragged it across his forehead. "I'm saying it was a damned waste."

Livia's and Robbie's nurses managed to take the three children to the park for a bit of fresh air in the early afternoon. The nurses, two sensible girls, reported that the city was eerily quiet, though there were horses drawn up before a number of houses, poised for flight. The children were a bit subdued but did not appear overly alarmed. After they'd been fed, they were happy to settle down in the hall beside the healthier of the wounded.

"Geoff says keeping one's spirits up is half the battle to recovering," Aline said, watching Colin and Robbie build a fort for Colin's lead soldiers in Christophe's sheets.

"I used to carry Colin about with me when I was nursing the wounded in Spain," Suzanne said. "It always seemed to cheer them. And it's rendered Colin wonderfully unflappable."

Simon and David returned a short time later, with a towheaded ensign with a head wound and a redheaded Highlander who had died on the journey into the city. Simon, who had been holding the dying man in his lap, sprang down from the carriage without speaking, cheeks streaked with damp.

"People are drinking beer in the suburbs," he said to Suzanne, when the towheaded boy had been settled in the hall with Aline, and they were in the kitchen gulping down cups of tea Cordelia had made. "Quite as though it were an ordinary Sunday."

"But a bit farther into the forest the road is littered with baggage." David stirred sugar into his tea as though he'd forgot what he was doing with his hands. "The wounded are picking their way over the wreckage and all too many have dropped in their tracks." He flung down the spoon, spattering tea over the deal table.

Simon tossed down a sip of tea as though he wished it were brandy. He had removed his coat and his shirt was soaked with blood. "We talked with one lieutenant who said that from what he had observed he didn't see how the French could be prevented from cutting straight through to Brussels. Of course he's only one man and didn't have a view of the whole field."

"But it's good you're ready to leave if necessary," David added.

Raised voices drew them back into the hall. A chestnut-haired woman in a blood-spattered white and green dress ran across the floor tiles to Suzanne. "Mademoiselle Garnier," Suzanne said, taking her hands.

"Forgive me, Madame Rannoch." Rachel's breath came quick and hard and her hair tumbled free of its pins. "I've found Henri. He was brought in on a cart and simply left in the street. Le Paon d'Or is already overflowing with soldiers, and you were closer. I thought perhaps—"

"Of course. Where is he?"

David and Simon went with Rachel to bring back the young Belgian lieutenant. He had a bandage round his head and a wound in his chest that looked to have been hastily dressed on the battlefield. "Could you get my medical box?" Suzanne asked Aline. "It's a mercy he's lost consciousness for the moment, but perhaps you'd hold him steady in case he stirs, Mademoiselle Garnier?"

Rachel nodded, eyes dark, mouth set with determination. Suzanne realized how very young she was. Probably little more than eighteen.

Suzanne cleaned the wound and found some bits of shell casing the battlefield surgeons had missed. Lieutenant Rivaux opened his eyes with a cry of pain when she was midway through. "Hush, Henri." Rachel tightened her grip on his shoulders and put her face close to his. "Madame Rannoch's almost finished. Do you want some brandy?"

"Rachel." His voice was a harsh rasp. "Thought I'd never see you again."

"Well, that was silly. You know where to find me."

"Not that." His pain-glazed eyes focused on her features. "Sure I was done for."

"You should have had more faith in yourself. I did."

He gave a weak laugh and tried to reach for her hand. Rachel curled her fingers round his.

Suzanne packed the wound with *boulettes* of lint to absorb the blood and secured a bandage over it. "You're a brave man, Lieutenant Rivaux. Thank you for making that so easy."

Aline poured a glass of brandy and gave it to Rachel to hold to Rivaux's lips.

"Stupid," he muttered. "Fell when the battle had barely begun. If it wasn't for Davenport—"

Porcelain shattered on the marble tiles as Cordelia, who had just come in from the kitchen, dropped the cup of tea she'd been carrying. She ran forward over the shards of porcelain and dropped down beside Rivaux, "Harry Davenport?"

"Yes." Rivaux's gaze focused on her. "He's a friend of yours?"

"He's my husband."

Rivaux's mouth curled in a faint smile. "He saved my life. Got me behind the lines. He was unhurt then, madame. It must have been—not long past noon, I suppose."

Hours ago, but Cordelia's face broke into a smile. She pressed his hand. "Thank you, Lieutenant Rivaux. Don't try to talk more."

Rivaux turned his head toward Rachel. "I asked Davenport to find you if I didn't make it. Couldn't give him a proper message, but he seemed to understand what I meant." He turned his gaze back to Cordelia. "I suppose it must be how he feels about you, madame."

Rivaux managed another sip of brandy, then collapsed against the pillows and closed his eyes, still gripping Rachel's hand.

David walked into the bedchamber he and Simon were sharing to find Simon bare chested, clutching the bloodstained shirt he'd been wearing.

He seemed not to have heard the opening of the door. David almost retreated. Instead he stepped forward and touched Simon's arm. "He was beyond our help. You made his last moments easier."

Simon started. "Who—Oh, you mean the Highlander who died on the drive back to Brussels. Yes, poor devil. Though I think some of the blood is Rivaux's." Simon flung the shirt aside and went to the chest of drawers. "How is he?"

"Rivaux? Asleep holding Mademoiselle Garnier's hand. Suzanne says he's at risk for wound fever, but she hopes she can pull him through."

"Suzanne's amazing. But she can't save all of them." Simon yanked open a drawer and tugged out a clean shirt. His hands froze on the linen. "Damn. Damn everything."

Without pausing to think, David went to his side and put his arms round him. Simon turned in his embrace and clutched him hard for a moment. Then he drew back and set his hands on David's shoulders. "Believe what you will, David, but try to believe I never meant to hurt you."

David met his lover's dark, steady gaze. "You didn't trust me."

"That's not true."

"What the hell do you call thinking I'd fight a duel?"

Simon gave a faint smile. "You have a point, I suppose. But I saw no need to cause pain where there was nothing to be done."

Frustration tightened David's throat. "I'd have known the truth."

"And where would it have got you?"

David drew a breath. The weight of who and what he was—Viscount Worsley, future Earl Carfax—pressed against his shoulders. It was a burden he'd carried since his uncle had died when David was eleven, so much a part of him he forgot it was there. Simon watched him with that familiar steady gaze that didn't judge, that had been the anchor in his life since he was eighteen.

There was a streak of blood on Simon's jaw. David lifted a hand and placed it against the side of his lover's face. "Looking at Mademoiselle Garnier and Rivaux—If anything happened to you—"

Simon caught his hand and pulled it against his mouth. "Well, then."

By the time Suzanne brought Rachel a bowl of soup and a glass of wine, Henri had fallen into sleep or lost consciousness.

Rachel took a mouthful of soup and set the bowl on the floor beside her, then gulped down a sip of wine. "Will he live?"

Suzanne looked into the naked fear behind that determined gaze and felt the weight of years descend upon her. "The wound is serious, and the fact that it wasn't attended to properly at first puts him at more risk for wound fever. But if we can hold infection at bay, he has a good chance of recovering."

Rachel nodded. "Thank you for being honest." She glanced round the hall. "I've seen a lot. But until today I hadn't seen death."

"One never really grows used to it," Suzanne said. "Which in its own way is an odd sort of relief." She glanced down at Rivaux. He looked even younger with his eyes closed and his face relaxed in sleep. "I'm glad you've stopped telling yourself you don't have a right to fuss over him."

Rachel brushed her fingers over Rivaux's hair. "Those sorts of distinctions seem very silly just now. Of course once we get through this—if we get through this—they'll be important again. But for the moment Henri is mine to fuss over."

"The moment is all we ever really have." Suzanne squeezed Rachel's hand and tried not to think about what might be happening at that very moment on the field of battle.

❧ 46 ❧

An odd quiet had come over the battlefield. At least it was quiet compared to the chaos of the cavalry charge. Shots still sounded to the right from Hougoumont and to the left from La Haye Sainte, on which the French had begun a determined assault. Malcolm swung down from Perdita and ran to help one of the stretcher parties carrying the wounded to makeshift hospitals behind the lines. Across the valley, the French were doing the same.

Eye-stinging black smoke hung over the field. Soldiers marched prisoners behind the lines, put bullets through the heads of horses too wounded to walk, rounded up riderless horses galloping among the injured or cropping the grass with fine disregard for the chaos. Malcolm paused to yell at an infantry sergeant pulling a watch from the pocket of a dead lieutenant. Then he knelt beside a dragoon with blood dripping from his mouth and the light fading from his eyes and took a letter and ring the young man begged him to send to his wife and son. Closer to the lines Malcolm closed the eyes of a lance corporal with whom he remembered sharing a flask of wine before the battle of Toulouse.

"If we lose La Haye Sainte the French will smash right through our center," Fitzroy said when Malcolm returned to the elm tree that served as Wellington's command post.

Malcolm glanced to the right. "I still see flames from Hougoumont."

"They're managing to hold out. The duke's told them to hold
on as long as they can but not endanger their lives from falling tim-
bers."

"Wellington looks calm." Malcolm had spotted the duke riding
among the troops on his chestnut horse Copenhagen.

"Looks. He must have taken his cloak on and off two dozen
times. Sure sign of disquiet. Good God. The madman." Fitzroy's
gaze went across the valley to the French ridge. "Ney's going to
send his cavalry at us without infantry support."

"Perhaps he thought it only sporting to even up the score when
we were so reckless with our own cavalry," Malcolm said.

Shouts of "prepare to receive cavalry" echoed along the Allied
line. The infantry began to form into squares. French cuirassiers
pounded across the valley and up the hill. Division after division
of heavy and light cavalry joined them. Wave upon wave, with no
supporting infantry or horse artillery. They met a checkerboard of
Allied infantry squares, four men deep, the front lines kneeling
with bayonet-tipped muskets pointed, the rear lines holding muskets ready to fire. Confronted with the bayonets, horses reared up
and dashed to the side.

With no supporting infantry to batter the squares, the French
cavalry wheeled and slashed, retreated, re-formed, charged again.
And again and again. The squares held steady. When a soldier fell,
his fellows pulled him into the center of the square and closed
ranks.

"Oh, Rannoch, good." Wellington thrust a paper at Malcolm as
shots whistled by. "Take this to Maitland. I've lost too damned
many aides-de-camp."

Malcolm tucked the paper into his coat and galloped toward
General Maitland, by instinct as much as sight. Guns thundered.
Bullets hammered against metal breastplates, sabres rang against
bayonets. Cannon smoke choked the air. Men screamed, horses
flailed, blood spurted, piles of dead and dying men and animals littered the ground.

He delivered the message to Maitland and made his way back

to Wellington, who was moving among the squares, pausing to ex-
hort the soldiers and offer encouragement. Wellington thrust another message at him, and he galloped on again in the choking
inferno, this time to the Prince of Orange. Sweat soaked through
his shirt. Smoke stripped his throat raw.

"We tried to save La Haye Sainte," Billy said when Malcolm
reached him, eyes fever bright in his pale face. "Alten ordered two
battalions of the King's German Legion to attack in line. Ompteda
objected, but I told him—It should have worked."

"It's done, sir." March laid a hand on Billy's arm. "You can't refine upon it."

Malcolm held out the dispatch. "Remember, sir. One moment
at a time."

March, his face set in harsh lines, rode part of the way off with
Malcolm. "When Billy insisted Ompteda follow Alten's order to
form line, Ompteda stared at him as though he'd received a death
sentence. After a moment he said that then he would try to save
the lives of his two nephews. Fourteen and fifteen."

"Did they survive?"

"Yes, but Ompteda and dozens of others didn't. And God knows
how many were taken prisoner."

"Try to keep him steady, March. It's all you can do."

March nodded. "The others?"

He meant the rest of the "family," Wellington's staff from the
Peninsula. "Fitzroy's fine," Malcolm said. "I just saw him with the
duke. I saw Gordon about an hour ago rallying some Hanoverians
and Canning half an hour or so before that. I saw Freemantle and
Davenport some time after the cavalry charge. The time starts to
blur."

March gave a brief nod.

"Your brothers?" Malcolm asked. "I don't think I've seen
George since the start of the battle." George Lennox was also an
aide-de-camp to Wellington.

"I haven't, either. I can only hope Father and William have the
wit to keep out of fire. Edgar?"

"I haven't seen him since this morning."

On the way to deliver another message to Sir Colin Halkett, Malcolm turned his head to see a French cuirassier galloping straight at him. He dashed into a nearby square, which opened to receive him, then quickly drew closed. The ranks were thinned, scarcely two deep now. Inside, red-coated men lay on the ground, some twisted in an agony of death, some groaning with wounds. A man in his shirtsleeves bent over them.

"Geoff." Malcolm swung down from Perdita.

Geoffrey Blackwell's gaze skimmed over Malcolm as he finished tying a bandage round the arm of a young private. "Are you—"

"Unhurt." Malcolm dropped down beside Blackwell. "Just delivering messages."

"A lot of message deliverers have lost their lives today." Blackwell cast a glance round the square. "I'd give a great deal to have Suzanne here."

"So would I." Malcolm shook his head. "Odd. A man should want to protect his wife from this."

"Not a man who knows his wife as well as you do." Blackwell crawled over to an ensign who was curled on his side, his ribs exposed. "Let's have a look at you, lad."

"Shall I stay?" Malcolm asked.

"Get your message delivered. I'll manage."

A quarter hour later, Malcolm drew up beside Wellington and Fitzroy. "Billy ordered another line attack. Or rather Alten ordered it, but Billy backed him up."

Wellington grimaced. "Ney's going to come straight at our center now La Haye Sainte has fallen. And we don't have the heavy cavalry left to oppose him. If—"

A hail of sniper fire came from La Haye Sainte. "A bit hot," Wellington murmured. And then, in a different tone, "Fitzroy?"

Fitzroy was clutching his right arm. Malcolm grabbed his friend as he swayed in the saddle. "I'll be all right, sir," Fitzroy murmured, face drained of color, blood spurting from his arm.

"So you will when you've seen a surgeon," Wellington said. "Get him behind the lines, Malcolm."

* * *

Pounding feet and shouts echoed through the Rue Ducale.

Cordelia looked up from changing Christophe's dressing. "I think they're saying, *'Les français sont ici,'* again. I suppose one of these times it could prove to be true."

Simon and David ran outside to check and returned to report that the Cumberland Hussars had apparently fled the battlefield and galloped through the forest of Soignes and into Brussels through the Porte de Namur.

"They went pelting down the Rue de Namur and through the Place Royale with scarcely a thought for the people in their wake," Simon said. "Shouting that the French were hard on their heels. No French have yet materialized."

Suzanne nodded, scarcely sure whether to be relieved or alarmed.

"Right," Cordelia said. "If we don't need to take immediate flight, we should see about dinner. Has anyone eaten today?"

None of them had, at least not more than a mouthful. Suzanne was usually good about forcing herself to eat even during a crisis, but food had been the last thing on her mind all day. Yet when Cordelia and Simon assembled leftover soup, slightly stale bread, and scrambled eggs, she managed to force down a few bites.

They were still at the table when Addison came in with the news that fifteen hundred French prisoners had been marched into the city, along with two captured French eagles. "I saw complete strangers shaking each other by the hand at the sight," he said. "However, I also spoke with Mr. Legh, the MP for Newton, who had been at the battlefield. He said the battle looked to have been going as badly as possible. He intends to keep his horses at the door, so he can take flight for Antwerp at a moment's notice."

"Any other news?" Aline scanned his face with anxious eyes.

"Not about any one of our friends in particular, Mrs. Blackwell. But—"

"It's all right, Addison." Suzanne touched his arm. "Bad news is better than our imaginings if we have no news at all."

Addison gave her a faint smile. "I stopped at the Marquis Juarenais's and found Mr. Creevey also there in search of news. He told me that on his way round he'd met a Life Guardsman who had just come in from the battlefield and gave it as his opinion that he didn't see what there was to stop the French coming straight through to Brussels. Then we were shown into the drawing room, where we found Madame de Juarenais nursing a wounded officer from the Foot Guards. Griffiths, I learned later. A corporal knelt beside him picking bits of his epaulette out of his wound while Madame de Juarenais held her smelling salts to his nose. He murmured that he wouldn't trouble her for long, as the French were sure to be in Brussels tonight. Then he fainted dead away."

"It's difficult for any one soldier to have a sense of how the battle is going," David said into the silence that followed.

"Quite," Cordelia agreed. "Could you pass the wine, Simon? Addison, do take a glass."

Nothing to do but wait. Simon and David, who seemed much easier together since the afternoon, drove back toward Waterloo. Their rapprochement was a small bit of hope to cling to. Suzanne suspected she'd have gone mad without the wounded to tend to. Christophe continued to improve. Angus's wound was disturbingly red and oozing yellow pus. She wished quite desperately that she had Geoffrey Blackwell to consult with.

"Steady hands and clean instruments," Aline said, kneeling beside her. "That's what Geoff always says is most important."

Suzanne grinned at her young cousin-by-marriage. "How did you know I was wanting him quite desperately just now?"

Aline's hand curved over her stomach in that instinctive gesture Suzanne remembered so well from her own pregnancy. "Perhaps because I was. And for once for medical reasons. Among others."

Malcolm returned from taking Fitzroy behind the lines only to be dispatched by the duke with a message for Lord Edward Somerset, Fitzroy's elder brother, whose brigade had played a prominent role in the cavalry charge. He found Lord Edward by the side of the road with only two squadrons. "Pressed into service, Rannoch?" he asked, lifting his hand to shield his eyes against the slanting rays of the sun.

"Wellington's running short of aides-de-camp," Malcolm said.

"Fitzroy took a bad shot to the arm. But he was conscious and in good spirits when I got him off the field."

Edward drew in and released his breath. "Thanks."

Malcolm held out his message. "Where's your brigade?"

Edward glanced at the few men surrounding him. "Here," he replied.

Malcolm returned to Wellington to find him riding among the Brunswickers, attempting to rally the younger troops. Cannon and pistol smoke choked the air and bullets whistled by. Alexander Gordon had pulled his horse up beside the duke. "For God's sake, sir, you're an open target. This isn't fit for you."

Wellington wheeled Copenhagen round. "It's work that needs to be done, Gordon. Oh, Malcolm, good, I need you—"

The sound of a ball connecting with flesh interrupted him. Gordon tumbled from the saddle. Malcolm flung himself down beside his friend. Gordon's leg was a mess of blood and torn flesh.

Gordon seemed to have lost consciousness, but as Malcolm slid his arm beneath his shoulders he opened his eyes. "Glad you know about Stuart's ball at least. Wouldn't want us to part enemies."

"Don't be a damned fool," Malcolm said, lifting Gordon in his arms.

Two men with a stretcher arrived to take Gordon from the field. Wellington looked after his aide-de-camp for a moment with drawn brows, then thrust a paper into Malcolm's hand. "For the Prince of Orange."

Malcolm nodded and turned Perdita. Men and horses littered the ground, wounded, dying, dead. Bullets sang through the air, shells exploded, cannon rumbled. Beneath his coat, his sweat-soaked shirt was plastered to his skin. The smell of blood and powder, the screams of men and horses, the sight of gaping wounds and blown-off limbs had become monotonous reality. His own wounds from the past few days were a dull throbbing on the edge of his consciousness. He steered Perdita round two dead dragoons sprawled over the body of a horse with the lower part of its face shot off. Perdita was breathing hard, her sides damp with sweat, but she pressed on, surefooted and remarkably calm in the chaos. Malcolm patted her neck. With the part of his mind that could still think beyond the moment, he felt a flash of regret that he hadn't left her in Brussels and ridden a borrowed horse.

At last he caught sight of March through the smoke.

"Malcolm! Glad you're still alive."

"Gordon took a hellish shot to the leg," Malcolm said. "And I think Fitzroy's going to lose his arm."

March squeezed his eyes shut. His face was bone pale and smeared with blood.

"Where's Slender Billy?" Malcolm asked. "I have a message from the duke."

March jerked his head to the right. Then his gaze fastened on a lone rider approaching down the line. "I think that's Canning." He raised a hand in greeting.

Malcolm turned his gaze in the direction March was looking. Canning saw them and lifted his hand in acknowledgment. A moment later, grapeshot hit him in the stomach, and he fell from the saddle.

Malcolm and March touched their heels to their horses. Canning pushed himself up on one elbow as they swung down beside him. Pain glazed his eyes and blood seeped through his coat. His mouth twisted with the effort at speech. "The duke," he said in a choked voice. "Is he safe?"

"Unhurt. I just saw him." Malcolm slid an arm beneath Canning's shoulders.

"God bless him," Canning gasped. He turned his head toward March, who was kneeling at his other side, and reached for his hand, then looked between March and Malcolm. "God bless you both," he murmured, and went still, the light gone from his eyes.

March drew a breath that shuddered with grief and rage. When he lifted his gaze to Malcolm, tears glistened in the blood and dirt on his face. "Curzon died in much the same way. Only a few— God, I can't say how many hours ago it was. Damn this day."

The ground shook with the pounding of horse hoofs. The Prince of Orange flung himself down beside them. "Malcolm. March. Who—Oh God." He put his fingers to Canning's face. For a moment, they were all back in the Peninsula, laughing heedlessly over a flask of wine, danger quickening their blood but death still impossible to imagine.

"He's gone, sir." Malcolm touched the prince's arm. "We have to go."

Billy turned toward him. "We can't just—"

A bullet whistled through the air. Malcolm grabbed the prince but not quite quickly enough. Billy collapsed against him, blood spurting from his shoulder.

"Sir," Malcolm said. "Billy? Can you hear me?"

"Yes, of course." The prince struggled to sit up, then fell against Malcolm again, his breath quick and uneven. "I shall be quite all right in a moment."

"I'll get someone to carry you off the field, sir." March released Canning's hand, hesitated a moment, then plucked the Orange cockade from Billy's hat. "Wouldn't do to have you recognized."

Billy gave a weak smile. Blood dripped from his shoulder but not so quickly an artery had been struck.

March looked toward the trees from which the shot had come. "What the devil were the French doing shooting from there?"

Malcolm glanced at the trees, now still. "I don't think it was the French."

❧ 47 ❧

Georgiana and Sarah Lennox came to drink coffee in the Rue Ducale late in the evening, eyes bright with nerves.

"Father and William returned home about six," Georgiana said. "They reported that all was going as well as possible. But we stopped to see the Misses Ord on our way here. Hamilton had been to see them. Well, to see Mr. Creevey, their stepfather. He came into town with Adjutant General Barnes—Hamilton did, that is, I'm getting it all muddled. According to Hamilton, he— that is, Barnes—thinks the battle is quite lost." Georgiana took a quick gulp of coffee.

"But Mr. Creevey pointed out that Barnes was carried off the field at five," Sarah said, putting her hand over her younger sister's. "Goodness knows what's happened since then."

Georgiana gave a determined smile, but her lips trembled. "It isn't just the battle," she said, and then drew a sharp breath.

It was the fate of her brothers Lord March and Lord George, not to mention Sarah's unspoken love, General Maitland.

Fear seemed to thrum against the walls of the salon. Suzanne realized why. The sound of the guns had stopped. "It's over," Cordelia said, as she had two nights ago on the city walls. "Though God knows how long it will be until we know what's happened. More coffee?"

Georgiana lifted her cup with trembling fingers. "The lights are actually shining in the Théâtre de Monnaie, can you believe it? Mademoiselle Tennaux in something called *L'Eclipse à Colonne.* Who on earth could be heartless enough to go to the theatre tonight of all nights?"

"Someone who doesn't know any soldiers," Aline said.

"Someone who's hoping for a French victory," Cordelia added.

Suzanne stirred milk into her coffee. She couldn't imagine being able to sit through a play tonight of all nights.

Harry Davenport pulled his horse up beside Wellington. "The Fifth division is reduced from four thousand to closer to four hundred, sir. They have little chance of keeping their post."

Wellington cast a glance toward La Haye Sainte, from which the French were now peppering the Allies with musket balls. "We have no reinforcements to send. Will they stand?"

"I think so."

Wellington shot him a brief smile. "Never one to exaggerate, are you, Davenport? Tell them I shall stand with them until the last man." The duke tugged his watch from his pocket and cast a glance at the sky. "It's night or Blücher," he muttered. Then he thrust a paper at Davenport. "All right, off with you. This is for Maitland. Bonaparte's about to send in the Guard."

At least Maitland was still alive and might make it home to pretty Sarah Lennox. Three generals had been killed and five carried from the field that Harry knew of. He had begun to ask, "Who commands here?" whenever he rode up to a brigade with a message.

As he bent over Claudius's neck, he heard a stirring along the Allied line. A glance across the field made the reason plain. As Wellington had said, Bonaparte was at last sending in the Imperial Guard. The legendary elite troops, never defeated in battle, marched forward to the beating of drums, gleaming bayonets fixed. They moved over the undulating ground through a rippling curtain of cannon smoke, hidden for moments by the ground or the smoke only to emerge seemingly stronger and more implacable than ever.

By the time Harry had delivered his message to General Maitland, chaos engulfed the field again. The Allied infantry waited for the French columns in line, some of them, such as Maitland's men, lying flat on the ground to conceal their presence. Cannon thundered on both sides. Shells whistled through the air, exploded, or lay spitting and hissing on the muddy, bloody ground.

The French closed to within forty feet. "Now, Maitland!" Wellington's voice rang out over the cacophony of drums and shots. "Now is your time! Up, Guards! Make ready! Fire!"

Maitland's men sprang up from the ground and fired. Drumbeats, musket fire, and screams choked the air. Caught up in the confusion, Harry saw a familiar face in the smoky mêlée. "Ashton." He edged Claudius toward his brother-in-law. "What are you doing among the infantry?"

"Sent with a message. We're running short of staff officers." Ashton's voice sagged with exhaustion. Blood and dirt crusted his coat and his face glistened with sweat. "Glad you're alive, Davenport."

"It isn't over yet."

"I'm glad—" Ashton hesitated. "I know if I fall you'll help Cordelia look after Robbie. Thank you."

"Look, Ashton—"

But Ashton had already ridden off. Through the smoke, Harry saw a musket shot wing his brother-in-law's horse, saw Ashton tumble from the saddle and roll downhill. Harry urged Claudius forward in time to see a French grenadier rip through the cannon smoke, bearing down on Ashton with a bayonet. Harry fired off a shot, but he was at an awkward angle and it only grazed the grenadier's cheek. As Harry fought his way forward, knowing he was too far to save Julia's husband, a French infantry officer hurled himself forward and took the bayonet thrust. Ashton fired his pistol from the ground, bringing down the grenadier.

It was only when Harry flung himself down beside Ashton that he recognized the soldier on the ground beside him who had taken the bayonet thrust. Anthony Chase. In a blue coat. There was blue on both sides today, but that coat was unmistakably a French uniform.

"What the devil—" Ashton pushed himself up on his knees and bent over his childhood friend.

"Ask Davenport and Rannoch," Tony gasped. Blood dripped from his mouth and his eyes were already clouding. "No time to explain. Listen, Ashton. Look after Violet."

"But—"

"She wants you. She always has. And I think you want her."

"I don't—"

But as Ashton spoke, Tony's gaze froze, and his head flopped to the side. Ashton stared down at him for a long moment, then lifted a hand and closed his former friend's eyes. "Why in God's name—"

Harry touched his shoulder. "Explanations if we survive this, Ashton." Musket fire sounded on either side of them. They seemed to be in a gap between the French attack on the Allied right and another attack farther to the east. Ashton's horse had galloped down the hill toward them. Harry caught its bridle. The animal had a graze in its side but was otherwise unhurt. "Get back in the saddle before you're trampled." Harry pulled Ashton to his feet and swung back up onto Claudius. No possibility of moving Tony's body in the chaos.

Allied soldiers were advancing down the slope. Harry lost sight of Ashton as Allied and French soldiers spilled in from either side. Shouts of *"Vive l'empereur,"* "Form up," and *"Oranje boven"* cut the air. Out of the corner of his eye, Harry saw a flicker of movement in the smoke to his left. Pain exploded in his chest. He tumbled from his horse and gasped Cordelia's name into the mud.

The Imperial Guard had broken. Cries of *"la Garde recule"* sounded from the French ranks. Allied cavalry thundered down the ridge. Allied infantry followed. Malcolm, who had just delivered a message to Sir John Colborne, watched the Allied army, which had fought a defensive battle most of the day, at last advance. Three hussars galloped past him. A gust of wind stirred the smoke, and he caught sight of a muddy form in a dark blue coat sprawled on the slope below. A staff officer. A familiar-looking brown horse nuzzled the fallen man's arm. Malcolm urged Perdita forward. Brown hair. Something mocking and instantly recognizable about the small bit of profile showing. Malcolm swung down from Perdita, reached for Harry Davenport's wrist, and felt a faint pulse.

He turned Davenport over. Blood streamed from a wound in his chest. He gave a groan, then seemed to lose consciousness. Malcolm lifted him as carefully as he could.

Boots thudded against the ground. Malcolm looked up to see a chasseur leveling a musket at him.

They had lost. Raoul O'Roarke had known that even before he rode in the Guard's advance at Marshal Ney's side. They had seen troops approaching from the east. On Napoleon's orders, la Bédoyère had shouted that it was Grouchy bringing French reinforcements, but Raoul had been sure from the first that it was the Prussians, come at last to reinforce Wellington.

Still he fought, even now the seemingly invincible Guard had been pushed back. He heard shouts of *"nous sommes trahis"* from French soldiers who had realized the Prussians were at hand. Ney, his fifth horse shot from under him, wielded his sword with grim determination. For Raoul, the world had shrunk down to the few feet of ground in front of him. He slashed at a British hussar and saw a man in a brown civilian coat kneeling on the ground a few feet away. He held a fallen comrade in the dark blue coat of one of Wellington's staff officers. Good God. A chill went through Raoul. It was Malcolm Rannoch. And Raoul wasn't the only one who had seen him. A chasseur moved toward Malcolm, musket leveled.

Raoul didn't hesitate. He lifted his pistol and shot the chasseur in the back.

Georgiana and Sarah returned home in the still warm evening air, escorted by the footman who had come with them from the Rue de la Blanchisserie. Suzanne helped David and Simon settle a Prussian private they'd brought back from the road to Waterloo, gave some laudanum to Henri Rivaux, who was tossing restlessly, assisted Cordelia with changing Angus's bandages. She went upstairs to look in on the children. They were all sharing a room tonight, as they'd seemed comforted by being together. She found

Colin stirring fretfully, his blankets pushed down round his feet. She straightened the covers and stroked his hair until he flopped against the pillows. She touched her fingers to Livia's and Robbie's hair, surprised at how steadied she felt.

When she stepped into the passage raised voices assailed her from the hall below. She hurried to the stair head, pulse quickened. The light of the chandelier and lamps and candles flickered over the scene below. Christophe and two of the other wounded men were on their feet, cheering and slapping hands with the footmen. Aline was hugging Rachel. Addison was embracing Blanca. Cordelia, hair falling from its pins, had her arms round David and Simon.

"Wonderful news." David caught sight of Suzanne and moved to the base of the stairs, a surprisingly youthful grin splitting his face. "The French are in retreat. We've won."

❧ 48 ❧

Sunday, 18 June–Monday, 19 June

Such simple words. And it was over. The fighting, the struggle, the betrayals. All so she could stand at the head of a flight of mahogany stairs and hear the end of everything she had fought for pronounced by her husband's grinning best friend.

Suzanne ran down the stairs and flung her arms round David, burying her face in his shoulder. He swung her round in an exuberant circle. By the time he set her back on her feet, she had recovered her self-command. "Tell me. Where did you hear?"

"Stuart just sent word round. He had the news from Alten."

Suzanne shook her head. She could still not make sense of it. "I thought General Alten had been brought in wounded."

"He ordered one of his aides-de-camp to send word to him as soon as the battle was decided," Simon said.

Suzanne hugged Simon, holding on a little tighter than usual. "What else have you learned?"

"Nothing about anyone we know."

She nodded and reached out to hug Cordelia and then Aline. Rachel had dropped back down beside Henri, who was sitting up against the pillows, a smile creasing his face.

Simon and Cordelia opened champagne and handed it round in a variety of drinking vessels. Suzanne sipped champagne from a teacup, laughed, grinned, said and did everything that seemed appropriate.

Cordelia caught her eye. "I know. Such amazing news, and it won't mean anything to me if they don't come back."

"Quite."

"Drink some more champagne."

With the giddy atmosphere in the hall, it was a moment before Suzanne realized the door had opened. She turned round to see her husband standing just inside the door. She ran to him and flung her arms round him with the force of everything coursing through her.

Malcolm hugged her to him hard, but he spoke over her shoulder to David, Simon, and Addison. "Davenport's in the cart outside, badly wounded. I'm going to need help getting him in."

Suzanne drew back to see that Cordelia had taken two steps forward, parchment pale but all questions suppressed.

"It's serious," Malcolm said, meeting Cordelia's gaze. "But not beyond hope."

Cordelia gave a quick nod and snatched up a lamp. "Put him in my room."

Malcolm, David, and Simon carried Harry Davenport upstairs, while Addison saw to Perdita and Claudius, who had somehow survived the battle. Cordelia held the lamp to light the way. Suzanne set about gathering up lint, brandy, and clean cloths. Aline brought a bowl of warm water from the kitchen.

By the time they came into Cordelia's room, the men had got Harry's boots and coat off. He was moaning and twisting his head against the pillows but seemed unconscious of his surroundings.

"Bless you for the water." Cordelia dampened a cloth and sponged her husband's mud-caked face.

"He fell facedown," Malcolm said. "And it was some time before I got to him. I fear at least one horse trampled him. Blackwell says he has two broken ribs, but it's the wound in his chest that's really concerning. Blackwell said to tell you to change the dressing."

Suzanne pushed back the remnants of Harry's shirt, which had already been sliced neatly in two, probably by Geoffrey Blackwell.

She peeled back the dressing. Cordelia sucked in her breath. The wound was deep and perilously close to Harry's heart. But at least it was leaking clean blood. She cleaned it with brandy and applied a fresh dressing. He twitched but didn't waken from his feverish state. Cordelia held him steady, as Rachel had done earlier with Henri.

Suzanne bent over Cordelia and put her arms round her shoulders. "I'll have some tea sent up, and I'll be just downstairs should you need me. I've seen men much farther gone make a complete recovery."

Cordelia squeezed Suzanne's fingers. She didn't ask how many men in a similar state Suzanne had seen die, though the question lurked in her eyes.

Suzanne slipped out into the passage. Malcolm followed and pulled the door to behind him. For the first time since he'd come into the house, Suzanne looked properly at him. In the light from the candle sconces, she saw that his face was mud spattered and covered with a day's stubble. There was a red-brown smear just below his jaw. She put her hand up to it.

"I'm all right." He curled his fingers round her own. "I don't think it's mine."

"We heard the battle's won," she said, carefully calibrating a note of bright cheerfulness tempered by the horrors all round them.

Malcolm's mouth twisted. "At an intolerable cost."

The candlelight bounced off his eyes, revealing a hell starker than all the horrors of their years in the Peninsula. "Who?" she asked.

He swallowed. "Easier to ask who survived. Canning died of a stomach wound. De Lancey fell and last I heard no one had found him. Gordon lost his leg. He's in Wellington's bedchamber at Headquarters, and I doubt he'll last the night."

She sucked in her breath as though she'd received a blow to the gut. Gordon's infectious laughter echoed in her ears. She saw Canning's smile, heard Gordon's ironic voice, had a clear image of De Lancey bending over his young wife's hand. "Fitzroy?" she asked, holding her breath for the answer.

"He lost his arm. But Blackwell thinks he'll recover."

She squeezed her eyes shut. "March?"

"He was alive last I saw. He got Slender Billy off the field."

"The prince was wounded? Is he—"

"Alive at last report. He took a shoulder wound from a sniper. Who I think was aiming for me."

"Tony Chase?"

"So I suspect. Though I think any number of people would have quite cheerfully put a bullet through Billy in the course of the day. The damn fool ordered his men to form line instead of square again. It was like giving them a death sentence. The number who fell—"

"Malcolm." She tightened her fingers round his own. "Harry was right last night. Billy's failures shouldn't be on your conscience."

"Countless pointless deaths. If I'd been truly brave I'd have bashed him over the head and dragged him from the field." He caught her other hand in his, so tight she could feel the pressure of bone on bone. "The road from Waterloo is clogged with dead and dying men. Some were crushed under overturned wagons. Some are lying among the trees on the side of the road, unlikely ever to emerge. The number I passed without stopping—"

"Darling." She pulled her fingers free of his grip and took his face between her hands. "You can't save everyone."

"Of course not. It would be hubris to think so. Not to mention idiocy."

"But you still feel guilty when you can't."

He shook his head. "Wellington came through unscathed. But Blackwell told me Uxbridge had his leg shattered just at the end of the battle, when his horse was scarce more than a hand's breadth from Wellington's. He'll lose his leg." He drew a breath. "I was almost done for myself. When I was rescuing Davenport. A chasseur was coming straight at me."

A chill shot through her. "What happened?"

"Someone shot him in the back. Whoever it was, I'll be forever grateful to him."

She wrapped her arms round him and pressed her face into the hollow of his throat. "So will I."

Cordelia folded Harry's hand between her own and sat bolt upright in her straight-back chair. He was frighteningly pale, his hair and the brown stubble on his jaw stark against his ashen skin, but she thought his breathing seemed a bit easier. Or perhaps it was simply that she was desperate to latch onto some reason to hope.

She studied the rhythmic rise and fall of his chest and realized that this was the first time she'd properly watched him sleep. Even when they'd lived together, he would visit her room and then retire to his own to sleep, after the practice of fashionable Mayfair couples.

No, that wasn't quite true. She remembered once, early in their marriage, waking to the unexpected pressure of an arm flung across her and the feel of warm breath stirring her hair. She'd turned her head on the pillow to see Harry's face, relaxed in sleep in a way she'd never seen it in waking. She'd watched him for a few moments, an unexpected warmth welling up in her that might have been tenderness.

His gaze had flown open. For a moment it had lingered on her own, soft with warmth. Then reality came thundering back. Harry drew away, clutching the sheet over him. "Sorry," he'd mumbled. "Didn't mean to fall asleep."

She'd clutched at the sheet herself, feeling as though she'd been caught waltzing at Almack's without permission from the patronesses. Amazing how uncomfortable one could feel lying in bed with one's own husband.

If she'd reached out and caught his hand then, instead of watching as he struggled into his dressing gown and slipped from the room—Would anything have been different?

It all seemed so absurd now as she watched him fighting for his life. And yet if he recovered, if they tried to go on together—if he even wanted to—that was the world they'd go back to.

Suzanne brought her a cup of sweetened tea and gave her a hug. "I looked in on Livia. She's still sound asleep."

Cordelia forced herself to sip the tea, knowing she needed the strength. She had finished the cup and the sky was beginning to turn a pale charcoal beyond the window when Harry finally stirred. She thought it was the feverish restlessness again, but his gaze fastened on her face. His eyes were sleep clouded but focused. "Cordy?"

His voice came out rough and harsh, but it drove the fear from her lungs. "Good morning, Harry."

"What are you doing here?"

She dropped to her knees beside the bed so her face was level with his. "This is my room. You're in the Rue Ducale."

He frowned, shook his head slightly, winced. "Damned fool Rannoch. Damned generous fool. Thought I was done for."

"How much do you remember?"

His brows drew together. "Took a shot to the chest."

"Malcolm Rannoch found you on the battlefield. In the mud. Dr. Blackwell bandaged your wound."

"Hurts like the devil."

"You have two cracked ribs as well. Here." She reached for the laudanum. "This will help."

He pushed her hand away. "Is there news?"

"The battle's won. The French are in retreat."

A faint smile lit his eyes. "Thank God some good came of all the carnage." His gaze moved over her face. "Don't know if George survived—"

"That doesn't—"

"But I saw Tony Chase die in a French uniform. He took a bayonet meant for John Ashton."

Shock and relief that Johnny had apparently survived shot through her. Followed by an unexpected jolt of grief. She had an image of Tony as a seven-year-old boy, front teeth missing, climbing an apple tree.

"Sorry," Harry said. "He was your friend."

"A long time ago." She struggled to sort through the implications. "He died saving Johnny?"

"I think he did it for his sister."

Harry's eyes closed, and she thought he slept again. "Thank you," she murmured, more to herself than to him.

His eyes flew open. "For what?"

"For coming back."

"Damned ironic."

"What?"

"For the first time in my life I went into a battle wanting quite desperately to survive. And I very nearly didn't. May not."

"Don't talk foolishness, Harry. I have no intention of letting you die."

His eyes drifted closed again. "Never knew you so determined." His head sank deeper into the pillow. But as she returned to her chair to settle in while he slept, she heard him murmur, "Your name."

"What?" She leaned forward, not sure she'd heard him aright.

His eyes opened and fastened on her face for a moment, clear and focused. "Your name. Last thing I said before I lost consciousness with my face in the mud."

Henri Rivaux turned feverish in the early hours of the morning, thrashing on his pallet. Suzanne cleaned his wound, bathed it with an infusion of comfrey, and helped Rachel wash him with cool cloths to bring down the fever. Rachel worked with quiet determination, mouth set, though her lips trembled slightly. Another of the wounded, a sergeant in the Rifles, had died just after the news of victory. Simon and Addison had gone to arrange for his burial.

Malcolm touched her on the shoulder to murmur that he and David were going back to the battlefield to bring back more wounded and to try to learn what had become of his brother.

"Don't worry if we're gone for some time," Malcolm said, his fingers tightening on her shoulder. "The roads are an impassable hell. But the fighting's done. We won't come to mischief."

She nodded and turned her head to press her lips against his hand. The lowering truth was that she was oddly relieved to see him go. All the while she nursed the wounded and made sure there was food for the household and looked in on the children, a weight of sorrow tore at her chest. A sorrow she couldn't share with Malcolm, the man with whom she shared so much. A barrier had slammed up between them. A barrier that had been there from the moment they met, but that she had learned to ignore, to look past, to step through. Yet on this morning of victory for the Allies, it had never been more clear that he was a British gentleman and she was a French revolutionary.

Just after eight, she took Cordelia a tray of tea and toast. Colonel Davenport was asleep. "He woke briefly and seemed quite himself," Cordelia said, "though weak and in a great deal of pain."

"It's an excellent sign that he was coherent. Were you able to talk?"

Cordelia nodded. Her eyes held a mixture of hope, fear, and wonder, but she merely said, "How does Lieutenant Rivaux get on?"

"We've got the fever down. I think Rachel's going to keep him alive on sheer determination."

"I understand how she feels." Cordelia reached out and smoothed her husband's hair. "There's a blessed sort of clarity in the situation. They're hurt, and they need us. The barriers are down. It's crystal clear where we belong."

"And afterwards?" Suzanne asked.

Cordelia's eyes turned bleak. "Afterwards we're still going to live in the world we inhabited before the battle. But I'm not letting myself think that far ahead."

"Don't," Suzanne advised. "You'll ruin it before it's had a chance to properly begin."

Cordelia stared at her, like one looking into hell without flinching. "Some things are beyond forgiveness. Oh, perhaps they can be forgiven in a theoretical sort of way. One can make grand, sweeping promises in a moment of great emotion. But to live day in, day out with someone who's betrayed you in the worst way—I don't think that's possible. I don't think you would, either, on rational reflection. You're much too sensible a person."

Suzanne felt a knot of cold tighten round her heart. "That leaves aside the question of what sort of betrayal is the worst."

"I know what I did to Harry. If I didn't understand it before, I realized it these last few days in Brussels."

"Don't underestimate him," Suzanne said. "Or yourself."

Cordelia smiled but shook her head.

Suzanne went into the nursery where the children, probably the only people in the house to have got a good night's sleep, were breakfasting with Blanca and their nurses.

Colin greeted her with a cheerful smile. "We won."

Suzanne nearly vomited her tea and toast onto the gleaming nursery floorboards. She could feel Blanca's concerned gaze on her. Later they would have to talk. "Yes," she said, forcing a smile to her lips. "The Allies had a great victory."

"My daddy was hurt," Livia said.

"But he's doing very well." That was the thing about children. They forced you to keep going and not dwell on losses. "Your mummy's looking after him."

"Can I see him?"

"Perhaps in a bit. He's sleeping now." Suzanne touched Robbie's hair. "We hope your daddy will be here soon. He was well the last time your uncle Harry saw him."

Robbie nodded. "Lots of people died."

"A horrible number. We're very fortunate so many of the people we love survived."

After she left the nursery, she sat with Harry for a time so Cordelia could go in and reassure Livia and Robbie. Harry stirred occasionally but didn't waken. When Cordelia returned, Suzanne went into her own bedchamber, put on a gypsy hat, and tossed a mantilla into one of her larger reticules.

"I'm going out for a bit," she told Aline. "We need more laudanum."

Aline nodded. Her face was gray with exhaustion, but her eyes were lighter than they'd been last night. The worst was over. A shocking number of her friends were gone, but her husband was safe and the British had prevailed.

Horses no longer stood before houses in the Rue Ducale, ready for imminent flight. But more wounded men lined the streets, and Suzanne passed carts bringing in fresh casualties. She stopped to give water to the wounded until no more was left in the flask she carried.

She didn't stop at Madame Longé's. She was too exhausted to go through the motions now things were over to all intents and purposes. Which was foolish, because the need for secrecy would never be gone. But right now she didn't care. She was as drained and spent as she imagined a prizefighter would feel after a match. A losing match. She slipped into a gap between two houses, pulled off her gypsy hat and stuffed it into her reticule, and then replaced it with the mantilla.

Down the alley, along the familiar passage, up the stairs, to the door she had got to know so well during her months in Brussels. A part of her didn't really believe he'd be there, even when he answered her thrush call. But when she pushed open the door, she caught the familiar smell of his shaving soap, overlaid by stale sweat.

He pushed himself to his feet at her entrance but made no move to come toward her. The light slanting through the high windows showed her that apparently he had received no further hurt. She stared at the familiar bones of his face and felt the breath rush from her lungs. In his eyes, she saw desolation and shattered hopes that were the twin of her own. For a moment, she wanted to run and hide in his arms. Instead, she leaned against the closed door and said the words that most needed to be said. "I'm through."

❧ 49 ❧

Something flared in his eyes. Not surprise but a flash of acknowledgment that might have been sadness. "I thought as much."

She took two quick, determined steps into the room. Her mantilla slithered to the floor. "This isn't another attack of conscience. I'm done. I'm getting out. I'm not your agent anymore."

"Clearly stated."

She dropped down on the edge of the cot and gripped its wooden frame. She mistrusted that mild tone. "It's over." Her voice shook, beyond her control. "We lost."

"It's never entirely over." Raoul sat beside her, a few inches of gray blanket between them. "But we were certainly dealt a decisive blow. Not only has the game changed, it will be played on an entirely different board."

"Damn it, Raoul." She grabbed his arm. "It's not a game."

"Of course it is." He caught her wrist in a gentle grip. "A game with life-and-death stakes and people's future and liberty hanging in the balance."

"I'll still fight for the things I believe in," she said, perhaps a little too firmly, because she couldn't bear for there to be any doubt on this score. "But I'll only act openly as Malcolm's wife."

He nodded. "Knowing you, not to mention Malcolm, I imagine you'll be able to accomplish a great deal."

"I mean it. I won't dwindle into a wife."

His mouth curved in a faint smile. "I don't think you could if you tried." He looked at her for a moment. She had the oddest sense he was memorizing her features. "I think you've made a wise choice."

"For God's sake, Raoul." She pulled free of his grip. "What game are you playing? You're never so magnanimous without an ulterior purpose."

"We've never been in circumstances like these."

"I'm serious. I won't work as your agent anymore."

"I know. I'll miss you."

For some reason, that was when her throat closed and tears prickled the back of her eyes. She turned her head to the side, unable to bear the pressure of his gaze. "All these years. The fighting, the lying, the compromising. Twisting ideals to meet necessity. And this is where it got us."

"One can never see where it will take one. All one can do is hold on to what one believes in."

"Damn you, stop it with the platitudes." Her fingers dug into the coarse blanket. "You have to feel it, too. It's over. Bourbons on the throne of France for good, reforms repealed, monarchs grabbing for power. Castlereagh and Metternich and their ilk trying to turn the clock back on every shred of progress since the Revolution. Wasted years, wasted lives—"

Her chest ached from the lost purpose, wrenched from her at the news of the French defeat. The thing that had kept her going after the loss of her family, that had given her a focus, that had been the core of who she was. She couldn't seem to stop shaking. A sob tore through her.

Raoul's arms closed round her. She pushed against him, desperate to strike out at something. Then she drew a sharp breath and sobbed into his chest, clinging to him as though to her last remnants of herself, until the rage had drained from her, leaving her empty and winded.

"You can never let yourself think your work's gone for naught," he said, stroking her hair. "Or you'll go mad. Believe me, I speak from experience."

She drew back and looked up at him. "Ireland." She'd spent many evenings hearing him talk about the failure of the United Irish Uprising in 1798, anger and regret sharp in his voice.

"And the Revolution." Raoul had been a passionate supporter of the Revolution, but he'd found himself imprisoned in Les Carmes and had nearly gone to the guillotine. "One has to go on and do the best one can. Which I'm sure you'll continue to do."

"You make it sound so easy."

"Easy?" His voice cut with sudden force. "There's nothing easy about it. Do you think I haven't rethought every decision I've made a dozen times, haven't asked myself—" He shook his head. "But believe me, *believe me, querida*, you'll find a way to go on. Because there's no other choice."

She stared at him, memories coming thick and fast. His hands tossing her into the saddle or showing her how to load a pistol. His voice drilling her on court protocol or correcting her accent. His arm secure round her as she drifted into sleep. The steady trust in his eyes when he sent her on her first mission. "Are you saying this is what you want?"

"No." The short word held layers of meaning. "But I think it's what's best for you." He pushed her hair behind her ear with a tenderness that was somehow in a very different key from the days when they'd been lovers.

"Since when does what's best for any of us matter more than the cause?"

"My dear girl. I'm not nearly so single-minded or such a schemer as you make me out to be." He hesitated a moment. "Philippe was killed."

She bit her lip. Fresh tears stung her eyes. "I have a letter for his sweetheart."

"Do you want me to—"

"No. I know where to send it." She got to her feet and picked up her mantilla. "What will you do now?" she asked, running the black lace through her fingers.

"I'll manage."

She swung her gaze back to him. "You don't trust me anymore."

"I wouldn't say that." He got to his feet as well. "But our interests no longer neatly align. No sense in putting either of us in an awkward situation."

She nodded. Practicality, that was what was called for, and a cool head. She turned to the cracked looking glass and tried to pin her hair into some semblance of order.

Raoul leaned against the wall behind her. "In a few days or a few weeks you're going to feel an intolerable burden of guilt. Try to remember that guilt is a singularly wasteful emotion."

She met his gaze in the spotted looking glass. "Who says I'll feel guilty?"

"My intuition. You won't like the fact that you've betrayed your husband."

She gave a rough laugh. "I've been betraying Malcolm from the day I married him. The day I met him if it comes to that."

"But you could hide in the needs of the moment."

She jabbed a pin into her knot of hair, hitting her scalp. "I'm used to living with sins on my conscience."

"With peace you'll find you have leisure to dwell on the past. To question actions, to rethink decisions, to play the damnable game of what if."

She pushed two more pins into her hair and draped the mantilla over her head. "What makes you so certain?"

"Because I'm quite sure I'll be doing the same myself."

She spun round to look at the man who had always subsumed guilt to the goal in front of him. He returned her gaze. The scars in his eyes had never been plainer. "Raoul—"

He gave a faint smile. "Don't worry. It won't be the first time I've pieced my life back together."

She crossed the room to him, took his face between her hands, and kissed him on the lips for the first time since her marriage. For the last time. "Keep safe."

He squeezed her shoulders for a moment, as though catching onto the past, then released her. "Look after your family, *querida*."

*   *   *

Suzanne stepped back into the house in the Rue Ducale to the smells of beef tea and laudanum and the sound of a ball being tossed. Colin and Robbie were playing catch across Christophe's pallet. Rachel was spooning beef tea to Henri Rivaux, who protested feebly. Aline was changing Angus's dressing. The smile she gave Suzanne indicated that he was doing better. Brigitte came through the door from the kitchen with a tea tray.

Normal life, or at least what now passed for normal life. Raoul O'Roarke seemed a world away. She might never have been a Bonapartist spy. Save that the ache in her chest and the bitterness in her mouth told her she'd never forget.

With that uncanny instinct children often have, Colin ran across the hall and flung his arms round her knees. She scooped him up, held him close for a moment, then settled him on her hip, letting the solidness of his body and the milky smell of his skin pull her back to the reality of her life. However egregious her sins, she couldn't indulge in wallowing. She had obligations.

Malcolm and David returned just before dark with Edgar. He had a leg wound but no sign of fever or infection. They laid him on Malcolm's and her bed. When she checked his dressing, he opened his eyes and gave her a weak smile. "Malcolm is a capital brother."

"Yes, he is." She pressed a kiss to his forehead.

"Probably the most positive interaction Edgar and I've had since our mother died," Malcolm said when he and Suzanne were outside in the passage.

"I'm glad you found him. I mean, I'm glad he's all right, but I'm also glad you were the one to find him."

He gave a bleak smile. "Foreseeing neat tidy endings, Suzette?"

"Trying to take what we can from the wreckage."

He brushed his fingers against her cheek and studied her face for a moment. "Are you all right?"

She smiled and leaned her cheek against his hand. "Yes. Especially now you're back."

What else could she say?

* * *

Harry woke to the smell of barley water and beef tea. He opened his eyes onto an intent young face framed by a fall of pale blond hair.

"Mummy said I could come sit by you if I was quiet," Livia said. "Because you need to sleep." She frowned. "I didn't wake you, did I?"

"Not in the least. You were quiet as a sniper."

Livia grinned. "I sat very still. Do you want some broth? It'll make you better."

Cordelia moved into view. Her hair was pulled back into a simple knot, with the cropped bits escaping about her face uncurled, her cheeks were hollow, and purple shadows showed beneath her eyes. He couldn't remember when she had looked more beautiful. "Do you think you can sit up?" she asked.

He started to tell her not to be ridiculous and then realized that sitting up would indeed be a complicated maneuver. Cordelia perched on the edge of the bed, slid her arm under him, and bunched up the pillows, then half-held him while Livia carefully spooned the broth.

Pain shot through his cracked ribs, but he controlled his reaction to a wince. It took an absurd amount of strength to hold his head up. A ridiculous position to be in, but oddly he didn't mind as much as he would have expected. Perhaps that was because he was so tired.

"That'll do," he told Livia when he'd managed about half the broth in the cup. "No sense in pushing things. But you're an excellent nurse."

Livia's serious face brightened. Cordelia settled him back against the pillows.

"I was afraid you were going to die," Livia said.

"I was a bit concerned about it myself. I had a particular reason to want to survive this battle, you see."

"What?" Livia asked.

"I'd met you."

"Oh."

A small hand twined round his arm. A strange and wonderful

sensation. He squeezed Livia's fingers. His eyes drifted closed despite himself. When he opened them again, Cordelia was sitting beside the bed. "You were smaller when I fell asleep," he said.

"Livia's gone to have something to eat with the boys, but only after I assured her that she could see you again later. I hope you don't mind. I thought seeing you would reassure her."

"Difficult to imagine the sight of me like this reassuring anyone."

"One's imaginings are always worse than reality. And children are blessedly practical. Much more so than adults."

"Very true. And no, I don't mind. On the contrary." He turned his head on the pillow so he could see her better. The light from the window fell across one side of her face, showing lines about her eyes that hadn't been there five years ago and marks of strain that hadn't been there when he said good-bye to her at the Duchess of Richmond's ball. It wasn't only those on the field who'd been touched by the battle. "I meant it, you know," he added.

"What?"

"That having met Livia I wanted to come back. It's an odd thing, that sense of being responsible for another person. I'd never felt it before."

"No." Her gaze locked with his own. "Nor had I until she was born."

He let his head sink deeper into the pillows, his gaze still on her face. "I meant the other thing as well."

Her finely arced brows drew together. "Which thing?"

"Your name. My last word before I lost consciousness on the battlefield. For a moment I was one of those romantic idiots who can think of nothing but that he'll never see his wife again. War does damnable things to a man."

She turned her head away. To his amazement, he saw the prickle of tears against her skin. "Damn it, Harry, don't."

"I admit it's not the most elevated language, but I would have thought it would take more than that to make you cry. Haven't you been hearing the like from starry-eyed undergraduates since you were sixteen?"

"Don't turn me into something I'm not. You idealized me as all sorts of things I wasn't five years ago. Don't form another false picture of me now."

He tried to push himself up against the pillows and winced at the stab of pain through his chest. "Harry, no," she said, hands on his shoulders.

"I'm at too much of a disadvantage flat on my back."

She eased him up and propped the pillows beneath him. He set his shoulders against them and regarded her with a hard stare. "I'm not a fool, Cordy. Not such a fool as to think a kiss in a ballroom with bugles sounding in the distance and the fact that you're sitting by my sickbed have anything to do with our future."

"That's not—"

He grabbed her wrist, ignoring the fire that shot through his chest. "I don't know if you've been nursing me out of some sense of obligation, but for whatever reason you have my thanks."

Her gaze fastened on his face, wide with shock. "Harry, don't be silly."

"It's a reasonable assumption. Of course, you've been nursing all sorts of men—"

"Harry." She linked her fingers through his own. "For the past three days I've been consumed by the terror of losing you."

Something sang through him, something he'd never known or ever thought to feel. "Damned odd, considering—"

"I didn't have you to begin with. Quite. The irony isn't lost on me." Her gaze moved over his face. "I'm not a fool, either, Harry. I don't expect the past week to wipe away the past four years."

He inched up against the pillows. Amazing how much less it hurt. "I think the past is less important than the future."

"The past is always going to be there between us. I've done quite unspeakable things to you, Harry."

"I think you're puffing yourself up a bit. You haven't done anything half the wives in Mayfair haven't done."

"But their husbands aren't—That is—"

"I was in love with you. That made it worse. Granted. Go on."

She stared at their linked hands. "There'd be a sort of rosy glow at first. But eventually I'll do something or say something and you'll realize I haven't really changed. That I'm still the sadly commonplace woman you married in the first place."

"Are you saying you're planning to resume your affair with George Chase?"

"No, of course not, but—"

"Or with someone else?"

"That's not the point. My past is there. People are going to gossip. They're going to give you sad looks like they do William Lamb because you're saddled with an impossible wife."

"I've just survived a battle against Napoleon Bonaparte's army, Cordy. I think I can cope with the London gossips."

"And inevitably you'll remember. Some unthinking comment will bring it all flooding back. I don't want to find you looking at me across the breakfast things recalling past betrayals, knowing you're trapped but unable to say anything because we've papered over the past. Some cracks can't be papered over."

"All right." He rested his head against the pillows. "That's what you don't want. What *do* you want, Cordy?"

"I don't see—"

"It's a fair question. I don't want a wife who isn't happy. Do you want me to leave you free to go your own way? Do you want a divorce so you can marry again? I can afford it. I can make it as easy for you as possible."

"No, I told you—"

"Because I can be Livia's father without being your husband."

"That's not what I meant."

He kept his gaze steady on her face. "What then?"

Her brows drew together in the way he remembered from when she was trying to puzzle out a particularly difficult bit of translation. "What do *you* want, Harry?"

"Oh, that's easy." He tightened his fingers round her own. "I want the same thing I've wanted for five years. I want you, my darling."

❧ 50 ❧

"Malcolm." Billy turned his head against the pillow. The curtains were closed to allow the prince to rest, but the heat of the day leached into the room. The air smelled of toast, beef tea, and lavender. "Glad to see you alive."

"I could say the same." Malcolm looked down at his boyhood friend. The inexperienced general who had sent men to their deaths. Amelia Beckwith's lover.

"So many friends gone." Billy's fingers twisted in the fine linen sheet. "You know about Gordon?"

Malcolm nodded. "But Fitzroy looks as though he'll pull through."

"I heard he lost his right arm."

"He's already learning to write with his left hand. He'll be buried in paperwork again in no time. Apparently he made them stop and remove the ring Harriet gave him from his amputated arm before they carried it away."

Billy gave a weak smile, then searched Malcolm's face. "You haven't come to congratulate me on cheating death. Do you know what happened to Julia?"

"Not yet."

The prince regarded him in silence for a moment. "You'd better sit down, Malcolm." His gaze was dark in his pale face. "And then ask me whatever it is you've come to ask."

Malcolm dropped down on the edge of the bed. "Amelia Beckwith."

Billy's brows drew together. "Amy? What on earth does she have to do with—"

"You were her lover."

Billy flinched. "I was in love with Amy." He tried to push himself up against the pillows. "I wanted to marry her."

"But you didn't." Malcolm put a hand on Billy's shoulder to still him before he could do himself an injury.

Billy turned his head to the side, gaze fastened on the bar of light spilling between a gap in the curtains. "I was only eighteen. I wanted to elope to Gretna Green and damn the consequences, but Amy was afraid. I had to go to my parents for the Christmas holidays. I meant to tell my father, but somehow I couldn't bring myself to. Then I had to go to a damned house party in Devon. I wrote to Amy telling her to be patient. Perhaps one of my letters went astray. Somehow they—my parents—learned about us. I was summoned to London. They sent Rebecque to talk to me."

"I doubt I could have held out against such pressure at that age."

"No." Billy's voice cut with surprising force. "I refused to give her up. I stalked out and ordered my carriage. I got back to Carfax Court only to learn that Amy had died."

Malcolm studied his friend's indignant face. "Did you know Amelia was carrying your child?"

"*What?*" Billy pushed himself up, then winced in pain.

Malcolm gripped the prince's shoulders. "She confessed to a friend that she was pregnant just before she died."

"But—" Billy's eyes were wide with confusion. "Malcolm, Amy and I never—" He shook his head. "I wouldn't have. I was going to marry her."

Malcolm pulled up the pillows and settled Billy against them. "Scruples have a way of giving way to need. Especially when one's eighteen. I'm the last person who'd be scandalized by a love affair, Billy."

"I'm not saying it because you'd be scandalized. I'm saying it because it's the truth." Billy stared at Malcolm with mingled indignation and confusion. "What does this have to do with Julia?"

"Lady Julia may have uncovered information about Miss Beckwith's death."

The prince's eyes went wider still. "And you think—Malcolm, I got back to Carfax Court the day Amy died. Just after they found her in the lake." Remembered loss suffused his young face. "She couldn't have been carrying a child."

Billy's gaze held genuine torment. Malcolm drew a breath and placed his hand over Billy's own. "She couldn't have been carrying your child."

Suzanne had just finished changing Henri Rivaux's dressing when the door opened. She looked up, expecting Malcolm, and saw instead a slender figure in a lavender muslin gown and a chip straw hat standing on the threshold, looking about with an uncertain gaze.

It was Violet Chase. Suzanne got to her feet and went to meet the other woman. "Miss Chase. Do come in. I'm afraid we've quite abandoned any pretense of ceremony. Our footmen are too busy tending the wounded."

"Of course," Violet said. "I'm sorry to disturb you." Her gaze swept the hall and settled for a moment on Robbie, as usual sitting with Colin beside Christophe. "I came to see if you'd had any news of Captain Ashton."

"Colonel Davenport saw him alive and unhurt late yesterday," Suzanne said. "But nothing since then, I'm afraid."

Violet nodded, put her hand to her face, and burst into tears.

"Oh, my poor dear." Suzanne steered Violet into the empty study, exchanging a glance with Brigitte, who had emerged from the kitchen with tea for the wounded.

Inside the study, Suzanne pressed Violet into a leather armchair. Violet collapsed, hands pressed to her face, tears streaming between her fingers. Suzanne tugged a clean handkerchief from her sleeve and knelt beside the chair, waiting for Violet's tears to subside.

"I'm sorry," Violet said at last. "It's just so hard not knowing."

"I can well imagine." Suzanne put the handkerchief into her hand. "Captain Ashton is a capable soldier. From what my husband says it's still chaos at the battlefield. I wouldn't infer anything from none of us having heard from him."

Violet nodded, twisting the handkerchief between her fingers. "So many have fallen." She wiped her eyes with tugs of the handkerchief that were almost vicious.

"I'm sorry about Captain Chase," Suzanne said. "How is Mrs. Chase bearing up?"

"Almost frighteningly calm. But then Jane has much better self-command than I do. A Captain Flemming called on us last night with news of the battle and to give his condolences. That seemed to make her feel better."

Suzanne drew a breath, greatly relieved for Jane Chase's sake that Will Flemming had survived the battle.

"And Major Chase?" Suzanne asked.

"He came through without injury. He came to see us this afternoon. He got leave to return to Brussels and see Annabel and the children."

Brigitte knocked at the door with a fresh pot of tea. Suzanne poured a cup, stirred in liberal amounts of milk and sugar, and pressed it into Violet's hand. Violet managed a sip, sloshing some into the saucer. She cast a quick glance at the door. "What must they all think of me."

"With everything that's happened these past days, what anyone thinks seems singularly unimportant."

Violet opened her mouth as though to protest, then gave a sudden, desperate laugh. "How very true. And how odd to think that I would ever say so." She managed another sip of tea. "I heard Colonel Davenport had been wounded. How is he?"

"Weak but recovering. Cordelia's with him now. She's scarcely left him."

Violet's mouth twisted. "All the things Cordelia did to him, and yet she's had the right to worry and ask for news all this time and now she has the right to sit by his bedside and nurse him and no one can look askance at it because whatever she's done to him he's her husband."

"For what it's worth, Cordelia's been every bit as distressed these past days as you seem to be."

"I'm sorry, I didn't mean—" Violet bit her lip. "Of course I'm pleased Colonel Davenport is recovering." She stared into her tea for a moment. "Do you think he and Cordelia will actually patch things up?"

"I don't know. But they each clearly still have strong feelings when it comes to the other."

Violet hunched her shoulders, gaze on her tea. "Do you think one can ever get to the point where one forgets the horrid things a person has done?"

Suzanne took a sip from her own teacup and swallowed, hard. "Not forgets, perhaps, but finds one isn't sorry to remember."

"Forgiveness." Violet drew out the word, as though it was a foreign concept she couldn't quite comprehend.

"It's amazing what people can manage to forgive." Assuming they knew enough to even attempt to try.

Violet wiped at a trace of tea on the side of her cup. "I said some beastly things to Johnny when he got engaged to Julia. I can be horrid when I'm in a temper, and I was in a dreadful one. I think I wanted to provoke him into being angry back, so I'd have an excuse to hate him. Instead he just looked at me with this puzzled expression and said he'd never meant to hurt me. I saw something die in his eyes then. It was one thing when he chose Julia over me. This was worse. Like I wasn't the person he'd thought me to be." She cupped both hands round her teacup and took a quick swallow. "I don't think Johnny hates me anymore, but I don't know that he'll ever forgive me for that."

Suzanne choked back an hysterical laugh. "I very much doubt anything you said could be unforgivable, Miss Chase."

"You don't know. Not that it matters if he's all right. I swear I won't mind. That is, I'll try my best not to let it show." She tugged at the ribbons on her hat and jerked it from her head. "When

Johnny chose Julia I thought if he ever loved me in the future it wouldn't matter to me. How wrong I was."

Suzanne knew that Malcolm wouldn't have married her if he hadn't thought she'd been left orphaned and penniless by the war. Which he wouldn't have thought if she hadn't lied to him in the course of a mission. And yet for nearly a year now, she'd known, with a bone-deep certainty, that she loved him. And since last autumn in Vienna, she'd known he loved her. Or at least the woman he thought she was.

"Miss Chase—" Suzanne hesitated, a dozen possible platitudes trembling on her lips. "Try not to be too hard on yourself."

Violet gave a lopsided smile. "That sounds so ridiculously sensible."

"Mother's logic."

A rap sounded on the door. "Forgive me, madame," Brigitte said. "But there's a gentleman asking for you. Captain Ashton."

Violet gasped and nearly dropped her teacup. A moment later, John Ashton stepped over the threshold and gave a formal bow. "Mrs. Rannoch. Forgive the interruption. I've only just got leave. I saw Robbie in the hall. I wanted to thank you for your kindness—"

He broke off as his gaze fell on Violet, who had pushed herself to her feet.

"Johnny—" Violet stretched out a hand, then let it fall to her side. "I'm so glad you're all right."

"Unlike so many poor devils. Violet, I'm so sorry. That is—"

She gave a quick nod. "We know Tony was killed. Cordelia sent word."

"He took a bayonet thrust that should have killed me."

Violet's eyes widened. "I don't—"

"Nor do I. But I'll be forever grateful to him."

Suzanne moved to the door. "I should check on the children. Do have some tea, Captain Ashton. Miss Chase, I know I can rely upon you to look after him."

Ashton and Violet emerged from the study twenty minutes later, not touching but with a certain intimacy in the way Ashton held the door and Violet walked beside him, almost brushing his shoulder. Ashton knelt beside Robbie again while Violet hung back, gaze fixed on the two of them. "Tony sent Johnny back to me," she murmured to Suzanne. "That is, he sent him back. I don't understand—"

"Nor do I," Suzanne said. "I'd simply be grateful for what you can salvage from the wreckage."

When Ashton joined them, Suzanne offered to take him up to see Cordelia and Harry. But she hesitated at the base of the stairs, her hand on the newel post. "Captain Ashton. Did your wife ever say anything to you about Amelia Beckwith?"

"Amy?" It wasn't Ashton who responded, it was Violet. "What on earth does she have to do with any of this?"

"I'm not sure," Suzanne said. "But she and Lady Julia were confidantes."

"Yes, of course," Violet said. "We were all friends. But it was years ago." She moved toward the stairs then paused, fingering a fold of her muslin skirt. "It seems beastly now, but I was quite jealous of Amy. I think Julia was as well."

"Jealous?" Suzanne said.

"She kept claiming she knew what love was, while we were still stumbling about in the dark. She got all mysterious about it." Violet frowned. "And then at a party at Carfax House—it must have been just a fortnight or so before she died—she told me she'd thought she'd understood love, but it was so much more complicated than she'd ever guessed. That real love wasn't a fairy tale with a prince, it was finding a man one couldn't live without. After she died I wondered who on earth she'd been talking about. I asked Julia about it once, but she just went all quiet and changed the subject."

"I remember Amelia, of course," Ashton said. "Julia was most distressed when she died. But I don't recall Julia mentioning Amy in recent years. That is—"

"What?" Suzanne asked.

Ashton frowned at the molding on the wall opposite. "She did mention Amelia once. It was just after we came to Brussels. We'd come home from the Marquise d'Assche's. The first time we'd seen you and Rannoch in Brussels. Julia was taking a candle to go upstairs. She looked at me over the candle flame, and she said it was odd, she scarcely knew Malcolm Rannoch, yet he and she were the only two people Amy had confided in. She went upstairs before I could ask more." He cast a glance at Violet, then looked back at Suzanne. "I didn't realize Rannoch had known Amy that well."

"Nor did I," Suzanne said.

Suzanne met Malcolm in the hall on his return to the house half an hour later. "Darling. Amelia Beckwith. I think I know—"

He nodded. "So do I. I need you to come with me. I can't take Davenport in his condition."

"No," Suzanne agreed. "But we need to take Cordelia."

George Chase looked from Malcolm to Suzanne to Cordelia across the confines of the sitting room in his house in Brussels. In the early evening light spilling through the windows, Suzanne could see the pulse beating in his forehead. His eyes had a hurt, bewildered look one would swear was genuine. "I told you, Billy—"

"Billy swears he and Miss Beckwith weren't lovers in the physical sense," Malcolm said.

"And you believe him?"

"In this case, yes."

George spun away and strode across the room, boot heels thudding against the Aubusson carpet. "The more fool you."

"You called me *bienne aimée*," Cordelia said. Her voice was as raw as an oozing wound.

"Of course I did." George turned to look at her, gaze open and desperate. Despite everything she knew and suspected, for an instant Suzanne almost felt sorry for him. "I meant it."

"You'd never called me that before. And you only did it in your sleep. When you were tossing with troubled dreams." Cordelia drew a hard breath. "I don't think you were talking to me at all."

"That's absurd—"

"She threatened everything you'd built for yourself." Cordelia stared at her former lover as though she scarcely recognized him.

"Annabel, your secure fortune, your position in society, your military career—"

"For God's sake, Cordy, no." He lurched across the room and seized her shoulders. "It wasn't Annabel at all. I'd seen you. At your parents' house, before you and Davenport left for the Lake District. I knew I had to have you back. I couldn't let anything stand in the way."

Cordelia jerked out of his hold and took a stumbling step backward, eyes dark with revulsion. "Oh, my God."

"Cordy—"

Cordelia spun away and threw up into a Chinese vase on the table by the door. Suzanne put her arms round her friend's shoulders. Cordelia shuddered, as though her body could scarcely contain the horror of the realization.

"Billy was with his parents and then at a house party," Malcolm said, voice cool and controlled . "Amy was probably anxious, afraid he'd throw her over. You were there to comfort her. You were probably at Carfax Court a great deal to confer with Carfax. Amy told Violet real love wasn't a fairy-tale prince, it was finding a man one couldn't live without. Billy was the fairy-tale prince. You were the man she couldn't live without. And then she told you she was pregnant."

"And you—" Cordelia pulled away from Suzanne and spun round to face George. For a moment she simply stood there, holding him with her gaze. Something turned to ashes in the air between them. Not just an old love, but bonds that stretched back to childhood. "You killed her because she threatened the perfect life you'd built for yourself."

"No." The word seemed to be ripped from George Chase's throat. He stumbled toward Cordelia and stopped a hand's breadth away. "I told Amy we'd have to keep it secret, that there was no way out of my marriage to Annabel. Amy was distraught. When I tried to comfort her, she jerked away. She slipped. There'd been frost the night before. The ground was slippery. I reached for her, but she fell into the lake."

"And you didn't try to rescue her." Cordelia's voice was flat as hammered metal.

"I couldn't—"

"Don't, George." Cordelia gripped her elbows. Her gaze was sick with self-disgust.

"Amy had confided in Julia that she was pregnant," Malcolm said in the same calm voice. "I think in Brussels these past weeks Julia somehow realized you must have been the father. Did Julia threaten to reveal what she knew when she wanted out of the spy business?"

George drew a breath but bit back whatever he had been about to say.

"But Julia was wrong about one thing," Malcolm said. "I wasn't the other person Amy had confided in about her predicament."

Fear and surprise flickered in George's gaze. "I never—"

"You told your brother I knew about Truxhillo."

"I thought—"

"You couldn't have thought anything of the sort." Malcolm took a step toward the other man. "Because I didn't know about it. But you wanted to get rid of me."

George stared at him, face set in hard lines. "You can't possibly know that."

"It makes sense of the facts. Julia told her husband I was the only other person Amy had confided in. But I wasn't."

George squeezed his eyes shut. "Don't play games, Rannoch. Julia said Amy had told David's best friend."

"Oh, dear God," Malcolm said.

Suzanne sucked in her breath. "Simon."

"Of course. That's how Amy would have thought of him." Malcolm looked at George. "And based on that you decided to have your brother get me out of the way. So you told Tony I knew about Truxhillo. And when Tony tried to embroil Julia in his efforts to get rid of me, you told Julia to play along. That you'd make sure I wasn't actually killed. But Julia decided she wanted out. So you decided to get rid of both of us."

George returned Malcolm's gaze, his own as well defended as an infantry square. Beneath his desperation was a hardened agent. And a killer. "You can't possibly prove any of that."

"Not in a court of law perhaps."

Cordelia was still staring fixedly at her former lover. "I don't know why I never saw how weak you are," she said in a low voice. "You always took the easy way out. Marrying Annabel. Letting me convince you to go back to her. I don't know whether or not I could have survived in genteel poverty. But I'm quite sure you couldn't."

George's gaze jerked back to Cordelia. Something broke in the depths of his eyes. Suzanne had seen that look in the eyes of the wounded when they realized they were dying. "Cordy, I know I've lost—"

"I don't know if this makes things easier for you, George." Cordelia folded her arms in front of her. Her voice was harsh, the voice of one stripped of her last illusions. "God knows I don't want to make things easier for you. But for what it's worth, you lost me long since. I'm in love with my husband."

David pushed himself to his feet, spun away, and slammed his fist down on a mahogany table, sending two books thudding to the floor. "I'd like to kill him."

"But you won't." Malcolm got to his feet and went to his friend's side. "I know how you feel, David. Believe me. I felt much the same when we learned the truth about Tatiana Kirsanova's death last autumn. But I didn't act on those feelings, and you won't, either."

"Because I'm better than that?" David's mouth twisted.

"Yes. And because there's no point in compounding the tragedy by ruining your life and bringing scandal on your family."

David drew a breath of frustration. "My family—"

"And because you wouldn't do that to Simon."

David cast a quick glance at his lover. Simon looked steadily back at him.

Cordelia pushed herself to her feet. They were in Harry's bedchamber, gathered round his bed. Suzanne remained seated beside the bed and watched Harry and Simon, their gazes trained on Cordelia and David.

"I wanted to kill him myself," Cordelia said, touching David's arm. "You have no idea how badly. But it would have served little purpose. And we'll never know for a certainty if George set up the ambush that killed Julia or if it was Tony manipulated by George."

"And that matters?" David demanded.

"I'm afraid if Johnny thought George was responsible for Julia's death he wouldn't be able to refrain from violence. He'd ruin his life. And any chance he and Violet have of salvaging something from the tragedy."

David swallowed. His hands were curled into fists, but his shoulders were a fraction less tense. "So you want Ashton to blame Miss Chase's other brother?"

Cordelia moved back to the bed. "Tony died saving Johnny. That will make it easier for all of them to live with."

Harry twined his fingers round her hand.

David strode back to the bed and stood beside Simon. "I can't bear the thought of him getting away with it."

"He won't." Harry exchanged a look with Malcolm. "We'll make sure Wellington knows. And your father."

David shook his head, his jaw set. "There's not enough proof to bring him to justice."

"But his career will be over," Malcolm said. "You know how your father works. When Chase shows his face in England, he'll find himself quietly blackballed in society."

David's mouth curled. "So being thrown out of White's constitutes punishment?"

"For a man who values his position as much as George does," Cordelia said.

"Chase will be assigned to a backwater with no chance of advancement or sent into danger," Harry said. "Or both."

Malcolm put a hand on David's shoulder. "It may not be your idea of justice, David. Or mine. But between them your father and Wellington will see to it Chase's life isn't worth living."

❧ 51 ❧

Cordelia dropped into a leather armchair in the study beside Suzanne and reached for the teapot. "I'm not sure what happened to the man I married. He seems to have vanished. There's a damnably optimistic stranger lying in my bed upstairs."

Suzanne watched as Cordelia poured a cup of tea with fierce concentration. "What's Harry saying?"

"A lot of nonsense about the past not mattering. And that he wants me despite everything." Cordelia set down the teapot, spattering drops of tea on the tabletop.

"War can change people."

"In Harry's case it seems to have driven him mad." Cordelia grabbed the milk jug. "The idea that we could ever forget—"

"Perhaps you'll find you don't mind remembering." Suzanne thought back to her own wedding day. The close air in the embassy sitting room that served as a chapel, Malcolm's hand shaking slightly as he slid the ring onto her finger, her own hand trembling as she signed the marriage lines. Despite her torn feelings about why she had entered into her marriage, it was not an unhappy memory.

"Nothing can change the fact that our marriage was badly begun." Cordelia stirred her tea, clattering the spoon against the eggshell porcelain. "I took dreadful advantage of Harry. I married him for his money."

"A number of people marry for love and fall out of it. I don't see why the reverse can't be possible."

Cordelia drew a sharp breath. "And if Livia ever learns that George might be—"

"Her father?" Suzanne's fingers tightened round her teacup. Difficult to believe their confrontation with George Chase had been only yesterday. "Given what you've already been through, I think you and Harry will be able to handle that."

Cordelia flung down the spoon. "I don't—"

"Deserve him?" Suzanne bit back a bitter laugh. "Dearest, haven't you learned that no one gets what they deserve? Which is a very good thing for some of us."

Cordelia reached for her teacup. "Yes, but—"

The door from the passage was flung open. Rachel pushed through, then slammed the door shut behind her and leaned against the panels. "Henri's gone mad."

Cordelia set down her teacup. "Him too?"

"What's he done?" Suzanne asked.

Rachel's fingers curled against the polished mahogany of the door. "He says he wants to marry me."

Despite everything, Suzanne found herself smiling. "I knew Lieutenant Rivaux was a sensible man."

"It's insane." Rachel stalked across the room and flung herself into a chair beside Cordelia. "The Vicomte de Rivaux can't marry a whore. He'd be ruined."

"Hardly ruined." Cordelia poured a cup of tea with the ceremony of a hostess in her drawing room. "He might not be received certain places, but it's more you who'd be given the cut. It's amazing what a man can get away with."

Rachel shook her head. "It's not the life I want for him."

Cordelia handed the cup of tea to Rachel. "What sort of life does he want for himself?" She frowned, as though caught up short by her own words.

Rachel tossed down a swallow of tea. "That's not the point."

"It's a mistake," Suzanne said, "thinking one knows what's best for one's lover better than he does himself."

Rachel stared at her, brows fiercely drawn. "Don't tell me you think I should accept him?"

What could she say? *I was once a whore myself, and I don't think it's any bar to successful matrimony? I know better than anyone that a marriage can be flawed and still succeed? I need to believe you can be happy to have a shred of hope for myself?* "You'd be beginning with honesty," Suzanne said. "That's a great deal more than most people have."

Rachel shook her head, eyes armored against hope.

"Do you love him?" Cordelia asked.

"What's that to say to—"

"Do you—"

"I'm a whore."

"How many men a woman sleeps with has nothing to do with whom she loves. Believe me, I know." Cordelia tossed down a quick sip of tea. "Do you love Lieutenant Rivaux?"

"Of course," Rachel said as though the words were torn from her. "But—"

"Well then." Cordelia smiled again, a sudden, infectious, girlish smile, with none of her usual cynicism. "My husband just asked me what I wanted. I think you might ask yourself the same."

Cordelia leaned back in her chair, gaze on her husband. If someone had told her a month, even a week, ago that she'd feel an absurd rush of contentment simply watching Harry sleep, she'd have laughed in their face.

Harry's gaze flew open with that same lightning quickness with which his brain could dart from topic to topic. "I hate that I sleep so much. But I love waking up. It's such an amazing illusion to have one's wife look at one with such wonder."

"Who says it's an illusion?"

"I'm not a fool, Cordy."

An iron band squeezed her chest. "You've been the one who's been arguing that things could . . . that it could . . . that we could"— the words seemed to be stuck in her throat—"make it work."

His gaze shot over her face. "But I'm not fool enough to think you'd look at me with wonder after the first fortnight or so. Tolerant affection would be a great deal."

She swallowed. "I told George—" Her voice caught on his name.

"You don't have to talk about him." Harry's voice was rough. He reached for her hand.

"Yes, I do. I need you to know this. However disgusted I was to learn he was behind Julia's and Amy's deaths, whatever was between George and me ended long before. Because, as I told him, I'm in love with my husband."

For a moment, it was as though the breath had stopped in Harry's throat. Then his fingers tightened round her own. "You're sounding dangerously like a romantic, Cordy."

She returned the pressure of his hand, though she feared touching him was taking unfair advantage. "Harry, I can't promise you anything. That is, I can promise you'd be the only man in my bed, and I can promise that I'll try. But I can't promise that I won't make a hopeless mull of things. But—"

"Yes?" His gaze was trained on her face.

"But nothing would make me happier than if Livia and I could come and live with you."

Something sparked in his eyes that seared through the jaconet of her gown. "I don't see how anyone could object to a wife and daughter coming to live with a husband and father."

"No." Cordelia sucked in a breath, feeling as though she might shatter into a million pieces. "Harry—"

He had pushed himself up and was leaning forward, arm extended, in danger of falling off the bed. "I've been making a remarkable recovery. Especially after what you just said. Come here."

Moving to the edge of the bed and into the circle of his arm was the surest way to prevent him from tumbling off the edge of the bed.

His arm tightened round her. His breath brushed her skin and then his mouth closed over her own with a naked need that went beyond artifice and pretense, fear and uncertainty, forgiveness and betrayal.

"I'm terrified, Harry," she said a few moments later, her voice muffled by his dressing gown.

"So am I, my darling." His lips moved against her temple. "But I'm more terrified of life without you."

Suzanne cast a glance round the hall. Angus was finally winning the battle against infection, and Christophe would soon be well enough to return to his regiment. The rest of the remaining wounded looked as though they'd pull through. Upstairs Harry and Edgar were both mending. She went down the passage to the kitchen, and put the kettle on the range. Simon and David would be back soon from their visit to Fitzroy Somerset, and Malcolm would return from his call on Stuart. Tea was always welcome.

Over the whistling of the kettle, she didn't hear the opening of the door. The first she realized someone else had come into the kitchen was when Malcolm came up behind her and slid his arm round her waist. She released her breath and leaned back against him, seeking solace in the brush of his cravat against her cheek, the pressure of his arm round her waist, the stir of his breath against her hair. This was real, as real as her betrayal, and as much a part of who she was as being a French agent. The past might still hang over her, but she'd made her choice, and she knew where she belonged.

"Rachel's going to marry Rivaux," Malcolm said.

"I'm glad." She lifted her head and turned round to look at him. As well as she knew him, she wasn't entirely sure of his response to the news. She needed to look into his eyes, and she was terrified of what she might see.

Malcolm grinned. "I'm glad, too. I've never been much of a believer in young love, but they're enough to shake a cynic."

"Darling." Suzanne put her hands on his chest. "You're good at creating cover stories. Couldn't you create one for Rachel? So no one need know she ever worked at Le Paon d'Or? So she isn't ostracized?"

"I'm already working on the details. I was hoping you'd help me."

She reached up to press a kiss against his cheek. "You're wonderful, Malcolm."

"Why wouldn't I help Rachel? I'm very fond of her. Not to mention that I probably owe her my life." He set his hands on her shoulders. "I saw Stuart. It looks as though we'll be going to Paris once things are sorted here."

Paris under Allied occupation. She forced down a wave of anger at the image of foreign soldiers swarming over the Place du Carousel, the Bourbon flag flying, white cockades replacing the tricolor. She would manage. God knows she'd managed in the past.

She studied his face. His features were still scored with exhaustion. But it was his eyes that caught her. The gaze of a man who'd seen into hell and was clawing his way back to sanity.

"Men were dying all round me," he said in a quiet voice. "All I could think about was you and Colin. Getting back to you." He swallowed. "It wasn't my war, but I've spent so much of my life caught up in it. I had this sense that I needed to be there, to see it through to the end. But a part of me can't but wonder if I was wrong. If my first duty was to be with the two of you."

Her throat tightened. How odd that for all that divided them, in the midst of the battle their thoughts had been much the same. "It's difficult sorting out where one's duty lies," she said. "And often there's no clear answer."

His gaze moved over her face. "We live in a mad world and these past years it's been madder than usual. And yet somehow in the midst of it all I got you."

She linked her hands behind his head, using a playful smile to mask the feelings tearing through her. "Got stuck with me, you mean."

"I know I don't deserve you, sweetheart. And I know I don't say it often enough. But I'd be lost without you."

Tenderness and fear and wonder welled up in her throat. She took his face between her hands, memorizing the curve of his lips, the crinkles round his eyes, the bone-deep tenderness in the eyes themselves. Committing them to a memory she'd always carry with her, whatever was to come. "Well then," she said. "It's a good thing you have me. And I hate to break it to you, darling, but I don't see how you could get rid of me."

"You'll be the toast of Paris, you know."

The Bourbon court, ultra-Royalists in power, her friends imprisoned. It was going to be difficult, but she'd have him beside her. That counted for a lot. "Paris is going to seem positively tame after Brussels."

"I suspect adventure will find us. It always seems to, one way or another."

She kept a bright smile on her face.

For she knew his words were all too true.

HISTORICAL NOTES

As with *Vienna Waltz*, I have compressed the time line of historical events slightly for the purposes of this story. Sir Charles Stuart
gave a ball on 6 June. I have advanced the date of the ball to 13
June (the book begins after midnight, so technically the story
opens on the fourteenth). In combining real and fictional characters and events, I have of course had real historical people do and
say things that are not part of the historical record, though much of
the Duke of Wellington's dialogue in the book is taken from things
he is actually recorded to have said.

Lady Caroline Lamb went to Brussels to nurse her wounded
brother after Waterloo but was not in fact there in the time frame
of *Imperial Scandal*. She seemed such a perfect childhood friend
for Cordelia that I couldn't resist including her in the story.

Accounts of the Duchess of Richmond's ball differ as to the
order and location of events. I have relied chiefly upon the de-
scription given by Lady de Ros (the former Georgiana Lennox)
and Elizabeth Longford's account in *Wellington: Years of the Sword*.

In one of her letters, Harriet, Countess Granville, refers to
Emily Harriet Wellesley, Fitzroy Somerset's wife, as Harriet.
Based on this I have called Lady Fitzroy Somerset Harriet rather
than Emily in the book.

I knew from the first that I wanted to involve Malcolm in the
events of the battle of Waterloo. I was delighted in my research to
learn that there are accounts of Wellington, with many of his aides-
de-camp wounded, pressing civilians into service as message carriers.

SELECTED BIBLIOGRAPHY

Booth, John (compiler). *The Battle of Waterloo, containing a series of accounts published by authority, British and foreign.* London: J. Booth and T. Edgerton, 1815.

Cotton, Edward. *A Voice from Waterloo.* Brussels: Kiesling, 1895.

Creevey, Thomas. *The Creevey Papers: a selection from the correspondence & diaries of Thomas Creevey, M.P.* Edited by Sir Herbert Maxwell. London: Murray, 1904.

De Lancey, Magdalene. *A week at Waterloo in 1815.* London: John Murray, 1905.

de Ros, Georgiana. *A Sketch of the Life of Georgiana, Lady de Ros with some reminiscences of her family and friends, including the Duke of Wellington, by her daughter the Honorable Mrs. J.R. Swinton.* London: John Murray, 1893.

Frazer, Augustus. *The Letters of Colonel Sir Augustus Simon Frazer, K.C.B.* London: Longman, Brown, Green, Longmans, & Roberts, 1859.

Kincaid, John. *Adventures in the Rifle Brigade.* London: T. and W. Boone, Strand, 1830.

Longford, Elizabeth. *Wellington: Years of the Sword.* New York: Harper & Row Publishers, 1969.

Mercer, Cavalié. *Journal of the Waterloo Campaign.* London: Greenhill Books, 1989.

Miller, David. *The Duchess of Richmond's Ball 15 June 1815*. Staple-hurst: Spellmount, 2005.

Müffling, Friedrich Karl Ferdinand. *A Sketch of the Battle of Waterloo in which are added Official Dispatches of Field Marshal the Duke of Wellington; Field Marshal Prince Blücher; and Reflections upon the Battles of Ligny and Waterloo*. Brussels: Gérard, 1842.

Pratt, Sisson Cooper. *The Waterloo Campaign*. London: Swan Son-nenschein, 1907.

Weller, Jac. *Wellington at Waterloo*. London: Greenhill Books, 1967.

IMPERIAL SCANDAL

Teresa Grant

About This Guide

The suggested questions are included
to enhance your group's reading of
Teresa Grant's *Imperial Scandal*.

DISCUSSION QUESTIONS

1. Suzanne, Cordelia, Julia, Jane, and Simon all betray (or in Simon's case withhold information from) the men in their lives in different ways. How do the betrayals compare? Which do you think is the most devastating?

2. How do Henri Rivaux and Rachel Garnier help Cordelia and Harry come to certain realizations about each other? Do you think it's significant that Harry and Henri have the same name?

3. Which couple do you think has the most difficult path ahead: Suzanne and Malcolm, Harry and Cordelia, Rachel and Henri, Violet and Johnny? Why?

4. Did the revelation about Suzanne midway through the book surprise you? Why or why not? Did it change what you think of her as a character? (Including her actions in *Vienna Waltz* if you've also read it.)

5. Did you guess the murderer's identity? Why or why not?

6. How does being parents affect Suzanne's, Malcolm's, Cordelia's, and Harry's actions in the course of the book? Do you think their lives and relationships as couples would have evolved differently if they didn't have Colin and Livia?

7. Harry tells Henri Rivaux, "Some of us have been in the espionage game long enough to envy you your decency." Which of the spy characters do you think has most compromised him- or herself in their espionage work? Which do you think have managed to hold on to their integrity? Why?

8. Discuss how formality and social conventions break down in the household in the Rue Ducale in the course of nursing the wounded.

9. Compare and contrast Suzanne and Malcolm's relationship with Cordelia and Harry's, from their reasons for marrying to their betrayals to the challenges they face in *Imperial Scandal* and beyond.

10. How do childhood friendships color the way various characters interact—Malcolm and the Prince of Orange; Cordelia, John Ashton, and the Chases; Cordelia and Caroline Lamb; David, Malcolm, the Chases, and Cordelia? Does having known each other since the nursery make these characters more or less likely to see the truth of their present-day behavior and motives?

11. Compare and contrast the various farewells between the couples (Cordelia and Harry, Violet and Johnny, Jane and Tony, Aline and Geoffrey, Suzanne and Malcolm) at the Duchess of Richmond's ball. What do their different ways of saying farewell have to say about the characters and their relationships?

12. How do you think Malcolm would react if he learned the truth about Suzanne?

13. Malcolm, Suzanne, Harry, and Cordelia all claim not to be romantics. Perhaps they protest a bit too much. Which of them, or of the other characters in the book, do you think is the greatest romantic? Why?

14. Discuss how Malcolm and Suzanne are both torn between duty and personal relationships in the course of the story.

15. How does the hothouse atmosphere in Brussels with its frenetic round of parties and war looming ever closer on the horizon affect the personal relationships of the characters?

16. How do you think Suzanne and Malcolm's life would have played out if the French had won at Waterloo?

17. The battle doesn't leave anyone untouched. Which of the characters who survives the battle do you think has changed the most by the end of the book? Why?